LOST SOULS
OF
SAVANNAH
MORE ADVENTURES OF FLAGLER'S FEW

WRITTEN AND ILLUSTRATED BY
ANDRE R. FRATTINO

INKED BY RYAN ENGLISH

Pineapple Press, Inc.
Sarasota, Florida

Copyright © 2012 by Andre Frattino

All rights reserved. No part of this book may be reproduced in any form or by any means, electronic or mechanical, including photocopying, recording, or by any information storage and retrieval system, without permission in writing from the publisher.

Inquiries should be addressed to:

Pineapple Press, Inc.
P.O. Box 3889
Sarasota, Florida 34230

www.pineapplepress.com

Library of Congress Cataloging-in-Publication Data

Frattino, Andre R., 1984-
  Lost souls of Savannah : more adventures of Flagler's few / by Andre R. Frattino. -- 1st ed.
      p. cm.
  ISBN 978-1-56164-532-9 (pbk. : alk. paper)
  1. Parapsychology--Investigation--Comic books, strips, etc. 2. Graphic novels. I. Title.
  PN6727.F697L67 2012
  741.5'973--dc23
                        2012016370

First Edition
10 9 8 7 6 5 4 3 2 1

Design by Andre Frattino
Printed in the United States of America

IN HONOR OF . . .

MY GRANDMOTHER, WHO HAS BEEN AN EXAMPLE THAT JUST BECAUSE YOU GET OLDER DOESN'T MEAN YOU HAVE TO BE OLD.

MY MOTHER, WHO DRAGGED ME TO SAVANNAH, KICKING AND SCREAMING. THANKS, MOM!

SPECIAL THANKS TO . . .

ALYSSA CIACCIO, FOR SLINGING INK.

PIERCE MACIAIN, FOR TELLING ME THINGS I PROBABLY SHOULDN'T KNOW.

ENRICA JANG, FOR GUIDANCE AND SUPPORT IN THE WORLD OF COMIC BOOKS.

PINEAPPLE PRESS, FOR HELPING ME ACHIEVE MY DREAMS.

Introduction

Living in Savannah had a profound effect on me. To many transplants and tourists, Savannah was probably a pleasant place to visit, to set down roots or to retire, but to me Savannah was my salvation. It was Savannah that I moved to shortly after my father passed away and Savannah where I spent many years honing my artistic talents and developing *The Reaper of Saint George Street*. So when Pineapple Press allowed me to continue the Flagler's Few series, I knew of only one city I could set the sequel in.

In continuing with the focus of educating while entertaining, *Lost Souls of Savannah* is filled with historical facts and folklore. I spent six years as a tour guide in Savannah, so I knew what I was writing about better than most locals. However, setting it in the 1930s required me to do some deeper digging. Fortunately, I was lucky enough to rub elbows with Savannah natives who lived through the period and who loved to talk. My research culminated in a graphic novel that I think will give readers a thrilling Southern experience.

Lost Souls of Savannah also marks my first collaberation with artist Ryan English, a fellow Gainesville native who also attended the Savannah College of Art and Design for sequential art. I could not imagine a more fascinating angle than the team-up of two Alachua County residents whose lives were both changed in the Coastal Empire. Ryan's positive attitude and stellar ability to bring my pencils to life acted as a driving force for me throughout the making of this book and I could not imagine having developed it without him.

Finally, we come to Victor. When I originally developed the character for *The Reaper of St. George Street,* Victor was supposed to be the primary villain, an evil ghost bent on revenge. However, over time I couldn't help but mold the character into more of an anti-hero. Even though he was a two-dimensional character on paper, Victor had a charm I can't describe. Here was a tragic soul, set on a path he did not ask for, the darkness within threatening to consume him. I think maybe it's because I could relate to Victor in many ways. Maybe we all can.

-Andre R. Frattino

Introduction

Living in Savannah had a profound [illegible] and tourists [illegible] was [illegible] a pleasant place to visit, to sit down [illegible] to [illegible] Savannah [illegible] wanted to [illegible] Savannah [illegible] The Savannah [illegible] sequel to.

In [illegible] Savannah [illegible] went [illegible] in Savannah [illegible] in the [illegible] Fortunately, I was lucky enough [illegible] through the [illegible] graphic novel that I think [illegible] screen.

Lost Souls of Savannah [illegible] a fellow [illegible] College of Art and Design [illegible] angle than [illegible] residents whose [illegible] both [illegible]

Finally, we come [illegible] *The Ghosts of Savannah* [illegible] villain and [illegible] ghost [illegible] over [illegible] the character [illegible] Even though I [illegible] two-dimensional [illegible] a chord [illegible] was a tragic soul [illegible] the darkness within [illegible] trying to [illegible] because I could relate to Victor in many ways. Maybe [illegible]

[illegible] R. Frontino

CHAPTER
1

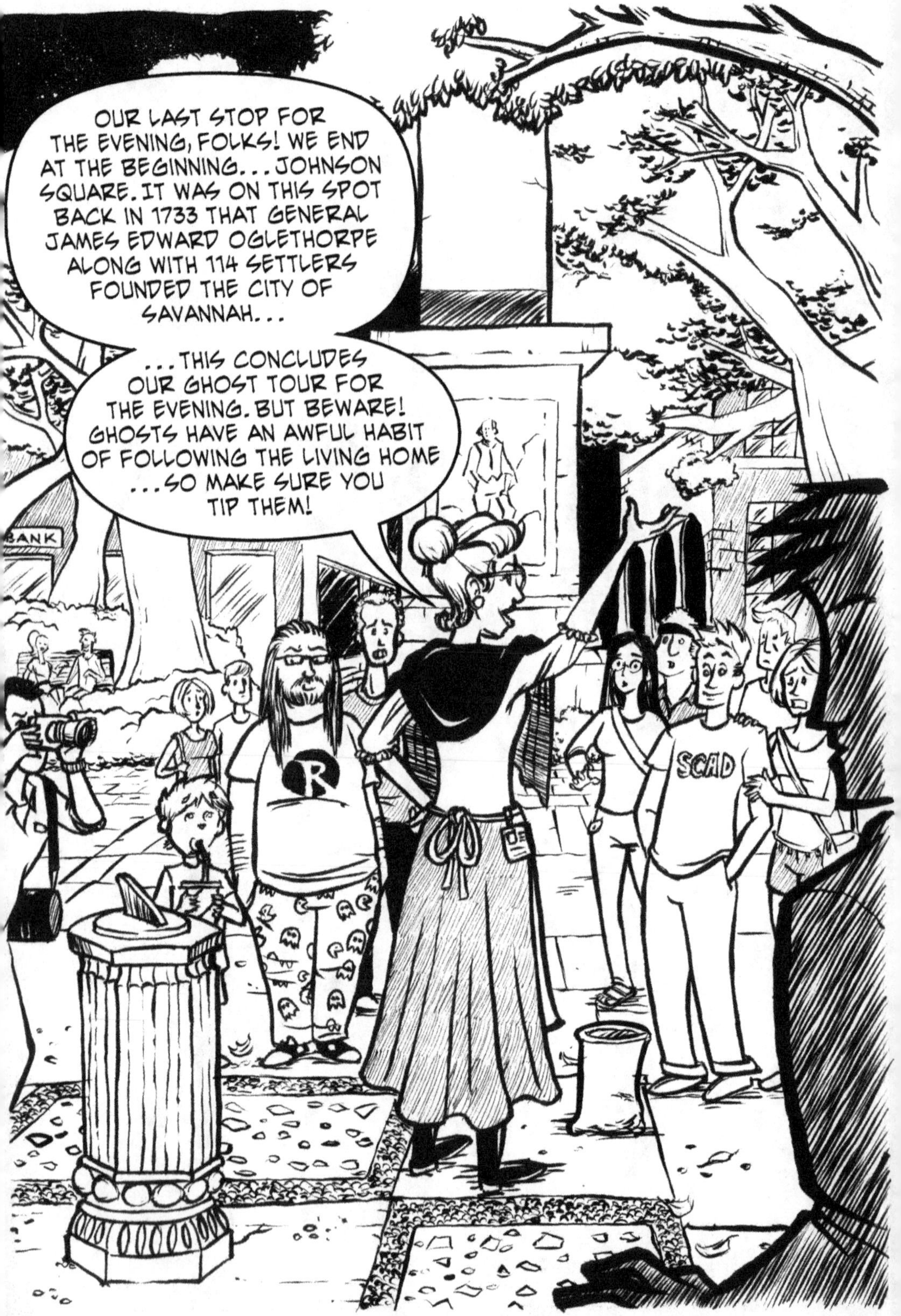
OUR LAST STOP FOR THE EVENING, FOLKS! WE END AT THE BEGINNING...JOHNSON SQUARE. IT WAS ON THIS SPOT BACK IN 1733 THAT GENERAL JAMES EDWARD OGLETHORPE ALONG WITH 114 SETTLERS FOUNDED THE CITY OF SAVANNAH...
...THIS CONCLUDES OUR GHOST TOUR FOR THE EVENING. BUT BEWARE! GHOSTS HAVE AN AWFUL HABIT OF FOLLOWING THE LIVING HOME ...SO MAKE SURE YOU TIP THEM!
BANK
R
SCAD

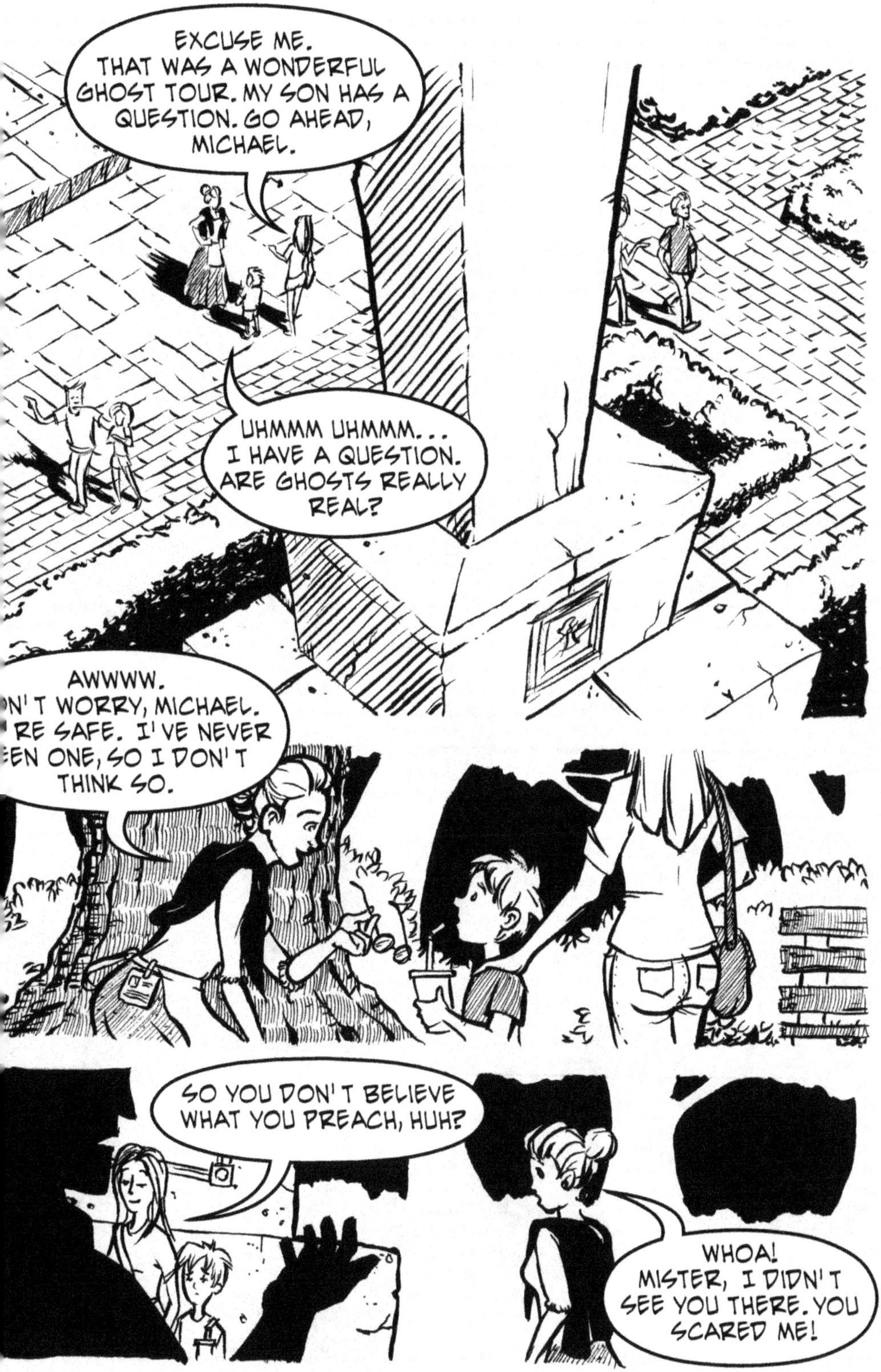
EXCUSE ME. THAT WAS A WONDERFUL GHOST TOUR. MY SON HAS A QUESTION. GO AHEAD, MICHAEL.
UHMMM UHMMM... I HAVE A QUESTION. ARE GHOSTS REALLY REAL?
AWWWW. N'T WORRY, MICHAEL. RE SAFE. I'VE NEVER EEN ONE, SO I DON'T THINK SO.
SO YOU DON'T BELIEVE WHAT YOU PREACH, HUH?
WHOA! MISTER, I DIDN'T SEE YOU THERE. YOU SCARED ME!

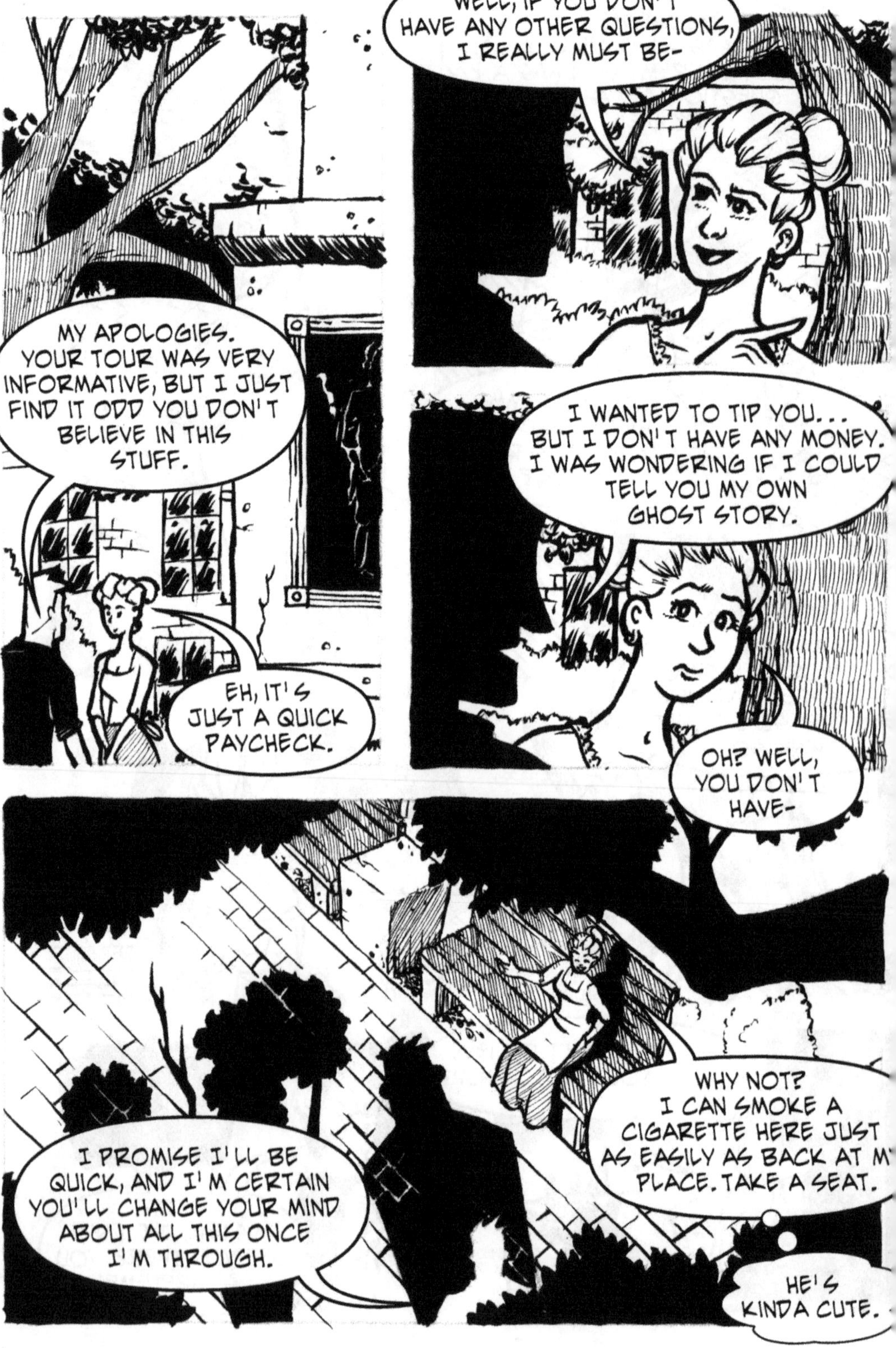

MY APOLOGIES. YOUR TOUR WAS VERY INFORMATIVE, BUT I JUST FIND IT ODD YOU DON'T BELIEVE IN THIS STUFF.
EH, IT'S JUST A QUICK PAYCHECK.
WELL, IF YOU DON'T HAVE ANY OTHER QUESTIONS, I REALLY MUST BE-
I WANTED TO TIP YOU... BUT I DON'T HAVE ANY MONEY. I WAS WONDERING IF I COULD TELL YOU MY OWN GHOST STORY.
OH? WELL, YOU DON'T HAVE-
I PROMISE I'LL BE QUICK, AND I'M CERTAIN YOU'LL CHANGE YOUR MIND ABOUT ALL THIS ONCE I'M THROUGH.
WHY NOT? I CAN SMOKE A CIGARETTE HERE JUST AS EASILY AS BACK AT M PLACE. TAKE A SEAT.
HE'S KINDA CUTE.

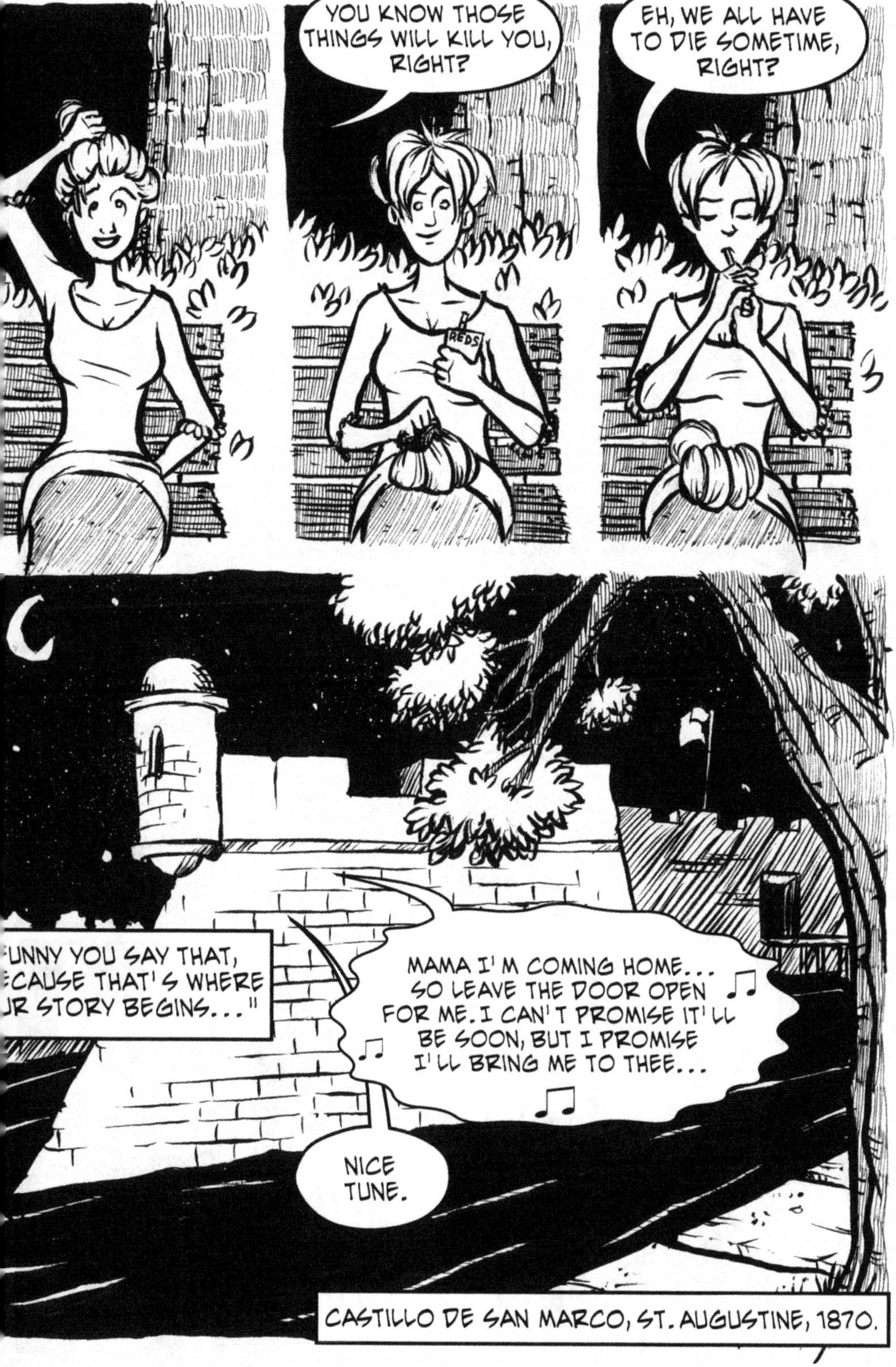
YOU KNOW THOSE THINGS WILL KILL YOU, RIGHT?
REDS
EH, WE ALL HAVE TO DIE SOMETIME, RIGHT?
UNNY YOU SAY THAT, CAUSE THAT'S WHERE R STORY BEGINS..."
MAMA I'M COMING HOME... SO LEAVE THE DOOR OPEN FOR ME. I CAN'T PROMISE IT'LL BE SOON, BUT I PROMISE I'LL BRING ME TO THEE...
NICE TUNE.
CASTILLO DE SAN MARCO, ST. AUGUSTINE, 1870.

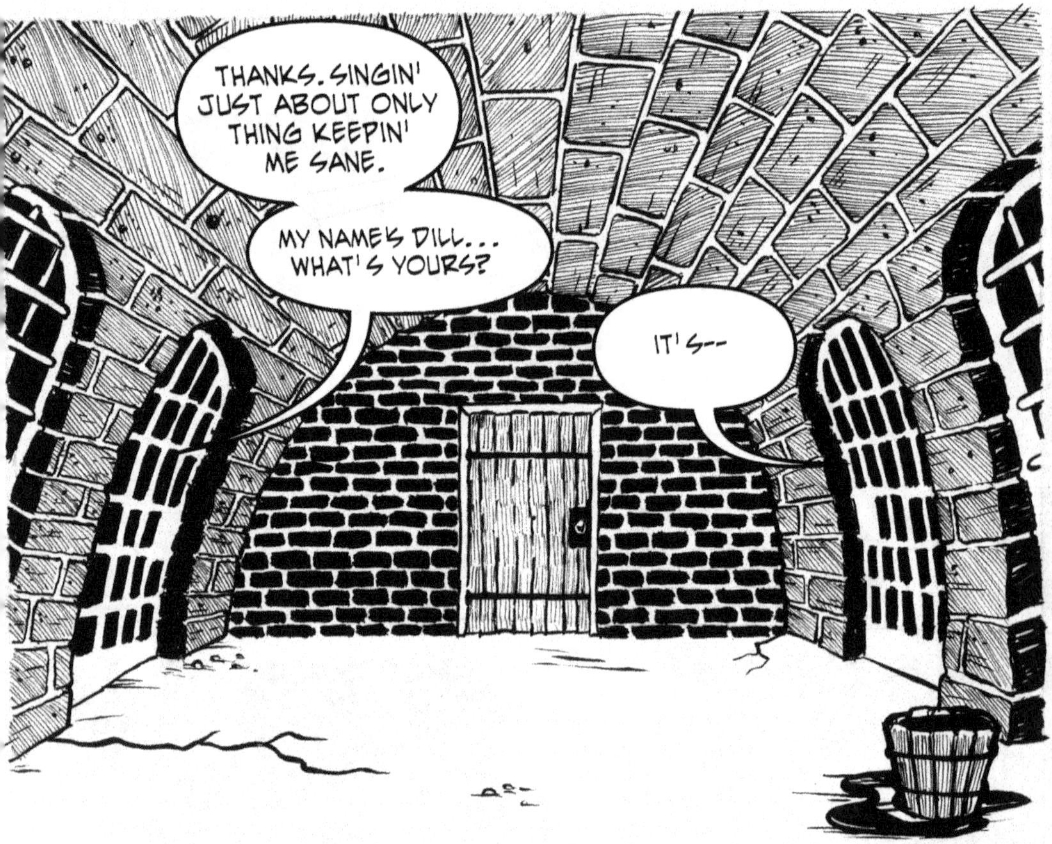
THANKS. SINGIN' JUST ABOUT ONLY THING KEEPIN' ME SANE.
MY NAME'S DILL... WHAT'S YOURS?
IT'S--

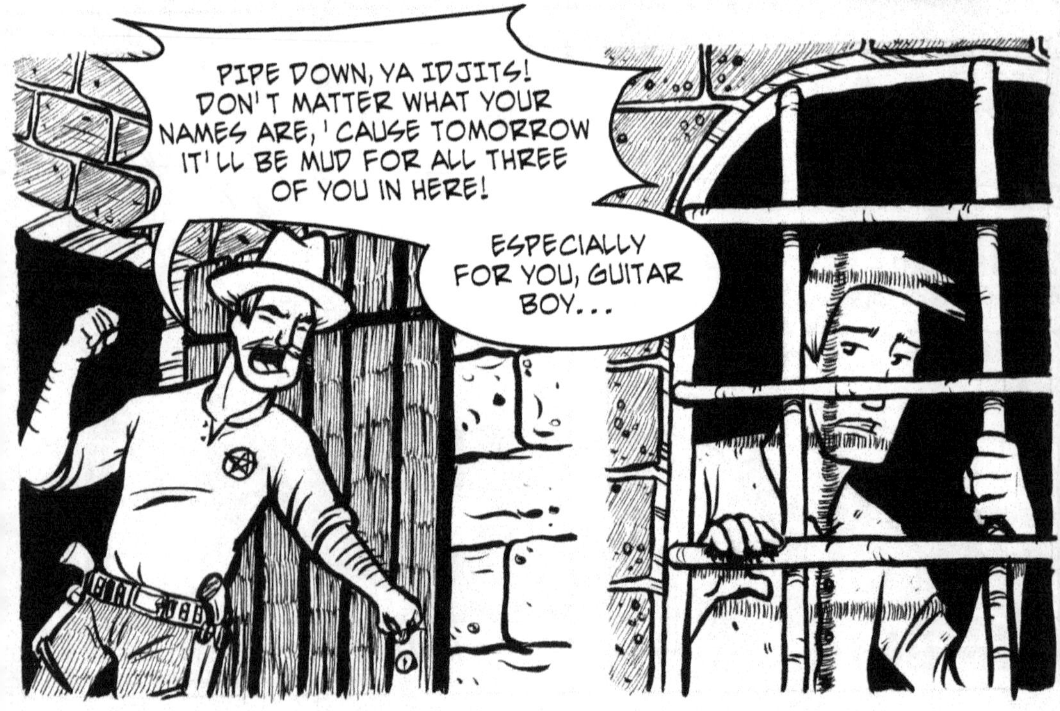
PIPE DOWN, YA IDJITS! DON'T MATTER WHAT YOUR NAMES ARE, 'CAUSE TOMORROW IT'LL BE MUD FOR ALL THREE OF YOU IN HERE!
ESPECIALLY FOR YOU, GUITAR BOY...

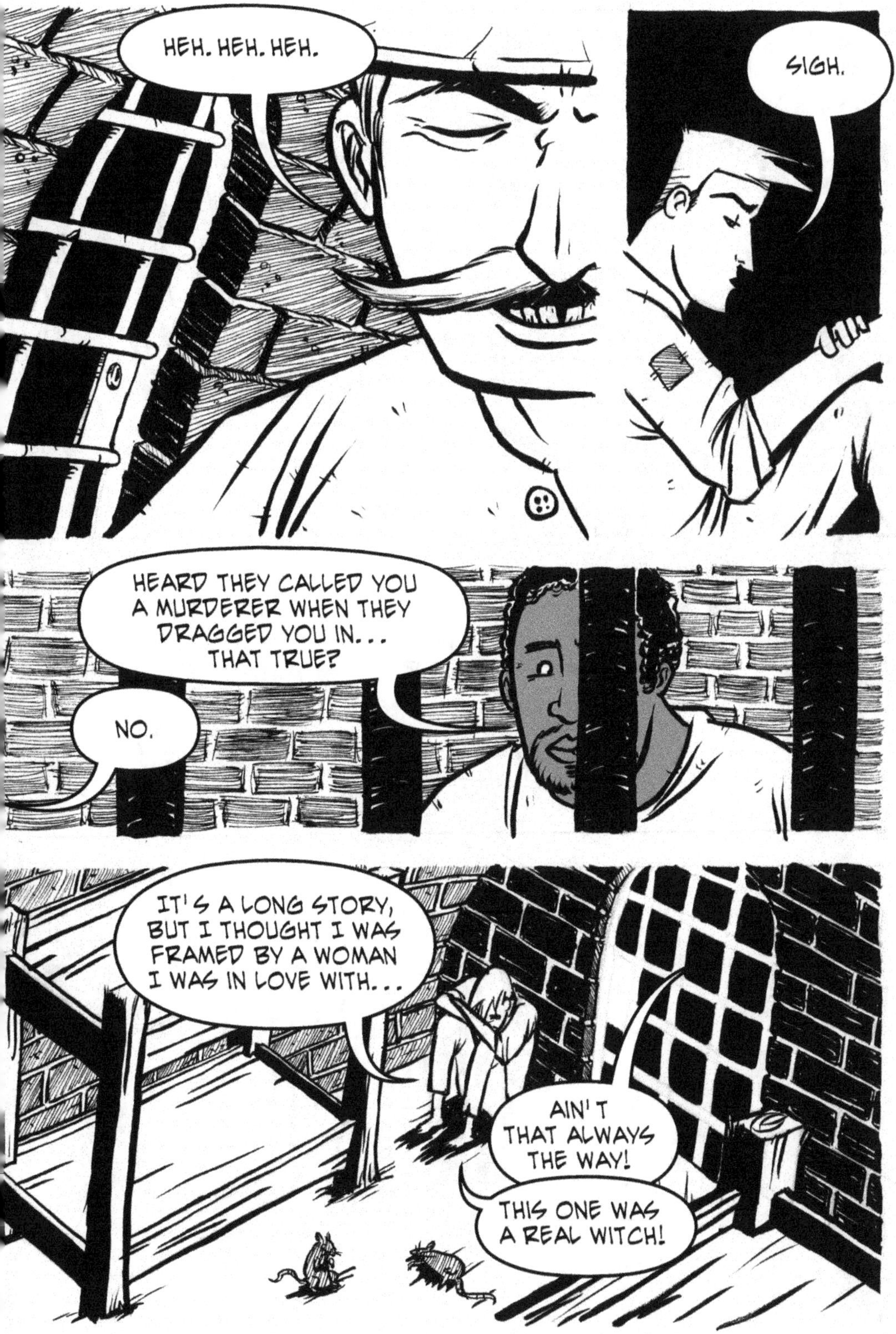
HEH. HEH. HEH.
SIGH.
HEARD THEY CALLED YOU A MURDERER WHEN THEY DRAGGED YOU IN... THAT TRUE?
NO.
IT'S A LONG STORY, BUT I THOUGHT I WAS FRAMED BY A WOMAN I WAS IN LOVE WITH...
AIN'T THAT ALWAYS THE WAY!
THIS ONE WAS A REAL WITCH!

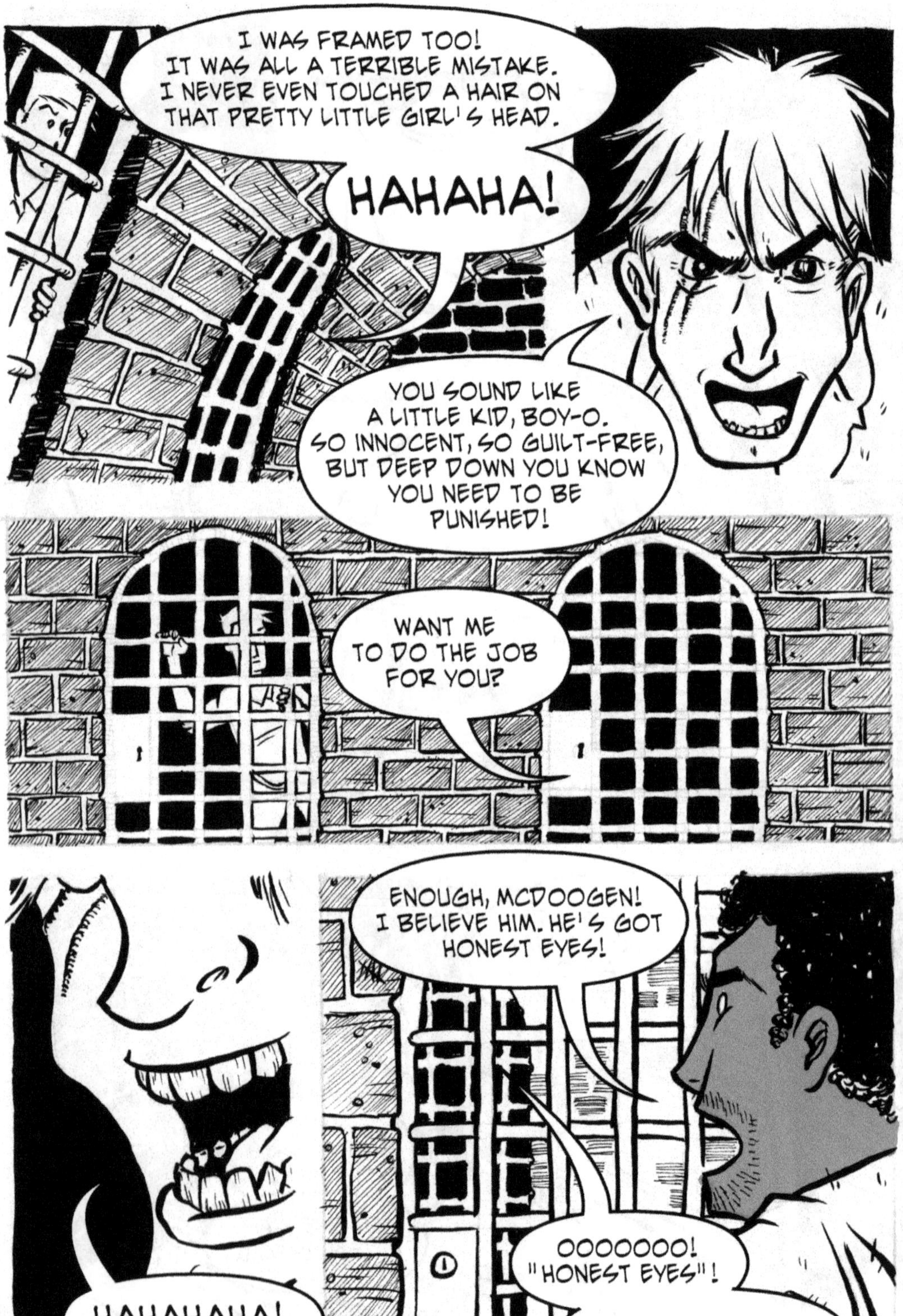
I WAS FRAMED TOO! IT WAS ALL A TERRIBLE MISTAKE. I NEVER EVEN TOUCHED A HAIR ON THAT PRETTY LITTLE GIRL'S HEAD.
HAHAHA!
YOU SOUND LIKE A LITTLE KID, BOY-O. SO INNOCENT, SO GUILT-FREE, BUT DEEP DOWN YOU KNOW YOU NEED TO BE PUNISHED!
WANT ME TO DO THE JOB FOR YOU?
HAHAHAHA!
ENOUGH, MCDOOGEN! I BELIEVE HIM. HE'S GOT HONEST EYES!
OOOOOOO! "HONEST EYES"!
HAHAHAHAHA!

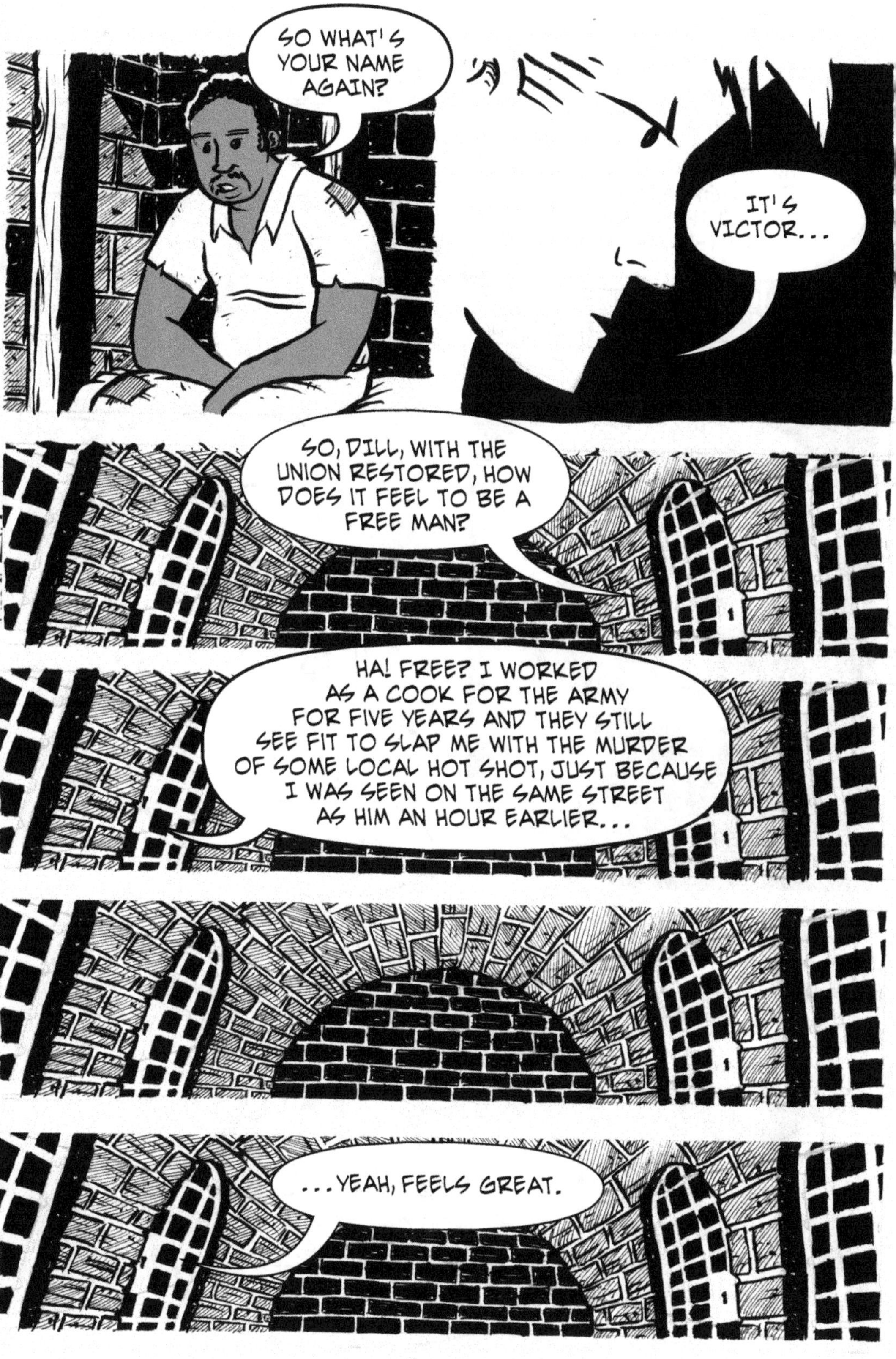
SO WHAT'S YOUR NAME AGAIN?
IT'S VICTOR...
SO, DILL, WITH THE UNION RESTORED, HOW DOES IT FEEL TO BE A FREE MAN?
HA! FREE? I WORKED AS A COOK FOR THE ARMY FOR FIVE YEARS AND THEY STILL SEE FIT TO SLAP ME WITH THE MURDER OF SOME LOCAL HOT SHOT, JUST BECAUSE I WAS SEEN ON THE SAME STREET AS HIM AN HOUR EARLIER...
...YEAH, FEELS GREAT.

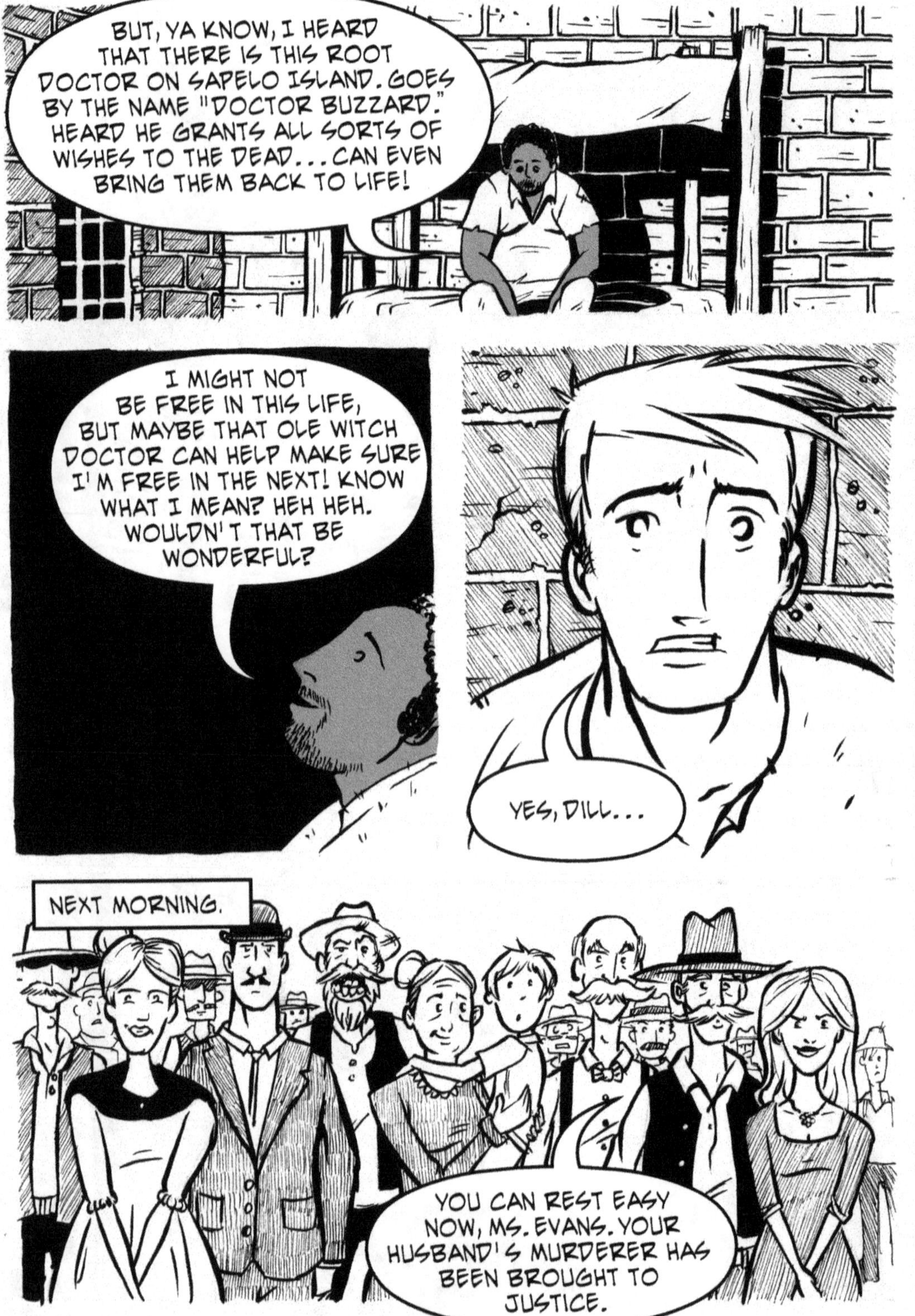
BUT, YA KNOW, I HEARD THAT THERE IS THIS ROOT DOCTOR ON SAPELO ISLAND. GOES BY THE NAME "DOCTOR BUZZARD." HEARD HE GRANTS ALL SORTS OF WISHES TO THE DEAD... CAN EVEN BRING THEM BACK TO LIFE!
I MIGHT NOT BE FREE IN THIS LIFE, BUT MAYBE THAT OLE WITCH DOCTOR CAN HELP MAKE SURE I'M FREE IN THE NEXT! KNOW WHAT I MEAN? HEH HEH. WOULDN'T THAT BE WONDERFUL?
YES, DILL...
NEXT MORNING.
YOU CAN REST EASY NOW, MS. EVANS. YOUR HUSBAND'S MURDERER HAS BEEN BROUGHT TO JUSTICE.

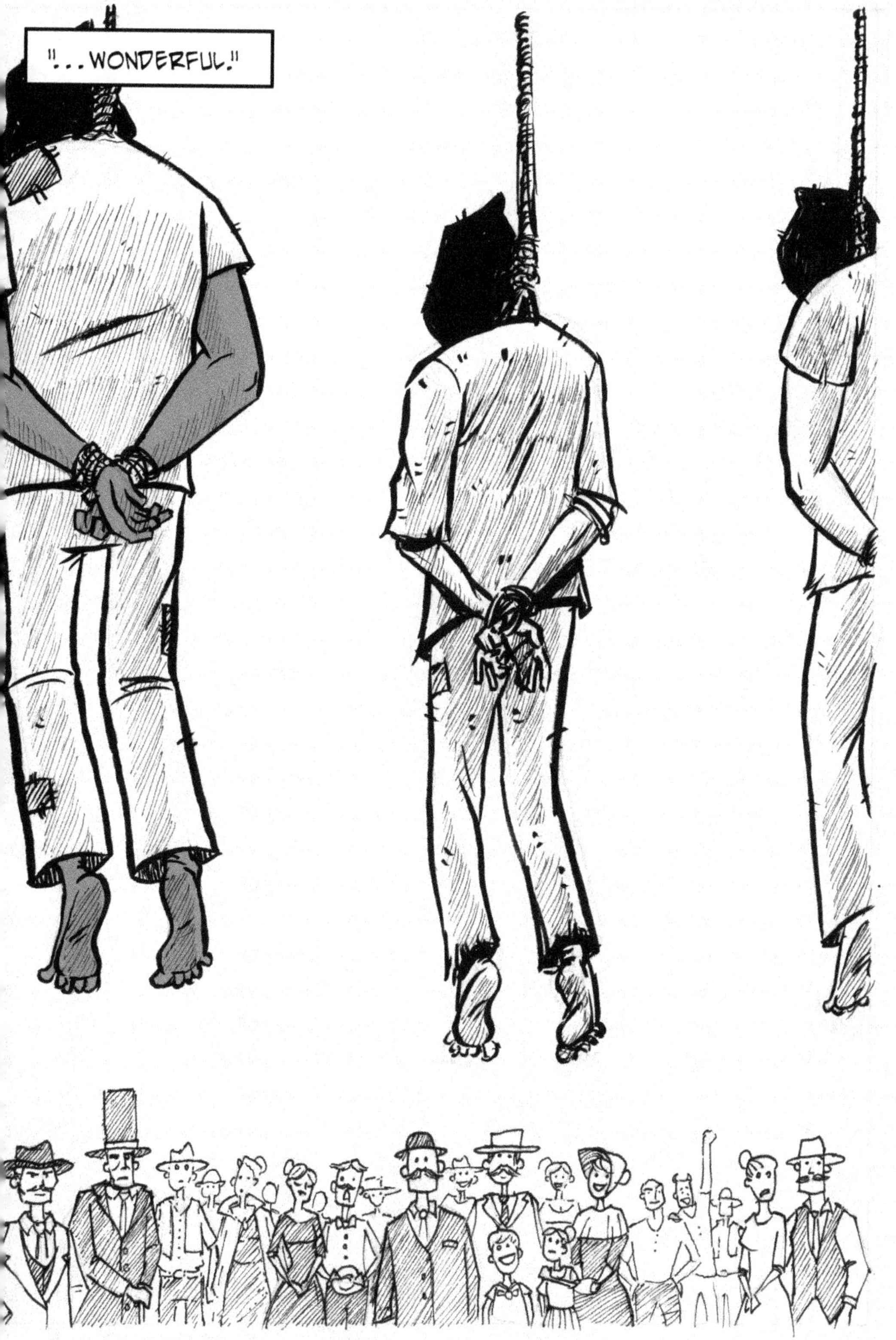
"...WONDERFUL."

CHAPTER
2

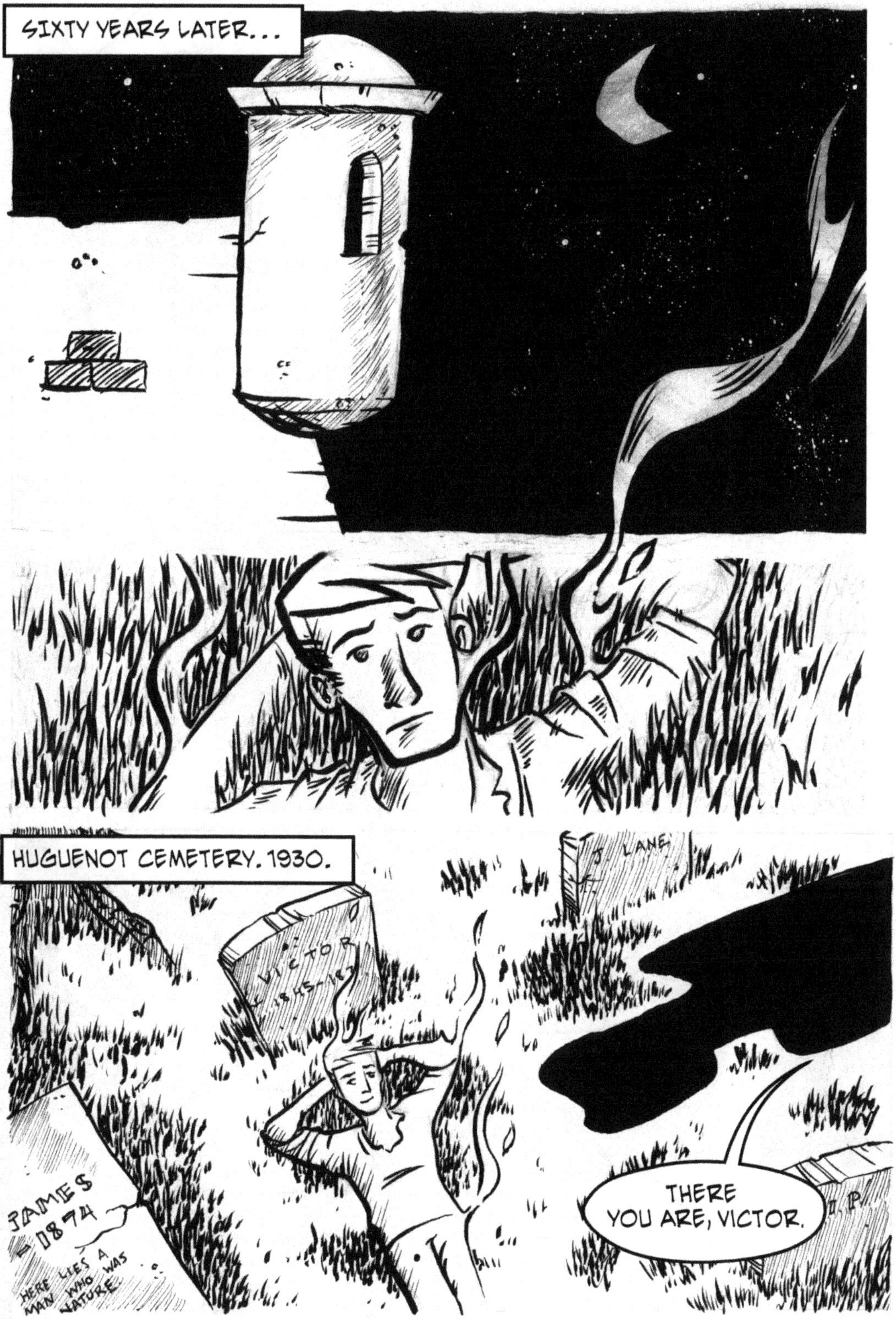
SIXTY YEARS LATER...
HUGUENOT CEMETERY. 1930.
VICTOR
JAMES 1894
HERE LIES A MAN WHO WAS NATURE
THERE YOU ARE, VICTOR.

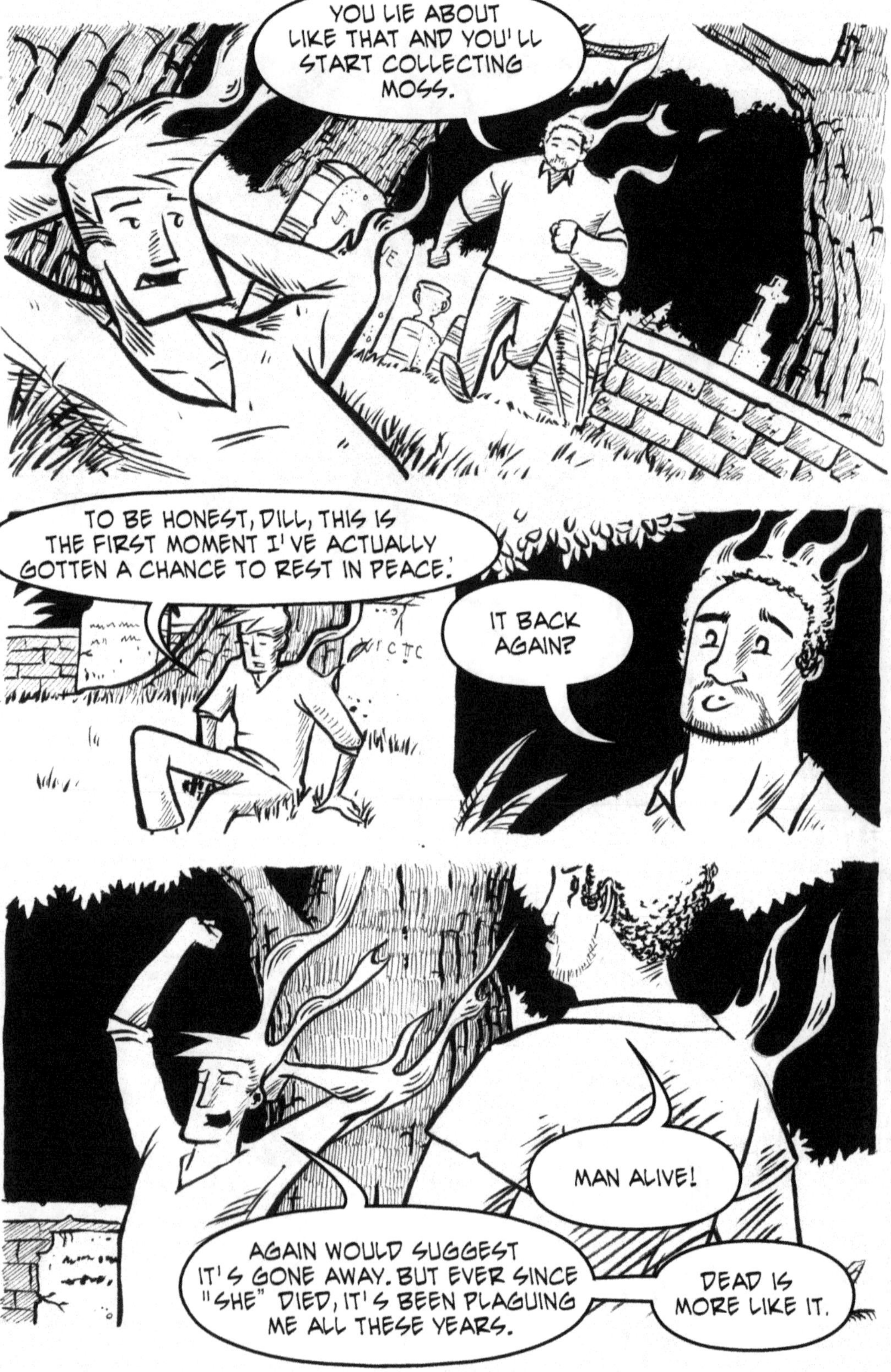
YOU LIE ABOUT LIKE THAT AND YOU'LL START COLLECTING MOSS.
TO BE HONEST, DILL, THIS IS THE FIRST MOMENT I'VE ACTUALLY GOTTEN A CHANCE TO REST IN PEACE.
IT BACK AGAIN?
AGAIN WOULD SUGGEST IT'S GONE AWAY. BUT EVER SINCE "SHE" DIED, IT'S BEEN PLAGUING ME ALL THESE YEARS.
MAN ALIVE!
DEAD IS MORE LIKE IT.

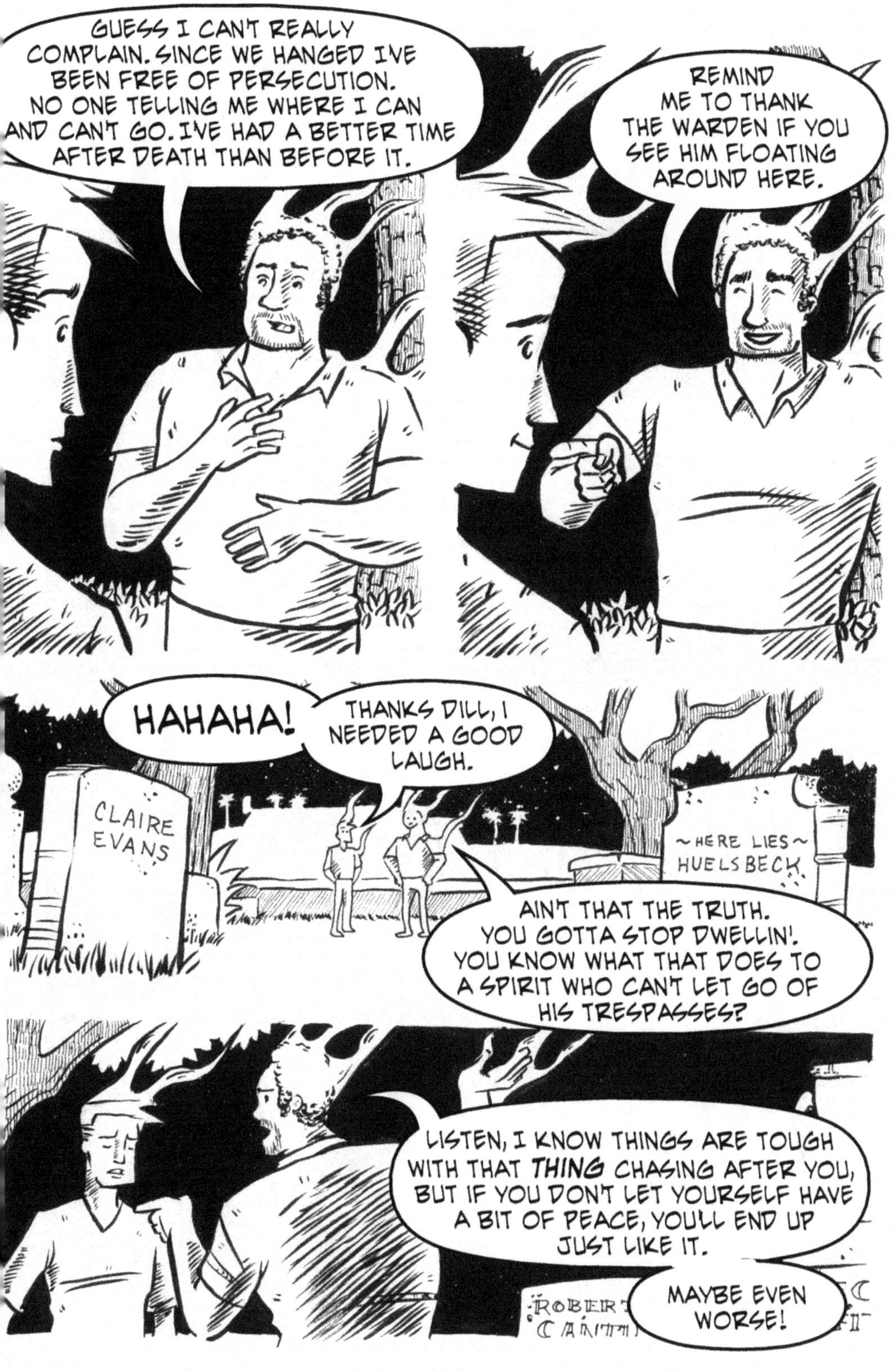
GUESS I CAN'T REALLY COMPLAIN. SINCE WE HANGED I'VE BEEN FREE OF PERSECUTION. NO ONE TELLING ME WHERE I CAN AND CAN'T GO. I'VE HAD A BETTER TIME AFTER DEATH THAN BEFORE IT.
REMIND ME TO THANK THE WARDEN IF YOU SEE HIM FLOATING AROUND HERE.
HAHAHA!
THANKS DILL, I NEEDED A GOOD LAUGH.
CLAIRE EVANS
~HERE LIES~ HUELSBECK
AIN'T THAT THE TRUTH. YOU GOTTA STOP DWELLIN'. YOU KNOW WHAT THAT DOES TO A SPIRIT WHO CAN'T LET GO OF HIS TRESPASSES?
LISTEN, I KNOW THINGS ARE TOUGH WITH THAT THING CHASING AFTER YOU, BUT IF YOU DON'T LET YOURSELF HAVE A BIT OF PEACE, YOU'LL END UP JUST LIKE IT.
MAYBE EVEN WORSE!

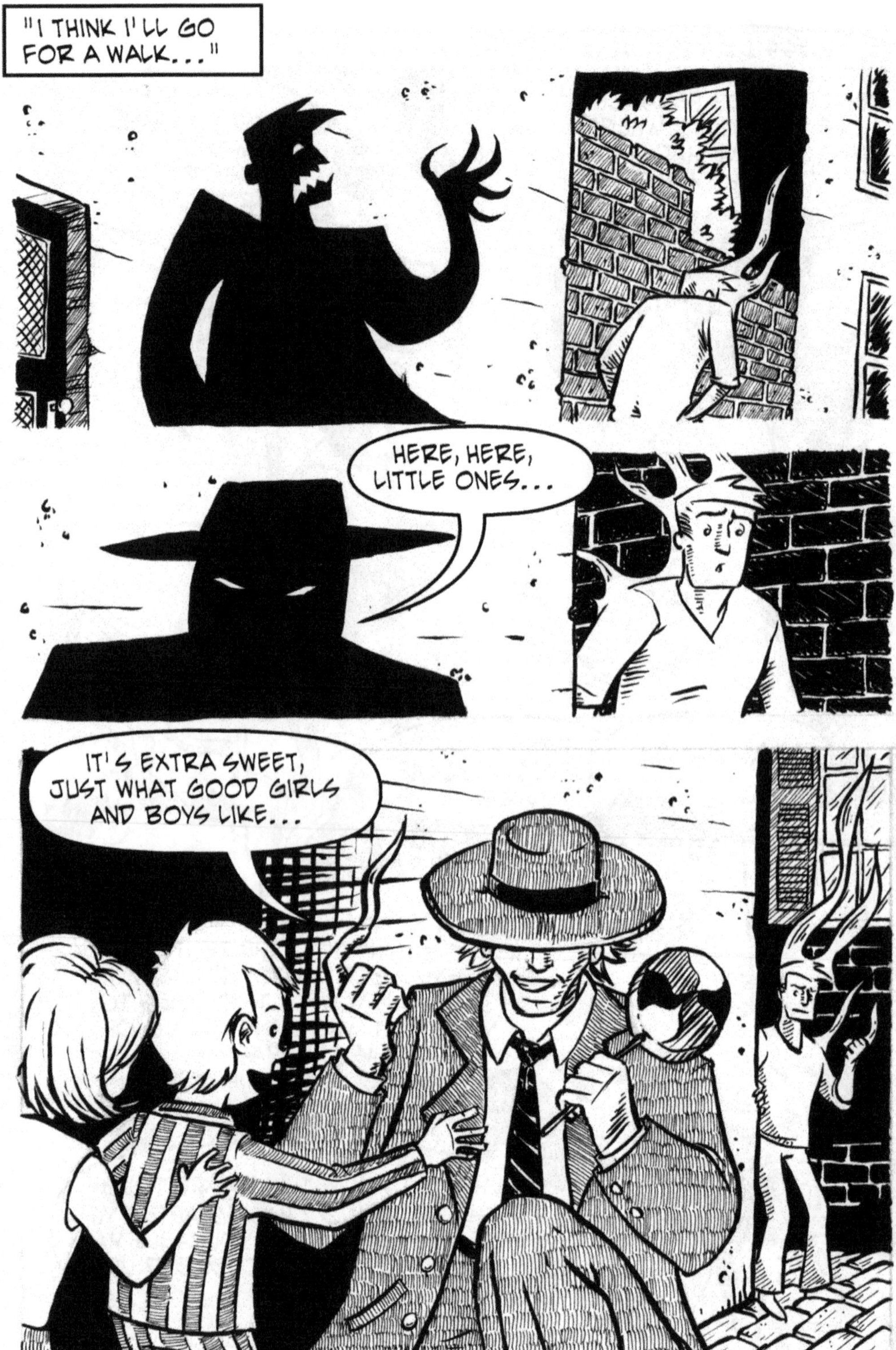
"I THINK I'LL GO FOR A WALK..."
HERE, HERE, LITTLE ONES...
IT'S EXTRA SWEET, JUST WHAT GOOD GIRLS AND BOYS LIKE...

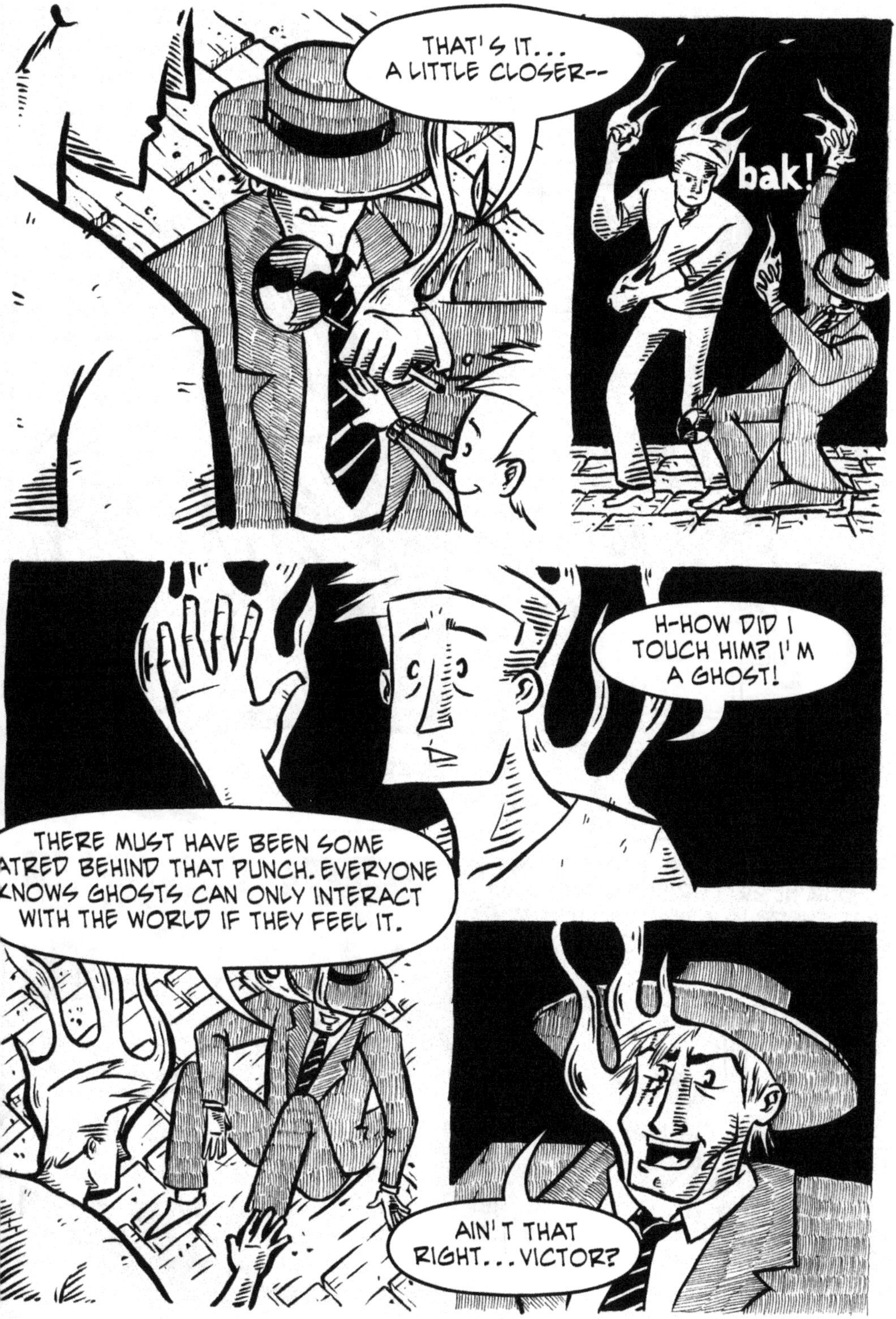
THAT'S IT... A LITTLE CLOSER--
bak!
H-HOW DID I TOUCH HIM? I'M A GHOST!
THERE MUST HAVE BEEN SOME ATRED BEHIND THAT PUNCH. EVERYONE KNOWS GHOSTS CAN ONLY INTERACT WITH THE WORLD IF THEY FEEL IT.
AIN'T THAT RIGHT... VICTOR?

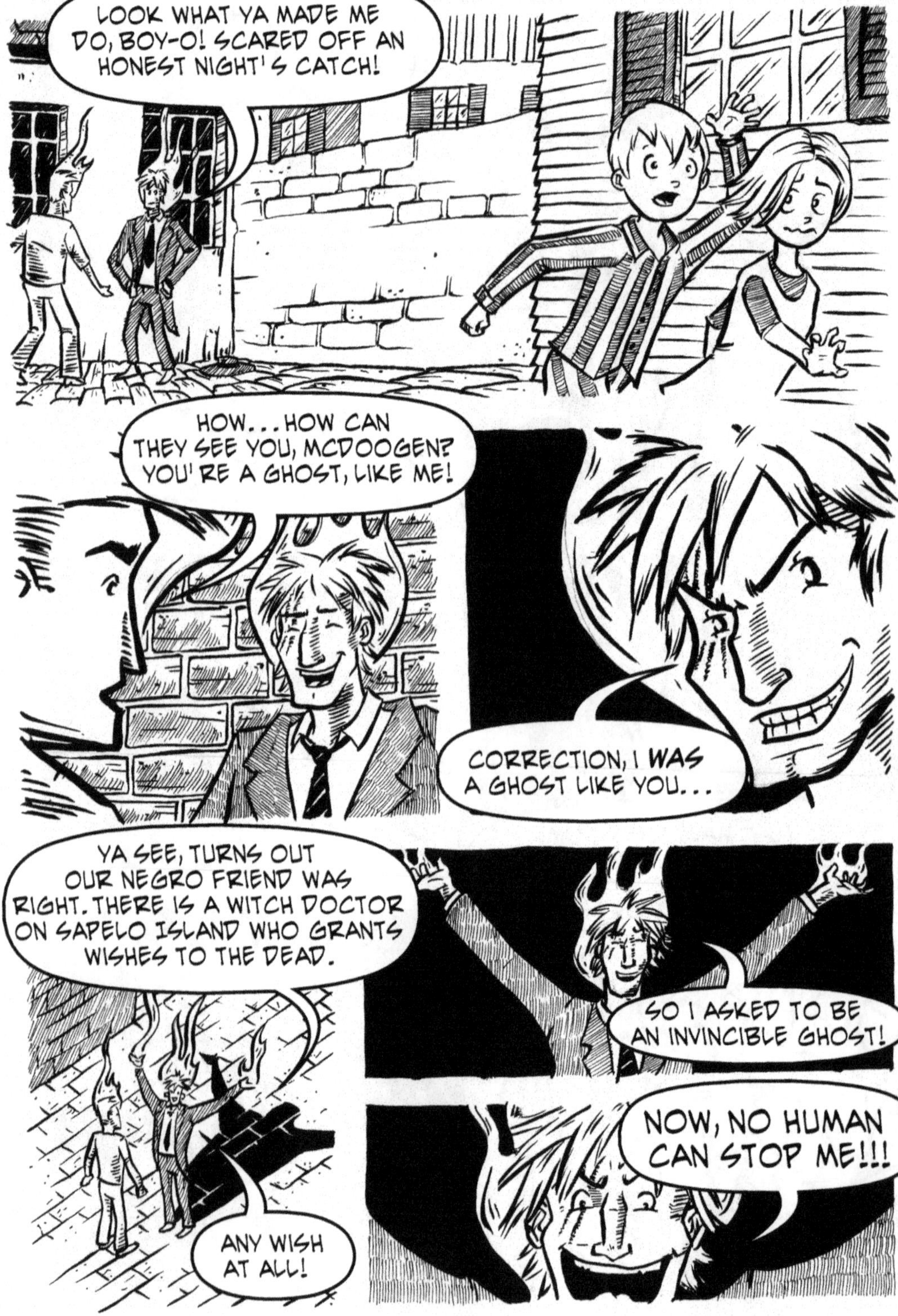
LOOK WHAT YA MADE ME DO, BOY-O! SCARED OFF AN HONEST NIGHT'S CATCH!
HOW... HOW CAN THEY SEE YOU, MCDOOGEN? YOU'RE A GHOST, LIKE ME!
CORRECTION, I **WAS** A GHOST LIKE YOU...
YA SEE, TURNS OUT OUR NEGRO FRIEND WAS RIGHT. THERE IS A WITCH DOCTOR ON SAPELO ISLAND WHO GRANTS WISHES TO THE DEAD.
ANY WISH AT ALL!
SO I ASKED TO BE AN INVINCIBLE GHOST!
NOW, NO HUMAN CAN STOP ME!!!

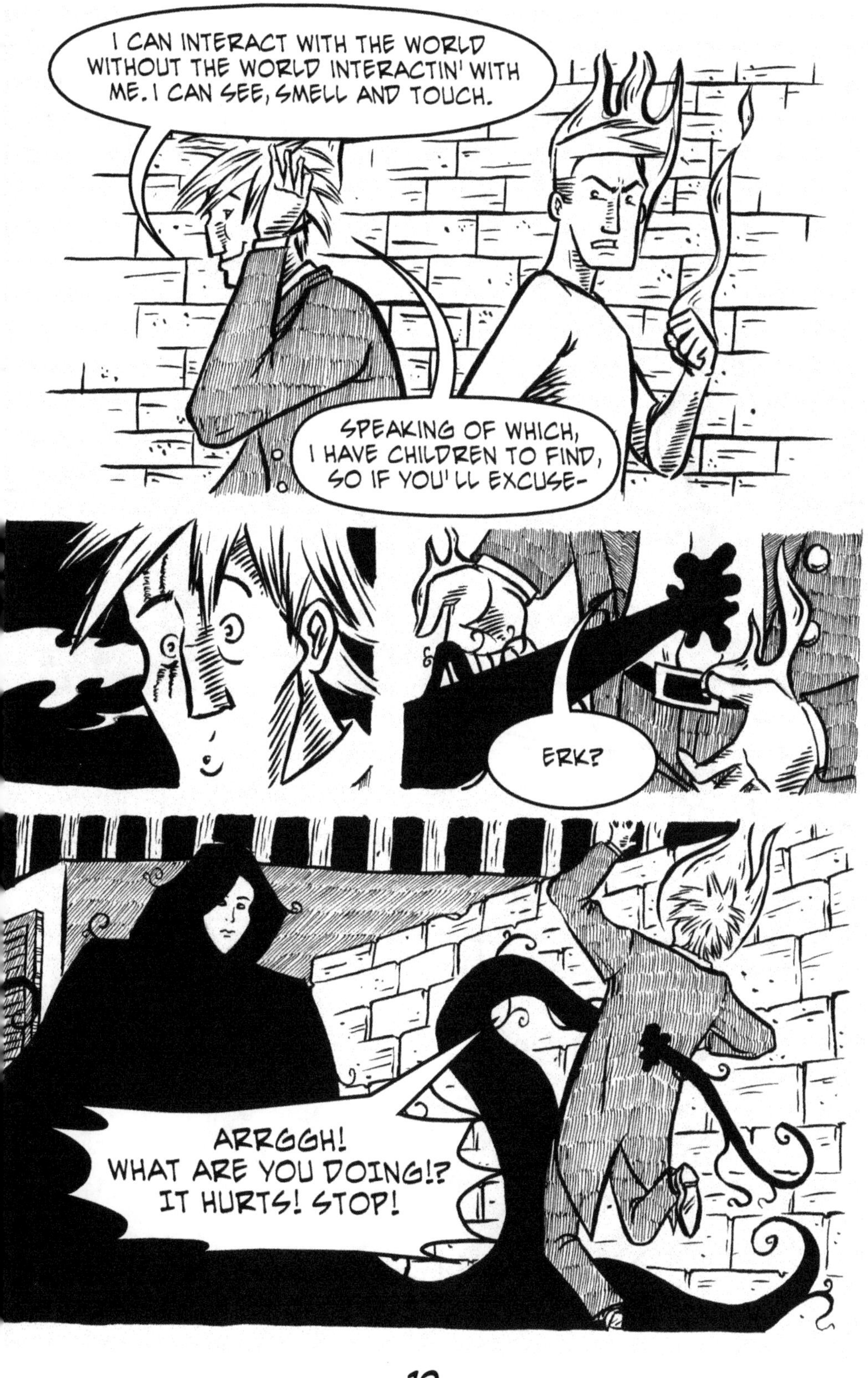
I CAN INTERACT WITH THE WORLD WITHOUT THE WORLD INTERACTIN' WITH ME. I CAN SEE, SMELL AND TOUCH.
SPEAKING OF WHICH, I HAVE CHILDREN TO FIND, SO IF YOU'LL EXCUSE-
ERK?
ARRGGH! WHAT ARE YOU DOING!? IT HURTS! STOP!

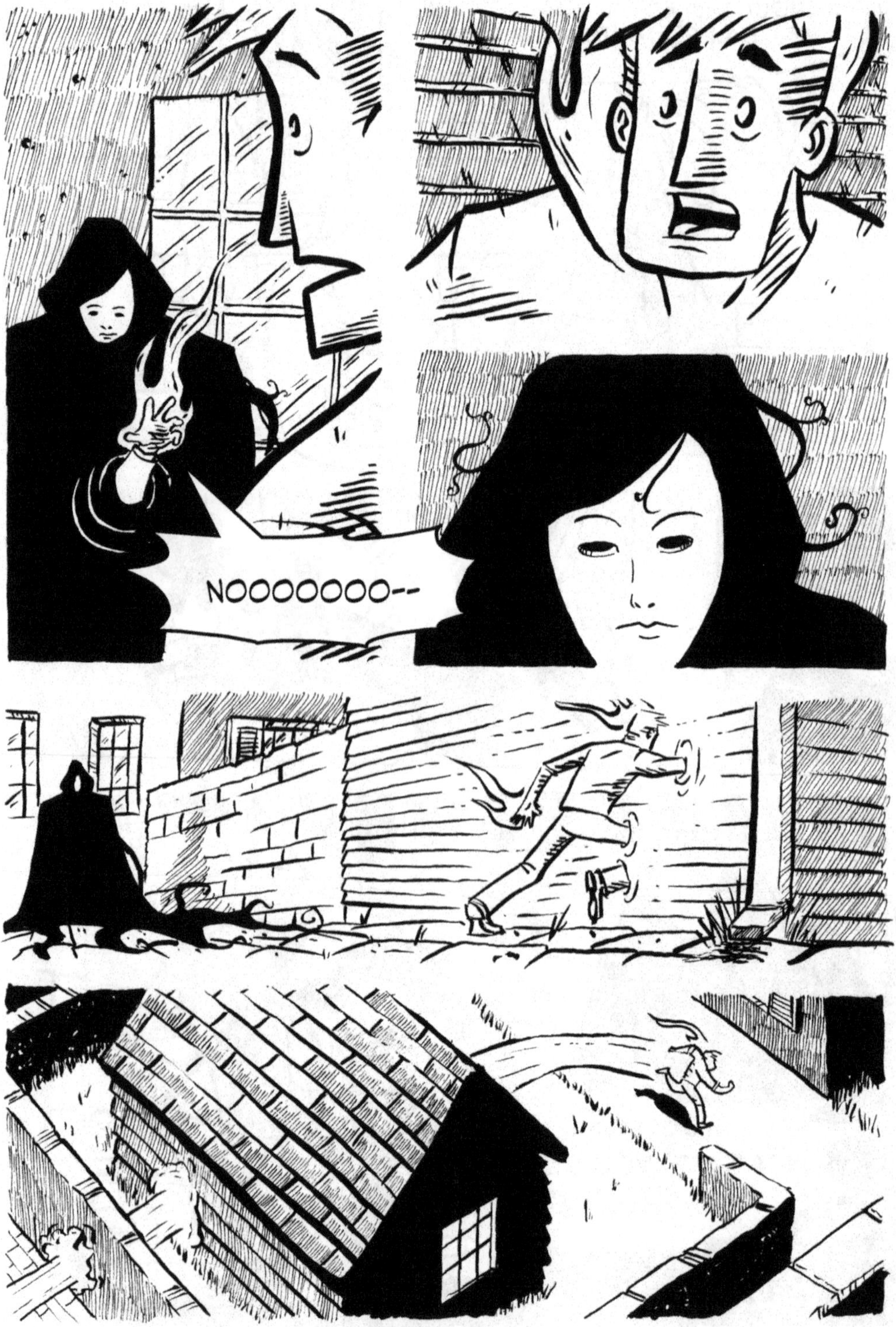
NOOOOOOO--

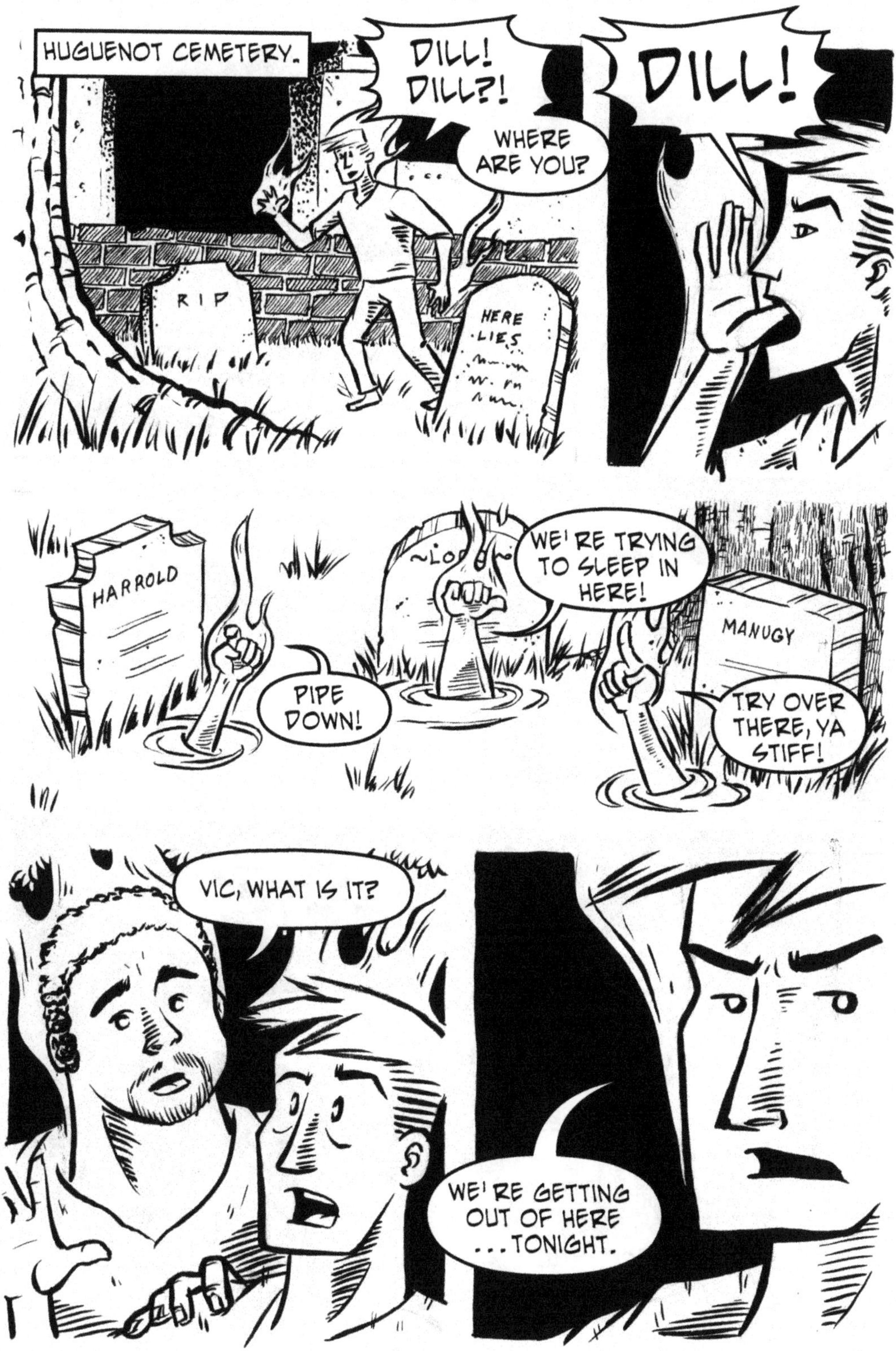
HUGUENOT CEMETERY.
DILL! DILL?!
WHERE ARE YOU?
DILL!
RIP
HERE LIES
HARROLD
MANUGY
PIPE DOWN!
WE'RE TRYING TO SLEEP IN HERE!
TRY OVER THERE, YA STIFF!
VIC, WHAT IS IT?
WE'RE GETTING OUT OF HERE ...TONIGHT.

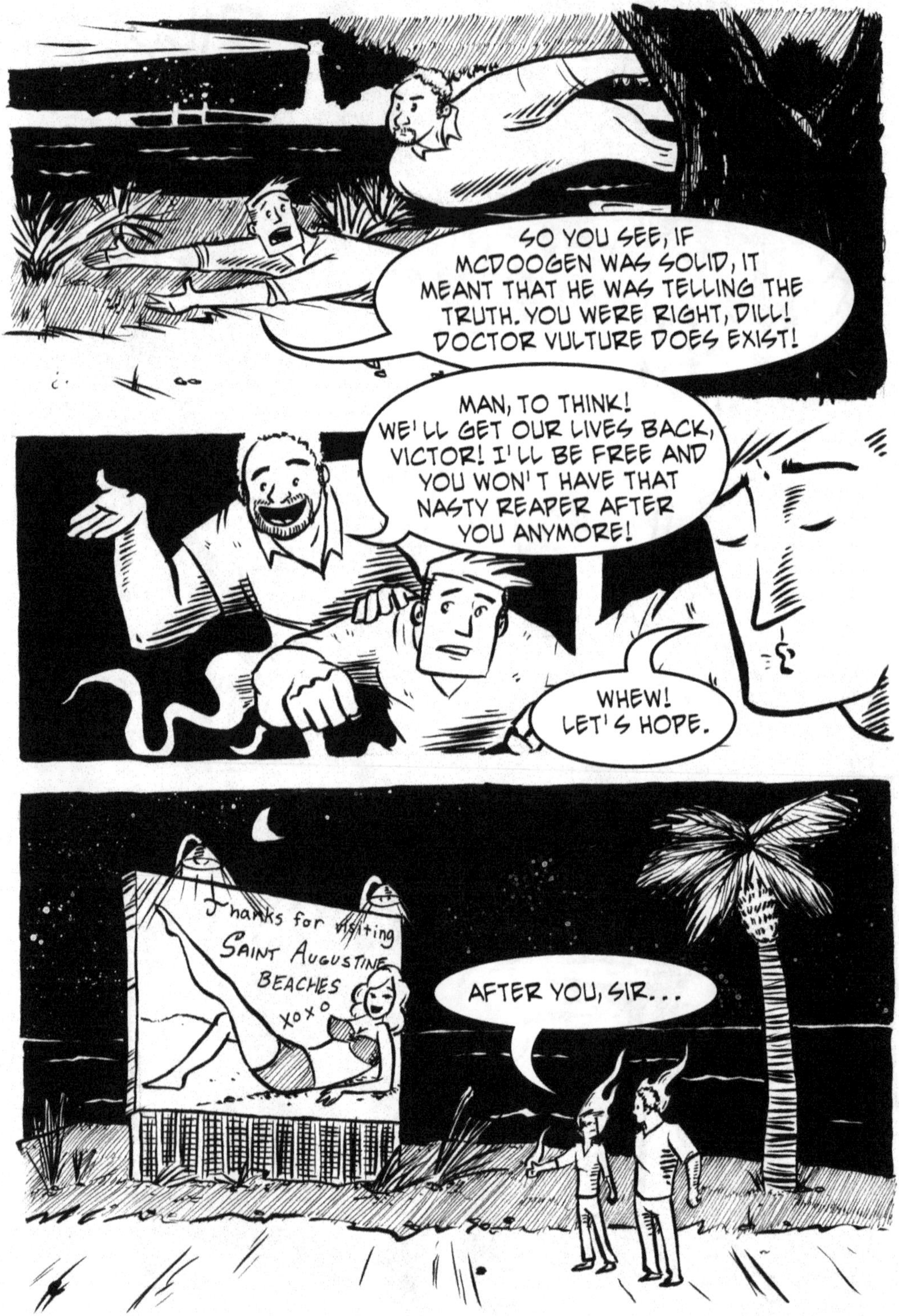
SO YOU SEE, IF MCDOOGEN WAS SOLID, IT MEANT THAT HE WAS TELLING THE TRUTH. YOU WERE RIGHT, DILL! DOCTOR VULTURE DOES EXIST!
MAN, TO THINK! WE'LL GET OUR LIVES BACK, VICTOR! I'LL BE FREE AND YOU WON'T HAVE THAT NASTY REAPER AFTER YOU ANYMORE!
WHEW! LET'S HOPE.
Thanks for visiting SAINT AUGUSTINE BEACHES xoxo
AFTER YOU, SIR...

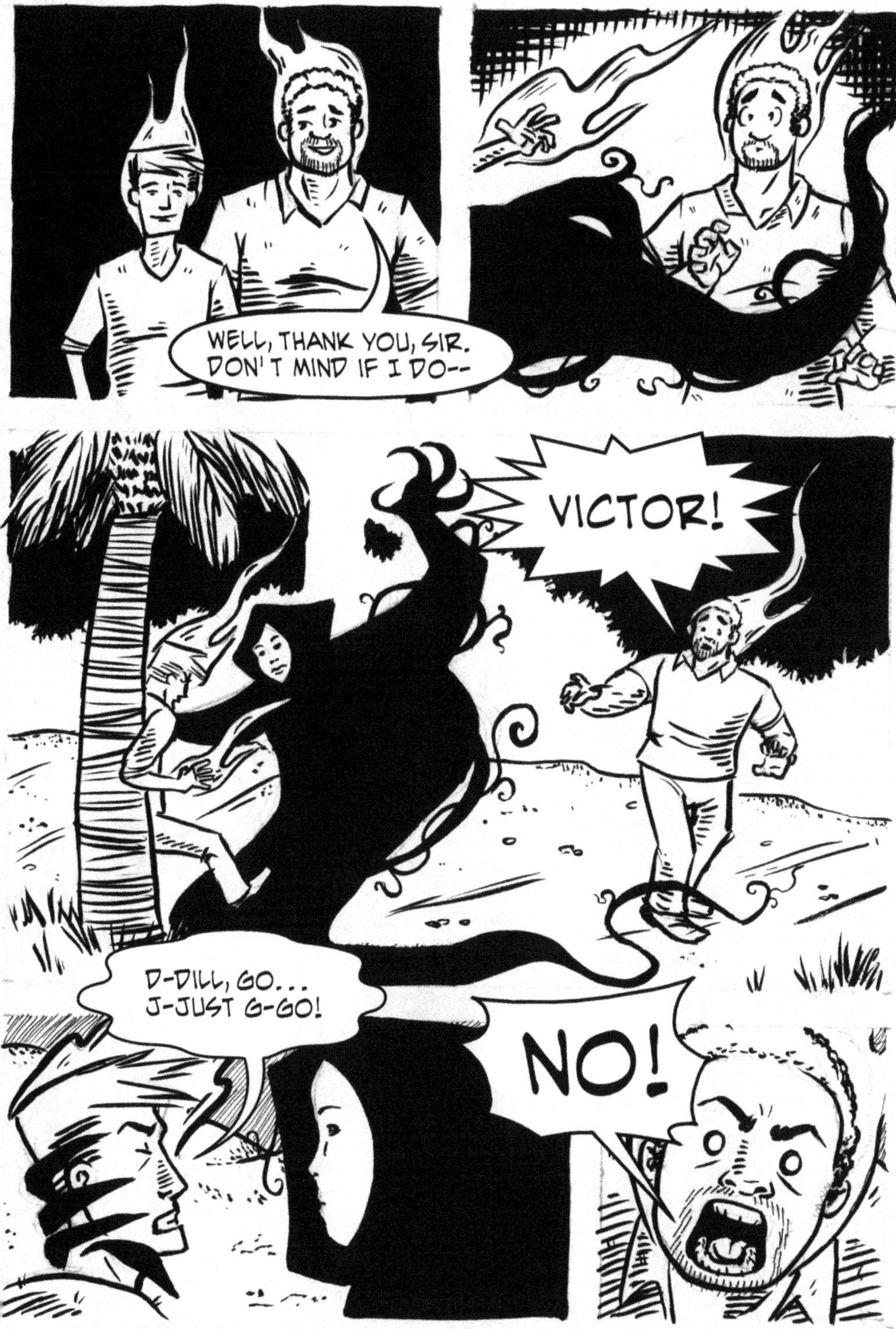
WELL, THANK YOU, SIR. DON'T MIND IF I DO--
VICTOR!
D-DILL, GO... J-JUST G-GO!
NO!

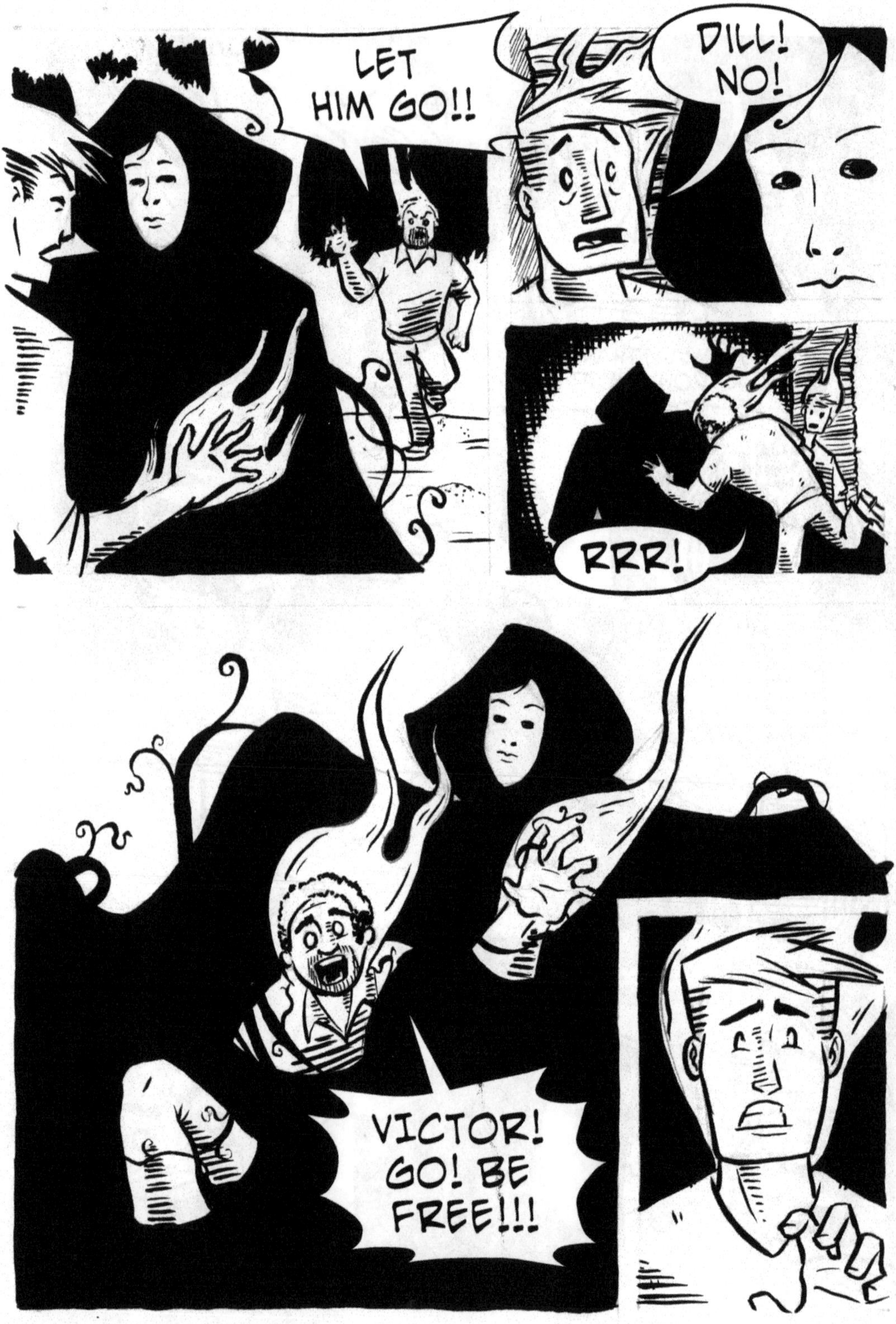
LET HIM GO!!
DILL! NO!
RRR!
VICTOR! GO! BE FREE!!!

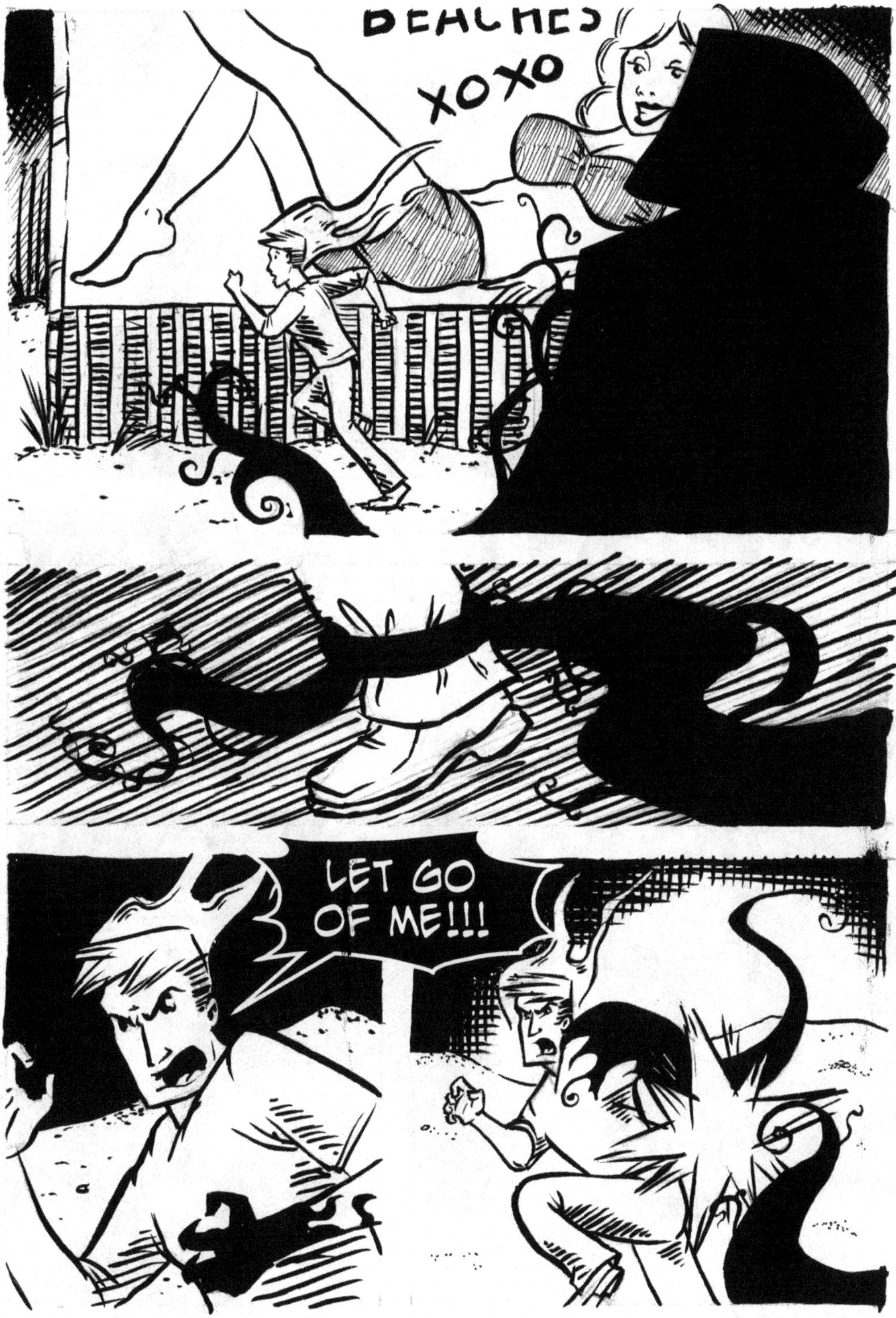
BEACHES
XOXO
LET GO OF ME!!!

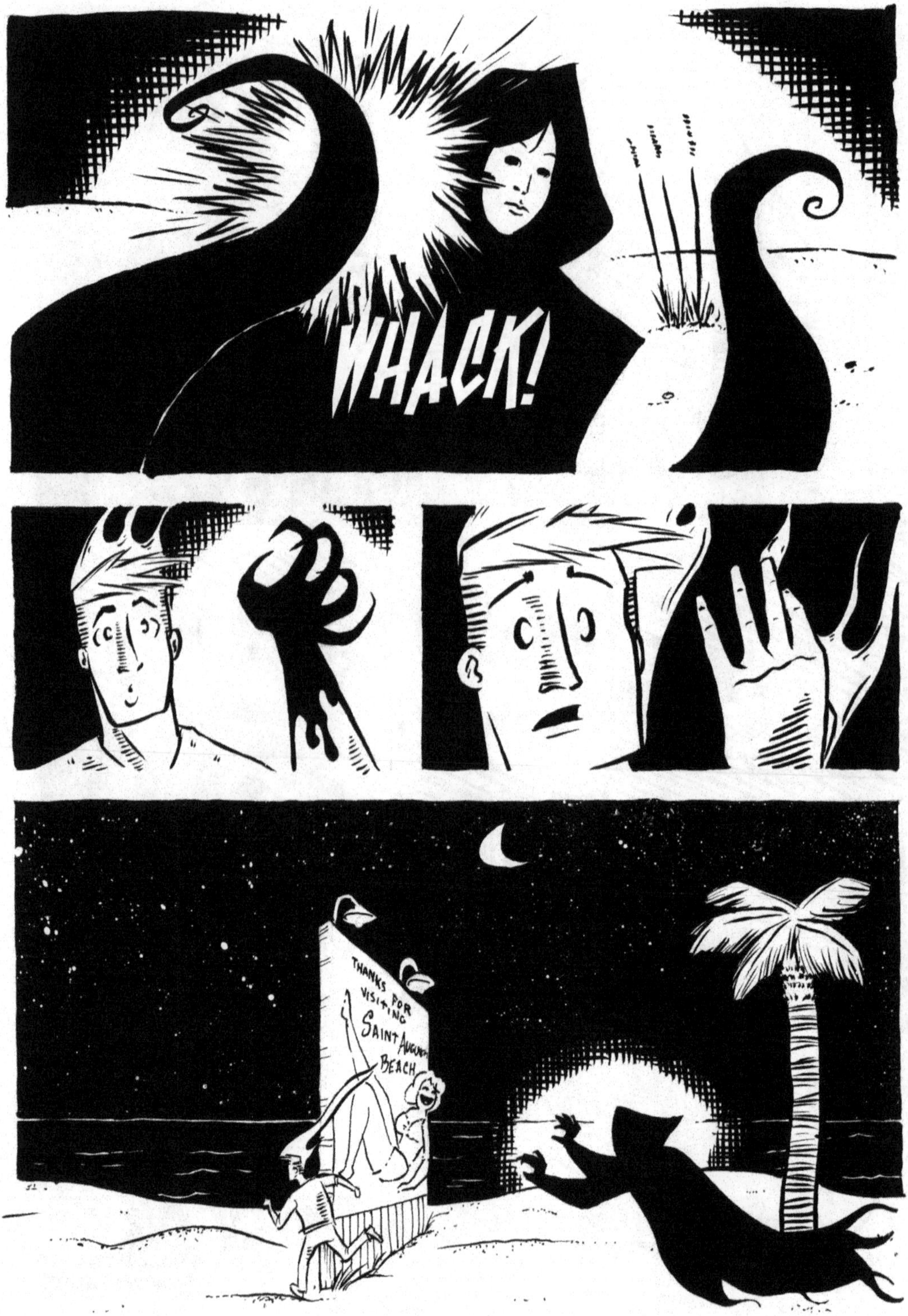
WHACK!
THANKS FOR VISITING SAINT AUGUSTINE BEACH

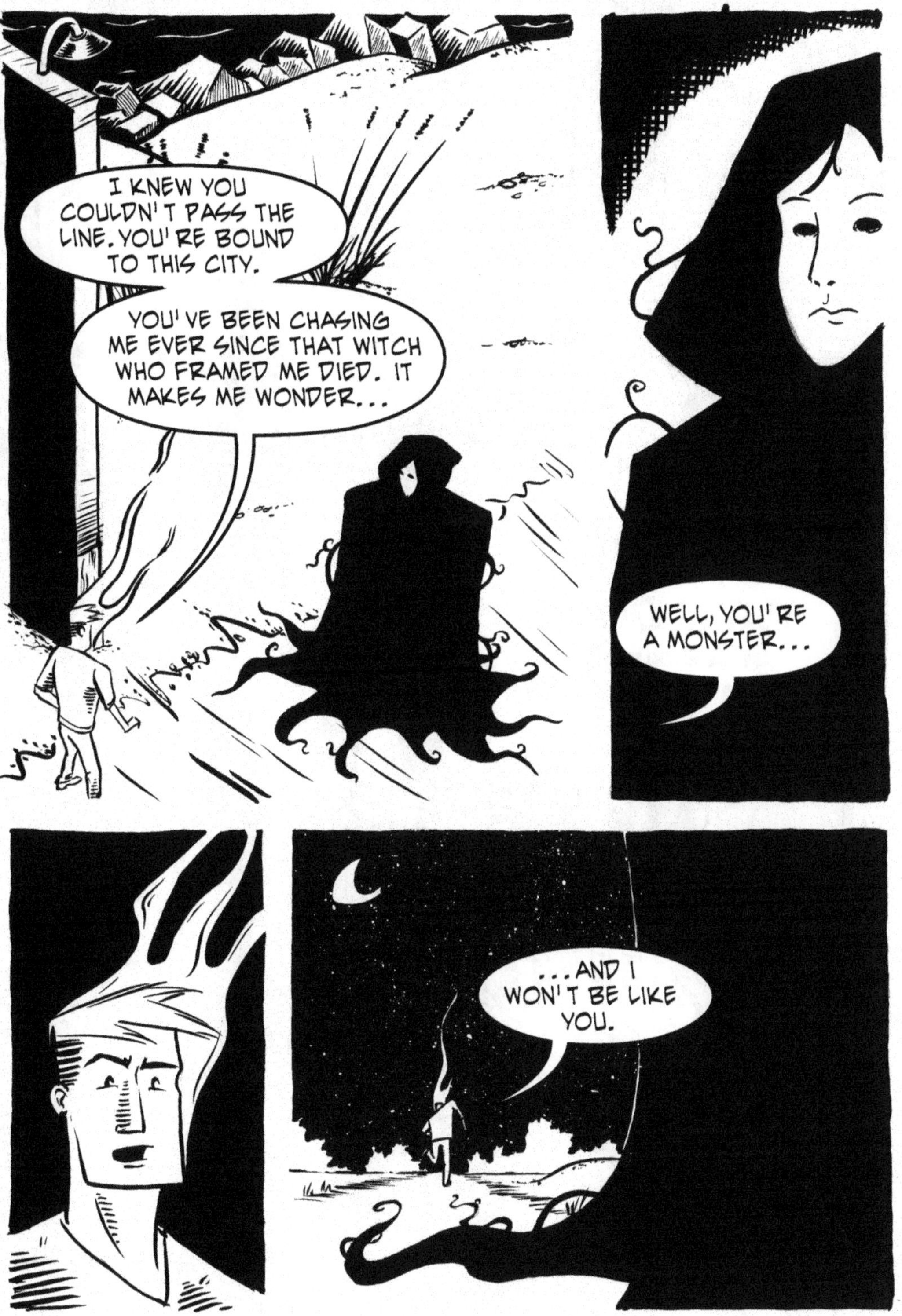
I KNEW YOU COULDN'T PASS THE LINE. YOU'RE BOUND TO THIS CITY.
YOU'VE BEEN CHASING ME EVER SINCE THAT WITCH WHO FRAMED ME DIED. IT MAKES ME WONDER...
WELL, YOU'RE A MONSTER...
...AND I WON'T BE LIKE YOU.

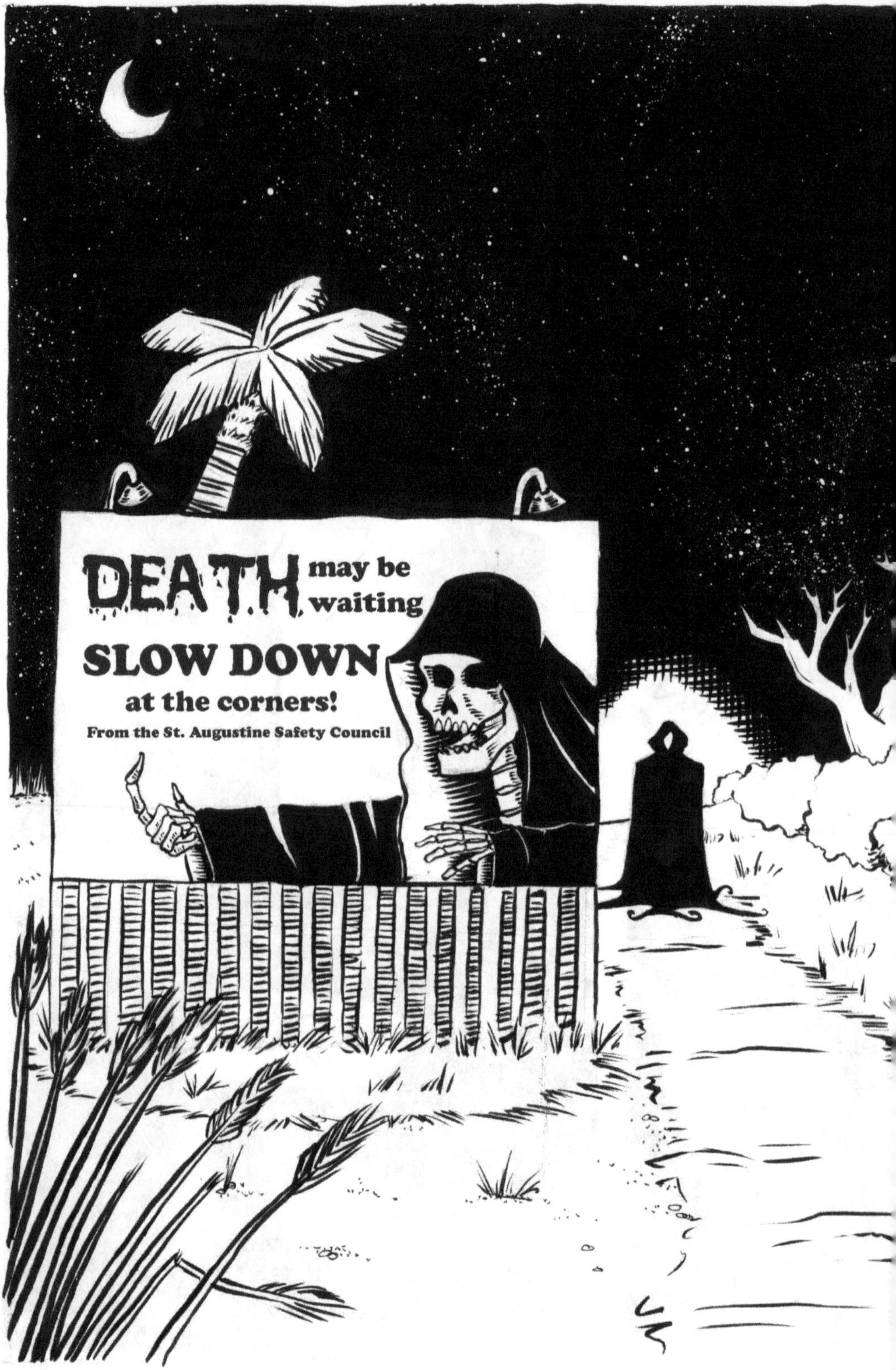
DEATH may be waiting
SLOW DOWN
at the corners!
From the St. Augustine Safety Council

CHAPTER

3

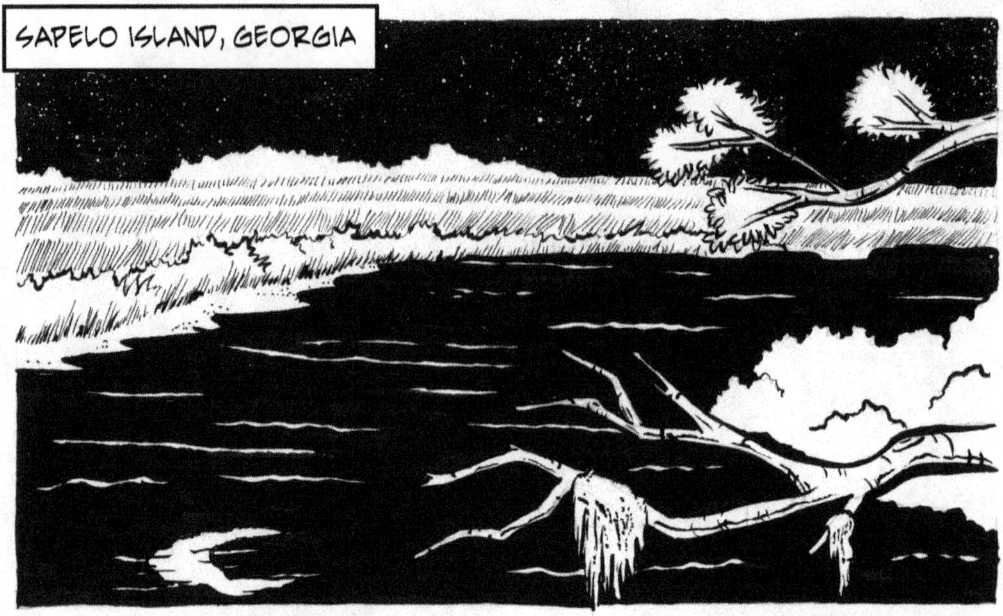
SAPELO ISLAND, GEORGIA

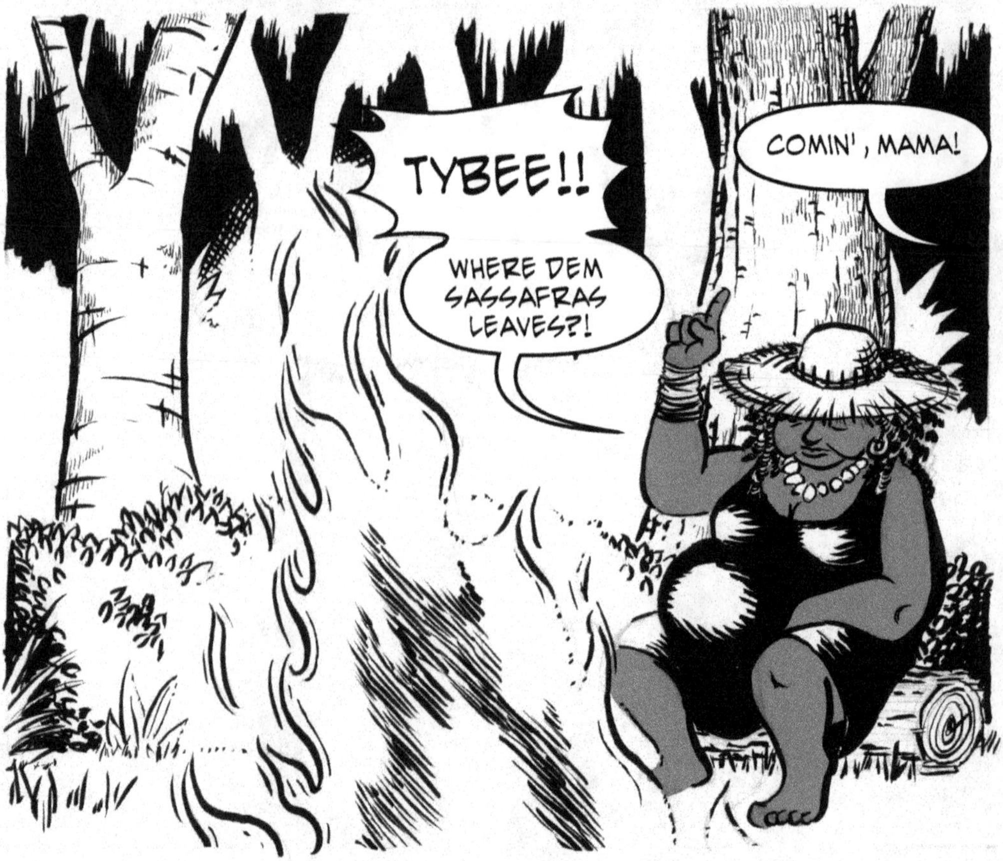
TYBEE!!
WHERE DEM SASSAFRAS LEAVES?!
COMIN', MAMA!

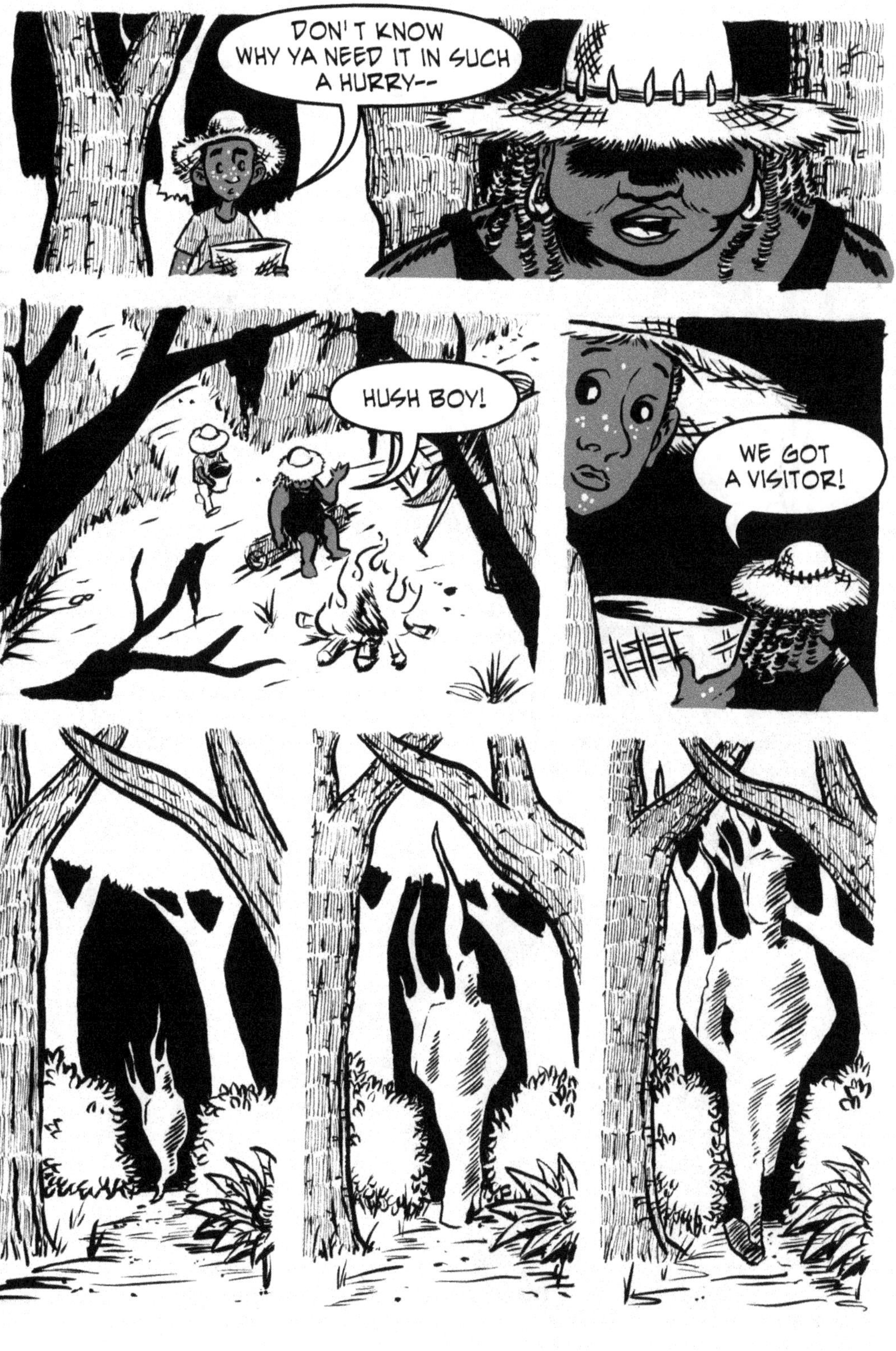
DON'T KNOW WHY YA NEED IT IN SUCH A HURRY--
HUSH BOY!
WE GOT A VISITOR!

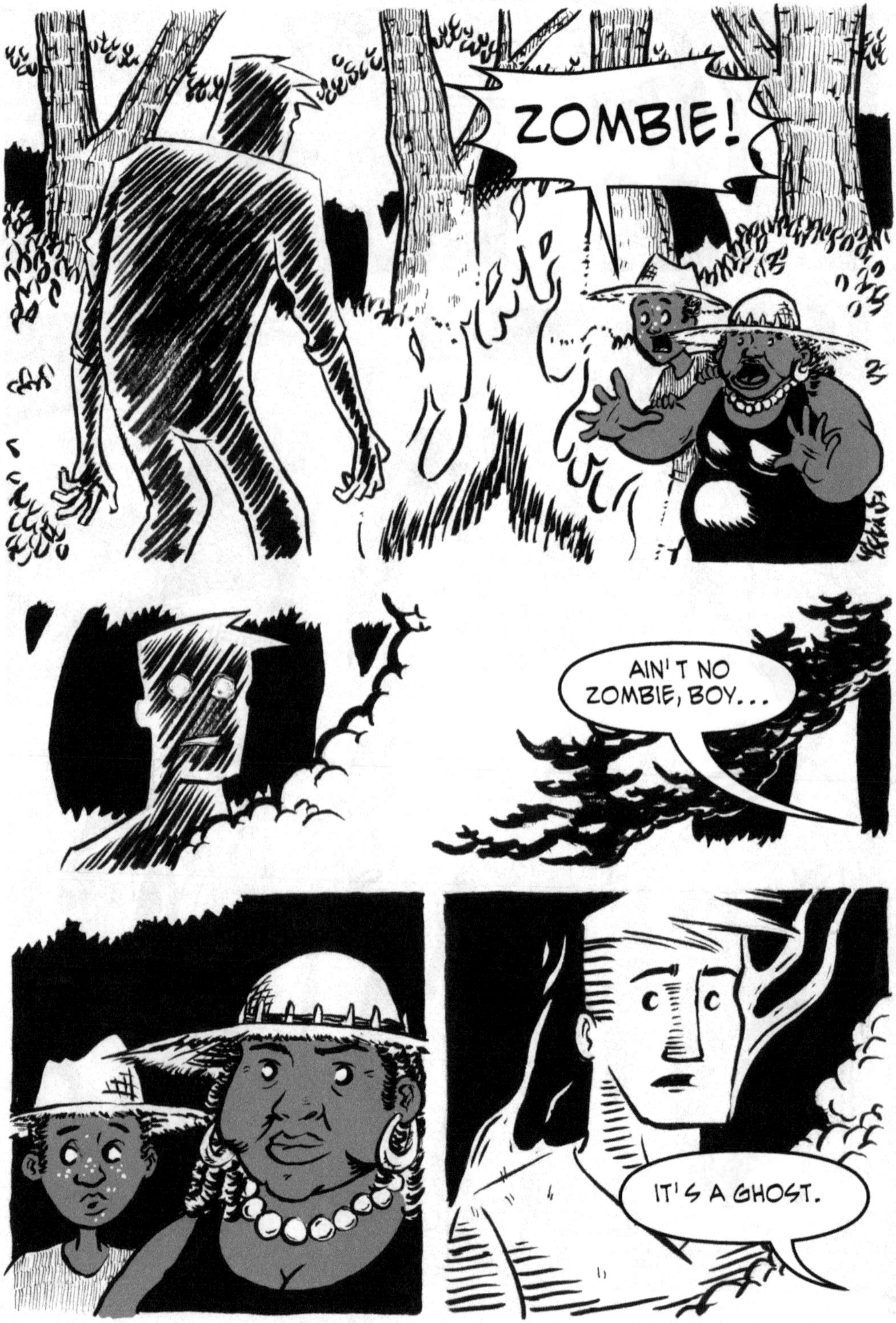
ZOMBIE!
AIN'T NO ZOMBIE, BOY...
IT'S A GHOST.

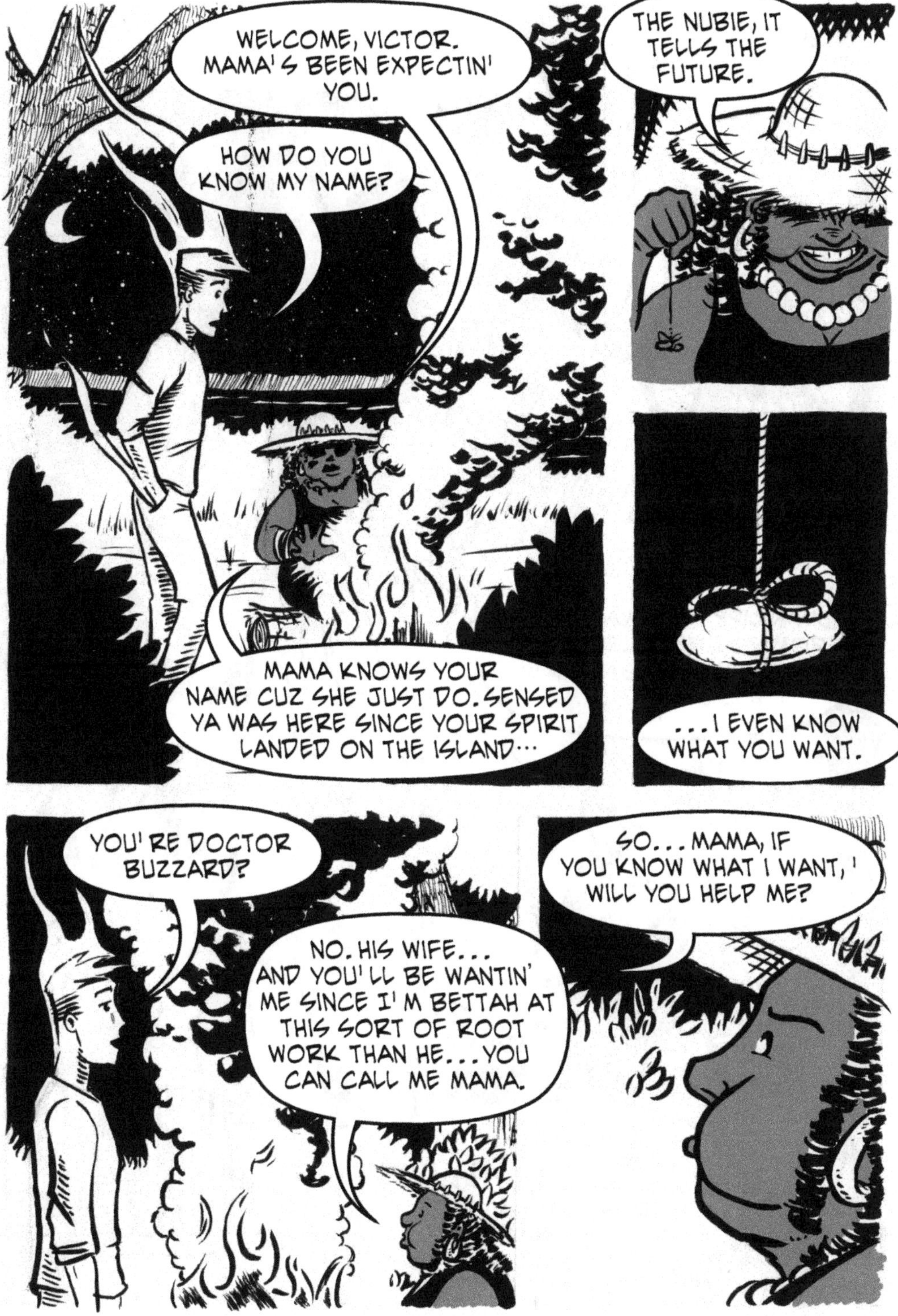
WELCOME, VICTOR. MAMA'S BEEN EXPECTIN' YOU.
HOW DO YOU KNOW MY NAME?
MAMA KNOWS YOUR NAME CUZ SHE JUST DO. SENSED YA WAS HERE SINCE YOUR SPIRIT LANDED ON THE ISLAND...
THE NUBIE, IT TELLS THE FUTURE.
...I EVEN KNOW WHAT YOU WANT.
YOU'RE DOCTOR BUZZARD?
NO. HIS WIFE... AND YOU'LL BE WANTIN' ME SINCE I'M BETTAH AT THIS SORT OF ROOT WORK THAN HE... YOU CAN CALL ME MAMA.
SO... MAMA, IF YOU KNOW WHAT I WANT, WILL YOU HELP ME?

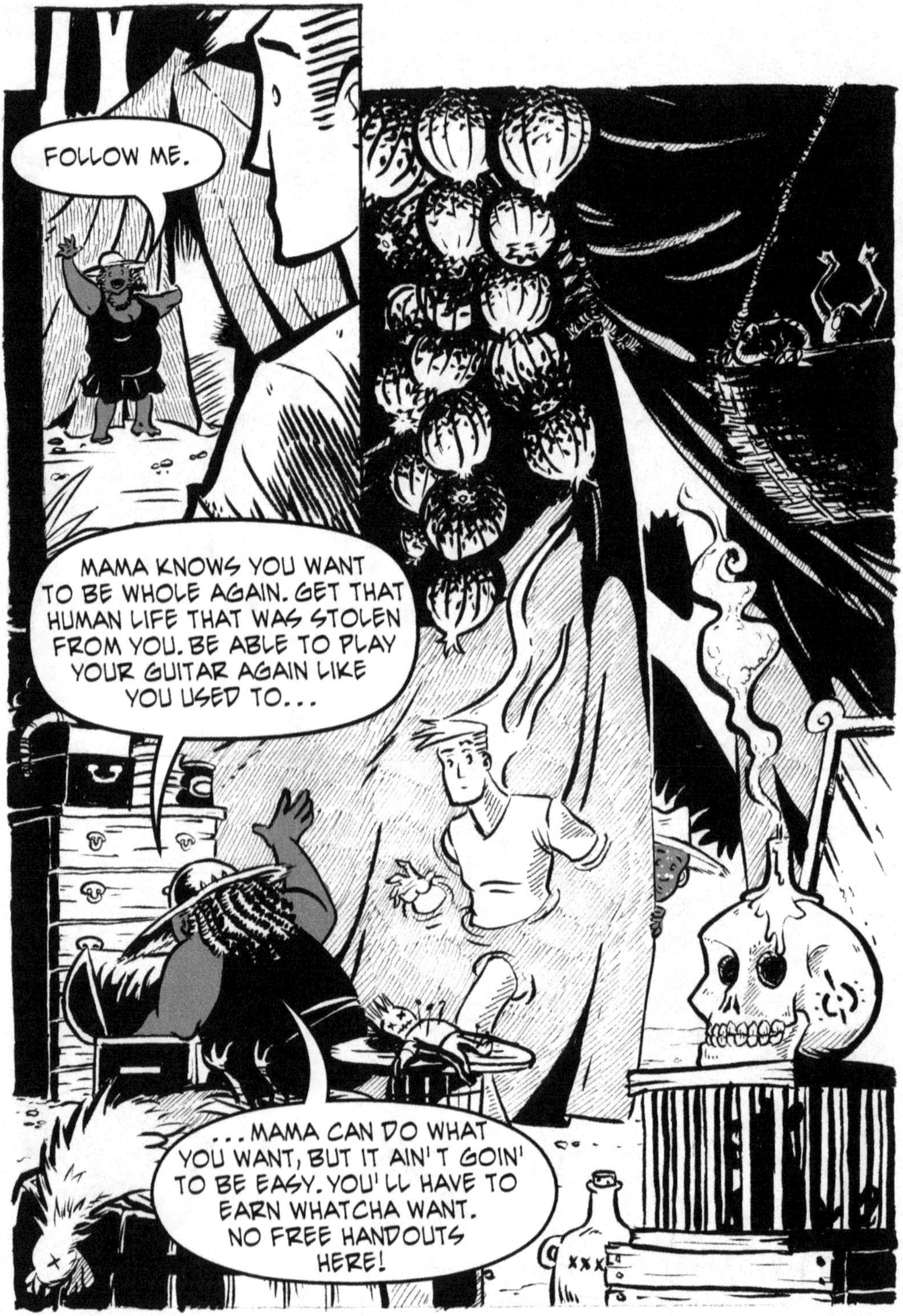
FOLLOW ME.
MAMA KNOWS YOU WANT TO BE WHOLE AGAIN. GET THAT HUMAN LIFE THAT WAS STOLEN FROM YOU. BE ABLE TO PLAY YOUR GUITAR AGAIN LIKE YOU USED TO...
...MAMA CAN DO WHAT YOU WANT, BUT IT AIN'T GOIN' TO BE EASY. YOU'LL HAVE TO EARN WHATCHA WANT. NO FREE HANDOUTS HERE!
XXX

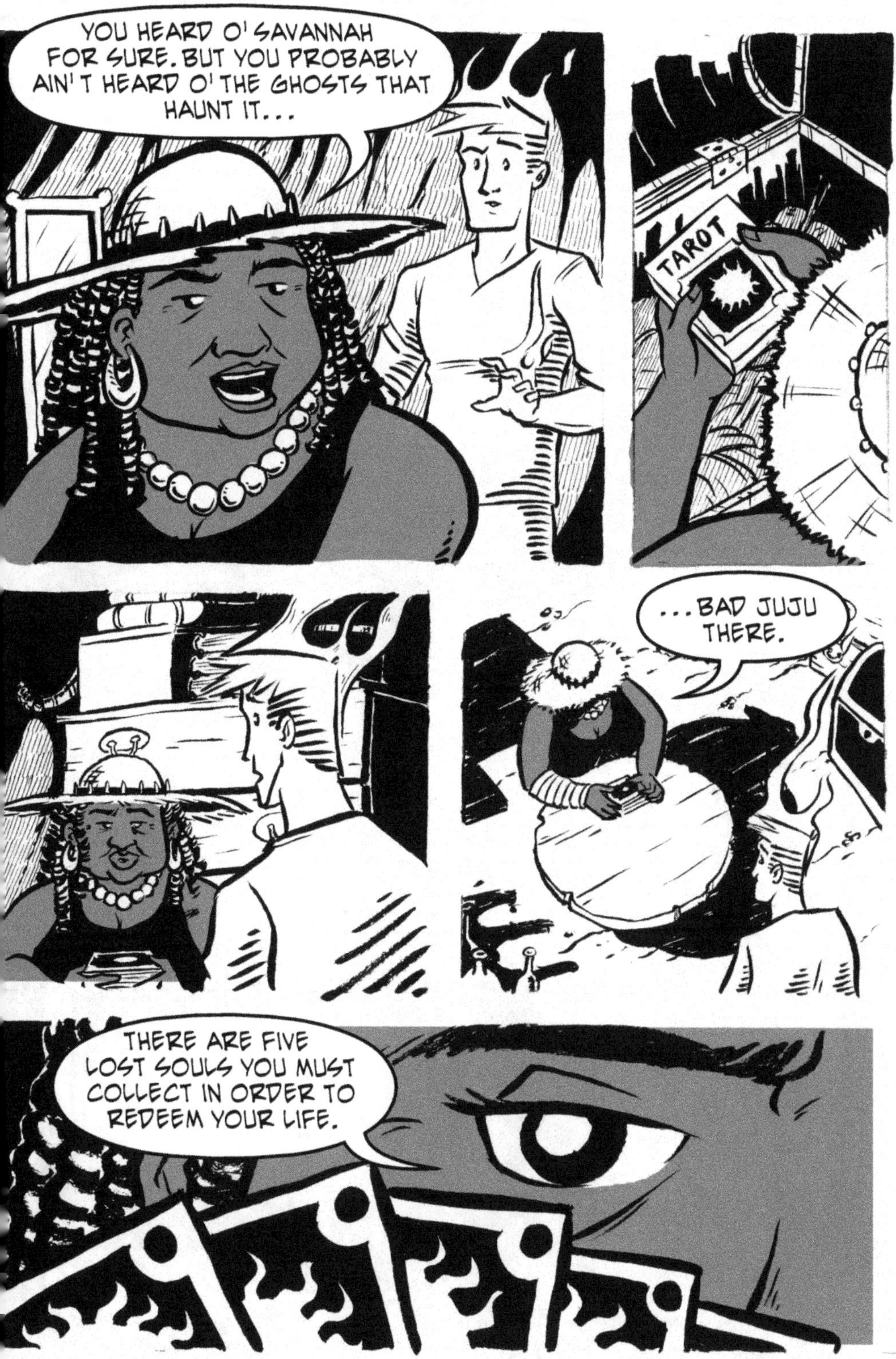
YOU HEARD O' SAVANNAH FOR SURE. BUT YOU PROBABLY AIN'T HEARD O' THE GHOSTS THAT HAUNT IT...
TAROT
...BAD JUJU THERE.
THERE ARE FIVE LOST SOULS YOU MUST COLLECT IN ORDER TO REDEEM YOUR LIFE.

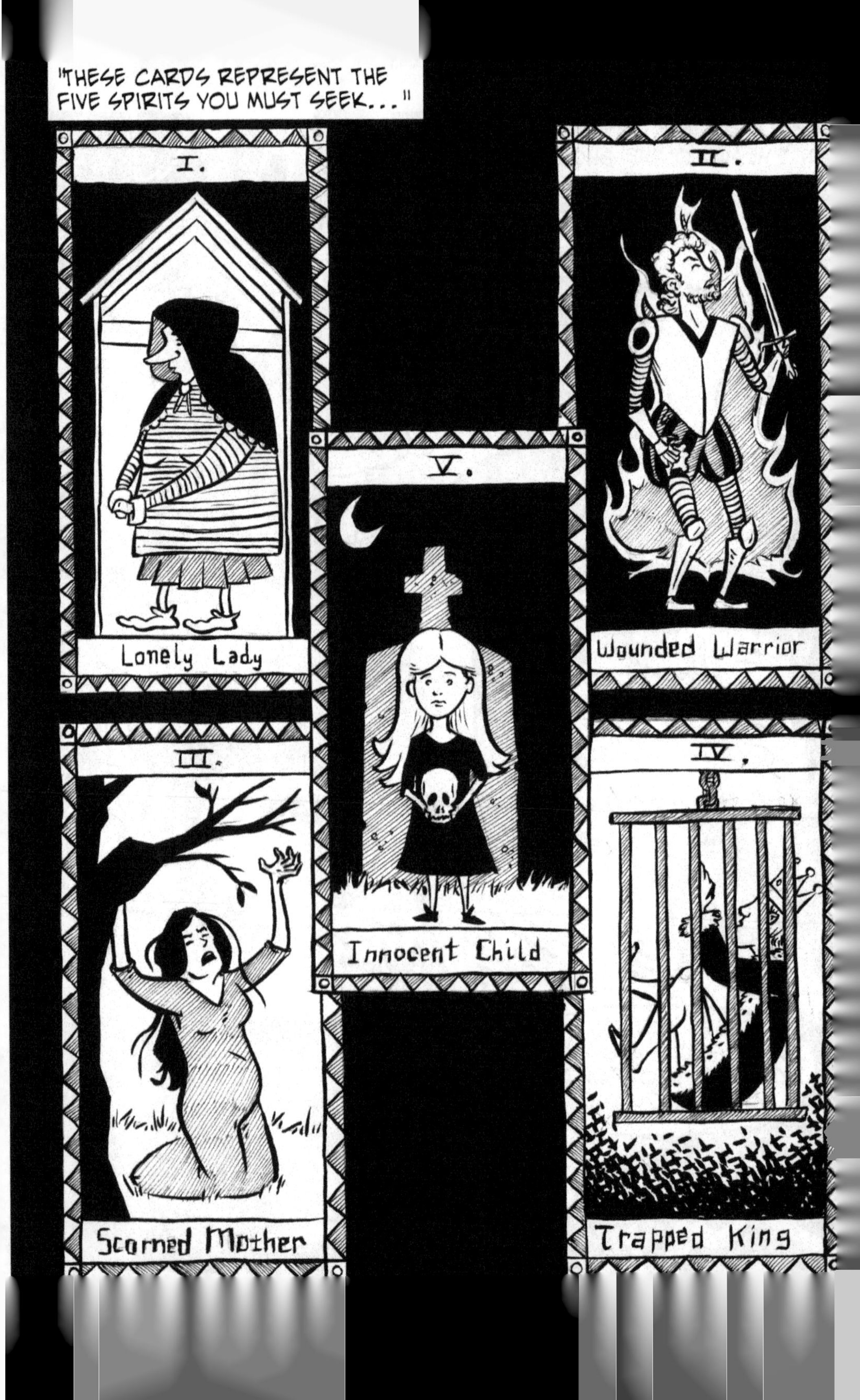
"THESE CARDS REPRESENT THE FIVE SPIRITS YOU MUST SEEK..."
I.
Lonely Lady
II.
Wounded Warrior
V.
Innocent Child
III.
Scorned Mother
IV.
Trapped King

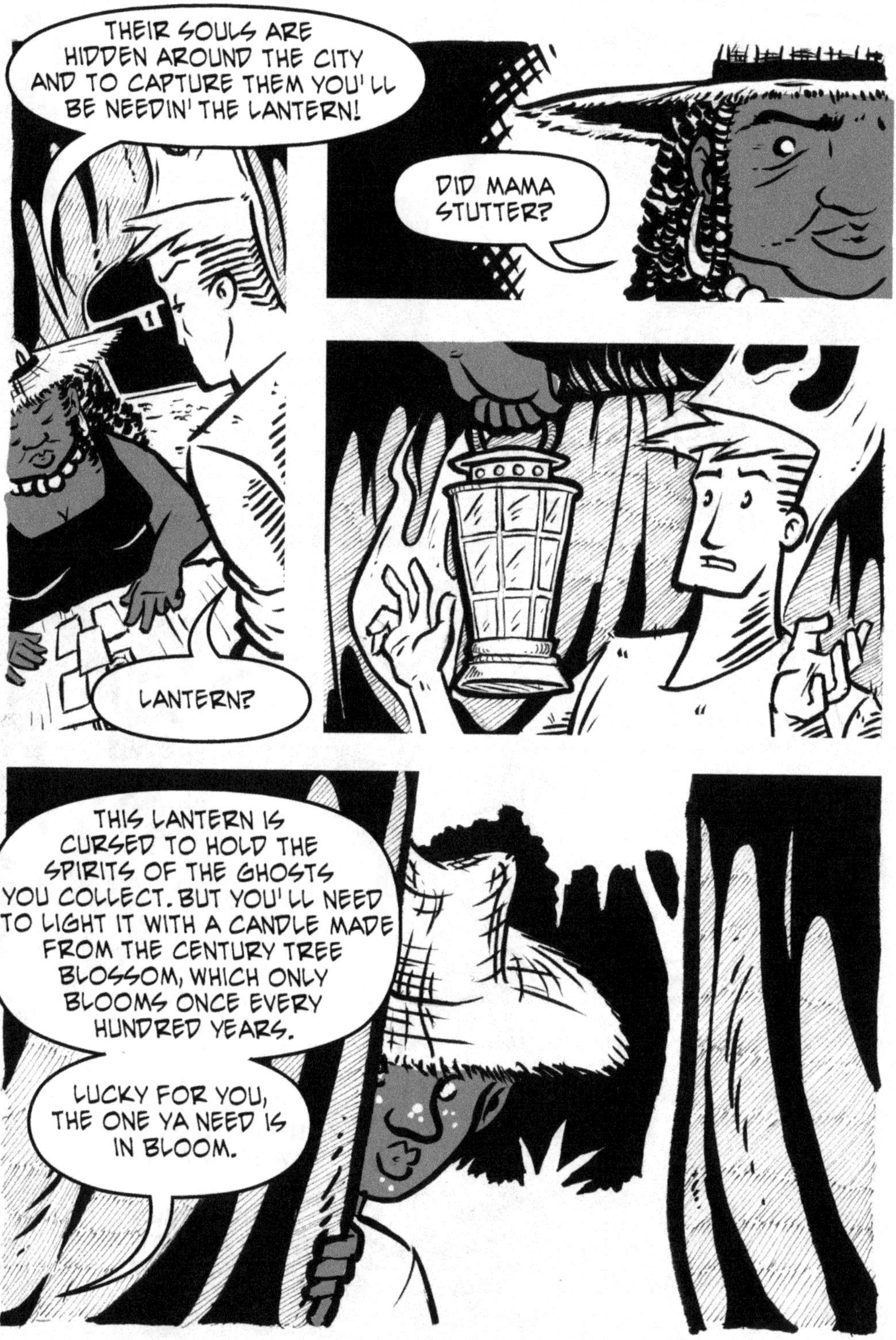
THEIR SOULS ARE HIDDEN AROUND THE CITY AND TO CAPTURE THEM YOU'LL BE NEEDIN' THE LANTERN!
DID MAMA STUTTER?
LANTERN?
THIS LANTERN IS CURSED TO HOLD THE SPIRITS OF THE GHOSTS YOU COLLECT. BUT YOU'LL NEED TO LIGHT IT WITH A CANDLE MADE FROM THE CENTURY TREE BLOSSOM, WHICH ONLY BLOOMS ONCE EVERY HUNDRED YEARS.
LUCKY FOR YOU, THE ONE YA NEED IS IN BLOOM.

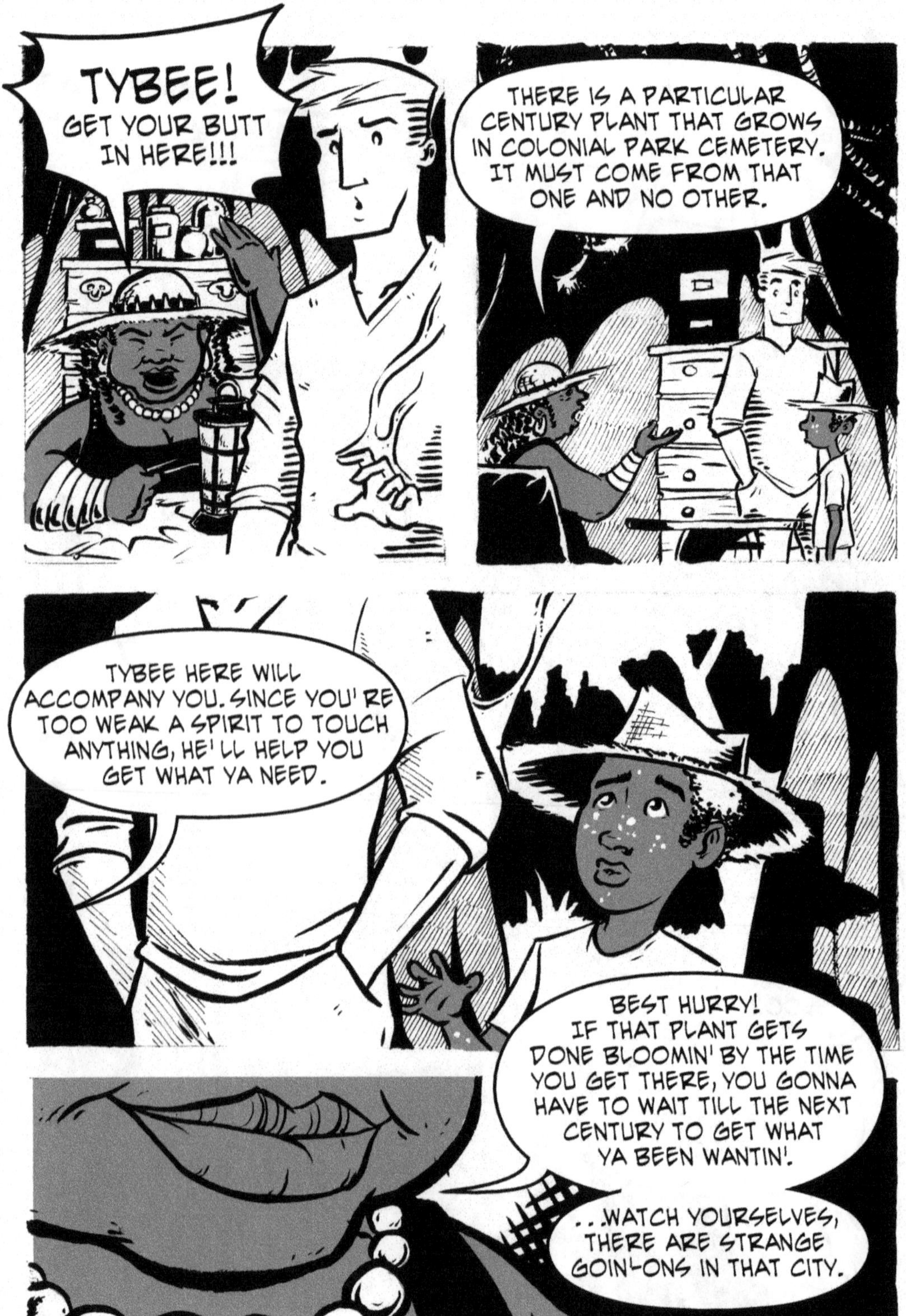
TYBEE! GET YOUR BUTT IN HERE!!!
THERE IS A PARTICULAR CENTURY PLANT THAT GROWS IN COLONIAL PARK CEMETERY. IT MUST COME FROM THAT ONE AND NO OTHER.
TYBEE HERE WILL ACCOMPANY YOU. SINCE YOU'RE TOO WEAK A SPIRIT TO TOUCH ANYTHING, HE'LL HELP YOU GET WHAT YA NEED.
BEST HURRY! IF THAT PLANT GETS DONE BLOOMIN' BY THE TIME YOU GET THERE, YOU GONNA HAVE TO WAIT TILL THE NEXT CENTURY TO GET WHAT YA BEEN WANTIN'.
...WATCH YOURSELVES, THERE ARE STRANGE GOIN-ONS IN THAT CITY.

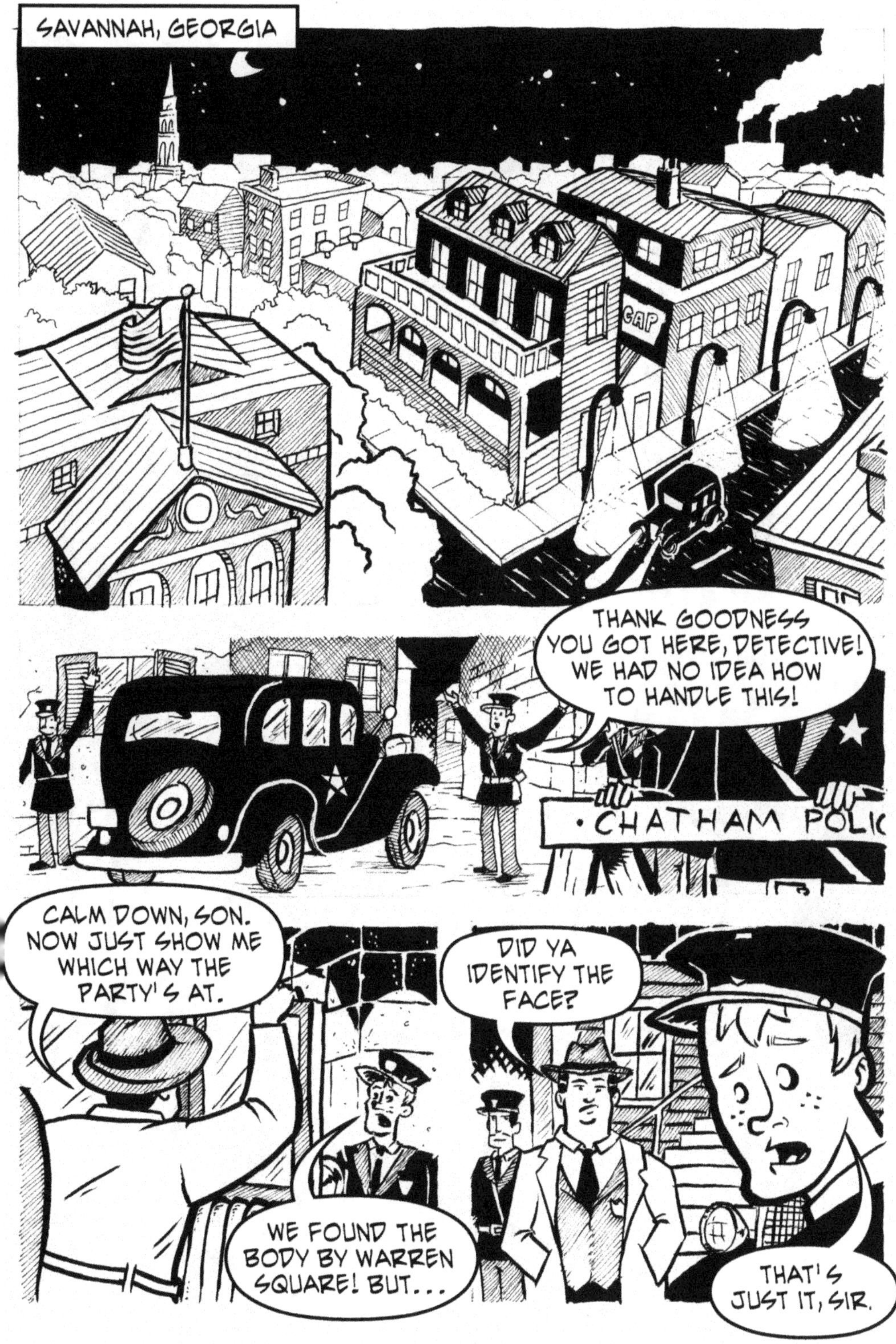
SAVANNAH, GEORGIA
GAP
THANK GOODNESS YOU GOT HERE, DETECTIVE! WE HAD NO IDEA HOW TO HANDLE THIS!
CHATHAM POLIC
CALM DOWN, SON. NOW JUST SHOW ME WHICH WAY THE PARTY'S AT.
WE FOUND THE BODY BY WARREN SQUARE! BUT...
DID YA IDENTIFY THE FACE?
THAT'S JUST IT, SIR.

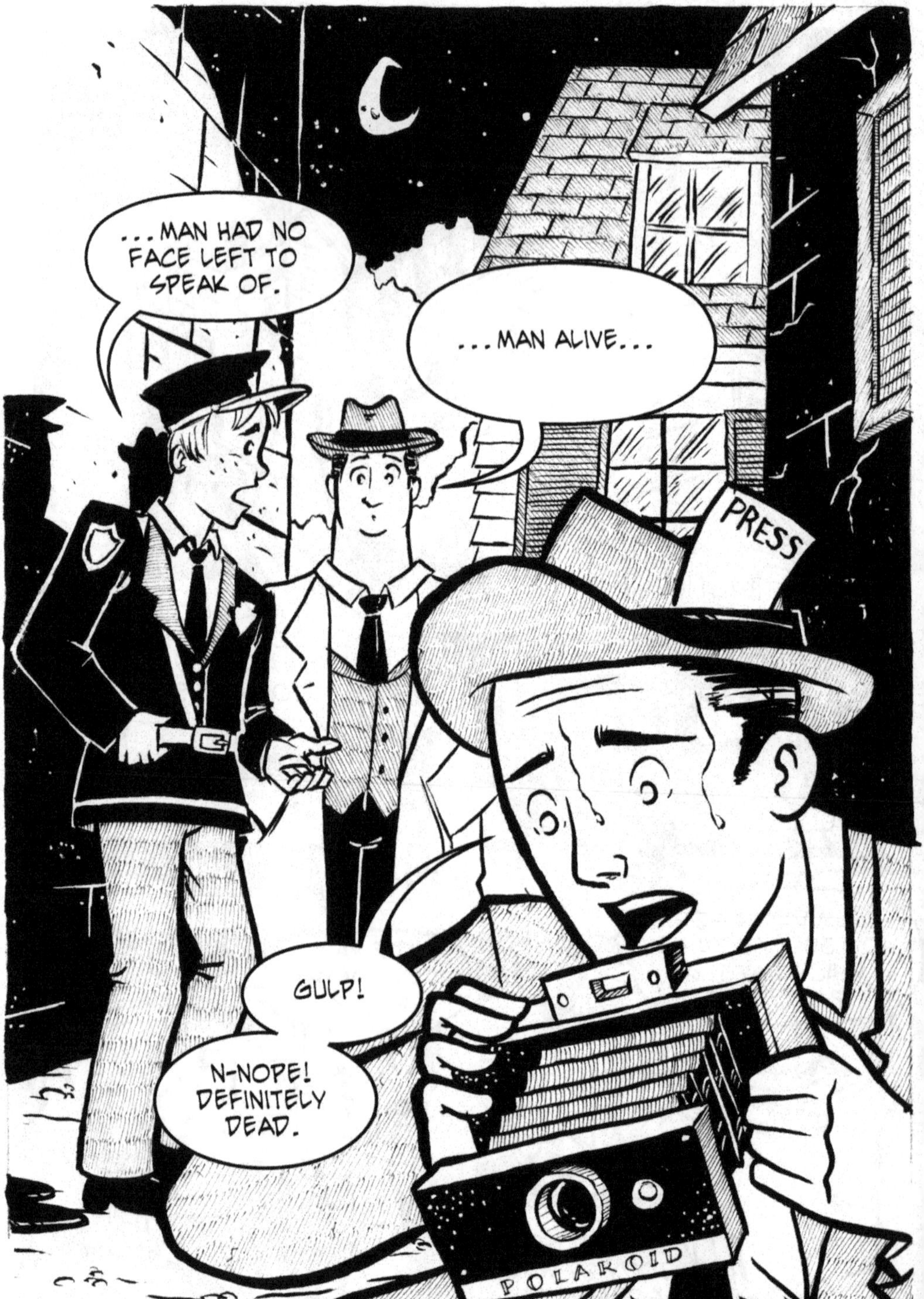
...MAN HAD NO FACE LEFT TO SPEAK OF.
...MAN ALIVE...
PRESS
GULP!
N-NOPE! DEFINITELY DEAD.
POLAROID

CHAPTER
4

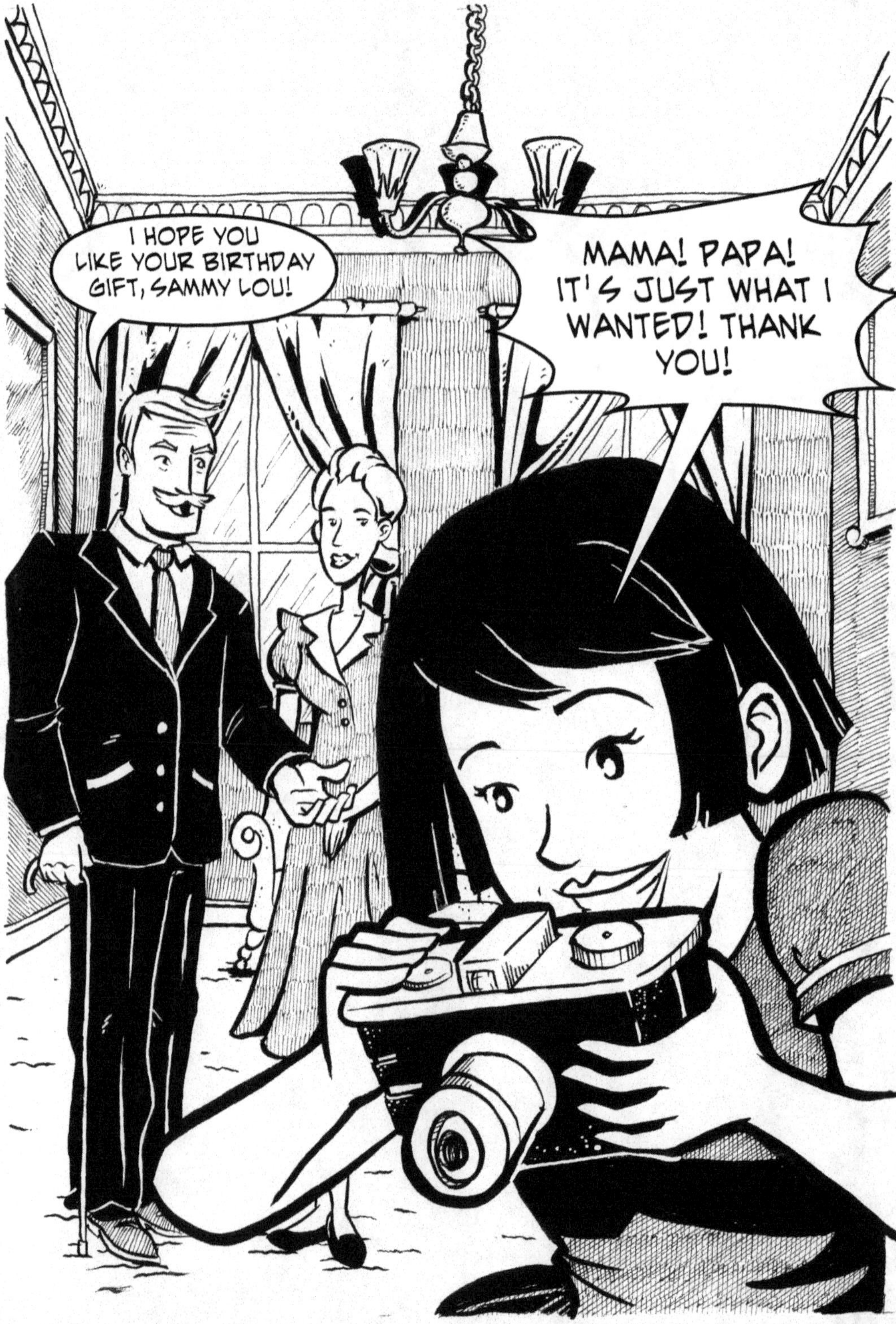
I HOPE YOU LIKE YOUR BIRTHDAY GIFT, SAMMY LOU!
MAMA! PAPA! IT'S JUST WHAT I WANTED! THANK YOU!

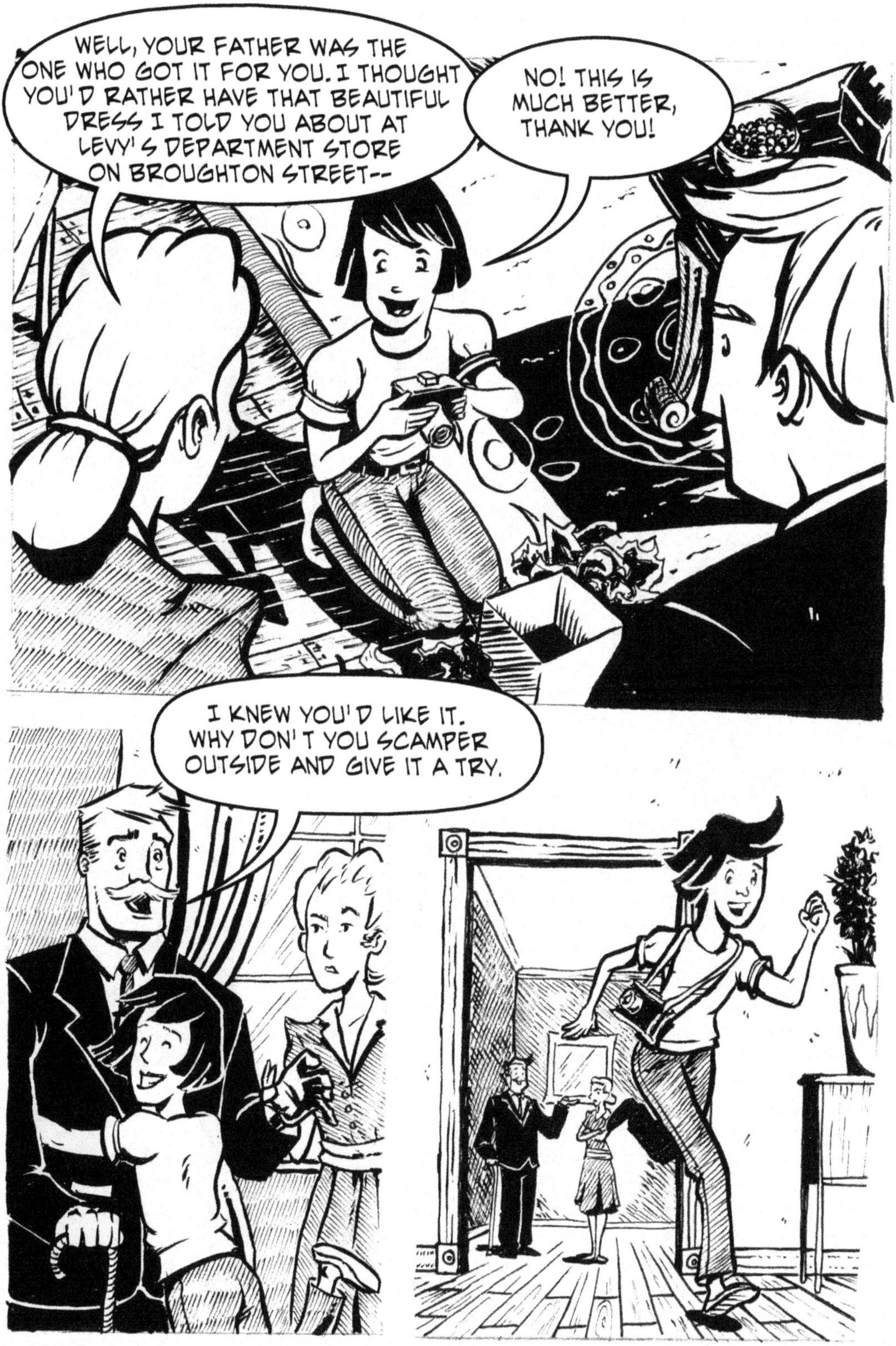
WELL, YOUR FATHER WAS THE ONE WHO GOT IT FOR YOU. I THOUGHT YOU'D RATHER HAVE THAT BEAUTIFUL DRESS I TOLD YOU ABOUT AT LEVY'S DEPARTMENT STORE ON BROUGHTON STREET--
NO! THIS IS MUCH BETTER, THANK YOU!
I KNEW YOU'D LIKE IT. WHY DON'T YOU SCAMPER OUTSIDE AND GIVE IT A TRY.

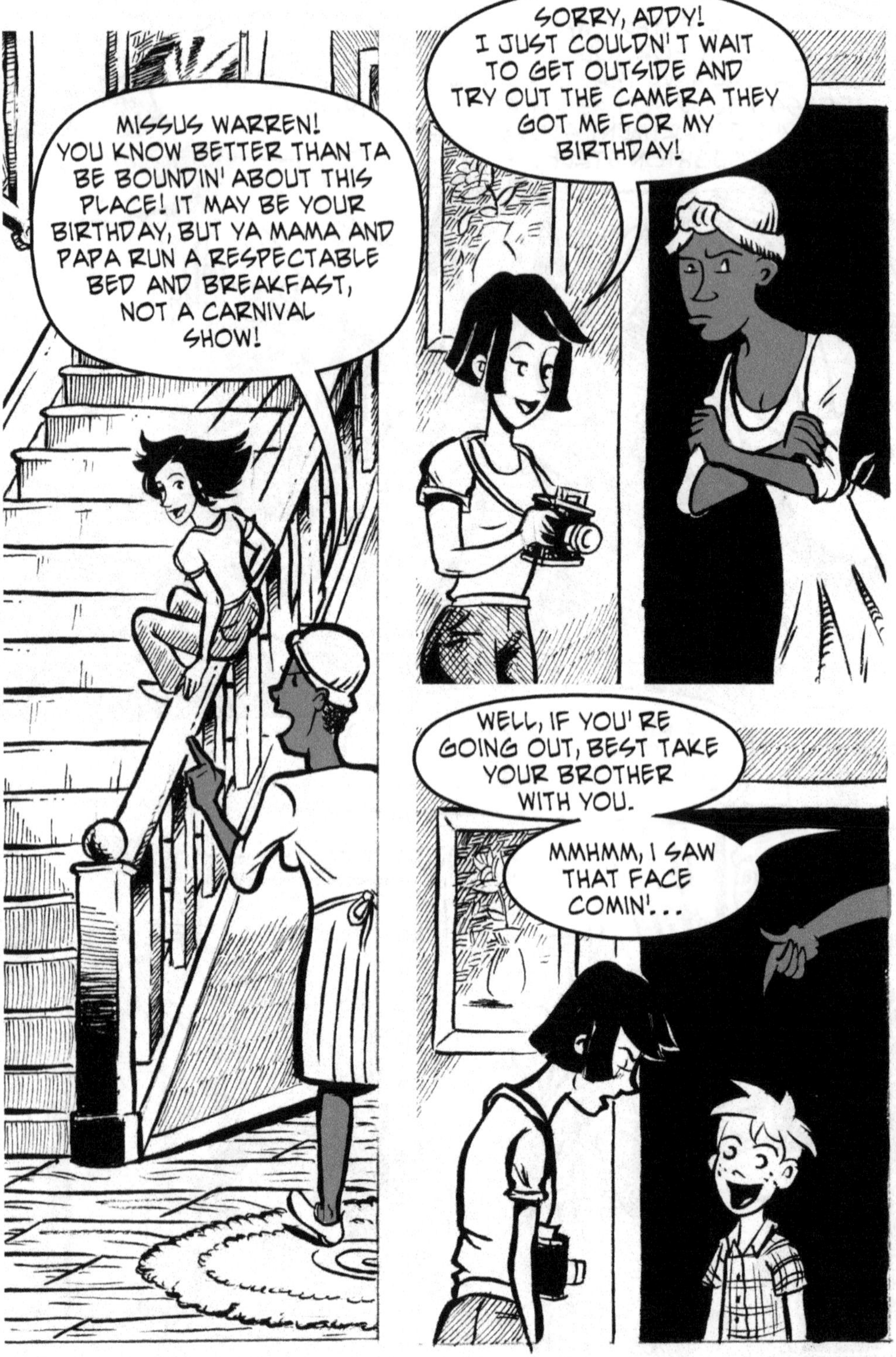
MISSUS WARREN! YOU KNOW BETTER THAN TA BE BOUNDIN' ABOUT THIS PLACE! IT MAY BE YOUR BIRTHDAY, BUT YA MAMA AND PAPA RUN A RESPECTABLE BED AND BREAKFAST, NOT A CARNIVAL SHOW!
SORRY, ADDY! I JUST COULDN'T WAIT TO GET OUTSIDE AND TRY OUT THE CAMERA THEY GOT ME FOR MY BIRTHDAY!
WELL, IF YOU'RE GOING OUT, BEST TAKE YOUR BROTHER WITH YOU.
MMHMM, I SAW THAT FACE COMIN'...

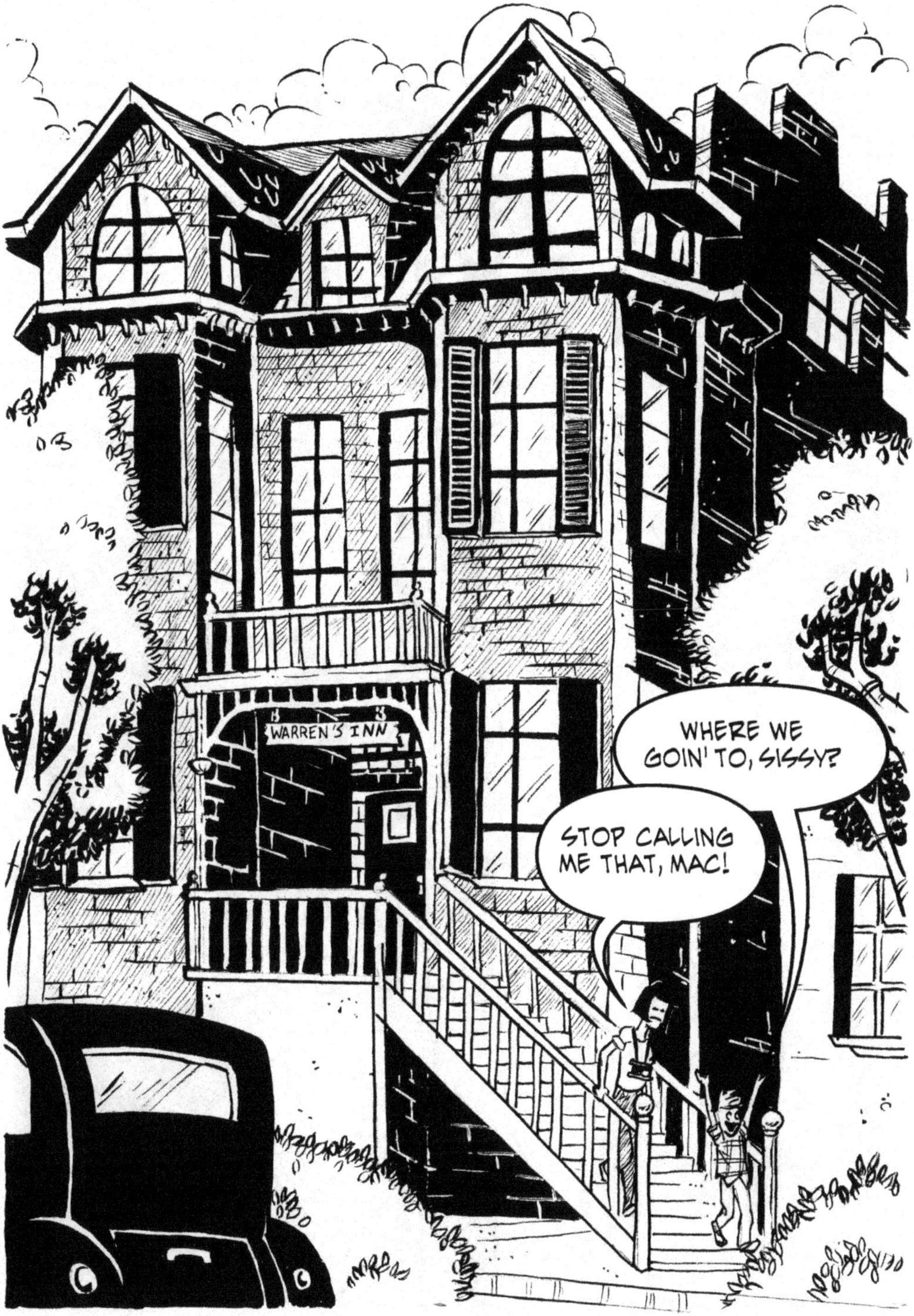
WARREN'S INN
WHERE WE GOIN' TO, SISSY?
STOP CALLING ME THAT, MAC!

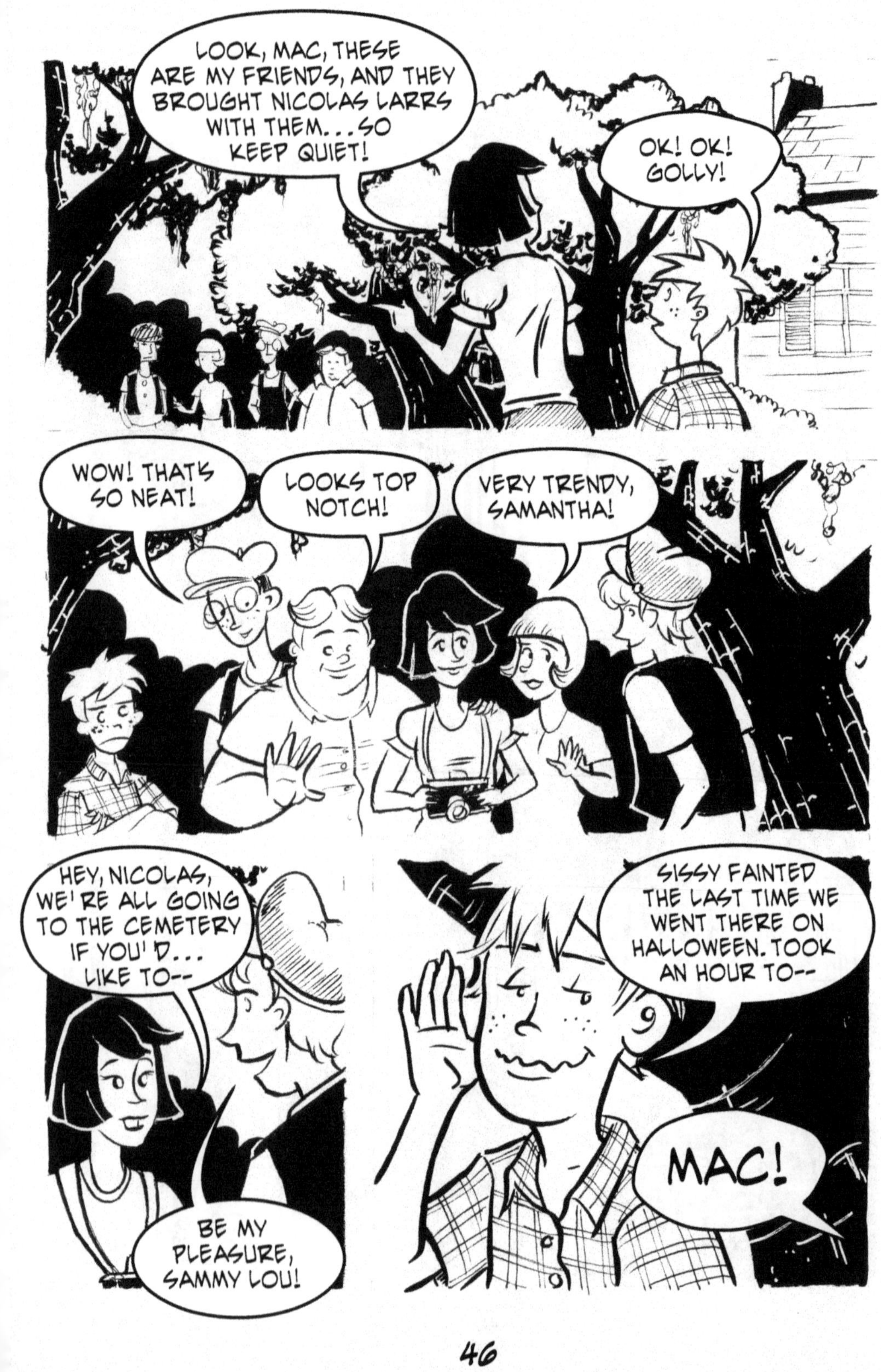
LOOK, MAC, THESE ARE MY FRIENDS, AND THEY BROUGHT NICOLAS LARRS WITH THEM... SO KEEP QUIET!
OK! OK! GOLLY!
WOW! THAT'S SO NEAT!
LOOKS TOP NOTCH!
VERY TRENDY, SAMANTHA!
HEY, NICOLAS, WE'RE ALL GOING TO THE CEMETERY IF YOU'D... LIKE TO--
BE MY PLEASURE, SAMMY LOU!
SISSY FAINTED THE LAST TIME WE WENT THERE ON HALLOWEEN. TOOK AN HOUR TO--
MAC!

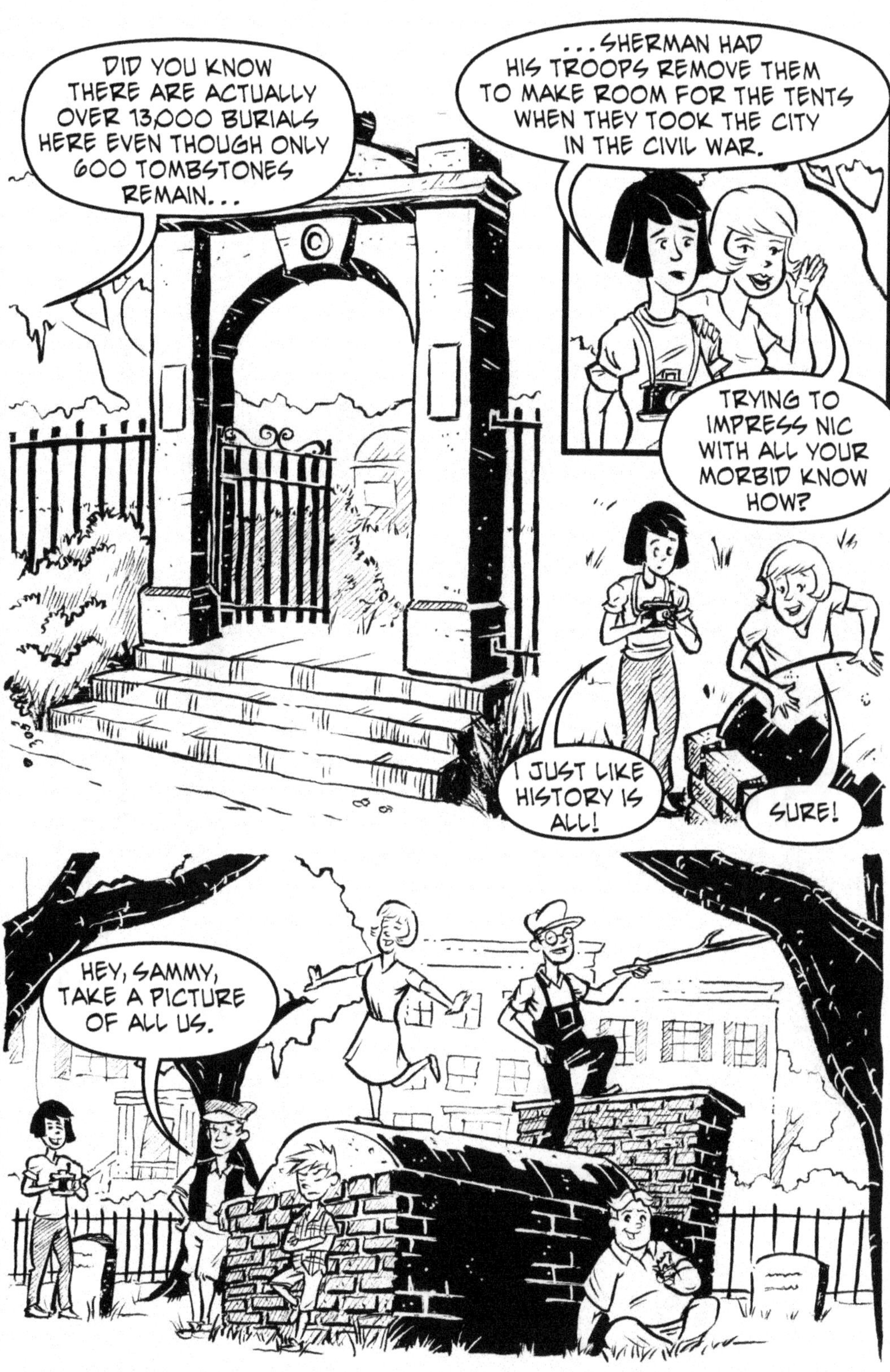
DID YOU KNOW THERE ARE ACTUALLY OVER 13,000 BURIALS HERE EVEN THOUGH ONLY 600 TOMBSTONES REMAIN...
...SHERMAN HAD HIS TROOPS REMOVE THEM TO MAKE ROOM FOR THE TENTS WHEN THEY TOOK THE CITY IN THE CIVIL WAR.
TRYING TO IMPRESS NIC WITH ALL YOUR MORBID KNOW HOW?
I JUST LIKE HISTORY IS ALL!
SURE!
HEY, SAMMY, TAKE A PICTURE OF ALL US.

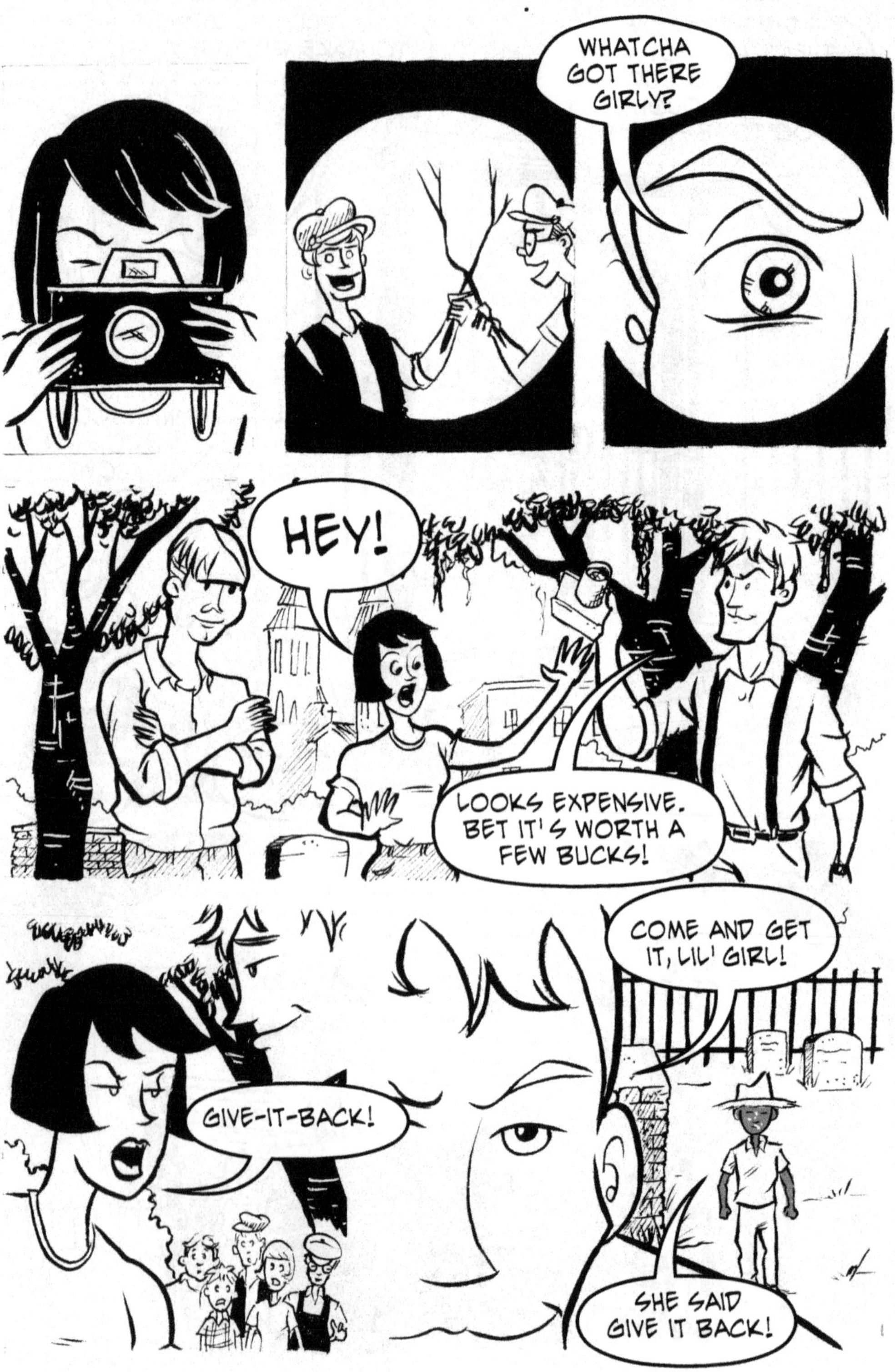
WHATCHA GOT THERE GIRLY?
HEY!
LOOKS EXPENSIVE. BET IT'S WORTH A FEW BUCKS!
GIVE-IT-BACK!
COME AND GET IT, LIL' GIRL!
SHE SAID GIVE IT BACK!

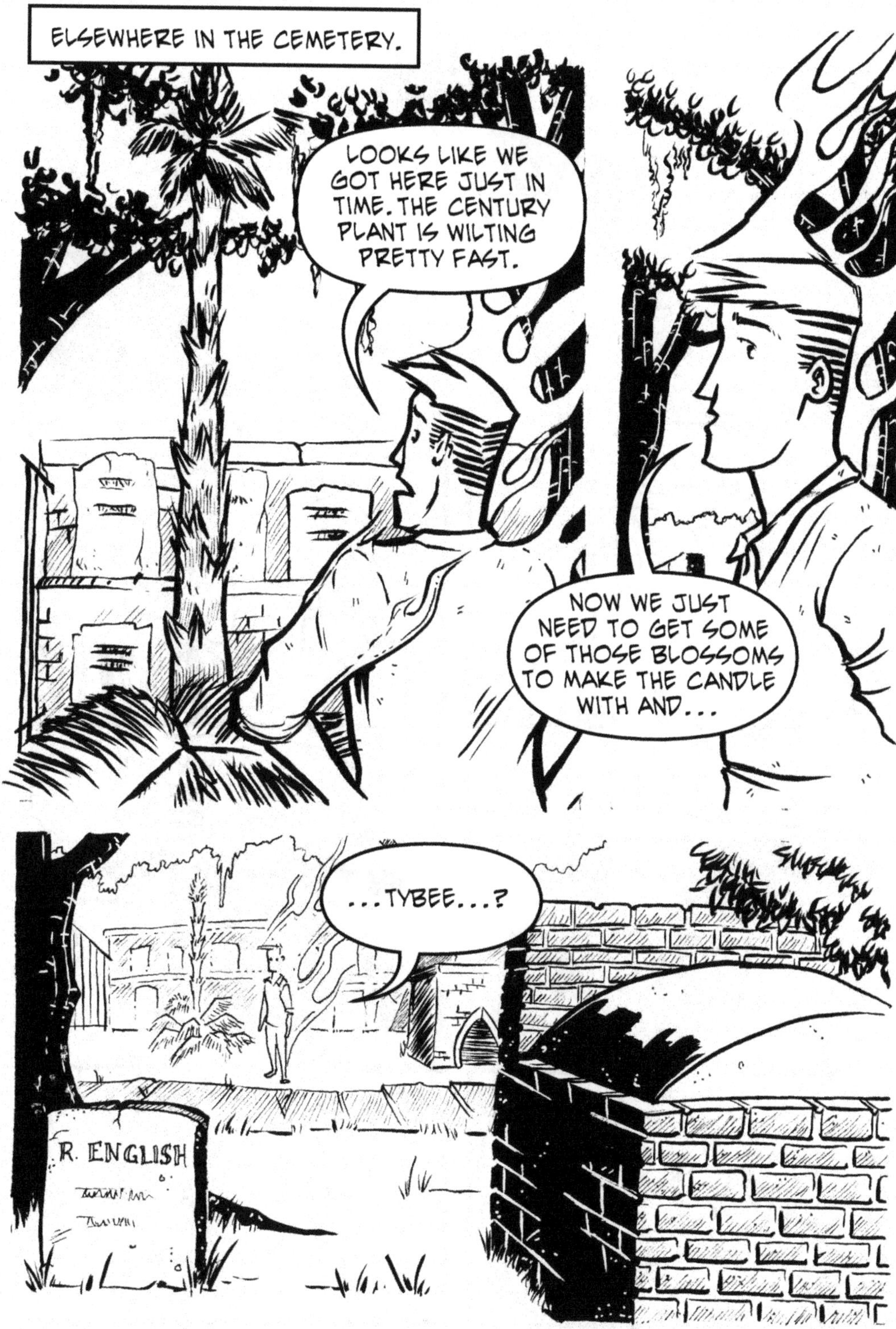
ELSEWHERE IN THE CEMETERY.
LOOKS LIKE WE GOT HERE JUST IN TIME. THE CENTURY PLANT IS WILTING PRETTY FAST.
NOW WE JUST NEED TO GET SOME OF THOSE BLOSSOMS TO MAKE THE CANDLE WITH AND...
...TYBEE...?
R. ENGLISH

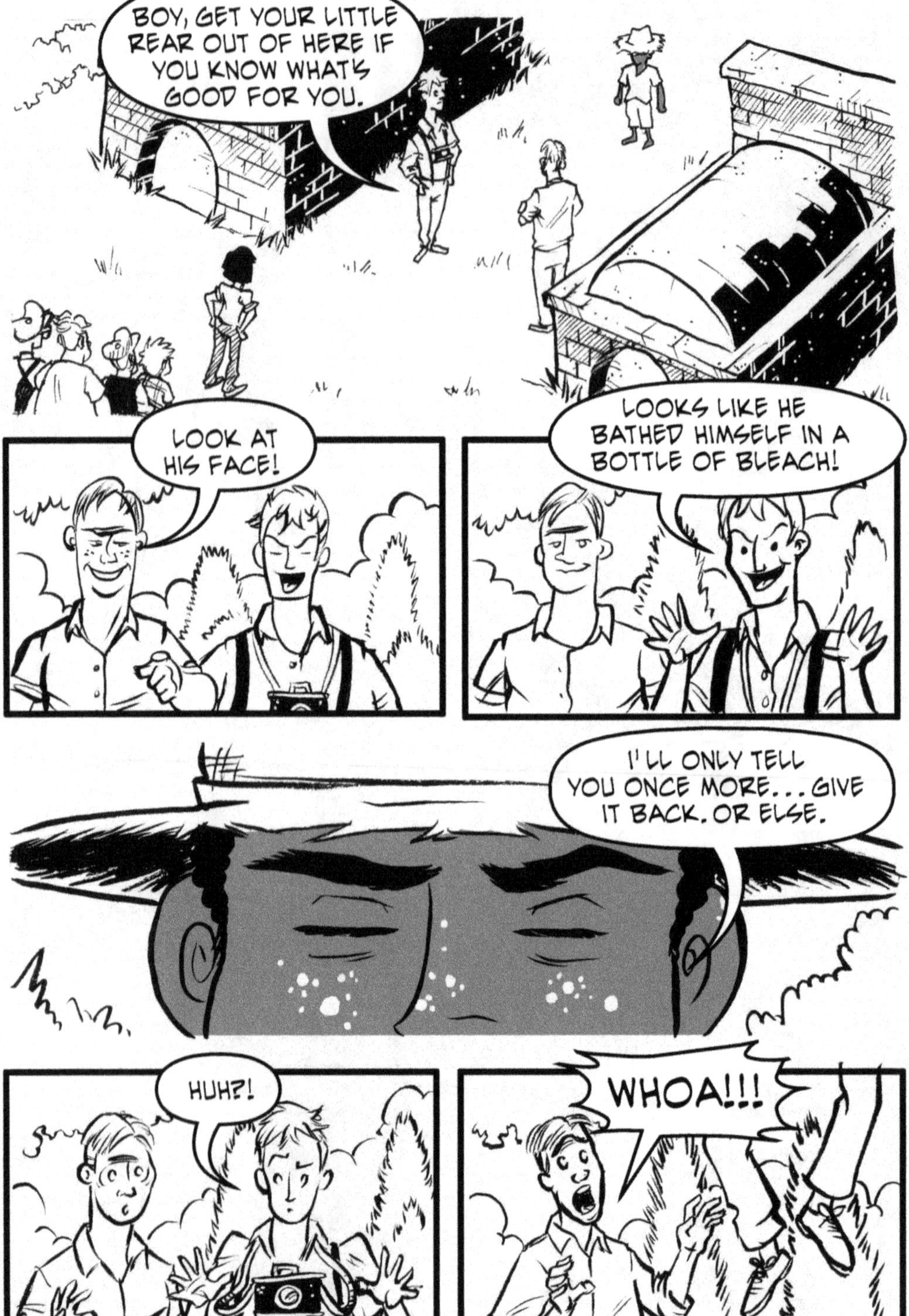
BOY, GET YOUR LITTLE REAR OUT OF HERE IF YOU KNOW WHAT'S GOOD FOR YOU.
LOOK AT HIS FACE!
LOOKS LIKE HE BATHED HIMSELF IN A BOTTLE OF BLEACH!
I'LL ONLY TELL YOU ONCE MORE... GIVE IT BACK. OR ELSE.
HUH?!
WHOA!!!

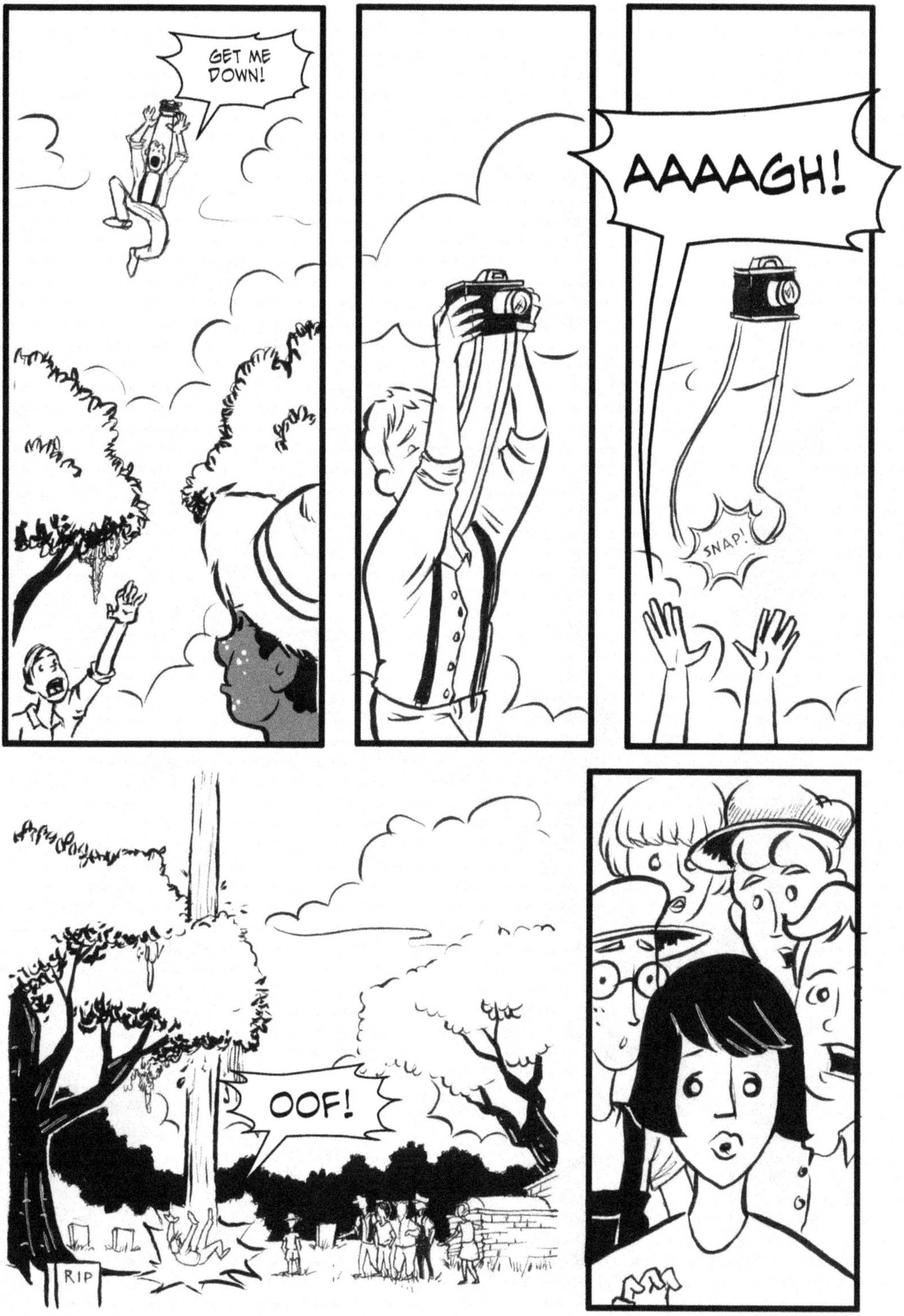
GET ME DOWN!
AAAAGH!
SNAP!
OOF!
RIP

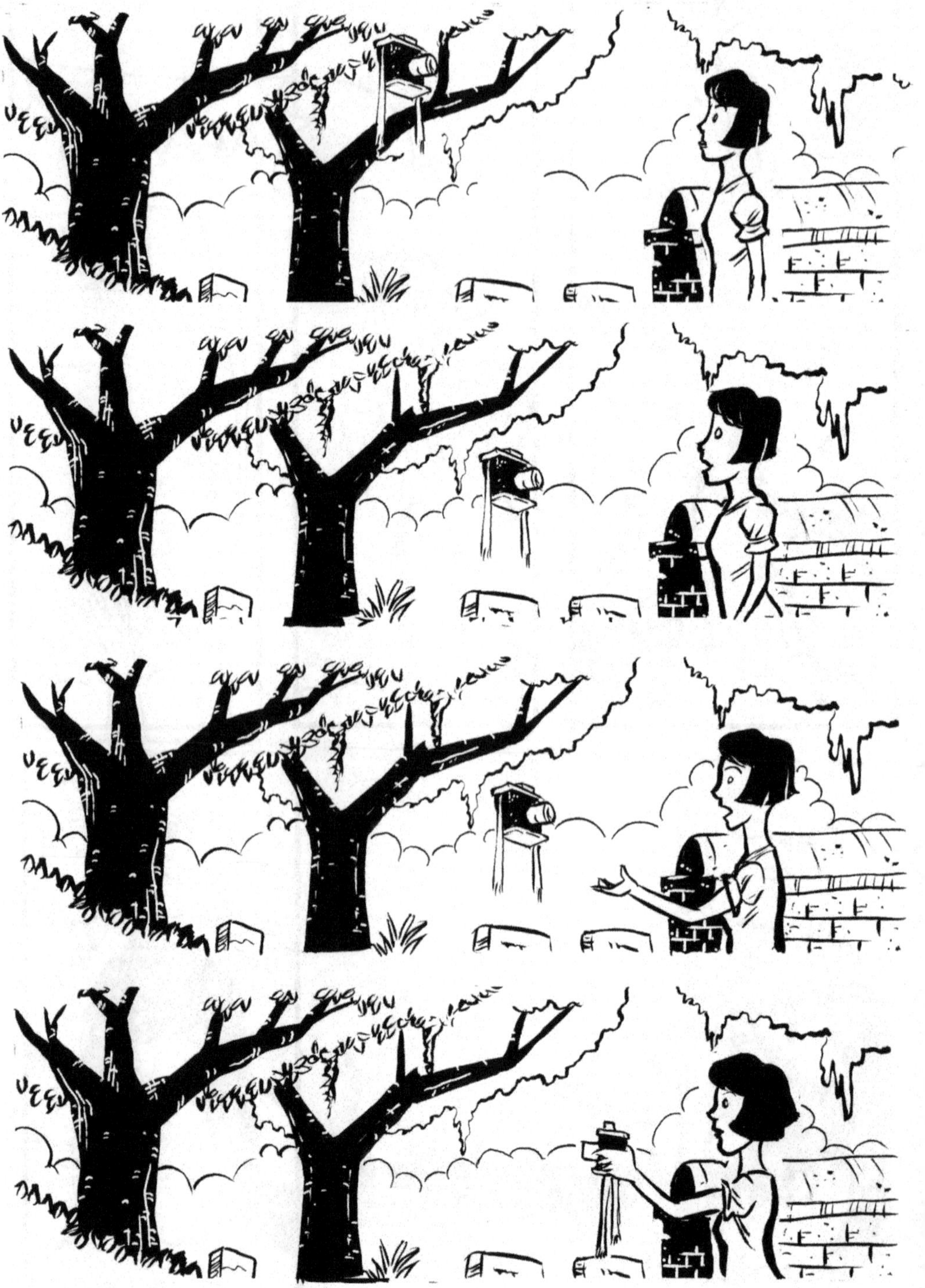

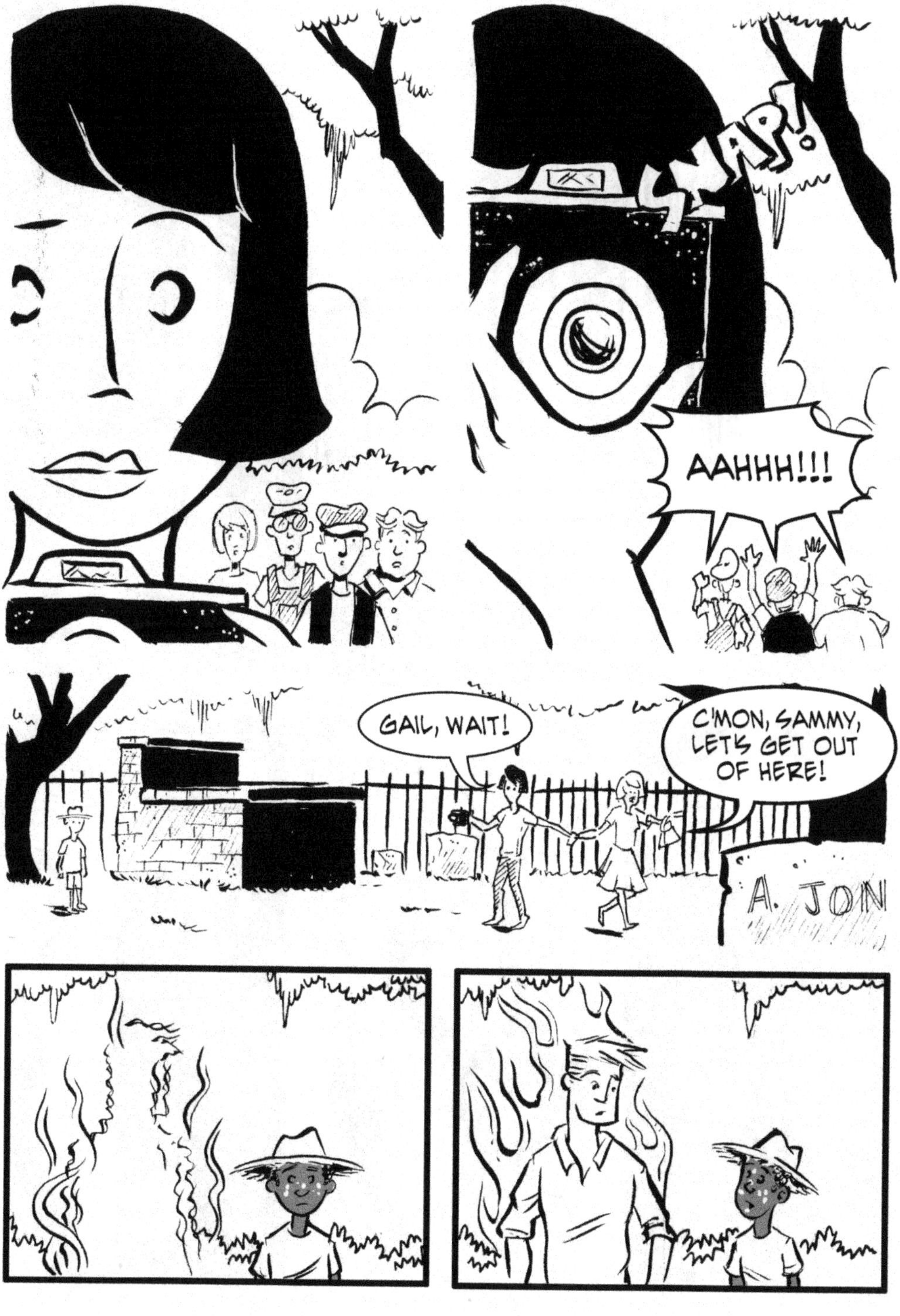
SNAP!
AAHHH!!!
GAIL, WAIT!
C'MON, SAMMY, LET'S GET OUT OF HERE!
A. JON

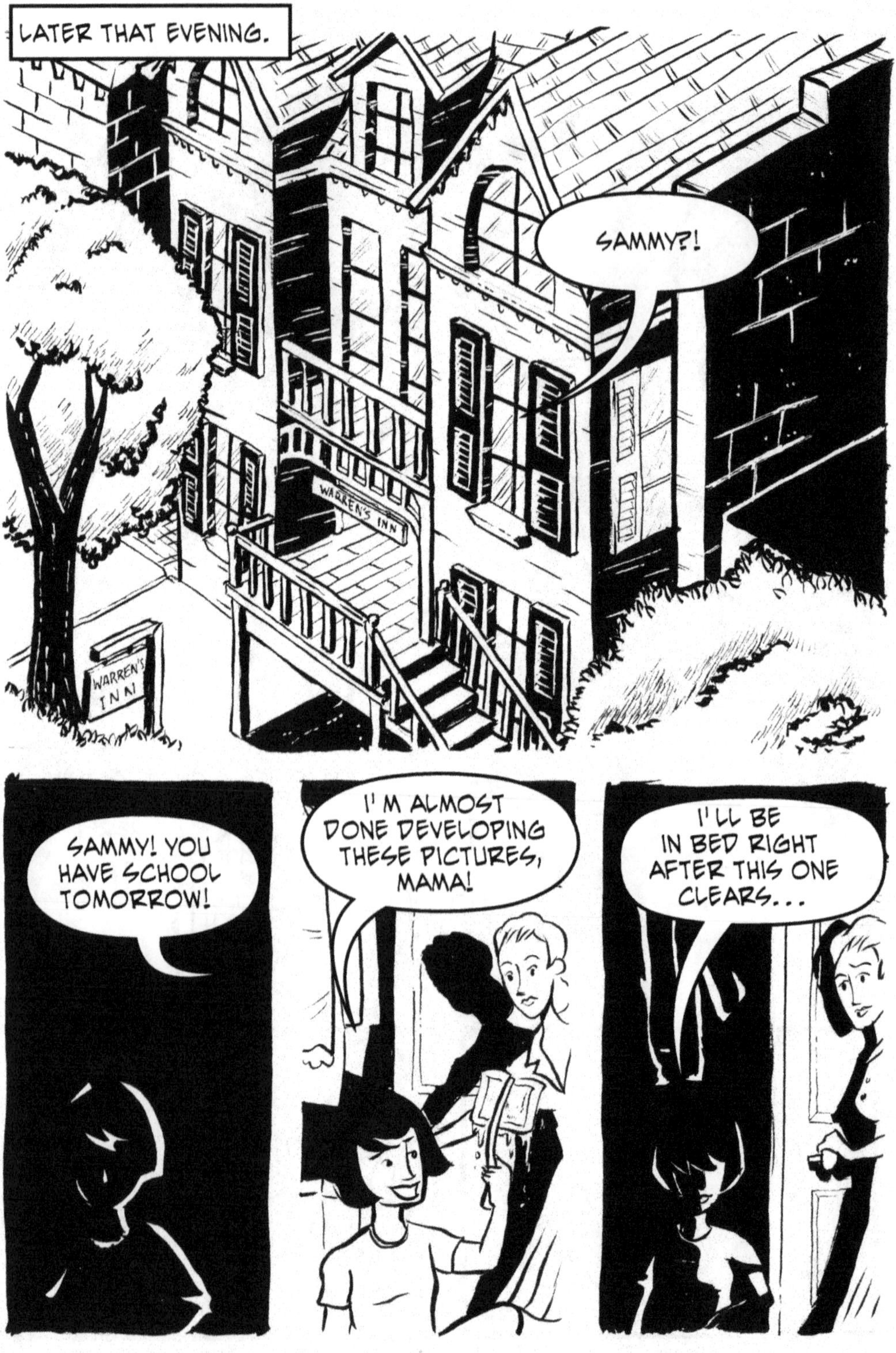
LATER THAT EVENING.
WARREN'S INN
WARREN'S INN
SAMMY?!
SAMMY! YOU HAVE SCHOOL TOMORROW!
I'M ALMOST DONE DEVELOPING THESE PICTURES, MAMA!
I'LL BE IN BED RIGHT AFTER THIS ONE CLEARS...

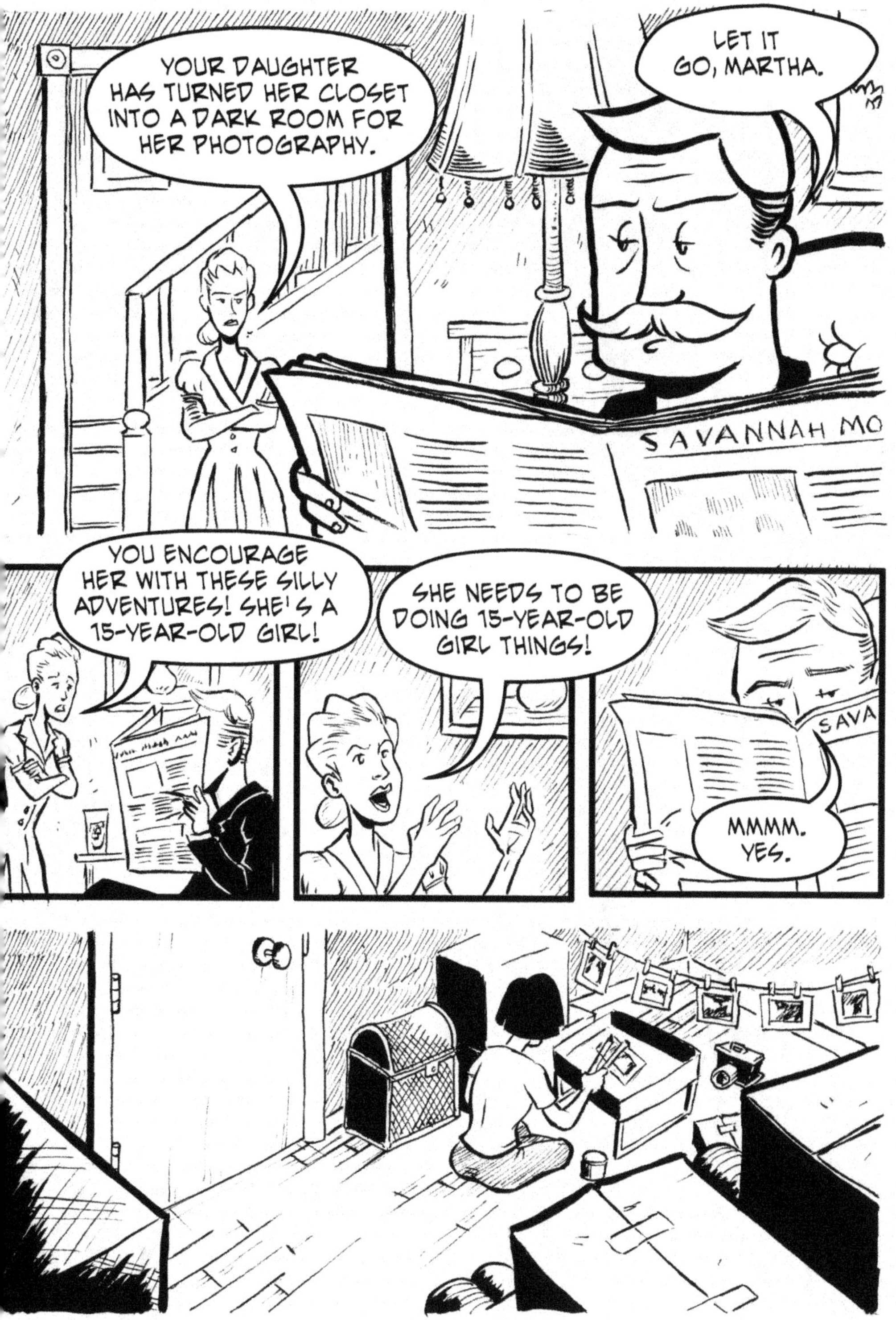
YOUR DAUGHTER HAS TURNED HER CLOSET INTO A DARK ROOM FOR HER PHOTOGRAPHY.
LET IT GO, MARTHA.
SAVANNAH MO
YOU ENCOURAGE HER WITH THESE SILLY ADVENTURES! SHE'S A 15-YEAR-OLD GIRL!
SHE NEEDS TO BE DOING 15-YEAR-OLD GIRL THINGS!
SAVA
MMMM. YES.

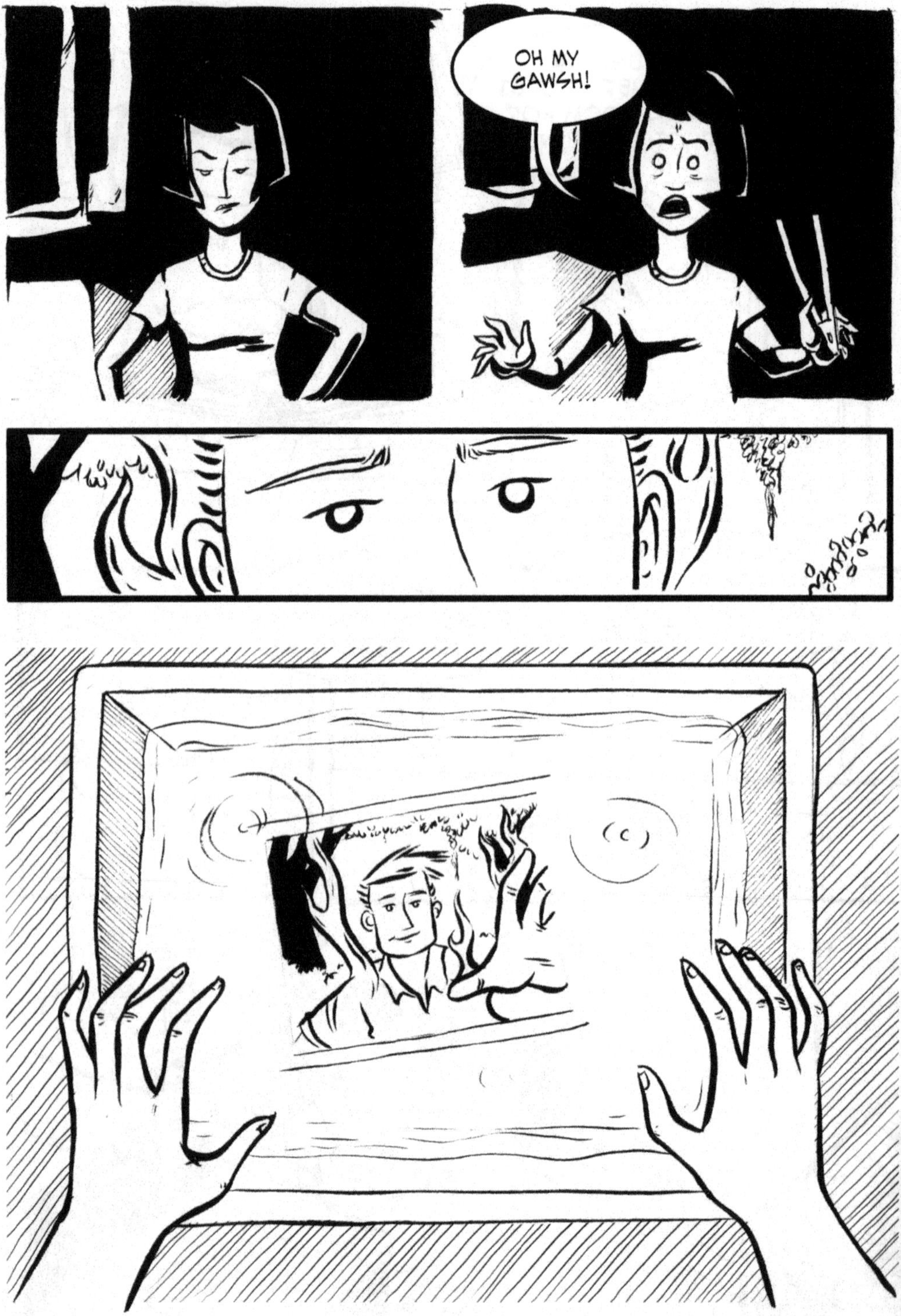
OH MY
GAWSH!

CHAPTER

5

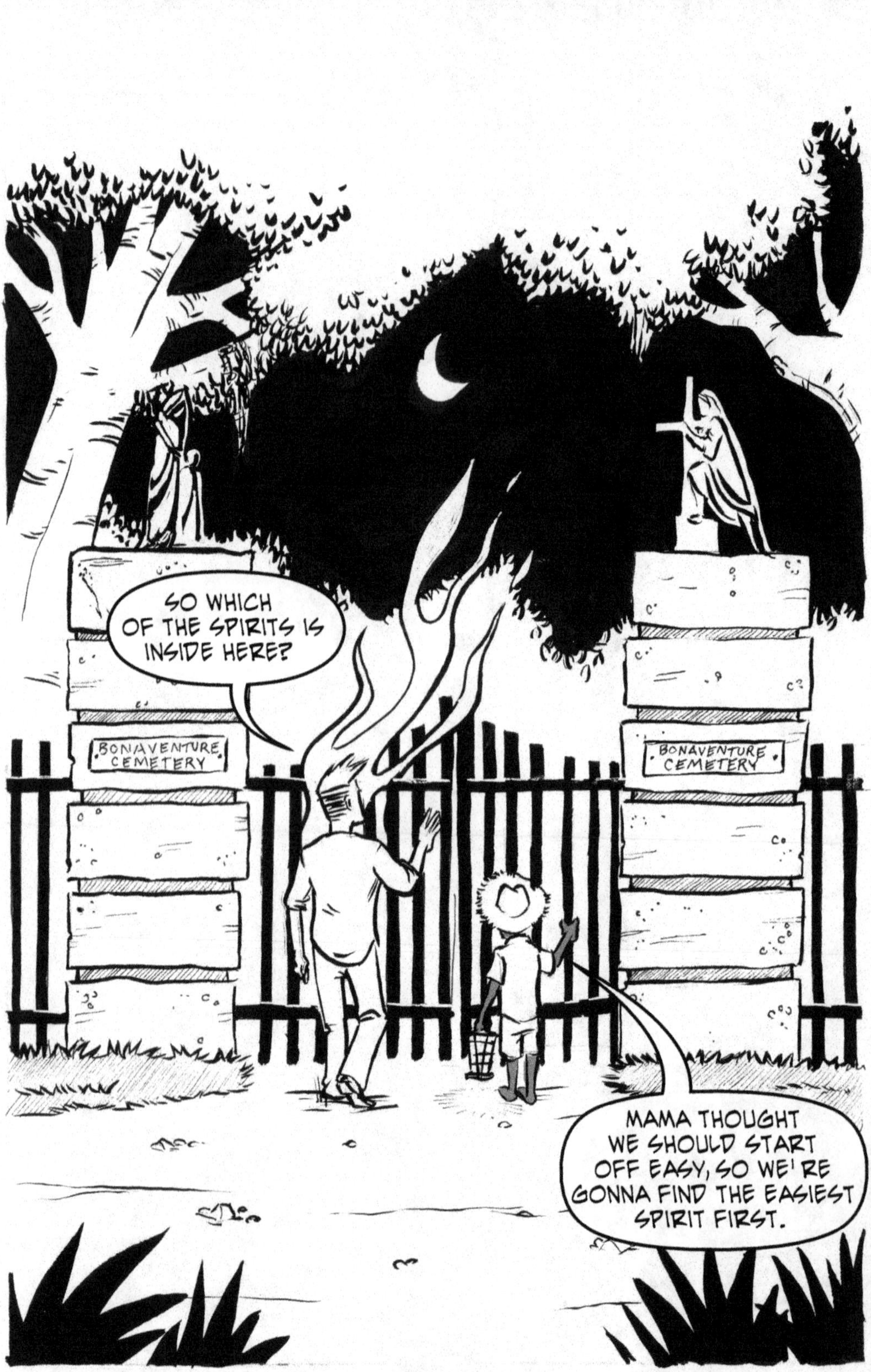
SO WHICH OF THE SPIRITS IS INSIDE HERE?
BONAVENTURE CEMETERY
BONAVENTURE CEMETERY
MAMA THOUGHT WE SHOULD START OFF EASY, SO WE'RE GONNA FIND THE EASIEST SPIRIT FIRST.

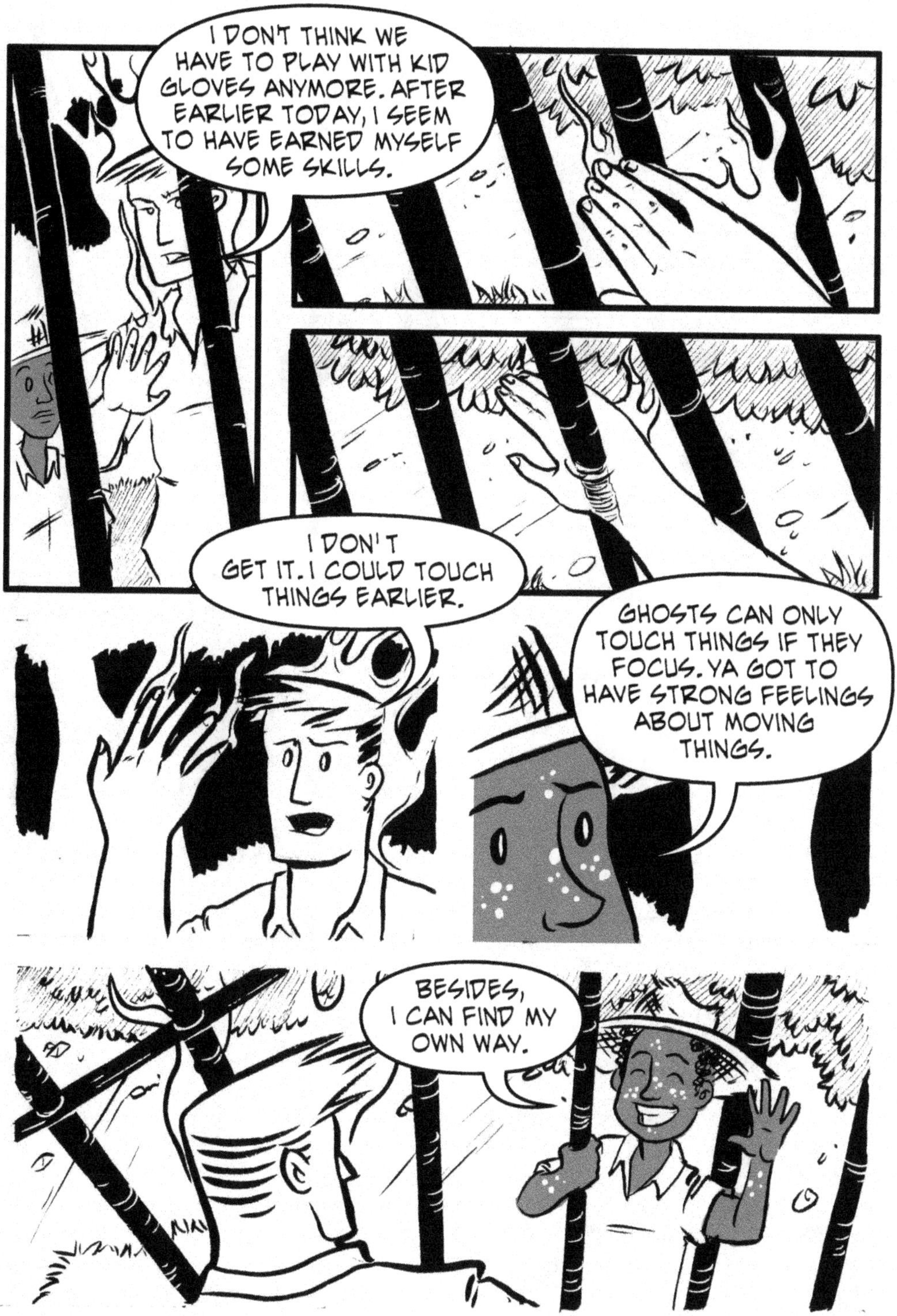
I DON'T THINK WE HAVE TO PLAY WITH KID GLOVES ANYMORE. AFTER EARLIER TODAY, I SEEM TO HAVE EARNED MYSELF SOME SKILLS.
I DON'T GET IT. I COULD TOUCH THINGS EARLIER.
GHOSTS CAN ONLY TOUCH THINGS IF THEY FOCUS. YA GOT TO HAVE STRONG FEELINGS ABOUT MOVING THINGS.
BESIDES, I CAN FIND MY OWN WAY.

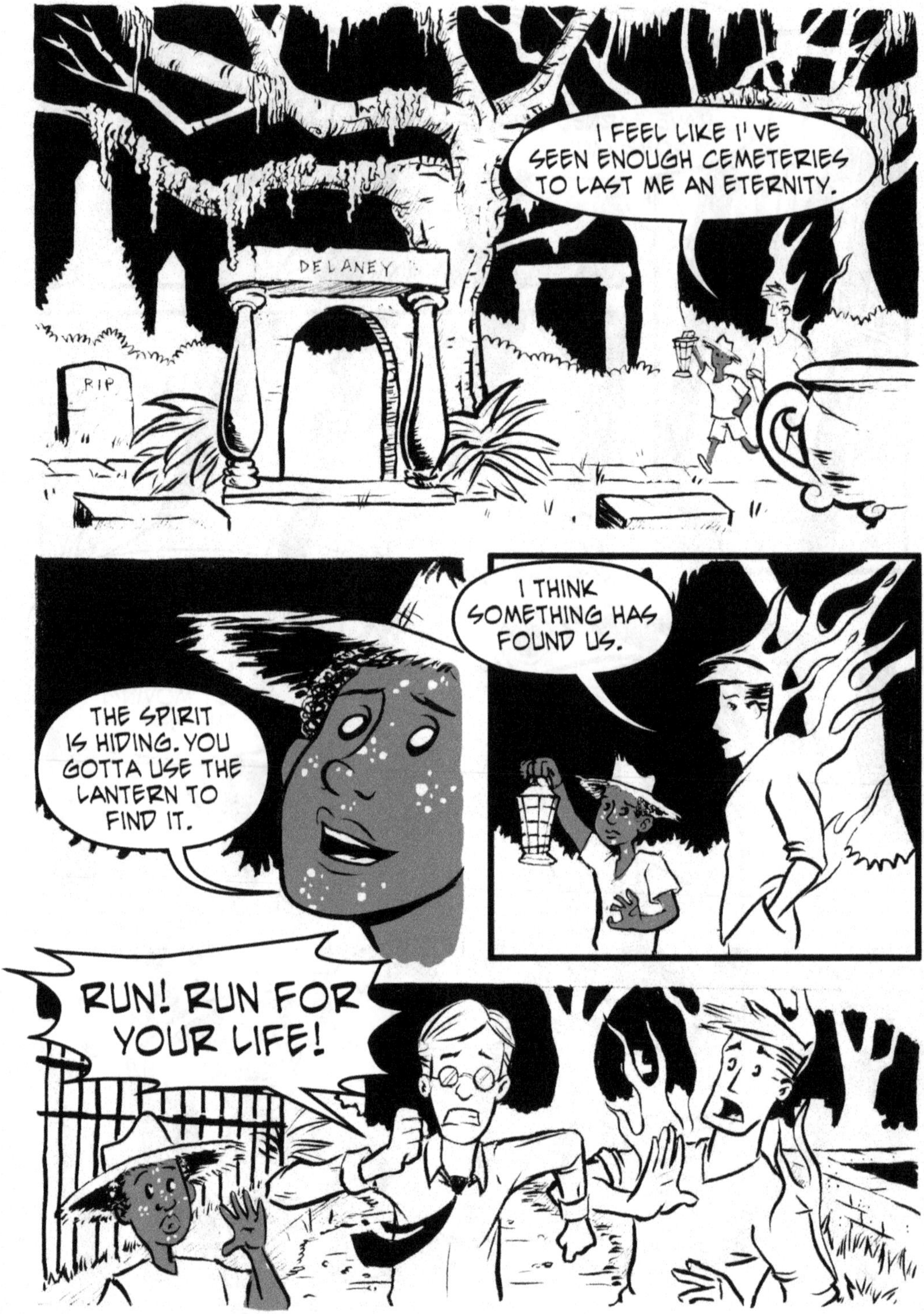

DELANEY
RIP
I FEEL LIKE I'VE SEEN ENOUGH CEMETERIES TO LAST ME AN ETERNITY.
I THINK SOMETHING HAS FOUND US.
THE SPIRIT IS HIDING. YOU GOTTA USE THE LANTERN TO FIND IT.
RUN! RUN FOR YOUR LIFE!

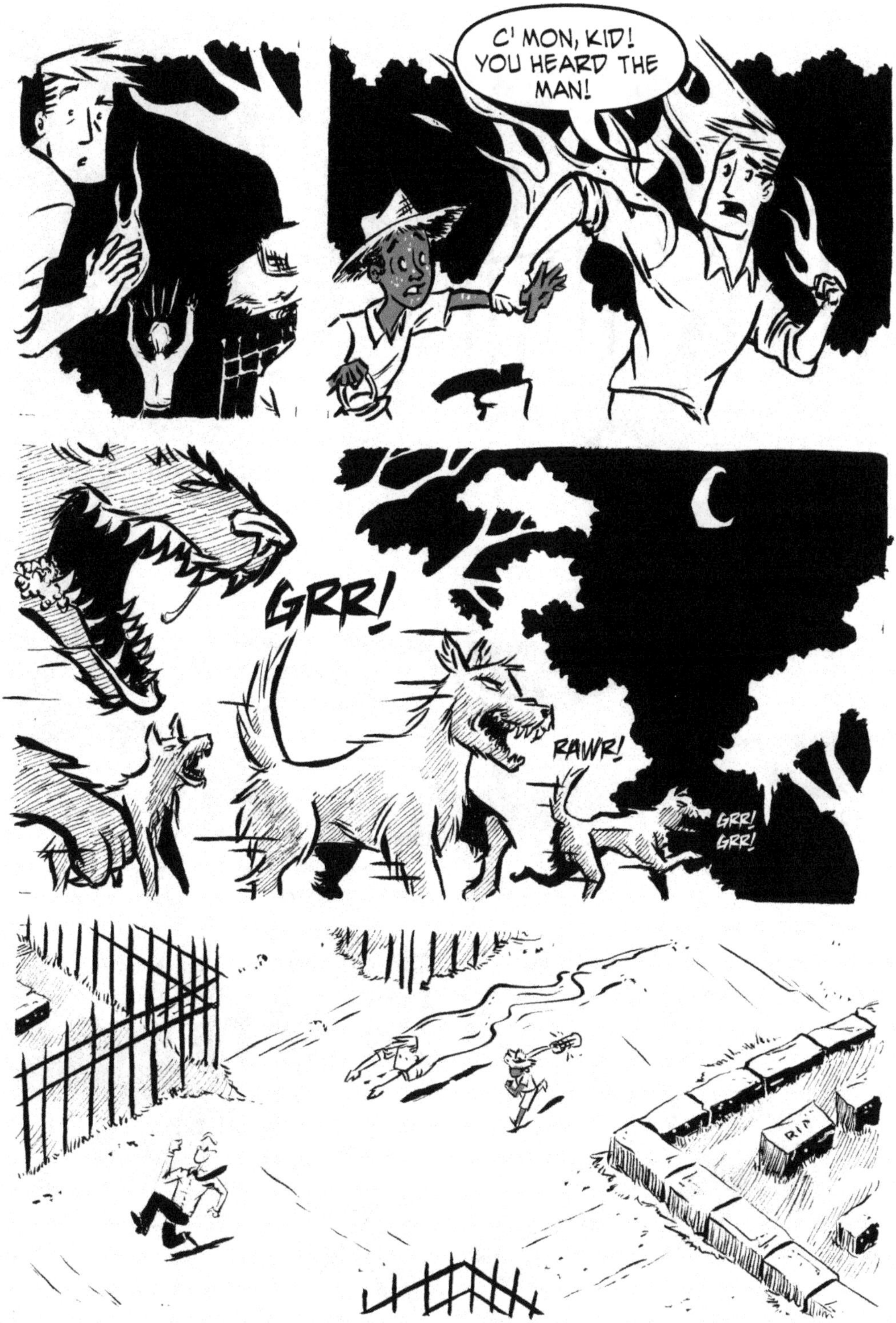
C' MON, KID! YOU HEARD THE MAN!
GRR!
RAWR!
GRR! GRR!
RIP

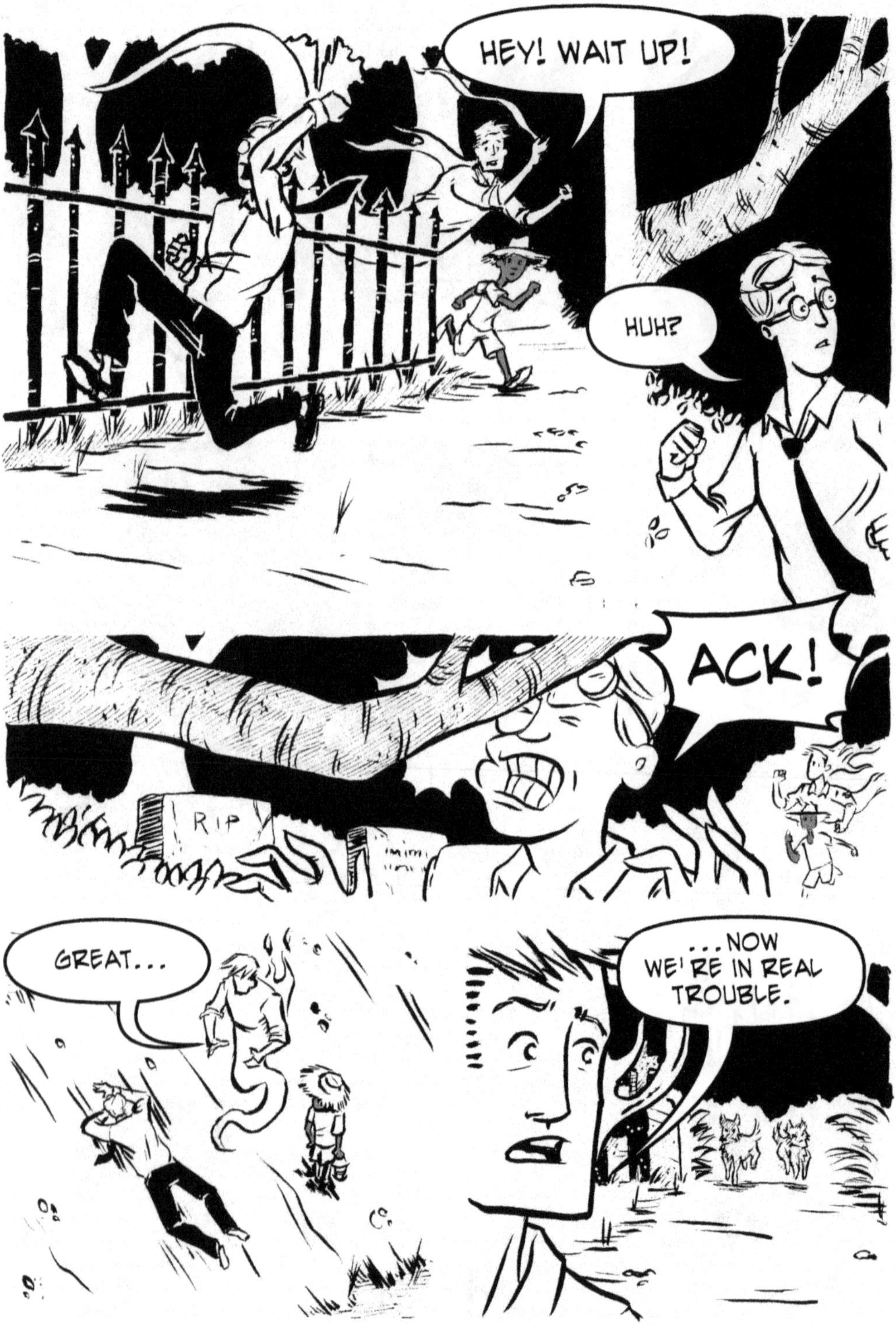
HEY! WAIT UP!
HUH?
ACK!
RIP
GREAT...
...NOW WE'RE IN REAL TROUBLE.

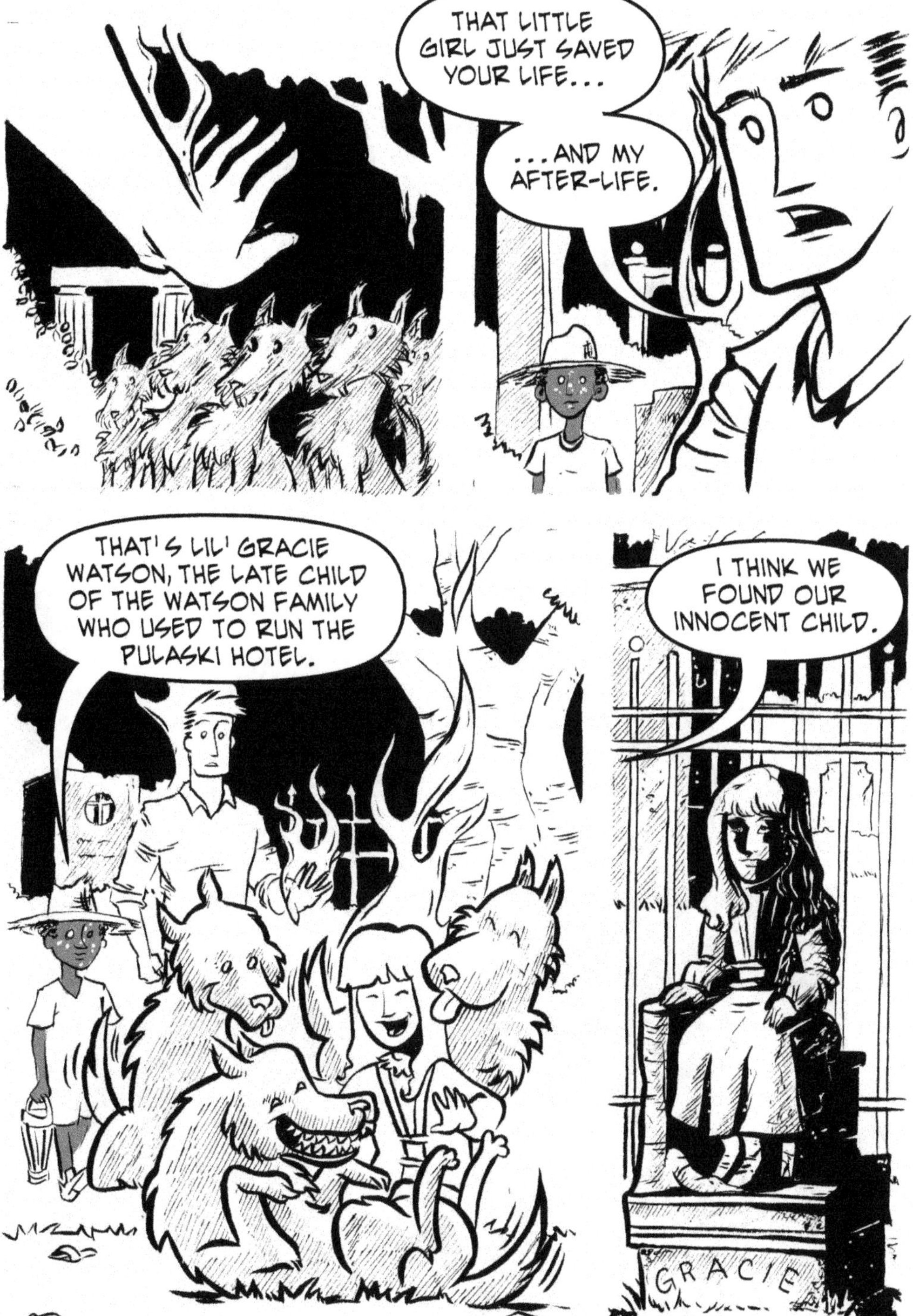
THAT LITTLE GIRL JUST SAVED YOUR LIFE...
...AND MY AFTER-LIFE.
THAT'S LIL' GRACIE WATSON, THE LATE CHILD OF THE WATSON FAMILY WHO USED TO RUN THE PULASKI HOTEL.
I THINK WE FOUND OUR INNOCENT CHILD.
GRACIE

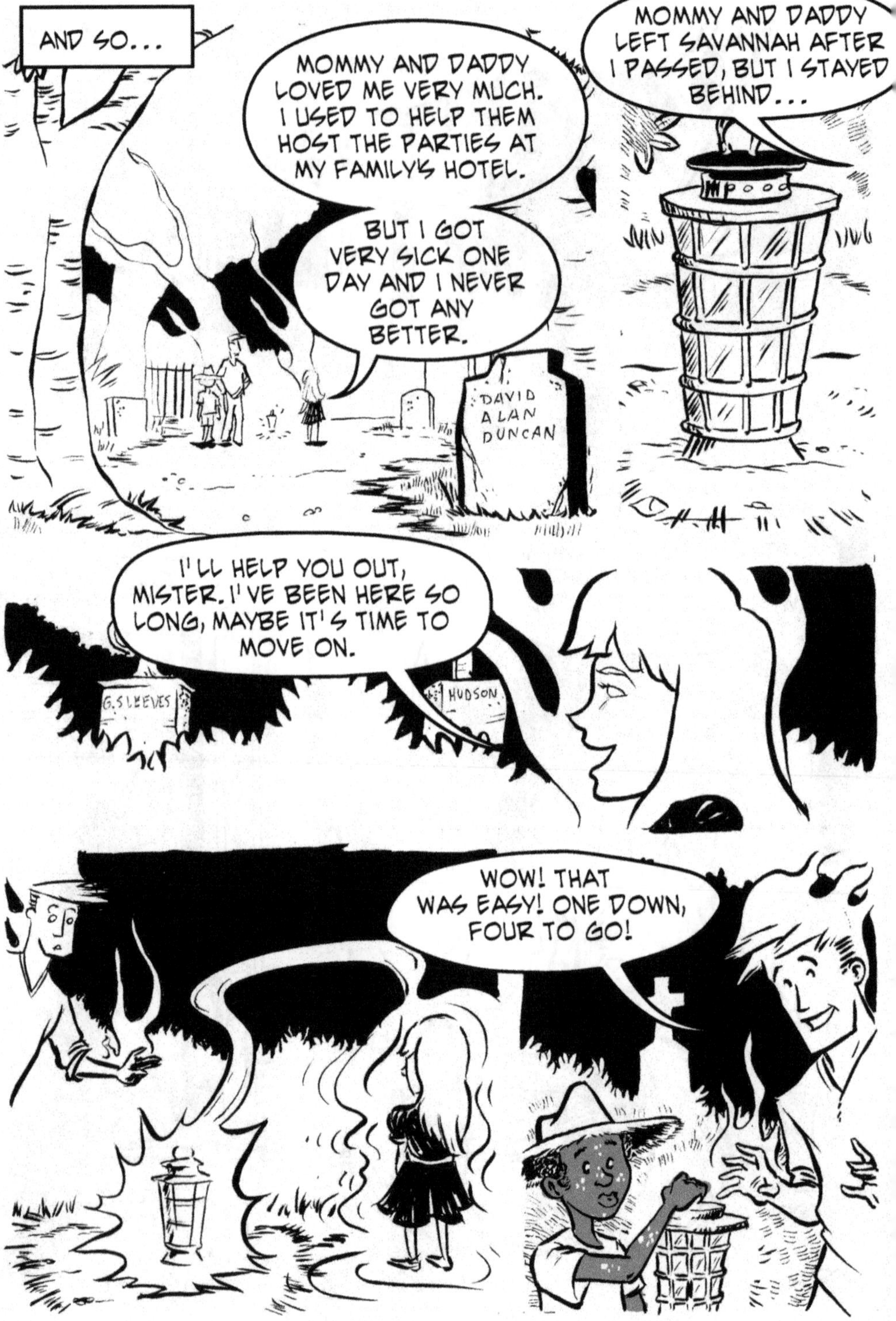
AND SO...
MOMMY AND DADDY LOVED ME VERY MUCH. I USED TO HELP THEM HOST THE PARTIES AT MY FAMILY'S HOTEL.
BUT I GOT VERY SICK ONE DAY AND I NEVER GOT ANY BETTER.
DAVID ALAN DUNCAN
MOMMY AND DADDY LEFT SAVANNAH AFTER I PASSED, BUT I STAYED BEHIND...
I'LL HELP YOU OUT, MISTER. I'VE BEEN HERE SO LONG, MAYBE IT'S TIME TO MOVE ON.
HUDSON
WOW! THAT WAS EASY! ONE DOWN, FOUR TO GO!

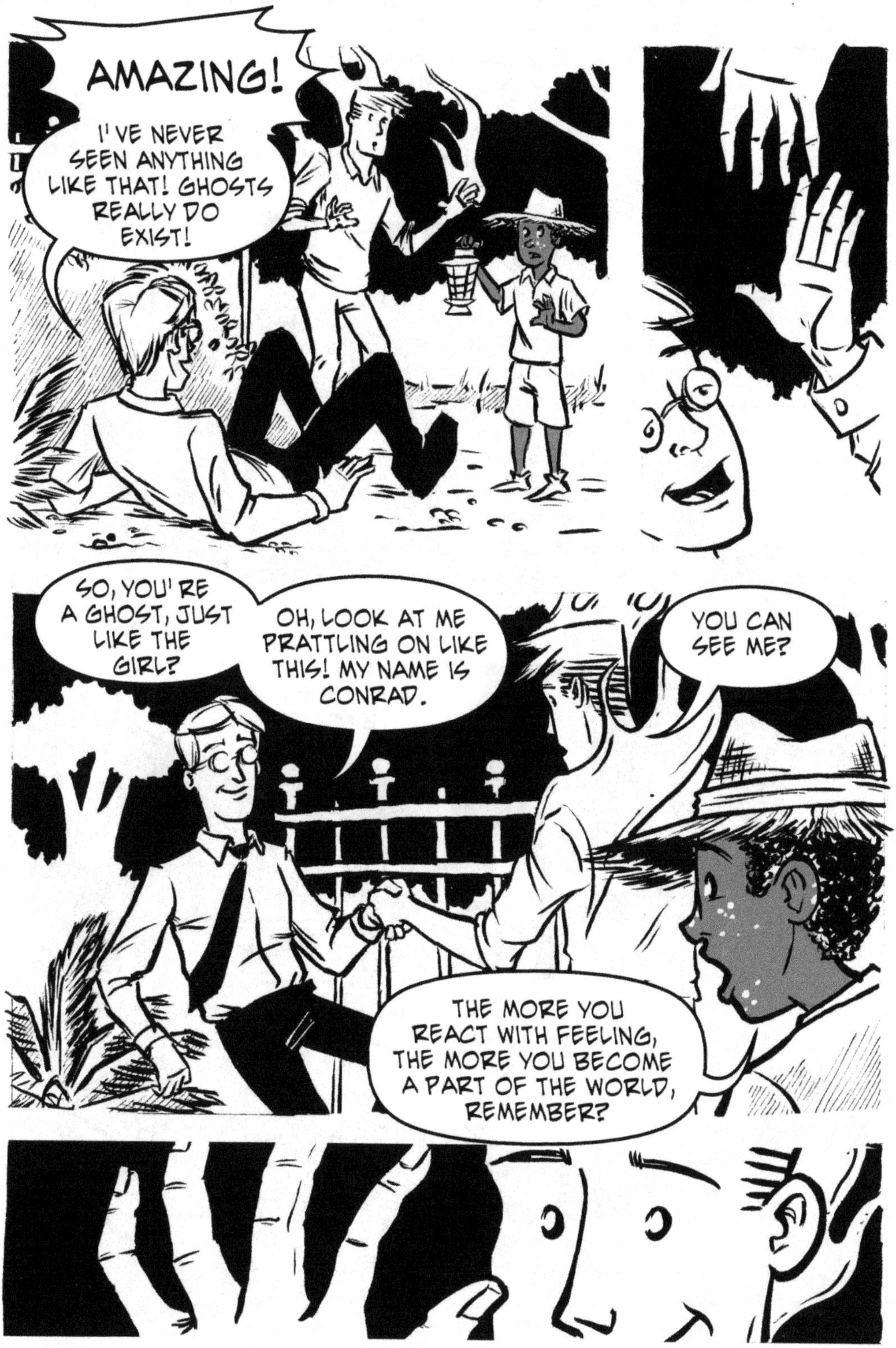
AMAZING!
I'VE NEVER SEEN ANYTHING LIKE THAT! GHOSTS REALLY DO EXIST!
SO, YOU'RE A GHOST, JUST LIKE THE GIRL?
OH, LOOK AT ME PRATTLING ON LIKE THIS! MY NAME IS CONRAD.
YOU CAN SEE ME?
THE MORE YOU REACT WITH FEELING, THE MORE YOU BECOME A PART OF THE WORLD, REMEMBER?

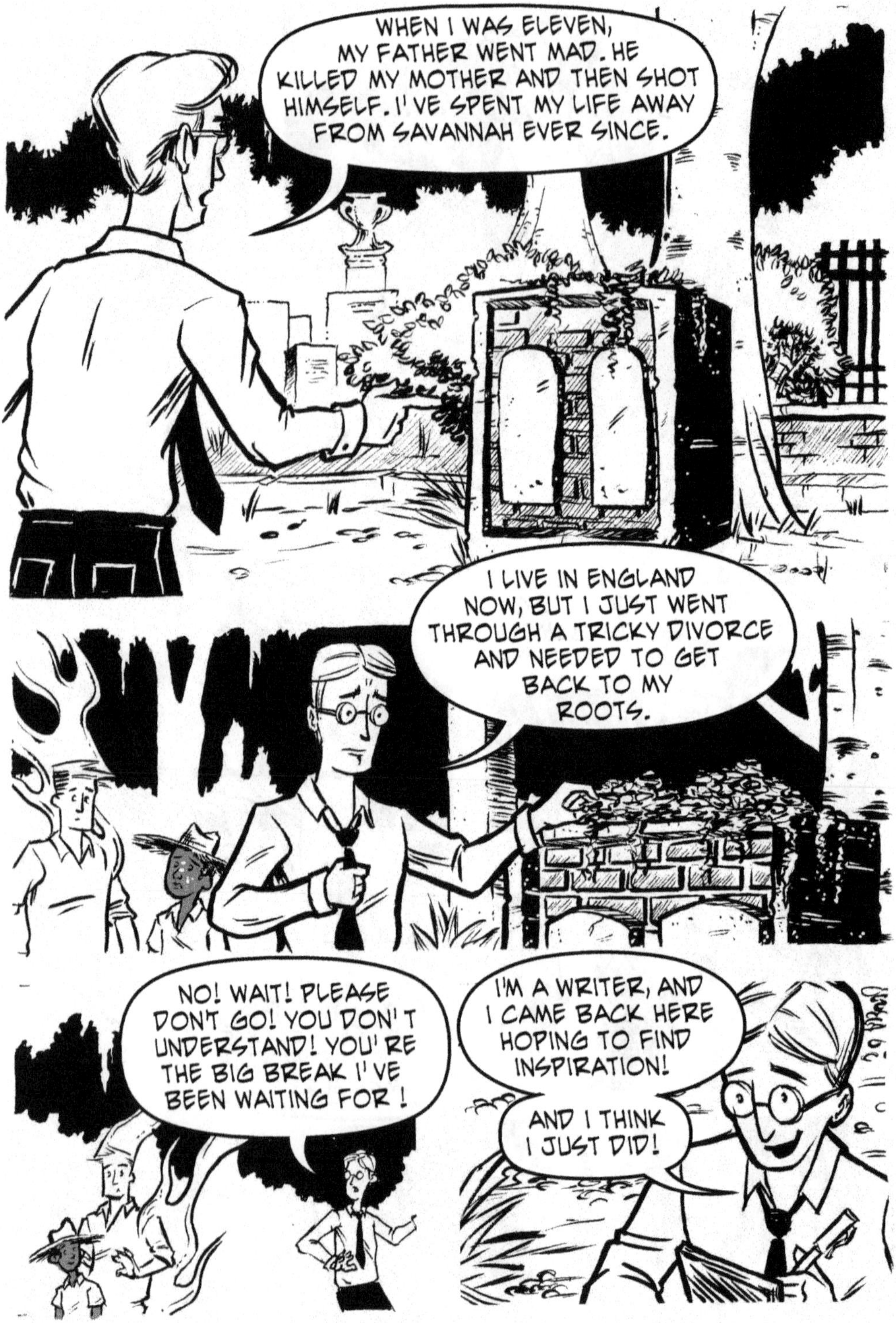
WHEN I WAS ELEVEN, MY FATHER WENT MAD. HE KILLED MY MOTHER AND THEN SHOT HIMSELF. I'VE SPENT MY LIFE AWAY FROM SAVANNAH EVER SINCE.
I LIVE IN ENGLAND NOW, BUT I JUST WENT THROUGH A TRICKY DIVORCE AND NEEDED TO GET BACK TO MY ROOTS.
NO! WAIT! PLEASE DON'T GO! YOU DON'T UNDERSTAND! YOU'RE THE BIG BREAK I'VE BEEN WAITING FOR!
I'M A WRITER, AND I CAME BACK HERE HOPING TO FIND INSPIRATION!
AND I THINK I JUST DID!

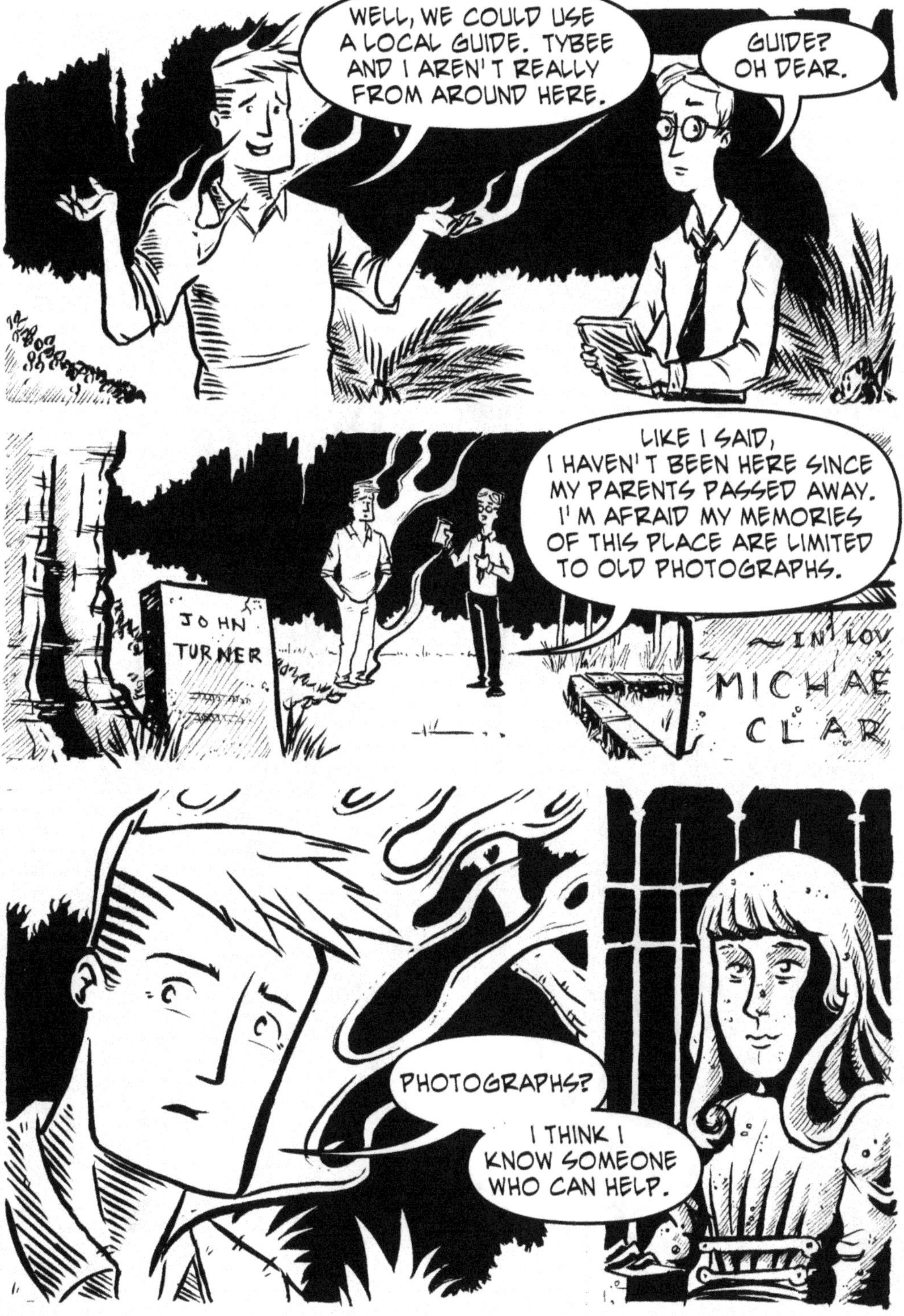
WELL, WE COULD USE A LOCAL GUIDE. TYBEE AND I AREN'T REALLY FROM AROUND HERE.
GUIDE? OH DEAR.
LIKE I SAID, I HAVEN'T BEEN HERE SINCE MY PARENTS PASSED AWAY. I'M AFRAID MY MEMORIES OF THIS PLACE ARE LIMITED TO OLD PHOTOGRAPHS.
JOHN TURNER
IN LOV
MICHAE
CLAR
PHOTOGRAPHS?
I THINK I KNOW SOMEONE WHO CAN HELP.

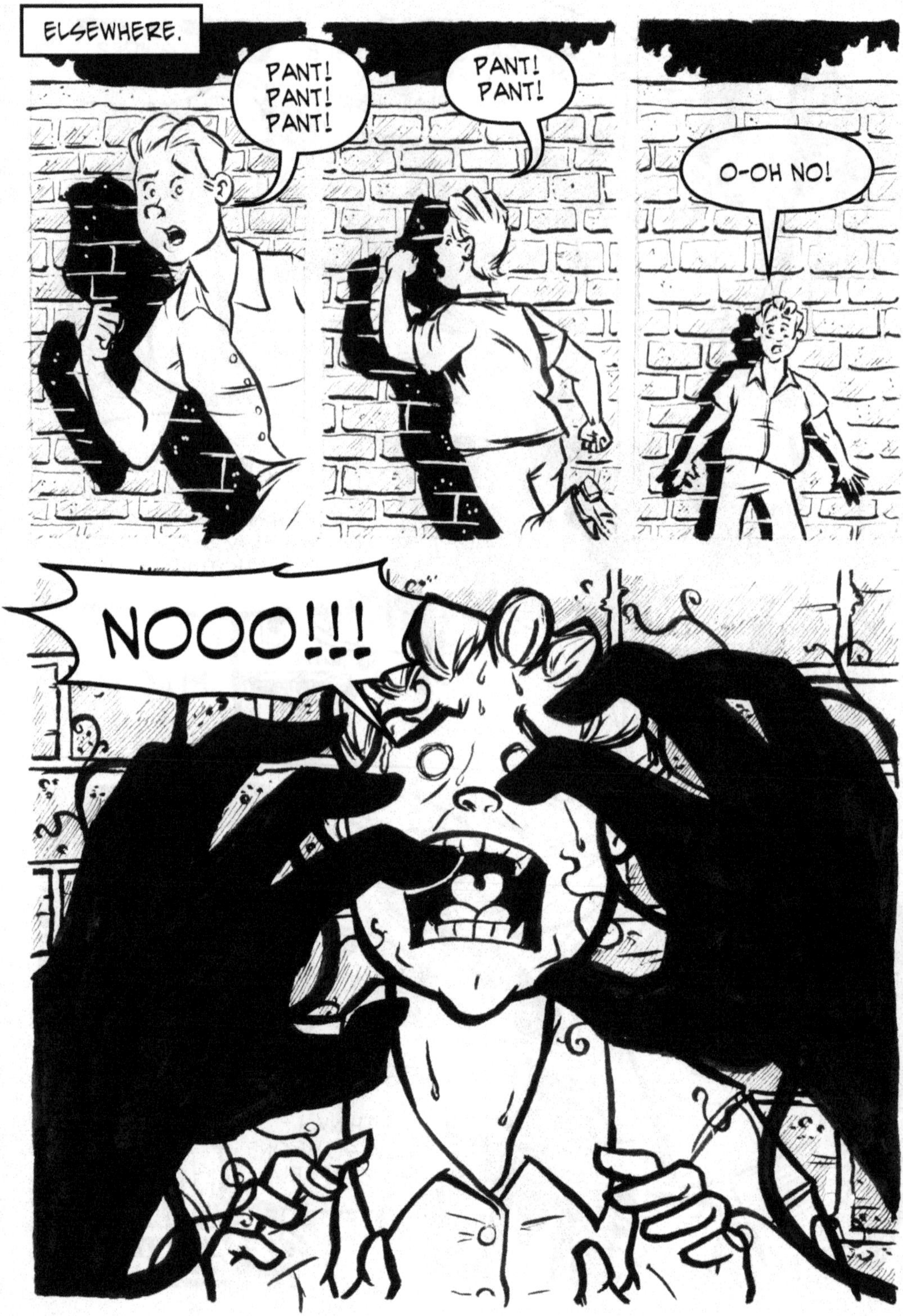
ELSEWHERE.
PANT! PANT! PANT!
PANT! PANT!
O-OH NO!
NOOO!!!

CHAPTER

6

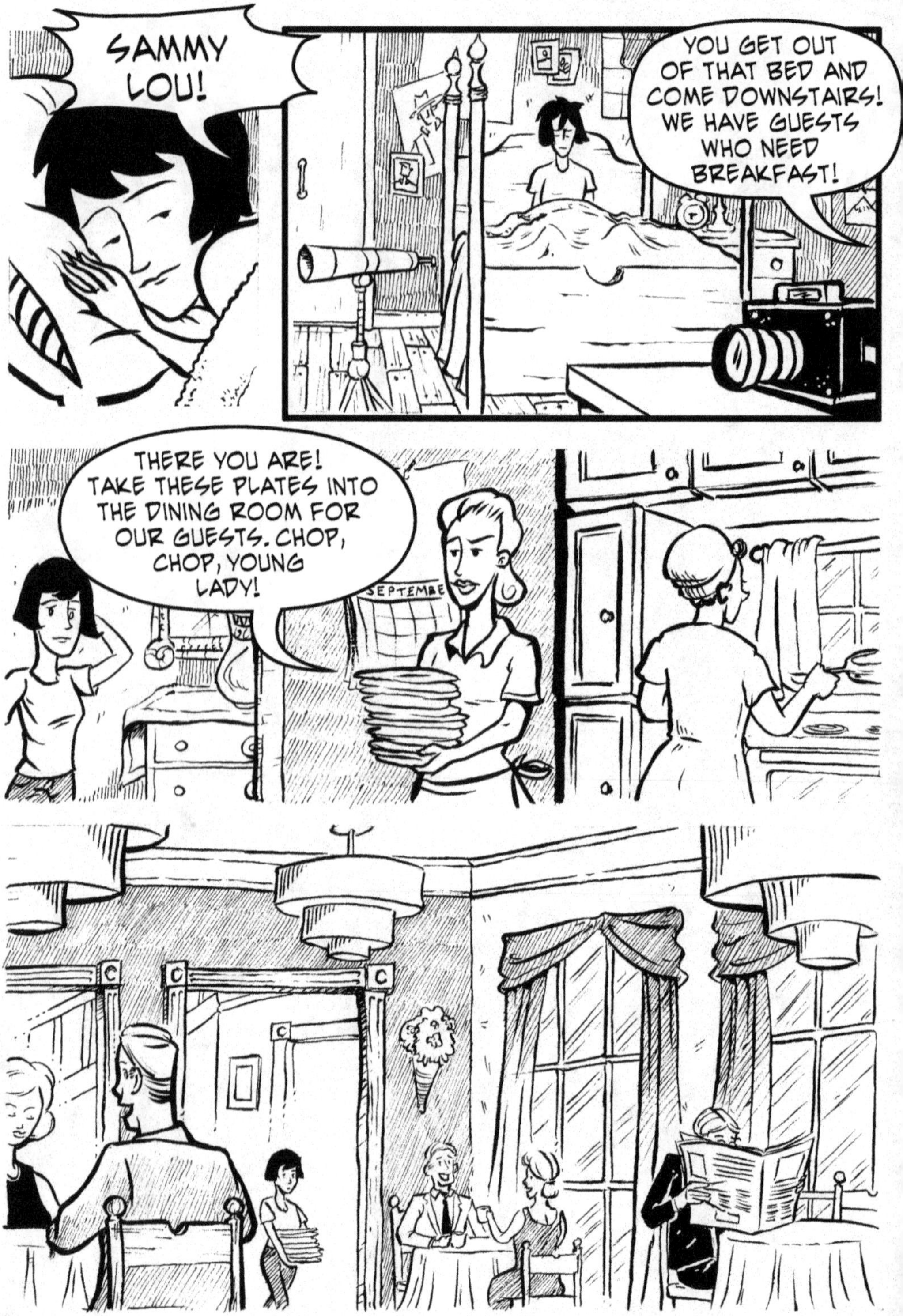
SAMMY LOU!
YOU GET OUT OF THAT BED AND COME DOWNSTAIRS! WE HAVE GUESTS WHO NEED BREAKFAST!
THERE YOU ARE! TAKE THESE PLATES INTO THE DINING ROOM FOR OUR GUESTS. CHOP, CHOP, YOUNG LADY!

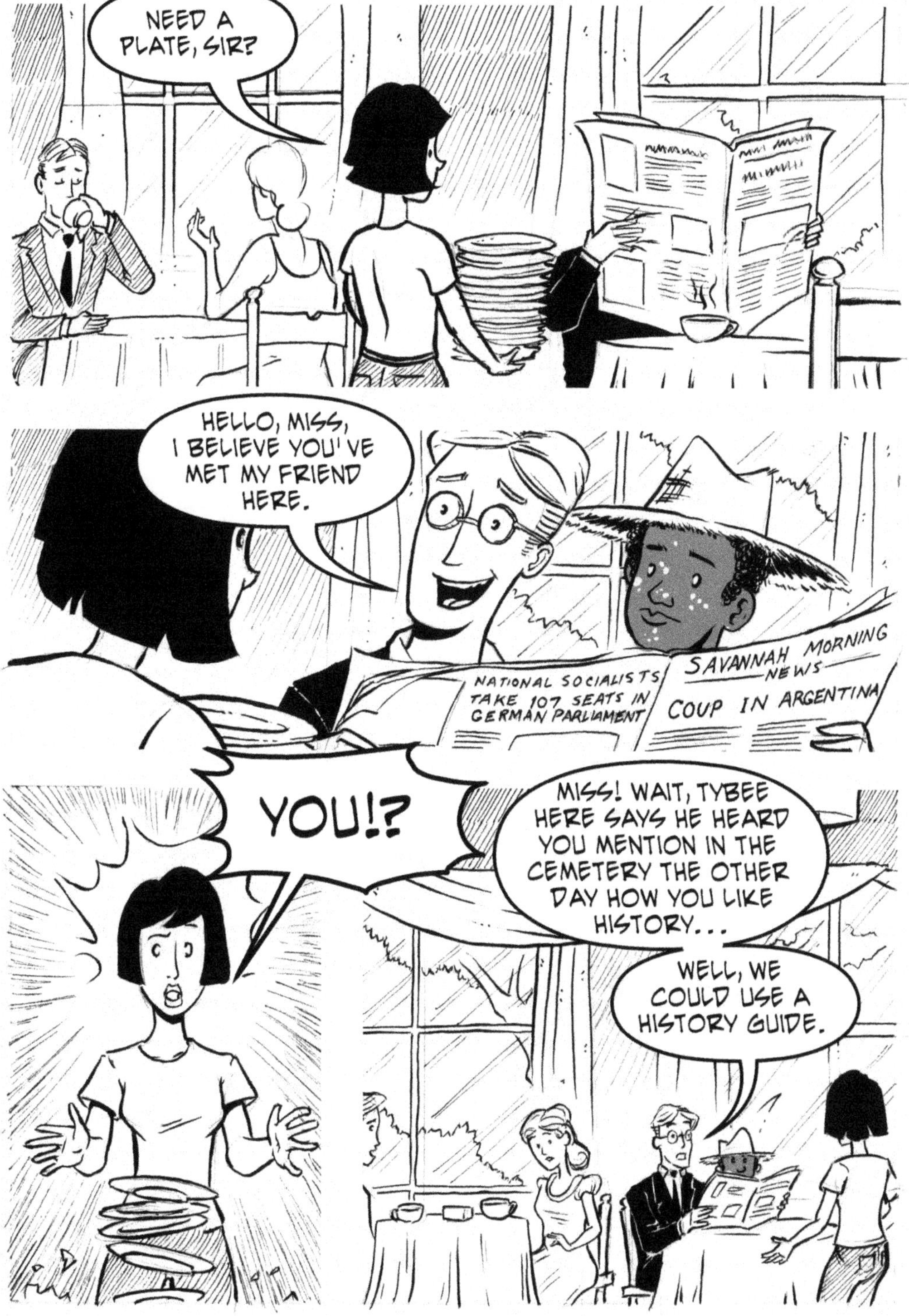
NEED A PLATE, SIR?
HELLO, MISS, I BELIEVE YOU'VE MET MY FRIEND HERE.
SAVANNAH MORNING NEWS
NATIONAL SOCIALISTS TAKE 107 SEATS IN GERMAN PARLIAMENT
COUP IN ARGENTINA
YOU!?
MISS! WAIT, TYBEE HERE SAYS HE HEARD YOU MENTION IN THE CEMETERY THE OTHER DAY HOW YOU LIKE HISTORY...
WELL, WE COULD USE A HISTORY GUIDE.

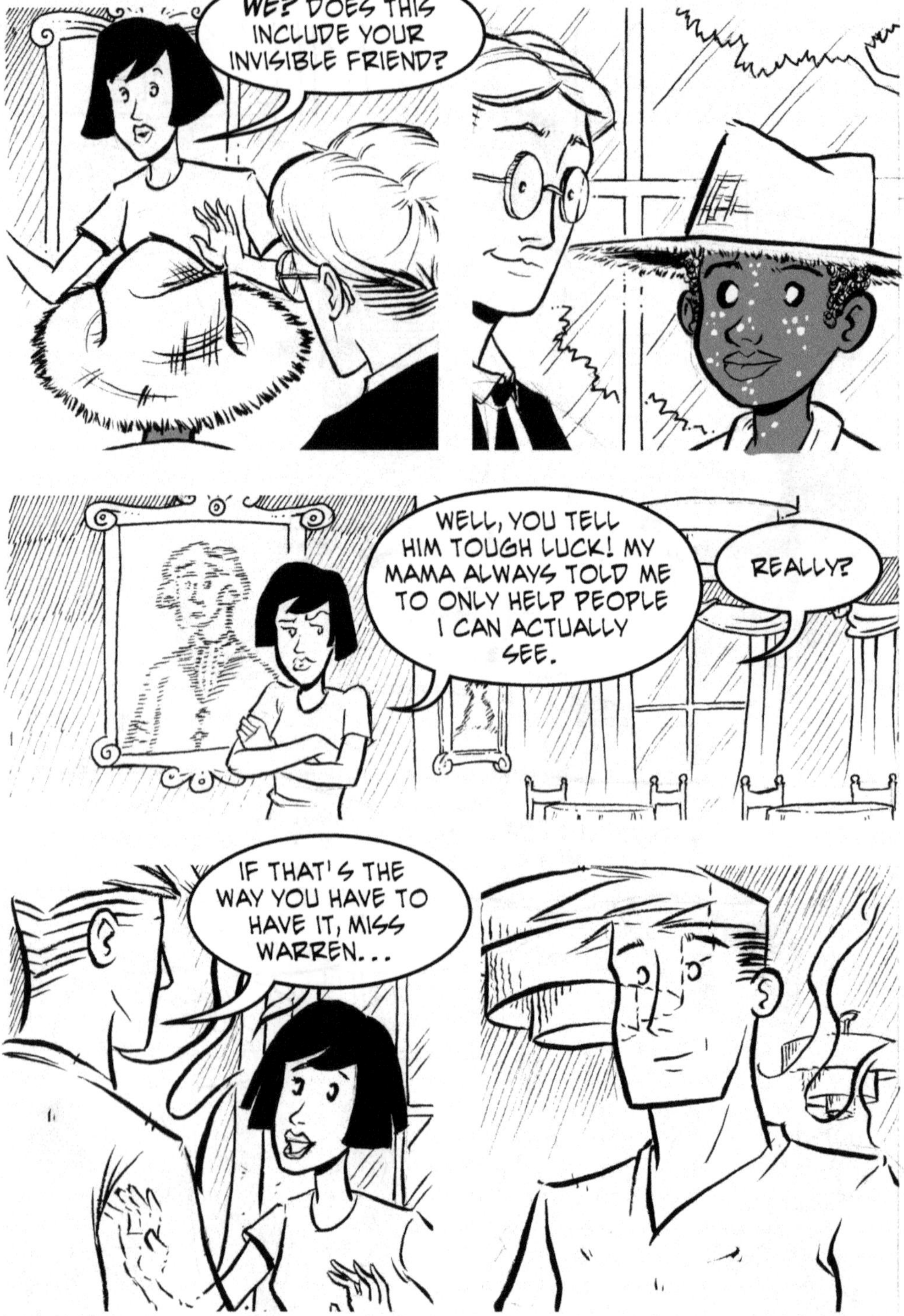
WE? DOES THIS INCLUDE YOUR INVISIBLE FRIEND?
WELL, YOU TELL HIM TOUGH LUCK! MY MAMA ALWAYS TOLD ME TO ONLY HELP PEOPLE I CAN ACTUALLY SEE.
REALLY?
IF THAT'S THE WAY YOU HAVE TO HAVE IT, MISS WARREN...

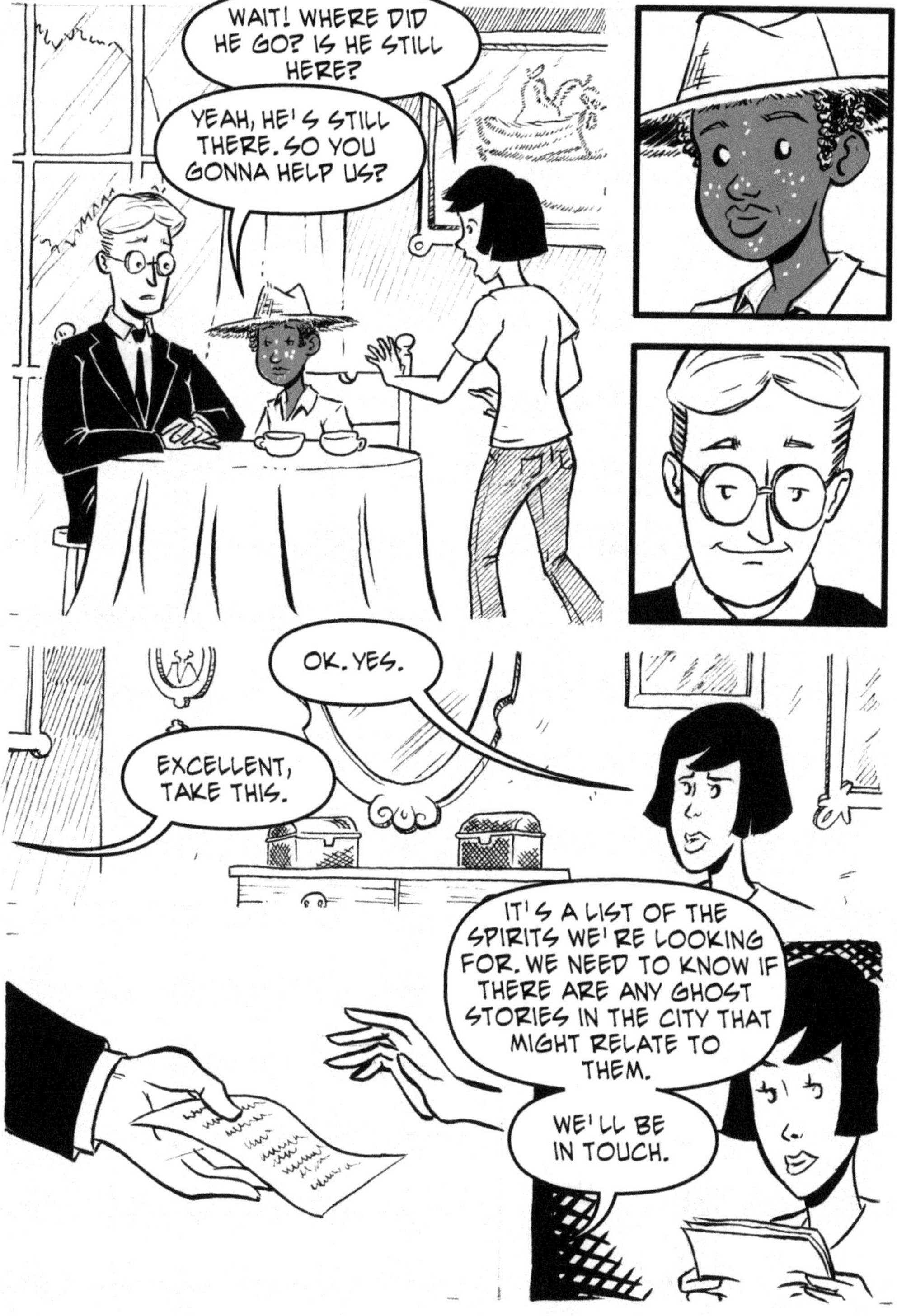
WAIT! WHERE DID HE GO? IS HE STILL HERE?
YEAH, HE'S STILL THERE. SO YOU GONNA HELP US?
OK. YES.
EXCELLENT, TAKE THIS.
IT'S A LIST OF THE SPIRITS WE'RE LOOKING FOR. WE NEED TO KNOW IF THERE ARE ANY GHOST STORIES IN THE CITY THAT MIGHT RELATE TO THEM.
WE'LL BE IN TOUCH.

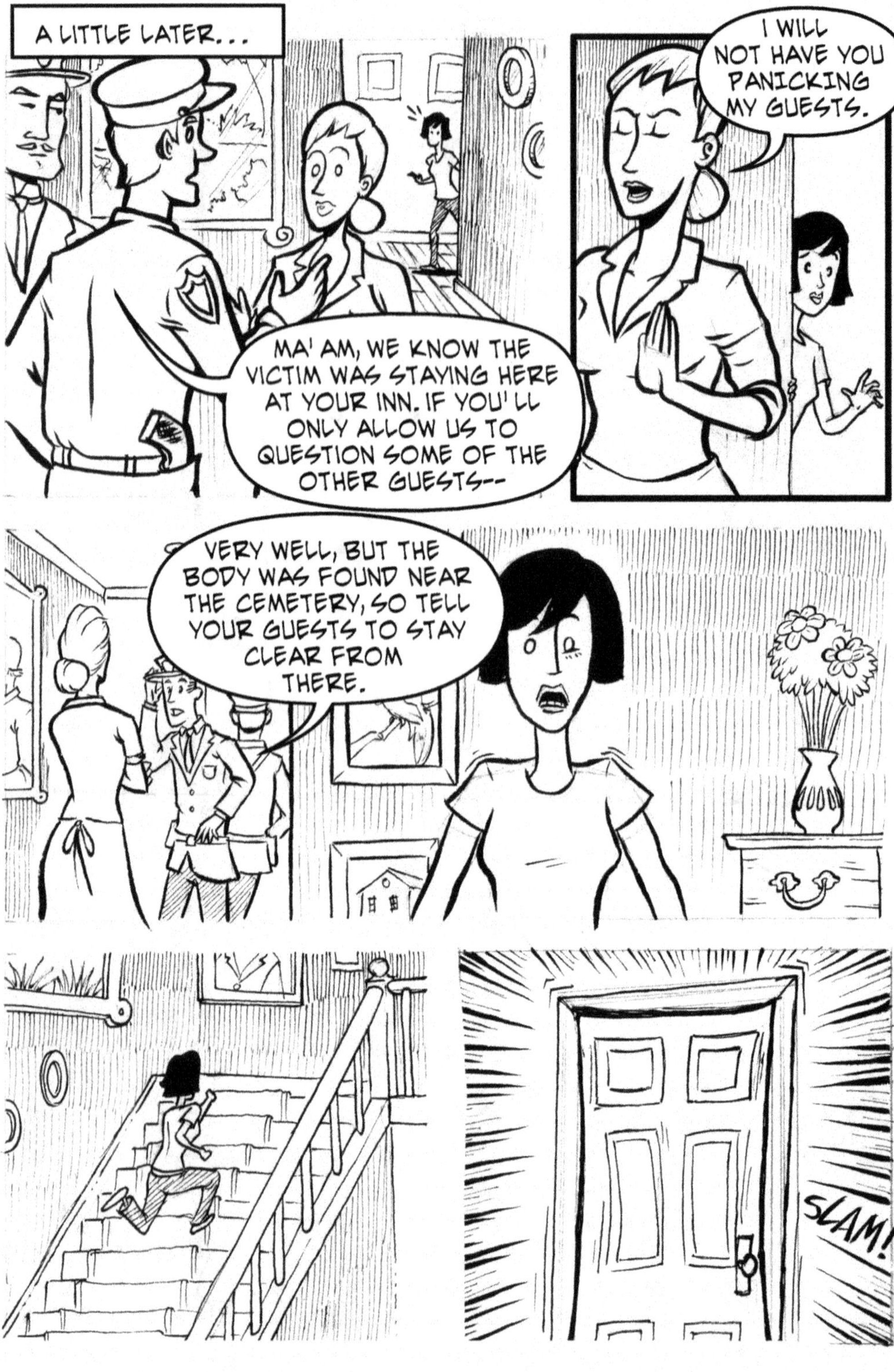
A LITTLE LATER...
MA' AM, WE KNOW THE VICTIM WAS STAYING HERE AT YOUR INN. IF YOU'LL ONLY ALLOW US TO QUESTION SOME OF THE OTHER GUESTS--
I WILL NOT HAVE YOU PANICKING MY GUESTS.
VERY WELL, BUT THE BODY WAS FOUND NEAR THE CEMETERY, SO TELL YOUR GUESTS TO STAY CLEAR FROM THERE.
SLAM!

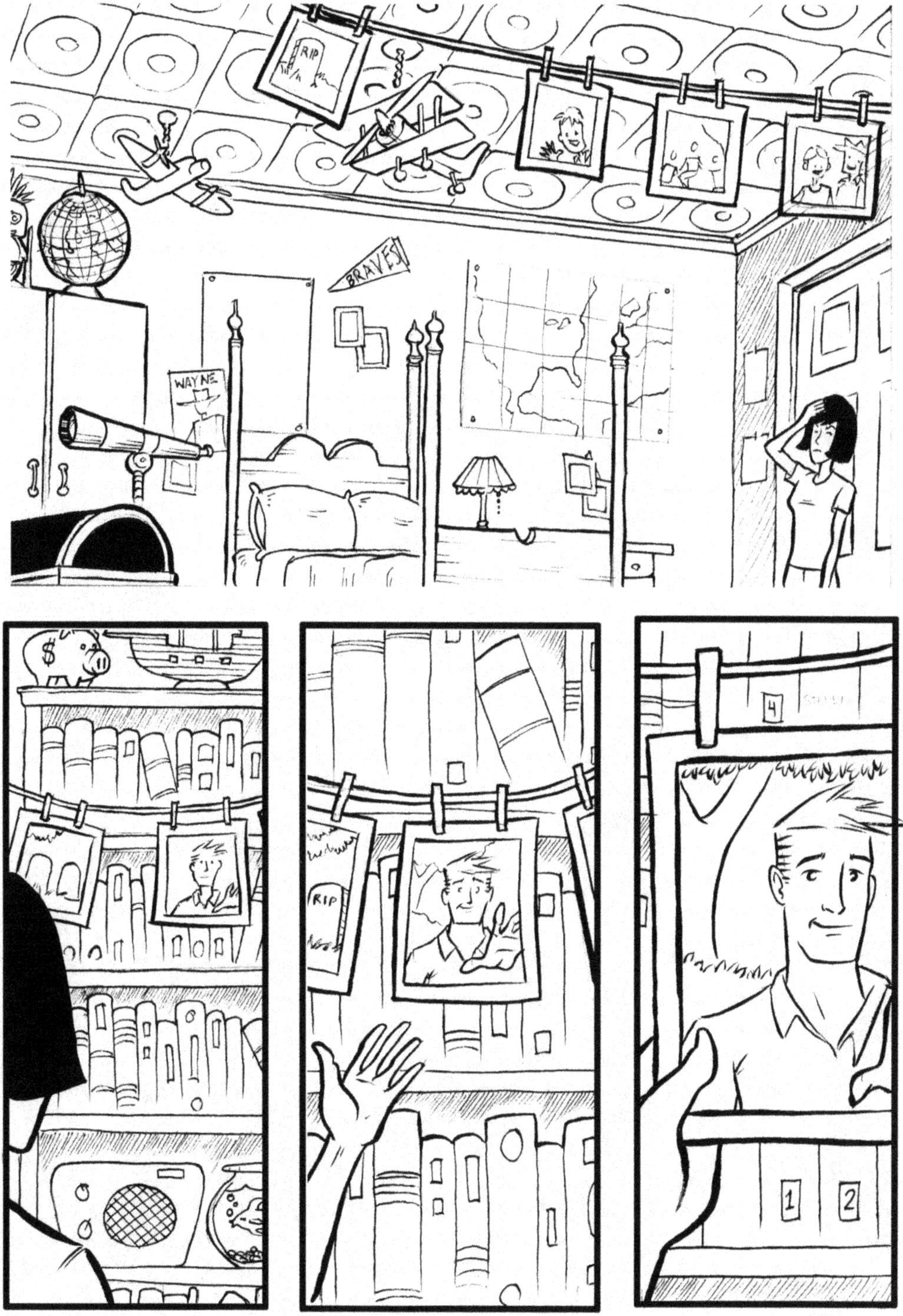
RIP
BRAVES
WAYNE
RIP
4
1
2

CHAPTER

7

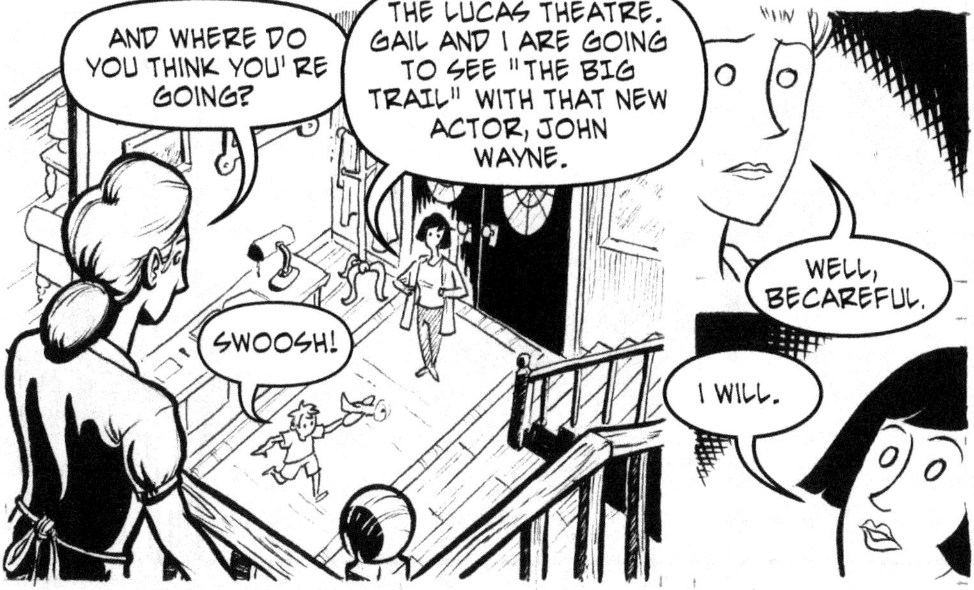
AND WHERE DO YOU THINK YOU' RE GOING?
THE LUCAS THEATRE. GAIL AND I ARE GOING TO SEE "THE BIG TRAIL" WITH THAT NEW ACTOR, JOHN WAYNE.
SWOOSH!
WELL, BECAREFUL.
I WILL.

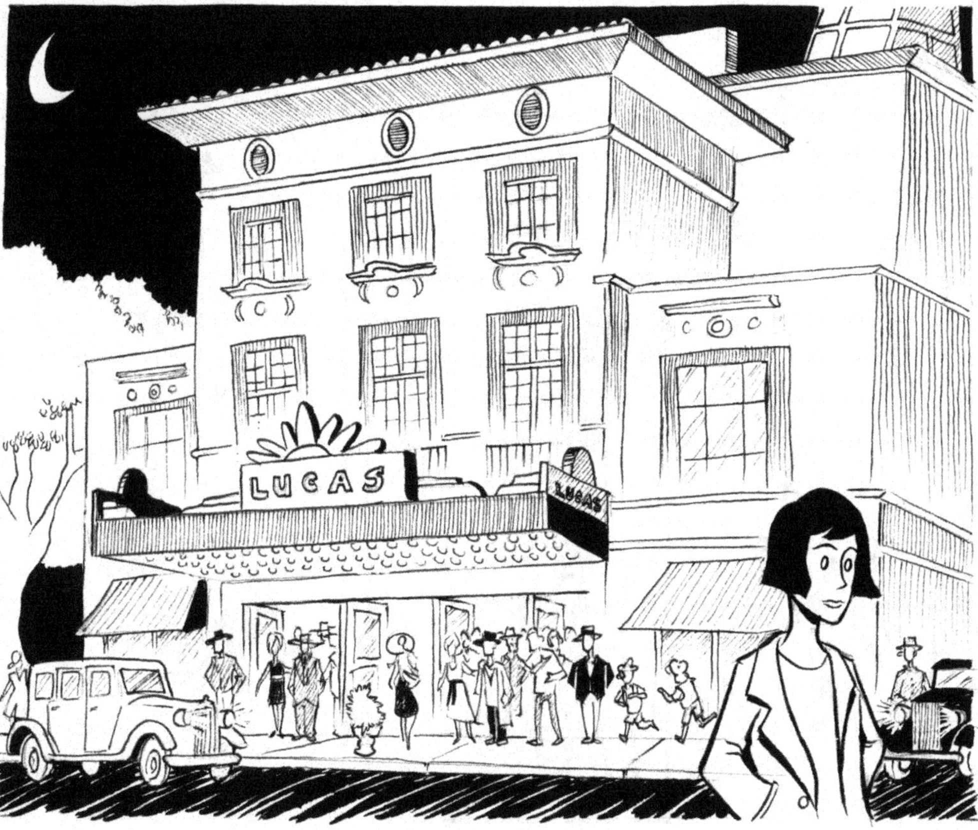
LUCAS
LUCAS

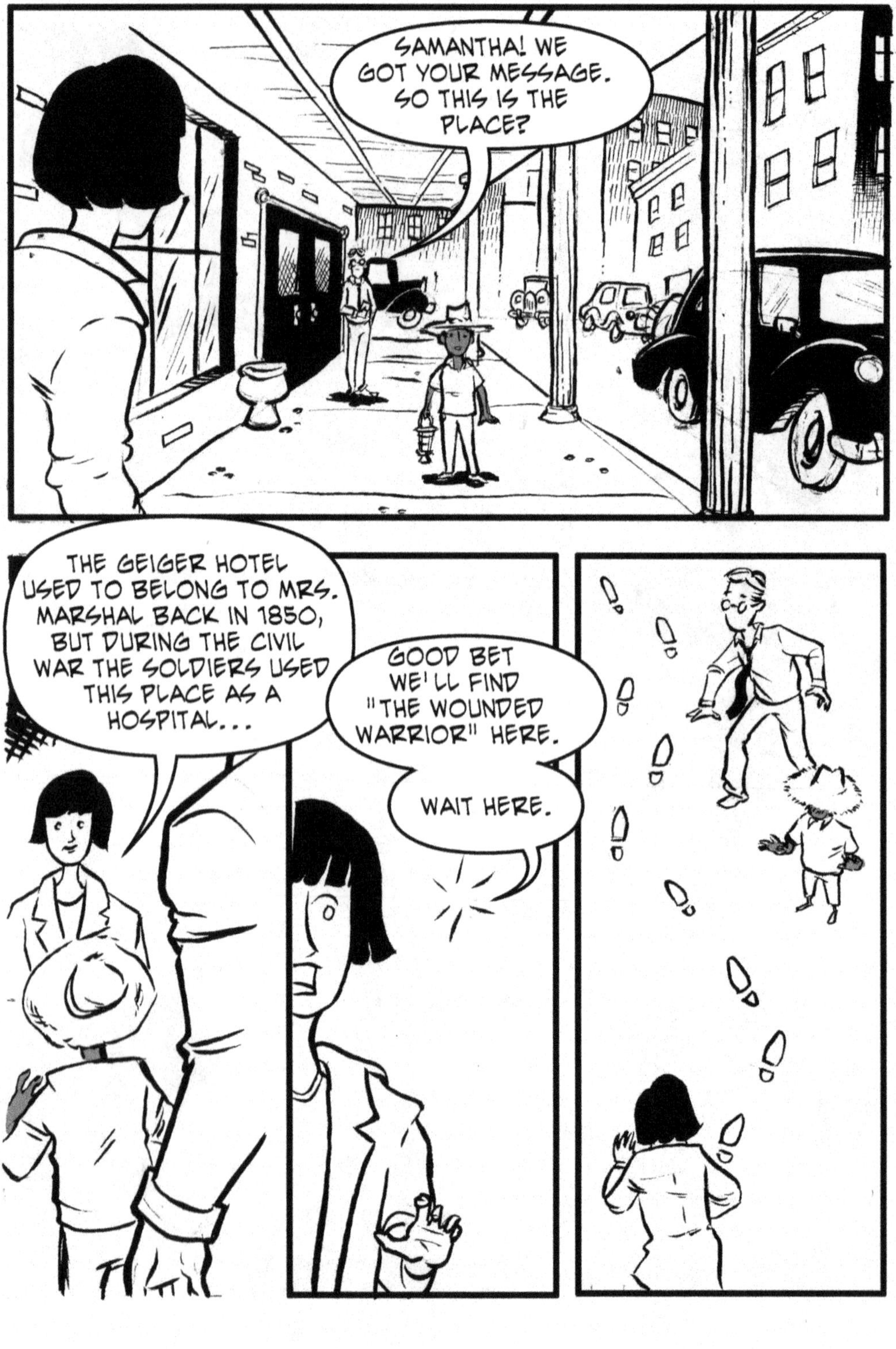
SAMANTHA! WE GOT YOUR MESSAGE. SO THIS IS THE PLACE?
THE GEIGER HOTEL USED TO BELONG TO MRS. MARSHAL BACK IN 1850, BUT DURING THE CIVIL WAR THE SOLDIERS USED THIS PLACE AS A HOSPITAL...
GOOD BET WE'LL FIND "THE WOUNDED WARRIOR" HERE.
WAIT HERE.

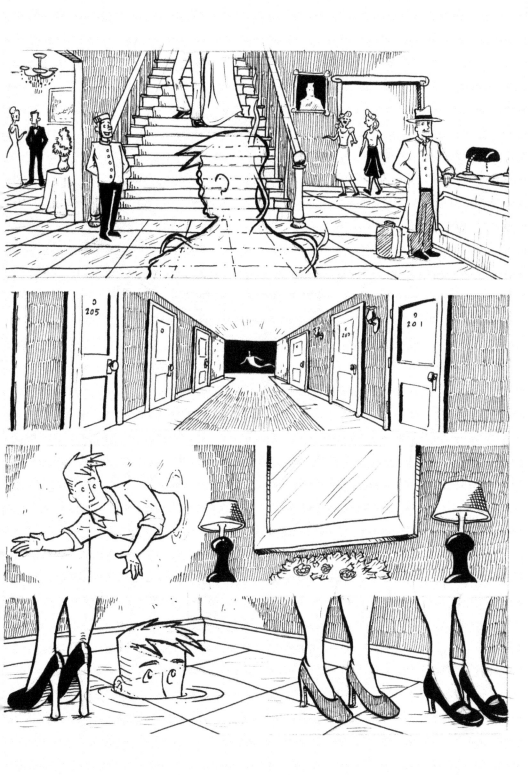

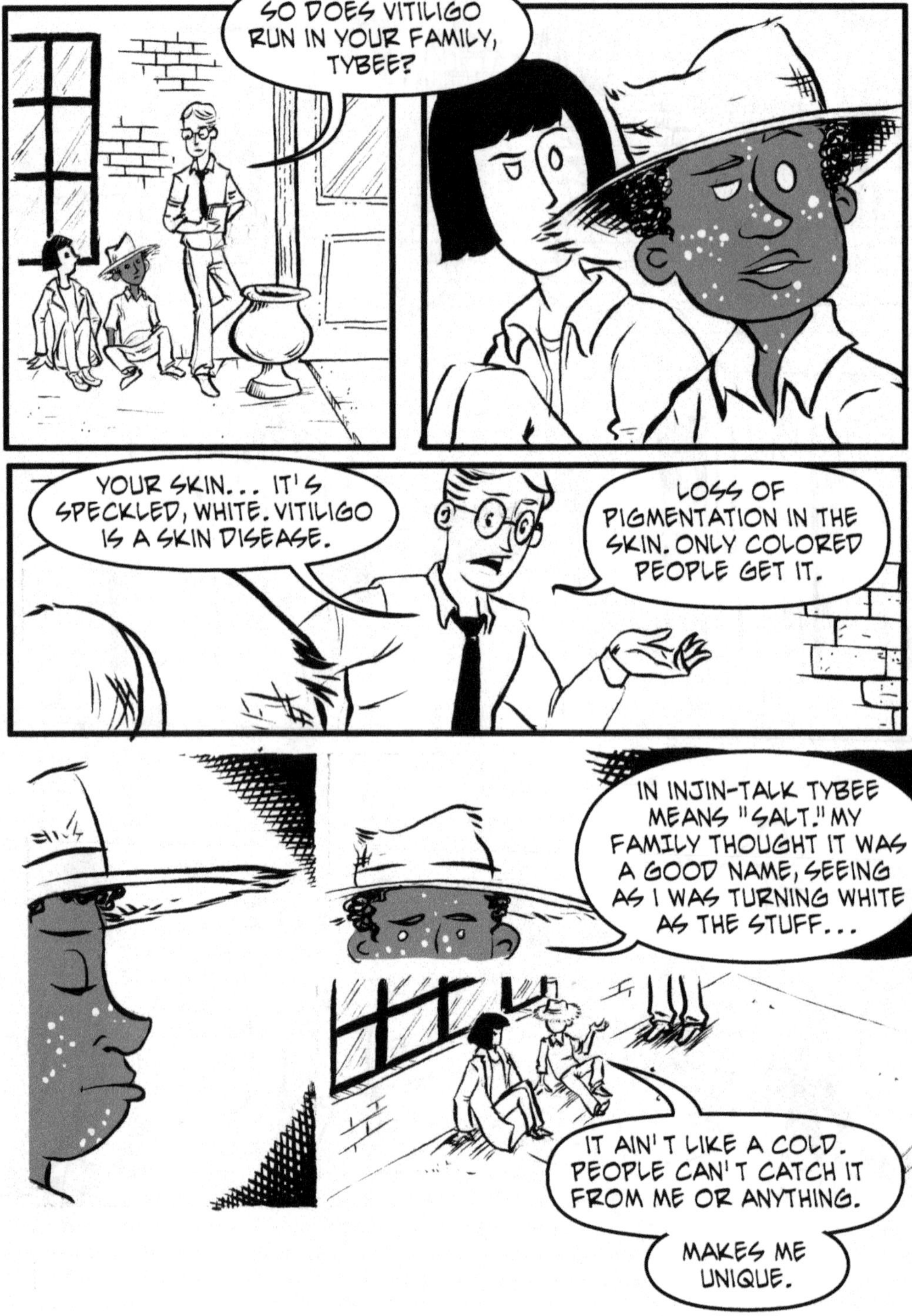
SO DOES VITILIGO RUN IN YOUR FAMILY, TYBEE?
YOUR SKIN... IT'S SPECKLED, WHITE. VITILIGO IS A SKIN DISEASE.
LOSS OF PIGMENTATION IN THE SKIN. ONLY COLORED PEOPLE GET IT.
IN INJIN-TALK TYBEE MEANS "SALT." MY FAMILY THOUGHT IT WAS A GOOD NAME, SEEING AS I WAS TURNING WHITE AS THE STUFF...
IT AIN'T LIKE A COLD. PEOPLE CAN'T CATCH IT FROM ME OR ANYTHING.
MAKES ME UNIQUE.

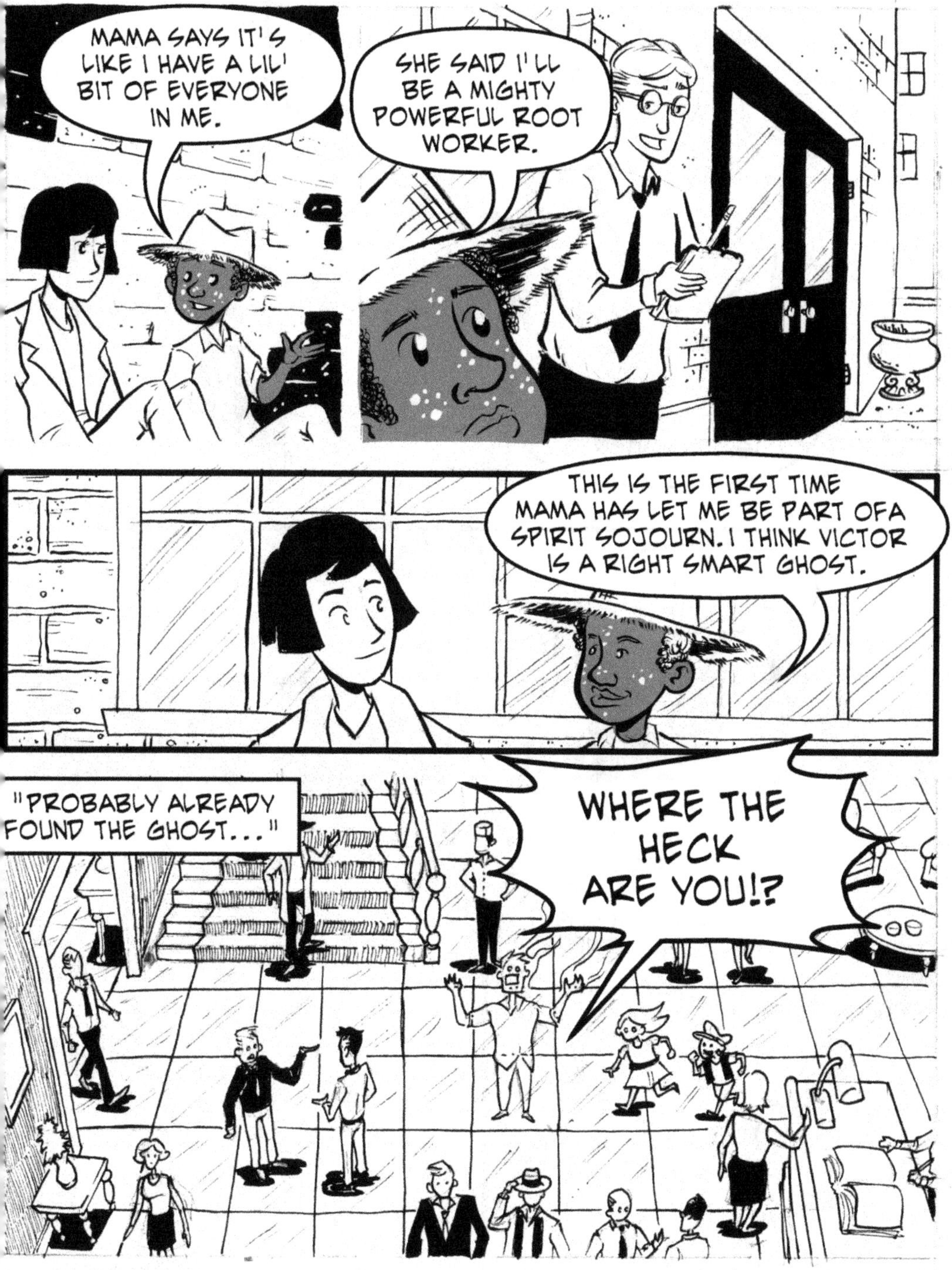
MAMA SAYS IT'S LIKE I HAVE A LIL' BIT OF EVERYONE IN ME.
SHE SAID I'LL BE A MIGHTY POWERFUL ROOT WORKER.
THIS IS THE FIRST TIME MAMA HAS LET ME BE PART OFA SPIRIT SOJOURN. I THINK VICTOR IS A RIGHT SMART GHOST.
"PROBABLY ALREADY FOUND THE GHOST..."
WHERE THE HECK ARE YOU!?

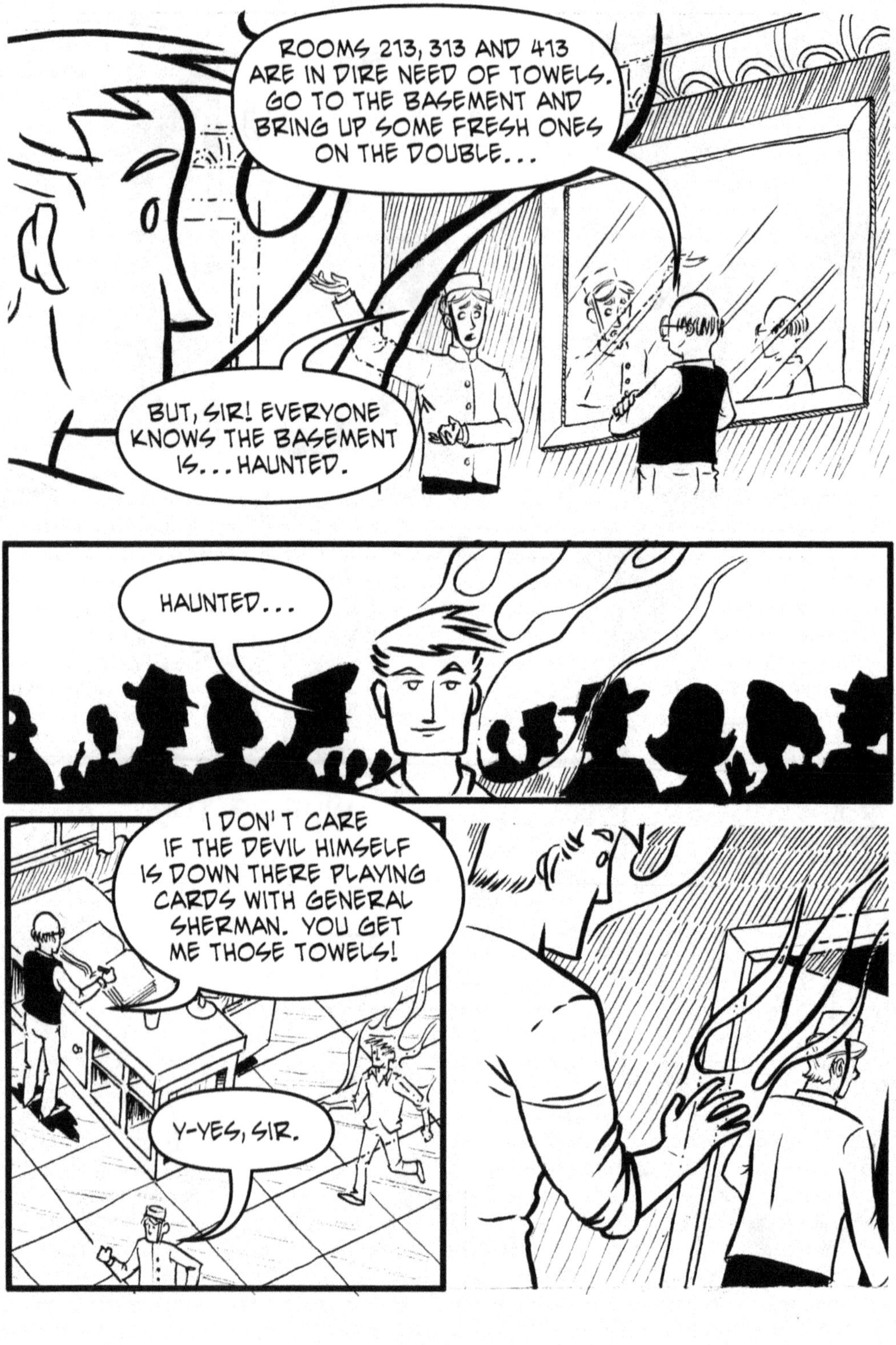
ROOMS 213, 313 AND 413 ARE IN DIRE NEED OF TOWELS. GO TO THE BASEMENT AND BRING UP SOME FRESH ONES ON THE DOUBLE...
BUT, SIR! EVERYONE KNOWS THE BASEMENT IS... HAUNTED.
HAUNTED...
I DON'T CARE IF THE DEVIL HIMSELF IS DOWN THERE PLAYING CARDS WITH GENERAL SHERMAN. YOU GET ME THOSE TOWELS!
Y-YES, SIR.

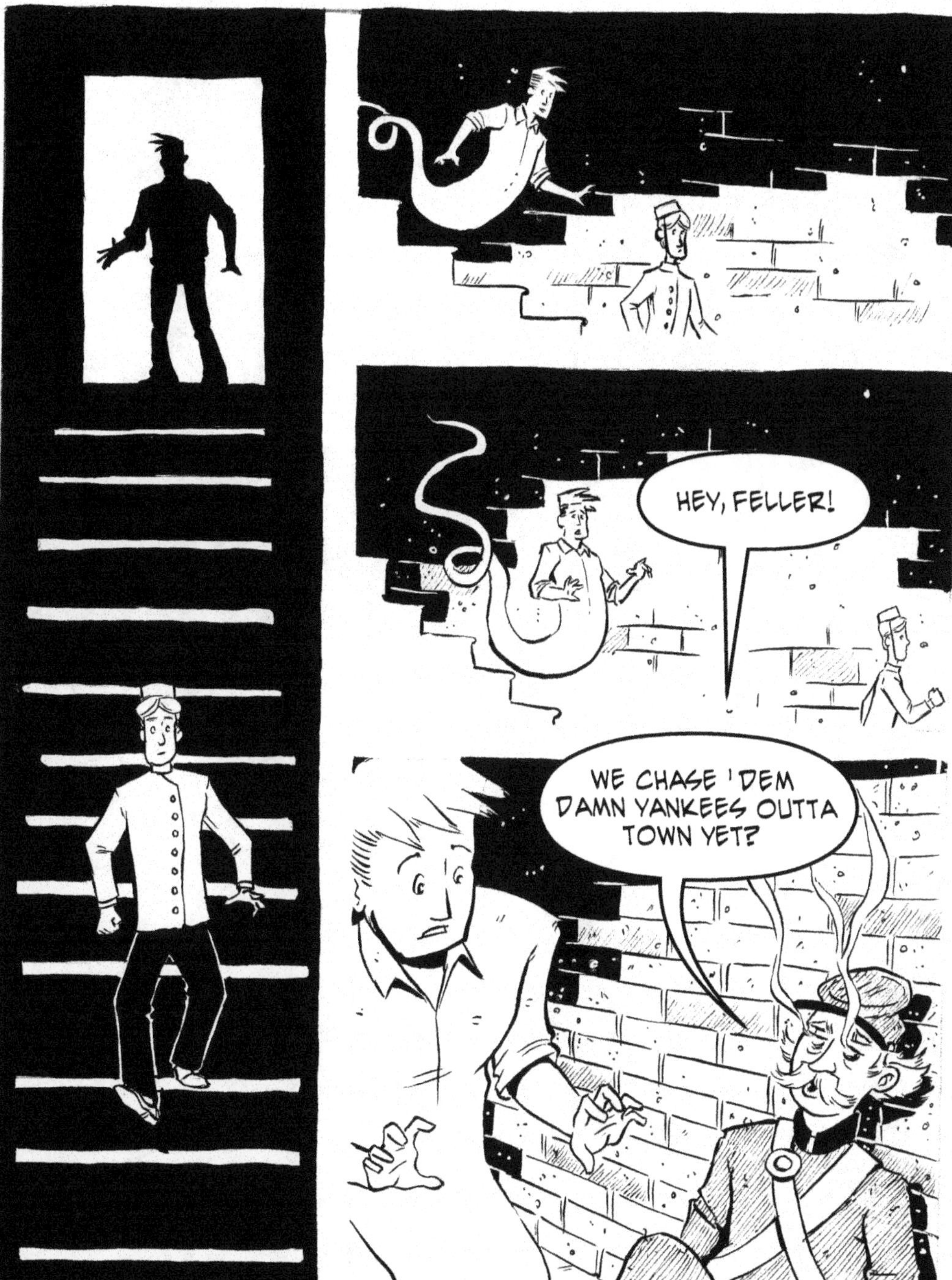
HEY, FELLER!
WE CHASE 'DEM DAMN YANKEES OUTTA TOWN YET?

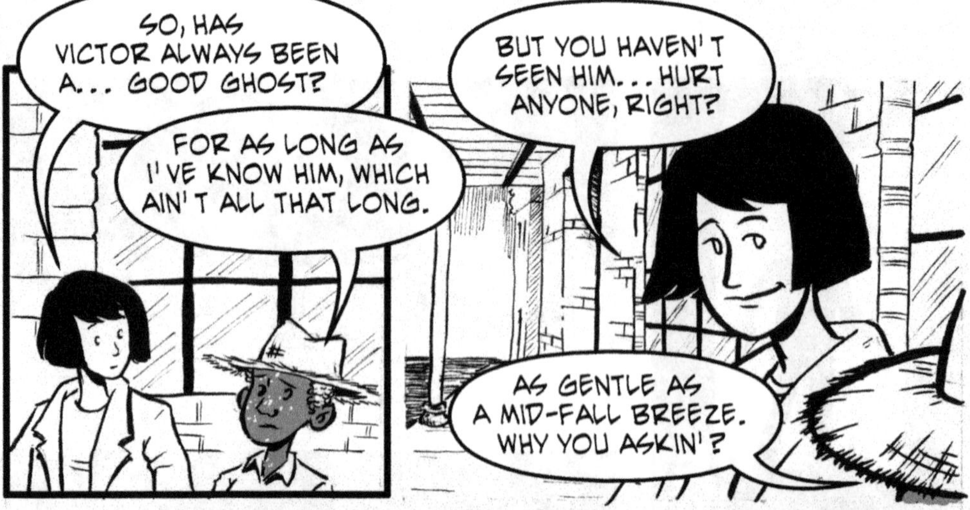
SO, HAS VICTOR ALWAYS BEEN A... GOOD GHOST?
FOR AS LONG AS I'VE KNOW HIM, WHICH AIN'T ALL THAT LONG.
BUT YOU HAVEN'T SEEN HIM... HURT ANYONE, RIGHT?
AS GENTLE AS A MID-FALL BREEZE. WHY YOU ASKIN'?

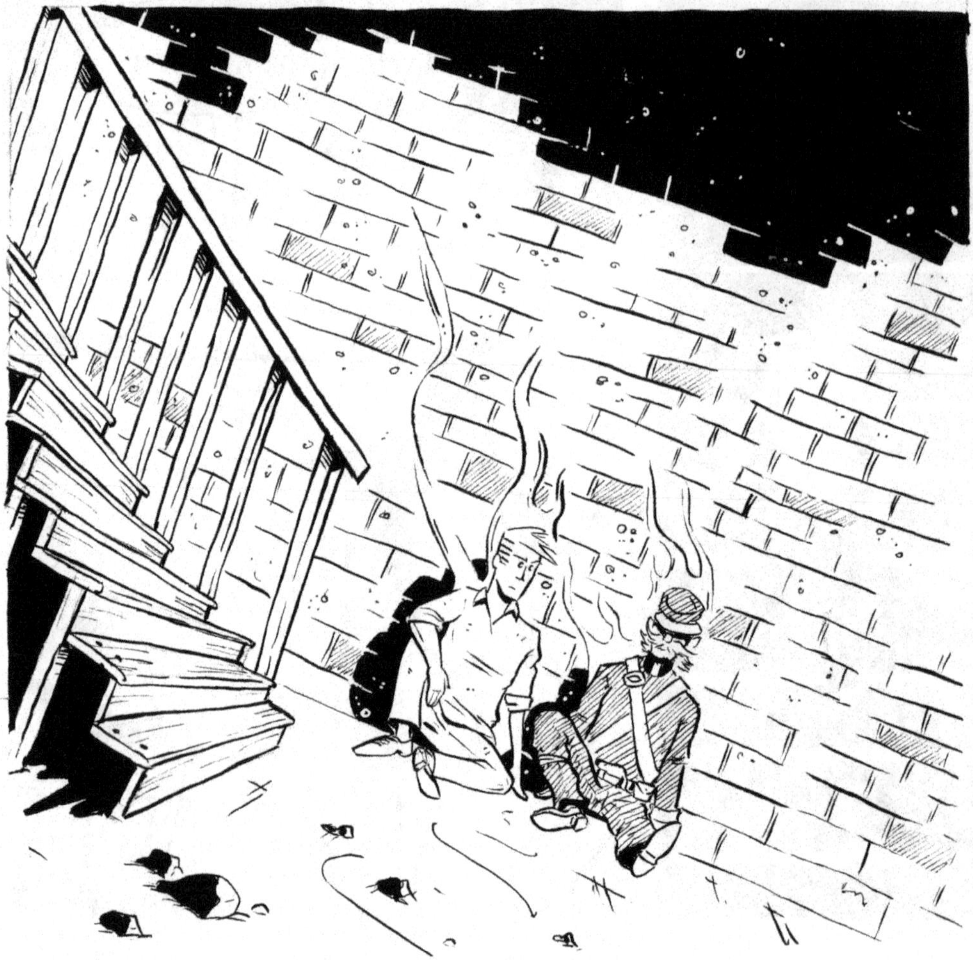

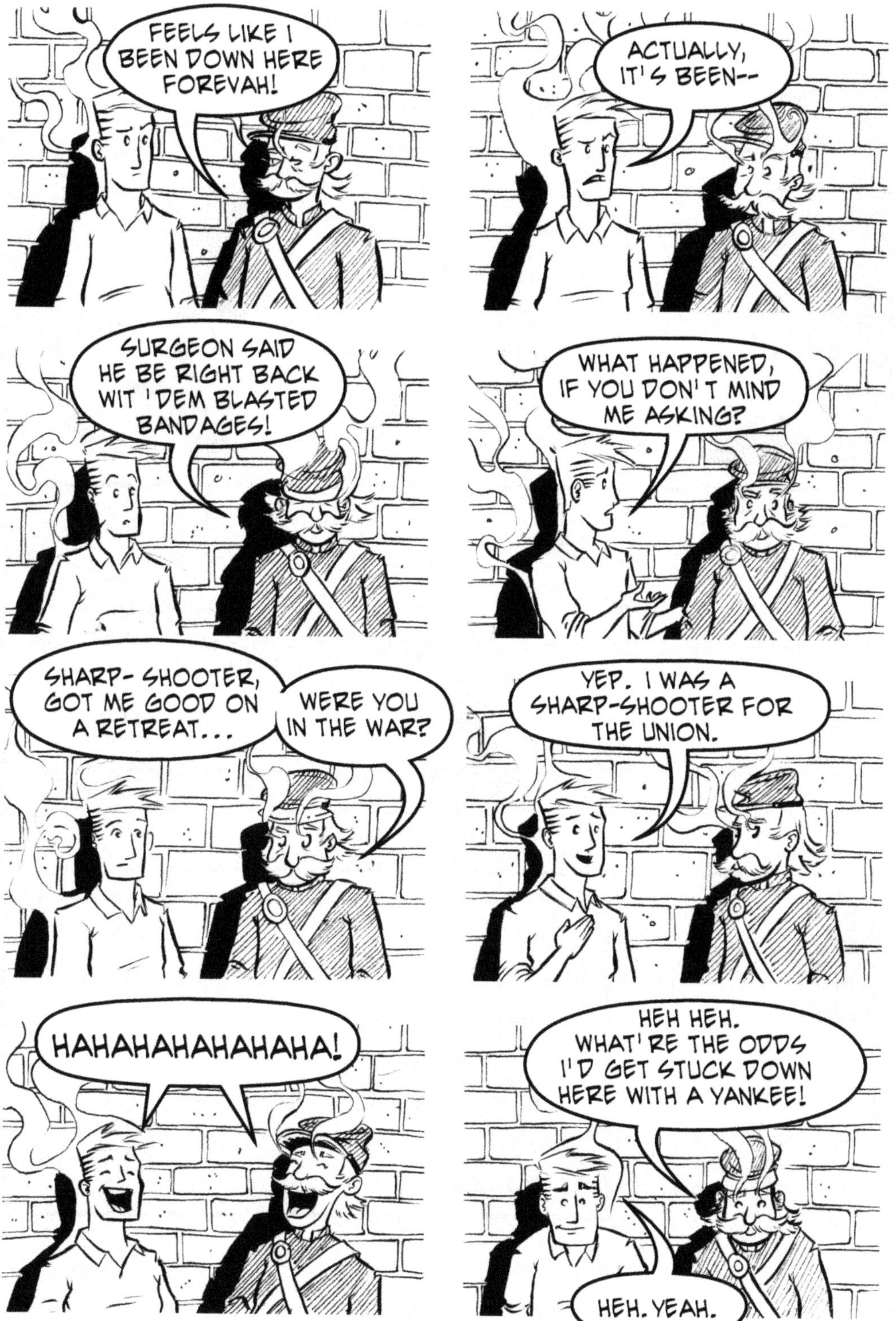
FEELS LIKE I BEEN DOWN HERE FOREVAH!
ACTUALLY, IT'S BEEN--
SURGEON SAID HE BE RIGHT BACK WIT 'DEM BLASTED BANDAGES!
WHAT HAPPENED, IF YOU DON'T MIND ME ASKING?
SHARP- SHOOTER, GOT ME GOOD ON A RETREAT...
WERE YOU IN THE WAR?
YEP. I WAS A SHARP-SHOOTER FOR THE UNION.
HAHAHAHAHAHAHA!
HEH HEH. WHAT'RE THE ODDS I'D GET STUCK DOWN HERE WITH A YANKEE!
HEH. YEAH.

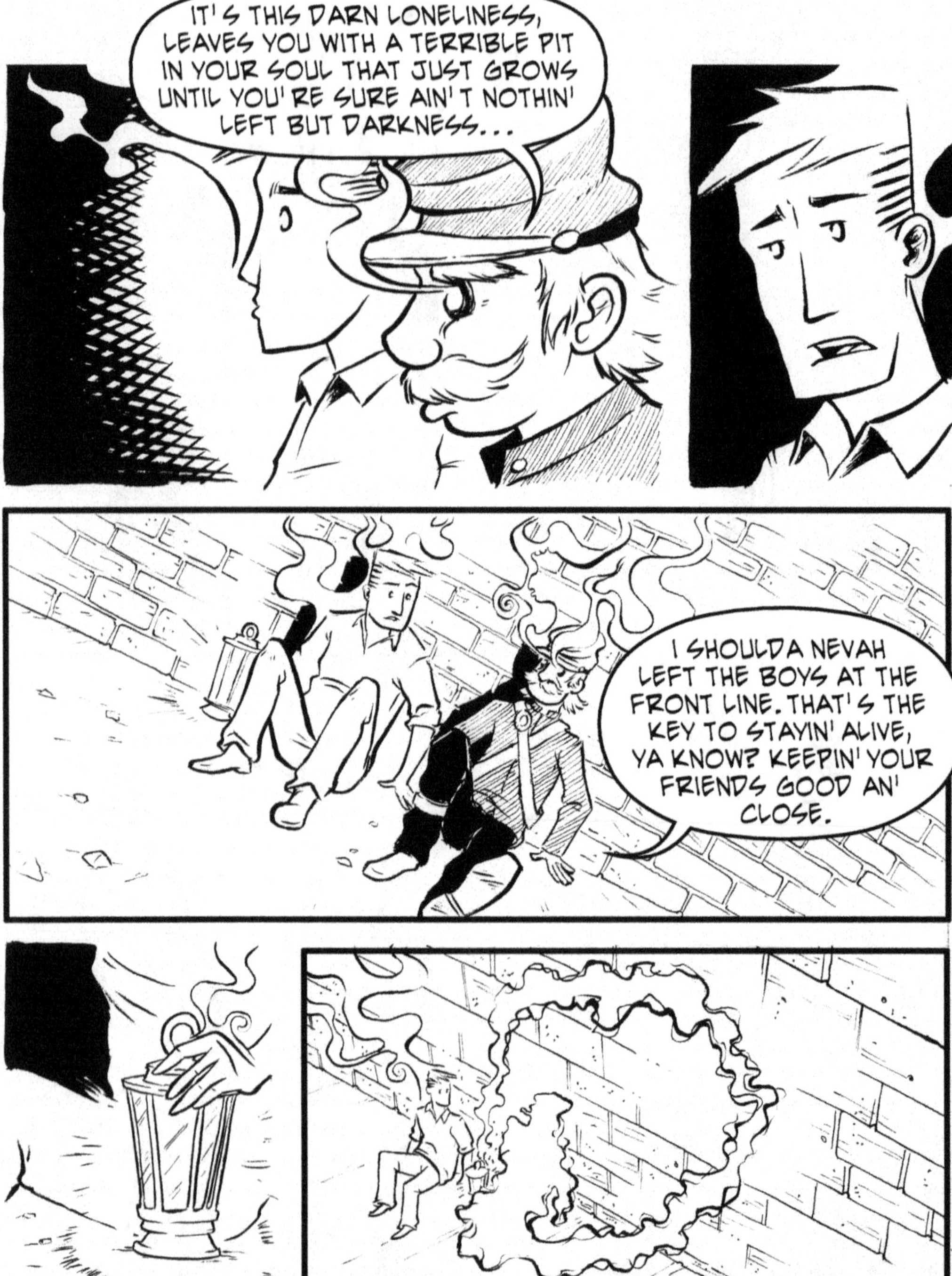
IT'S THIS DARN LONELINESS, LEAVES YOU WITH A TERRIBLE PIT IN YOUR SOUL THAT JUST GROWS UNTIL YOU'RE SURE AIN'T NOTHIN' LEFT BUT DARKNESS...
I SHOULDA NEVAH LEFT THE BOYS AT THE FRONT LINE. THAT'S THE KEY TO STAYIN' ALIVE, YA KNOW? KEEPIN' YOUR FRIENDS GOOD AN' CLOSE.

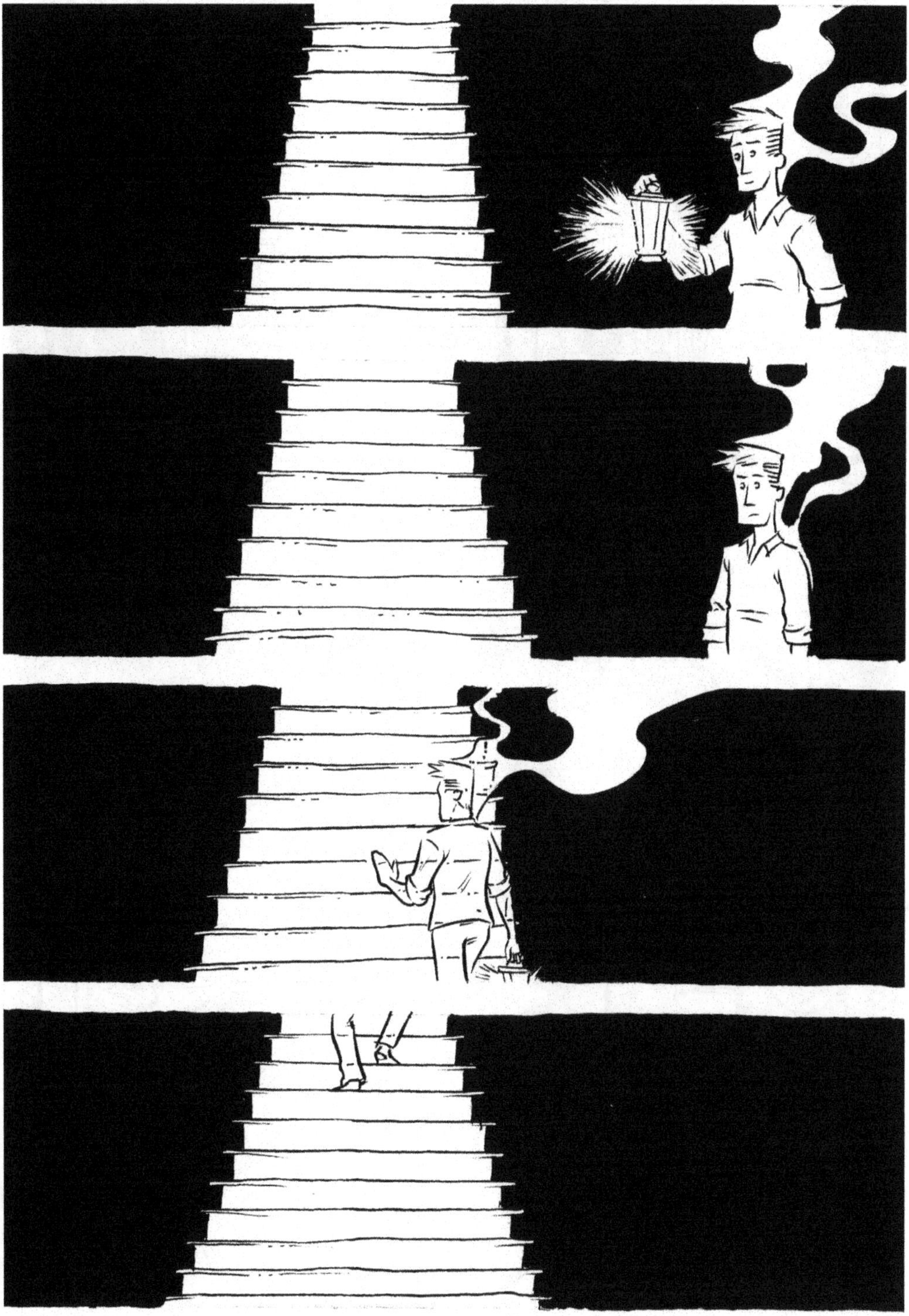

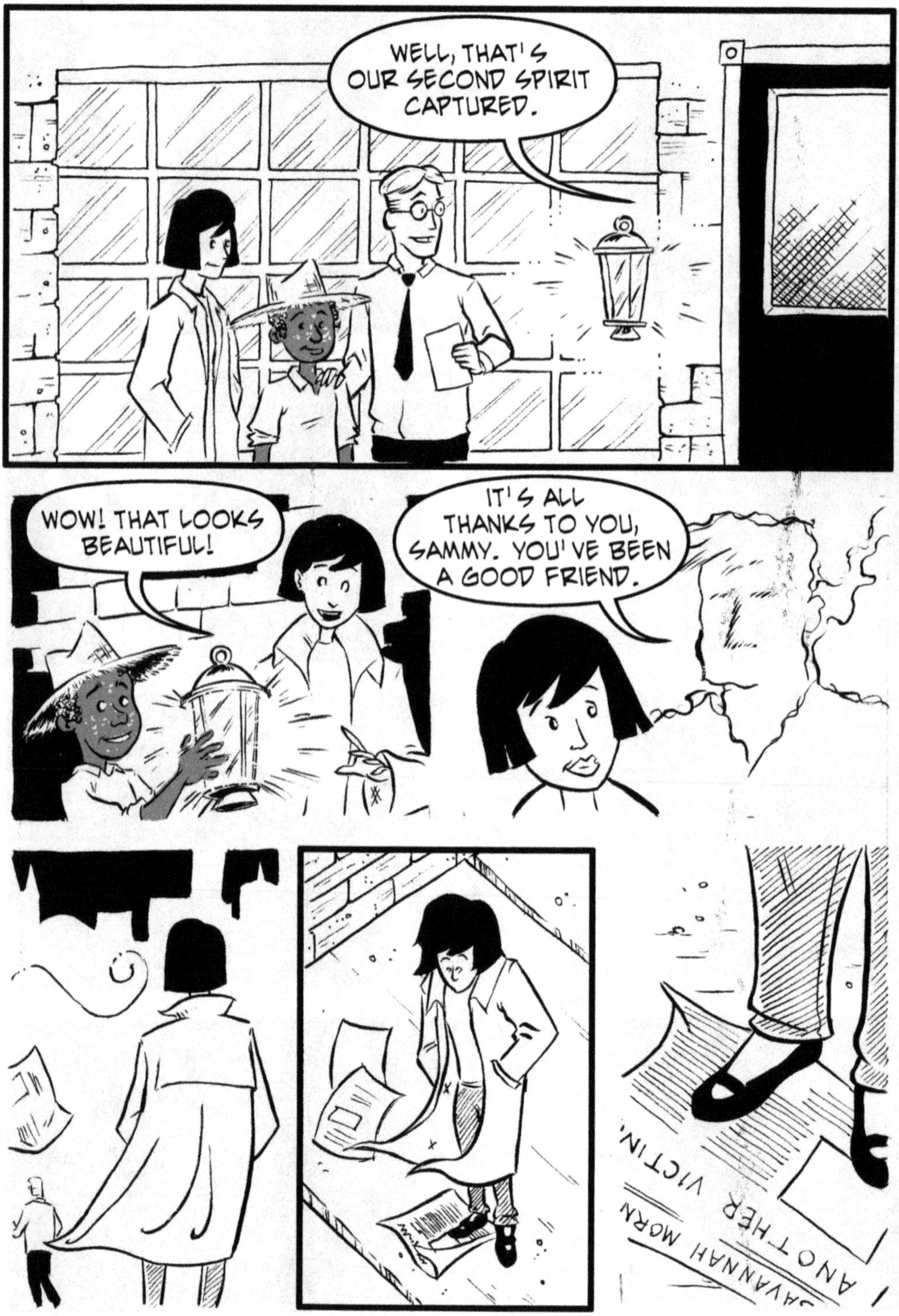
WELL, THAT'S OUR SECOND SPIRIT CAPTURED.
WOW! THAT LOOKS BEAUTIFUL!
IT'S ALL THANKS TO YOU, SAMMY. YOU'VE BEEN A GOOD FRIEND.

CHAPTER

7

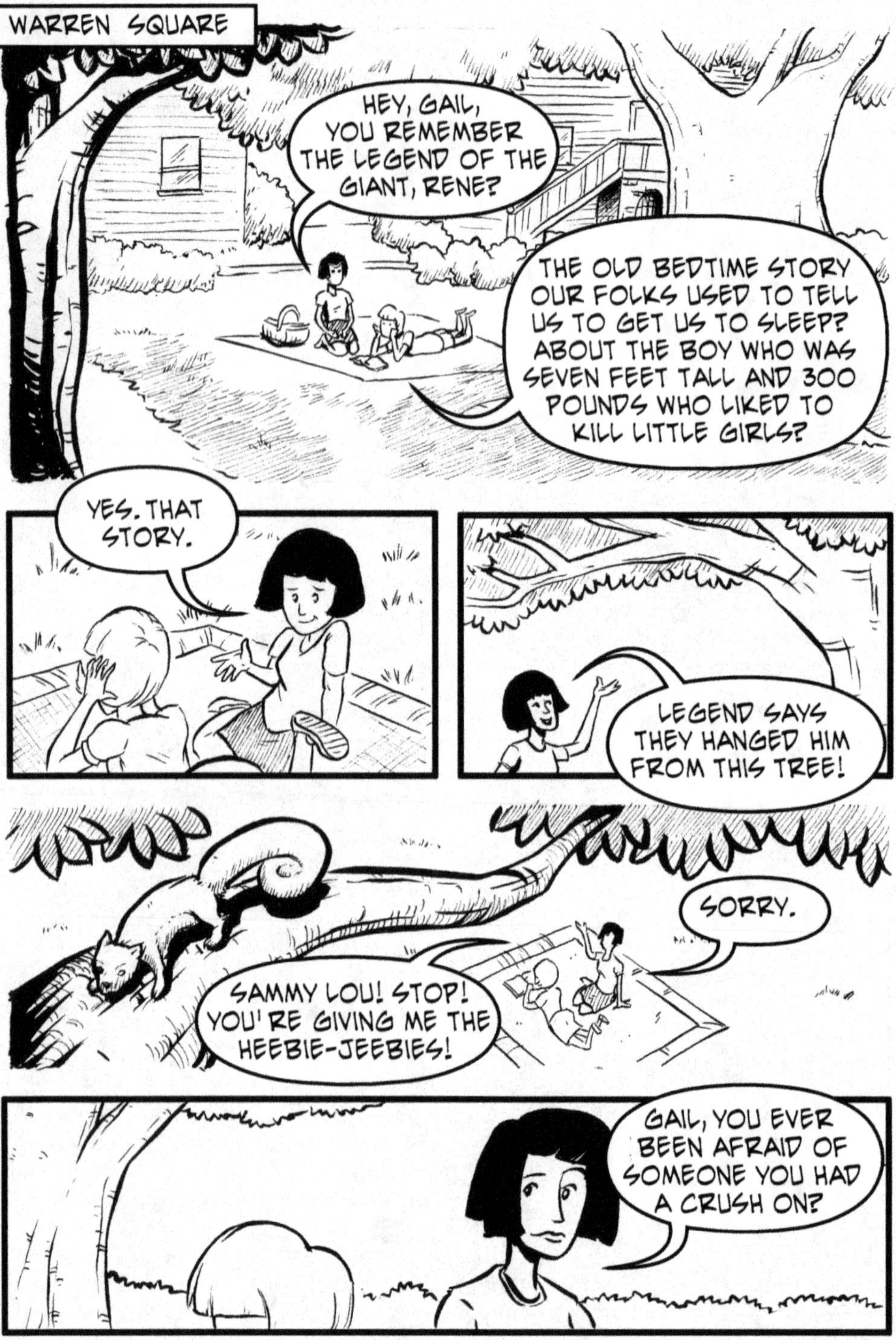
WARREN SQUARE
HEY, GAIL, YOU REMEMBER THE LEGEND OF THE GIANT, RENE?
THE OLD BEDTIME STORY OUR FOLKS USED TO TELL US TO GET US TO SLEEP? ABOUT THE BOY WHO WAS SEVEN FEET TALL AND 300 POUNDS WHO LIKED TO KILL LITTLE GIRLS?
YES. THAT STORY.
LEGEND SAYS THEY HANGED HIM FROM THIS TREE!
SAMMY LOU! STOP! YOU'RE GIVING ME THE HEEBIE-JEEBIES!
SORRY.
GAIL, YOU EVER BEEN AFRAID OF SOMEONE YOU HAD A CRUSH ON?

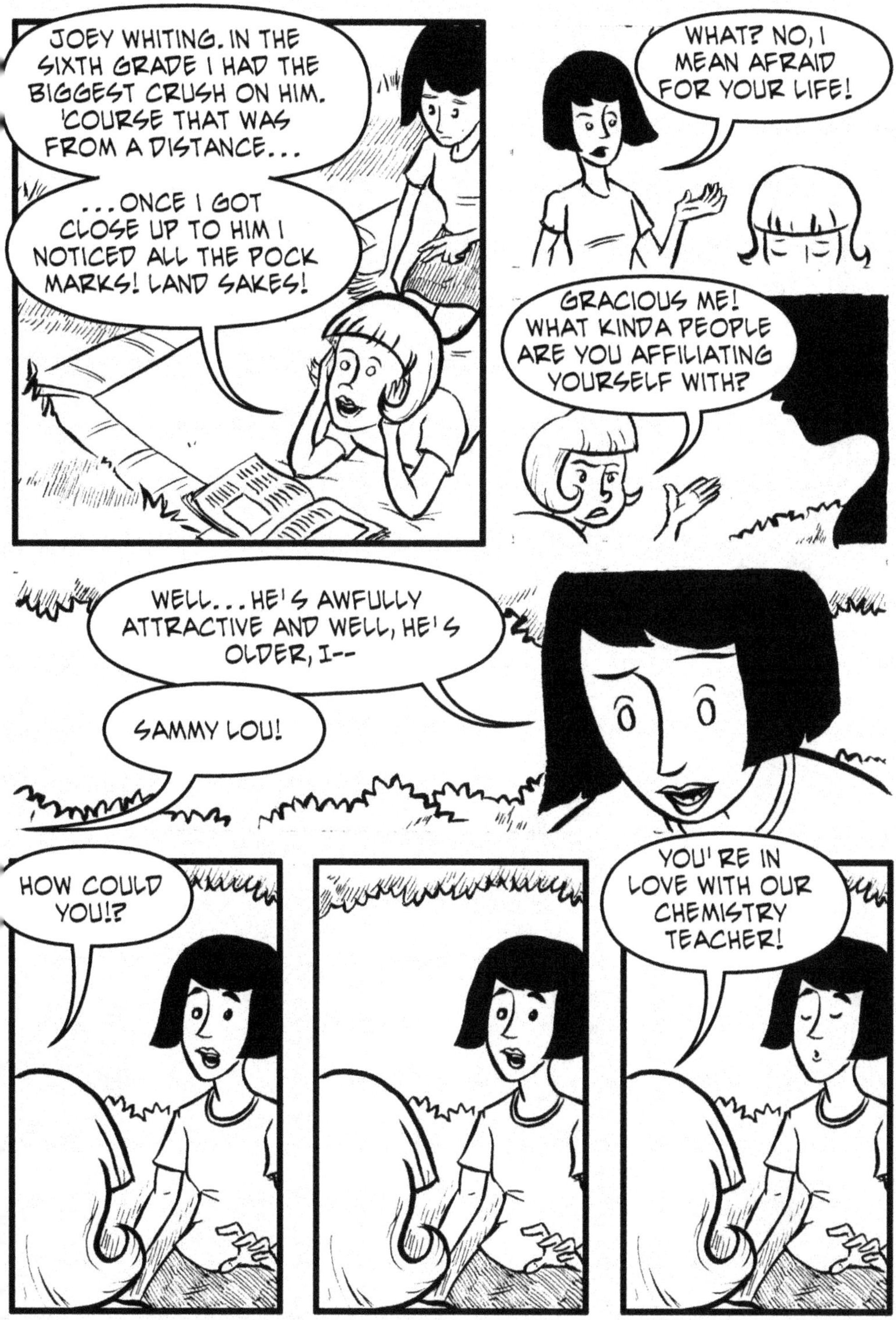
JOEY WHITING. IN THE SIXTH GRADE I HAD THE BIGGEST CRUSH ON HIM. 'COURSE THAT WAS FROM A DISTANCE...
...ONCE I GOT CLOSE UP TO HIM I NOTICED ALL THE POCK MARKS! LAND SAKES!
WHAT? NO, I MEAN AFRAID FOR YOUR LIFE!
GRACIOUS ME! WHAT KINDA PEOPLE ARE YOU AFFILIATING YOURSELF WITH?
WELL...HE'S AWFULLY ATTRACTIVE AND WELL, HE'S OLDER, I--
SAMMY LOU!
HOW COULD YOU!?
YOU'RE IN LOVE WITH OUR CHEMISTRY TEACHER!

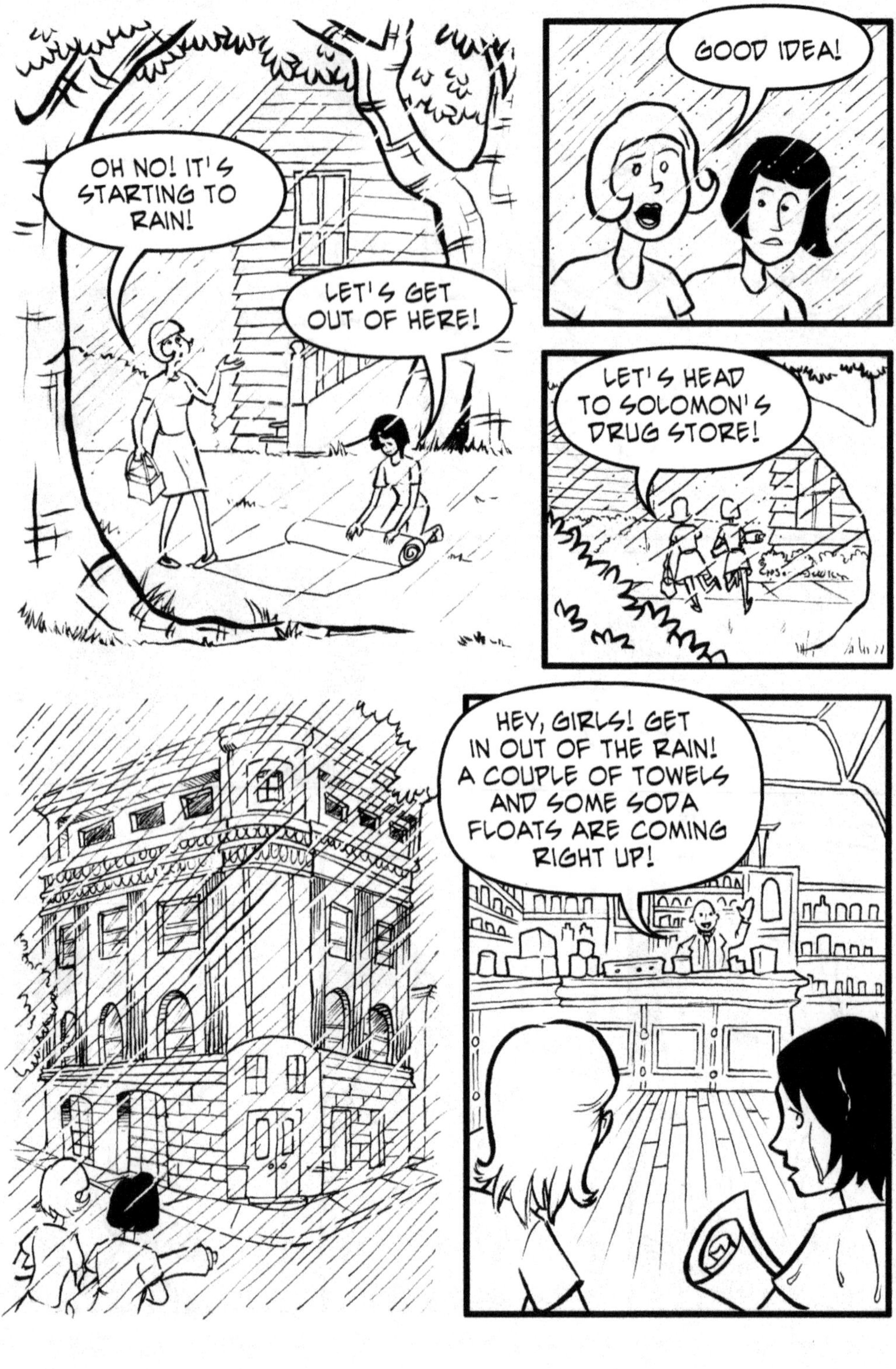
OH NO! IT'S STARTING TO RAIN!
LET'S GET OUT OF HERE!
GOOD IDEA!
LET'S HEAD TO SOLOMON'S DRUG STORE!
HEY, GIRLS! GET IN OUT OF THE RAIN! A COUPLE OF TOWELS AND SOME SODA FLOATS ARE COMING RIGHT UP!

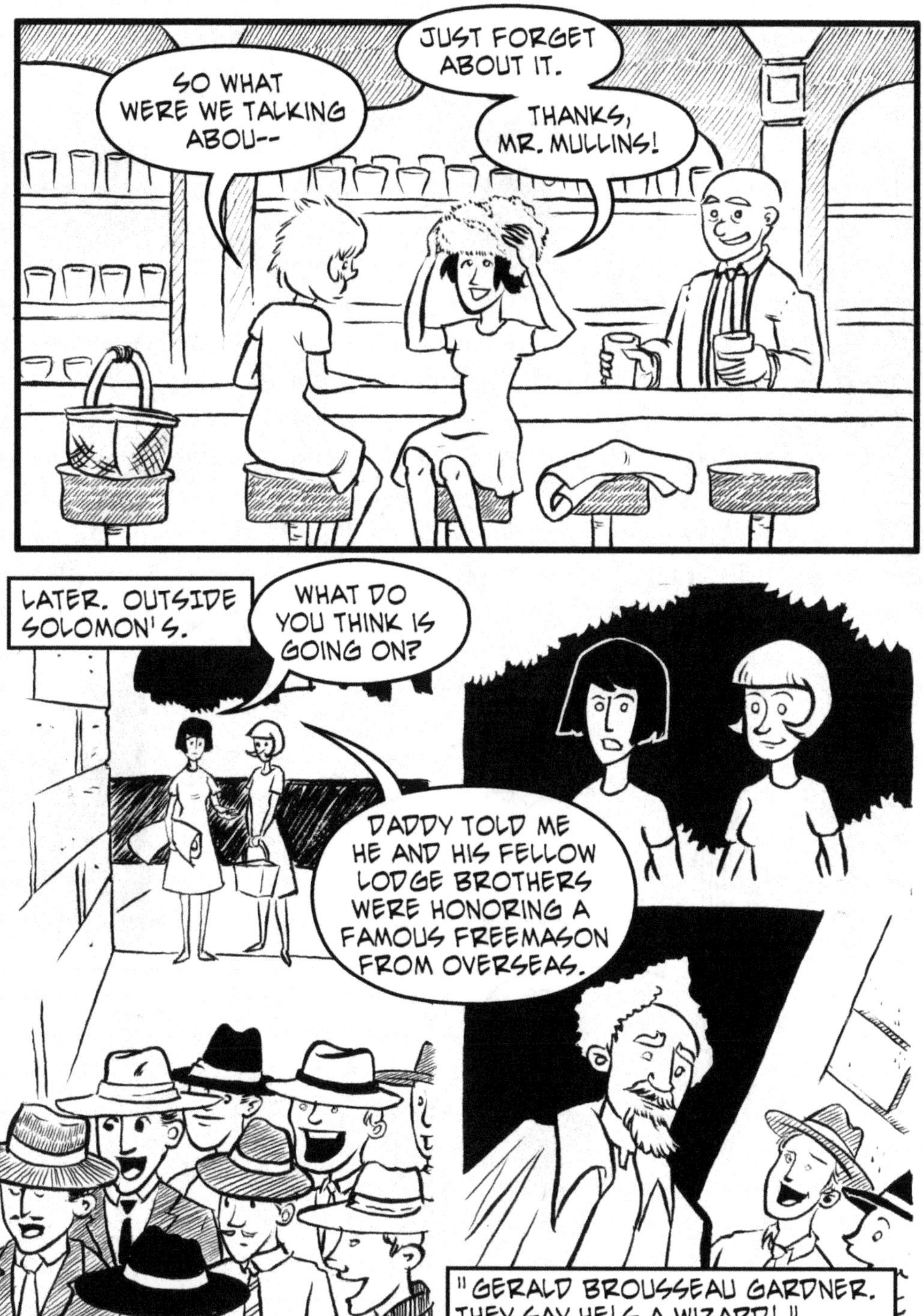
SO WHAT WERE WE TALKING ABOU--
JUST FORGET ABOUT IT.
THANKS, MR. MULLINS!
LATER. OUTSIDE SOLOMON'S.
WHAT DO YOU THINK IS GOING ON?
DADDY TOLD ME HE AND HIS FELLOW LODGE BROTHERS WERE HONORING A FAMOUS FREEMASON FROM OVERSEAS.
"GERALD BROUSSEAU GARDNER. THEY SAY HE'S A WIZARD!"

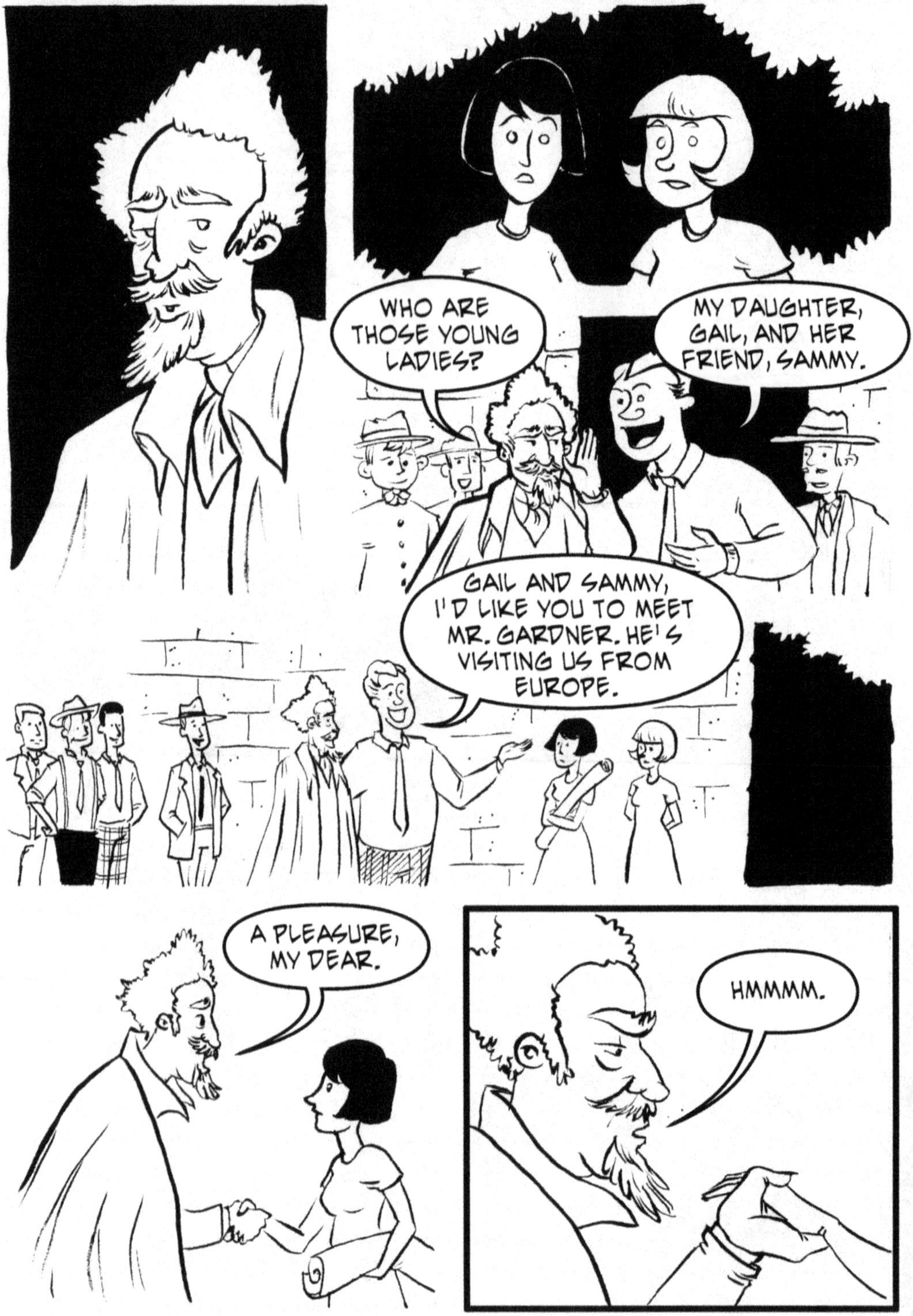
WHO ARE THOSE YOUNG LADIES?
MY DAUGHTER, GAIL, AND HER FRIEND, SAMMY.
GAIL AND SAMMY, I'D LIKE YOU TO MEET MR. GARDNER. HE'S VISITING US FROM EUROPE.
A PLEASURE, MY DEAR.
HMMMM.

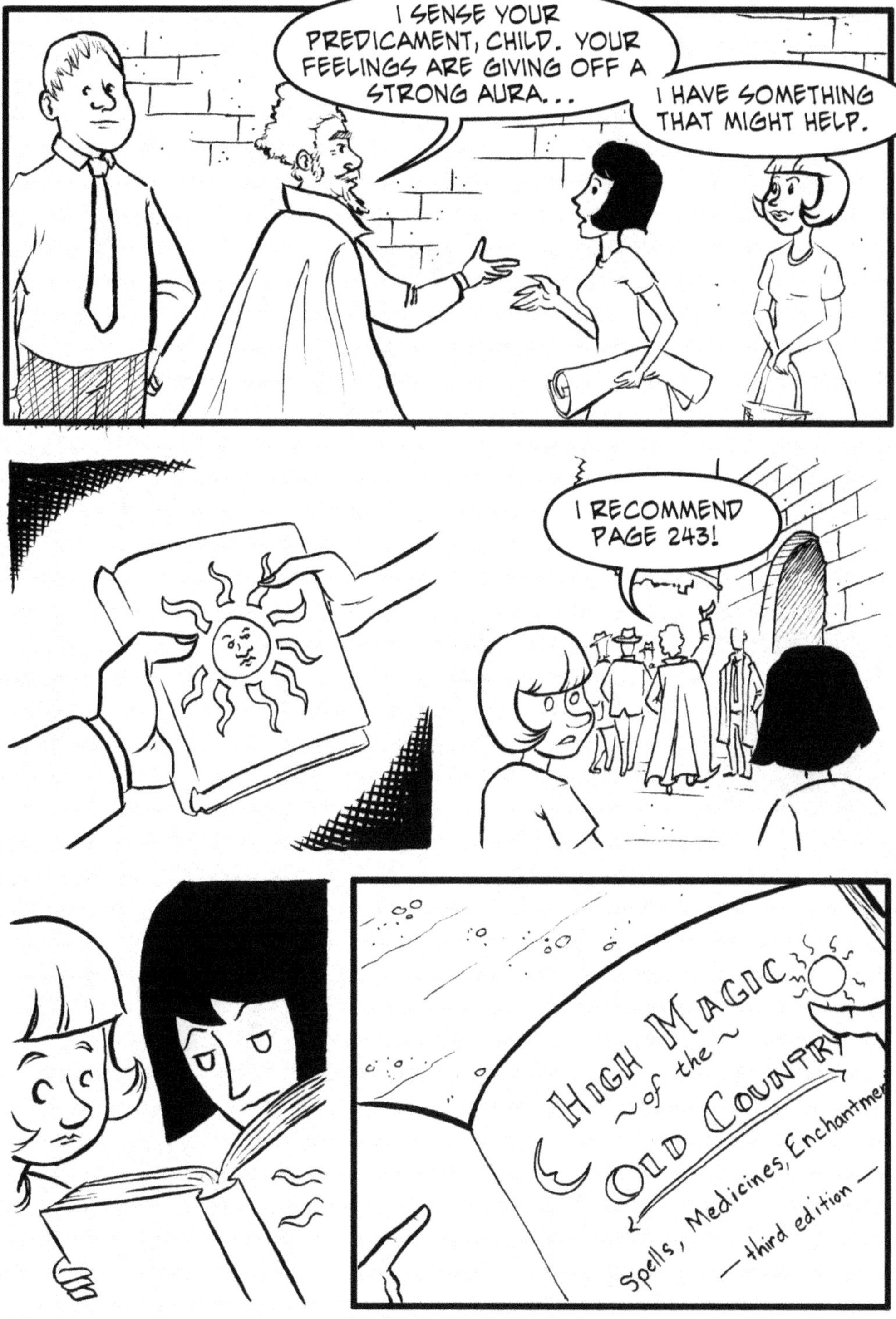
I SENSE YOUR PREDICAMENT, CHILD. YOUR FEELINGS ARE GIVING OFF A STRONG AURA...
I HAVE SOMETHING THAT MIGHT HELP.
I RECOMMEND PAGE 243!
HIGH MAGIC ~of the~ OLD COUNTRY
Spells, Medicines, Enchantme
— third edition —

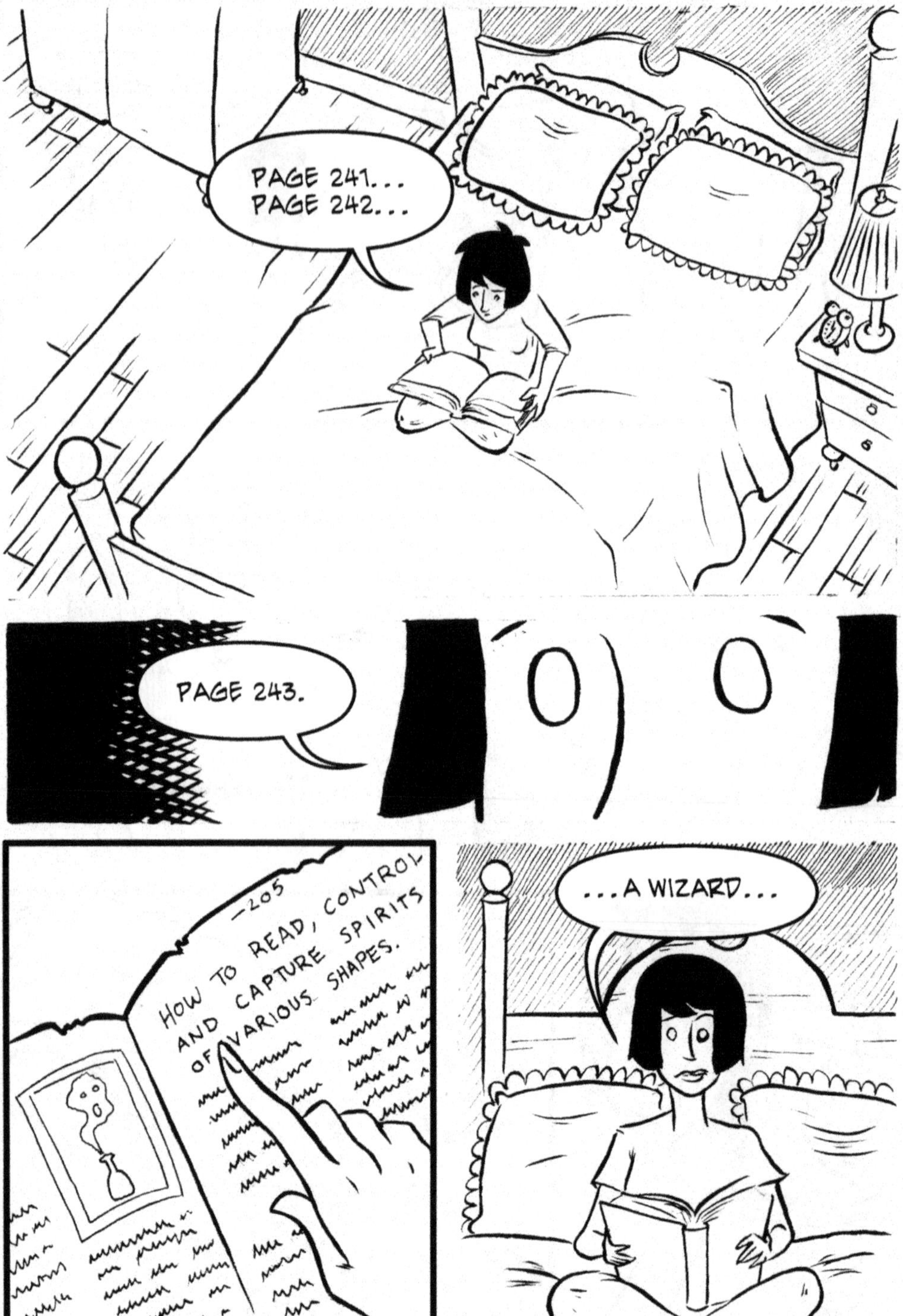
PAGE 241...
PAGE 242...
PAGE 243.
-205
HOW TO READ, CONTROL AND CAPTURE SPIRITS OF VARIOUS SHAPES.
...A WIZARD...

CHAPTER

8

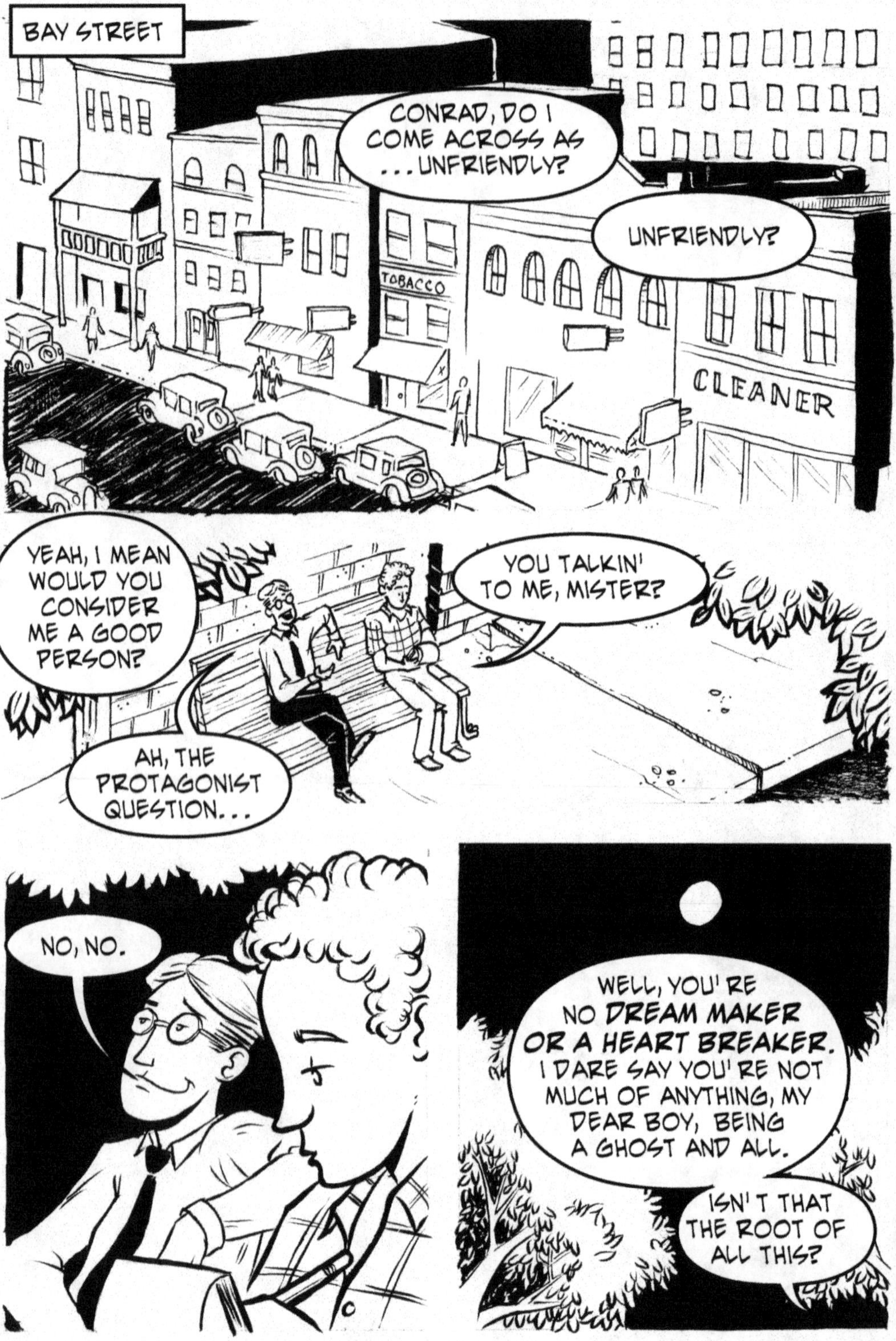
BAY STREET
CONRAD, DO I COME ACROSS AS . . . UNFRIENDLY?
UNFRIENDLY?
TOBACCO
CLEANER
YEAH, I MEAN WOULD YOU CONSIDER ME A GOOD PERSON?
YOU TALKIN' TO ME, MISTER?
AH, THE PROTAGONIST QUESTION. . .
NO, NO.
WELL, YOU'RE NO DREAM MAKER OR A HEART BREAKER. I DARE SAY YOU'RE NOT MUCH OF ANYTHING, MY DEAR BOY, BEING A GHOST AND ALL.
ISN'T THAT THE ROOT OF ALL THIS?

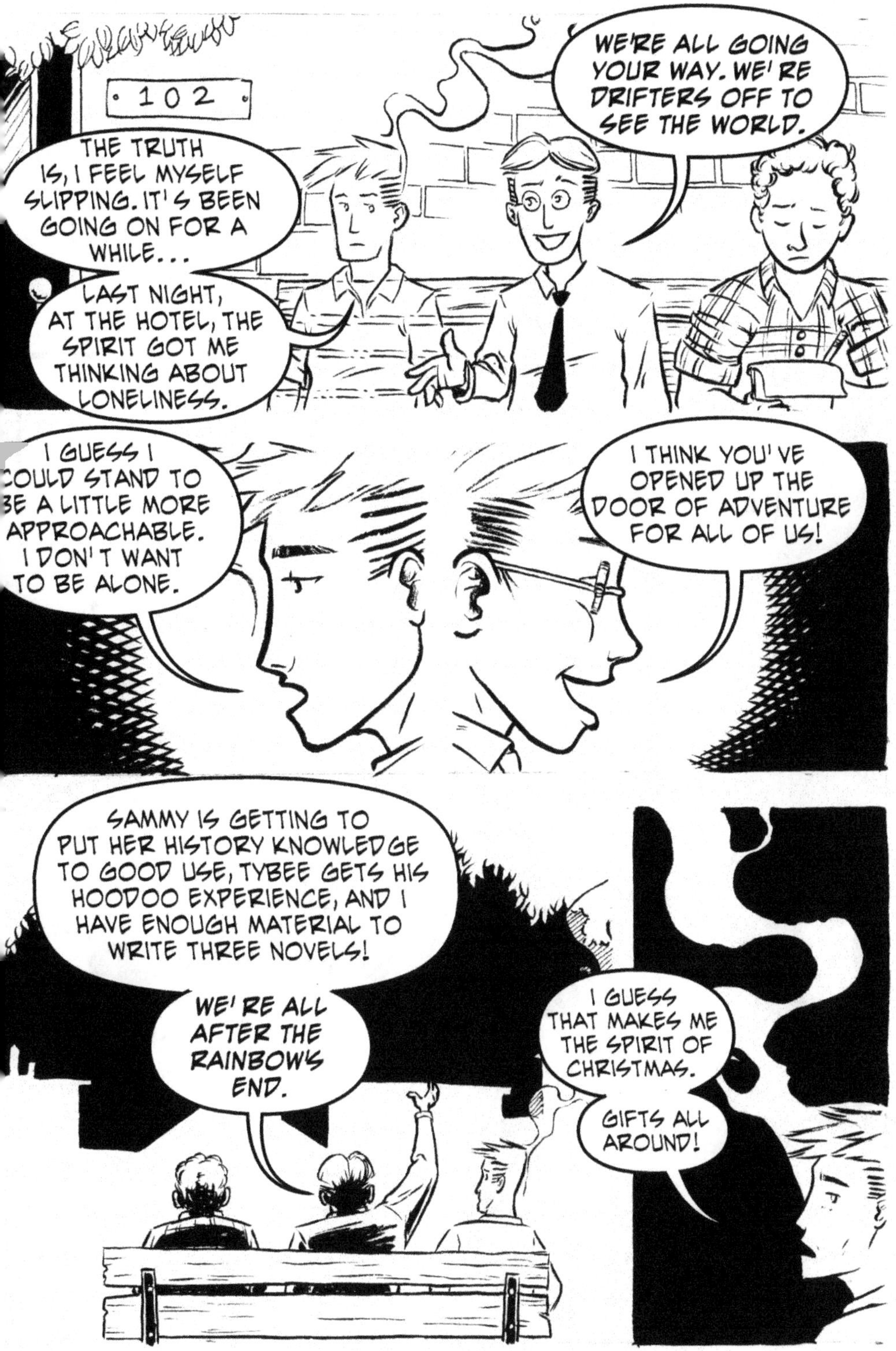
102
THE TRUTH IS, I FEEL MYSELF SLIPPING. IT'S BEEN GOING ON FOR A WHILE...
LAST NIGHT, AT THE HOTEL, THE SPIRIT GOT ME THINKING ABOUT LONELINESS.
WE'RE ALL GOING YOUR WAY. WE'RE DRIFTERS OFF TO SEE THE WORLD.
I GUESS I COULD STAND TO BE A LITTLE MORE APPROACHABLE. I DON'T WANT TO BE ALONE.
I THINK YOU'VE OPENED UP THE DOOR OF ADVENTURE FOR ALL OF US!
SAMMY IS GETTING TO PUT HER HISTORY KNOWLEDGE TO GOOD USE, TYBEE GETS HIS HOODOO EXPERIENCE, AND I HAVE ENOUGH MATERIAL TO WRITE THREE NOVELS!
WE'RE ALL AFTER THE RAINBOW'S END.
I GUESS THAT MAKES ME THE SPIRIT OF CHRISTMAS.
GIFTS ALL AROUND!

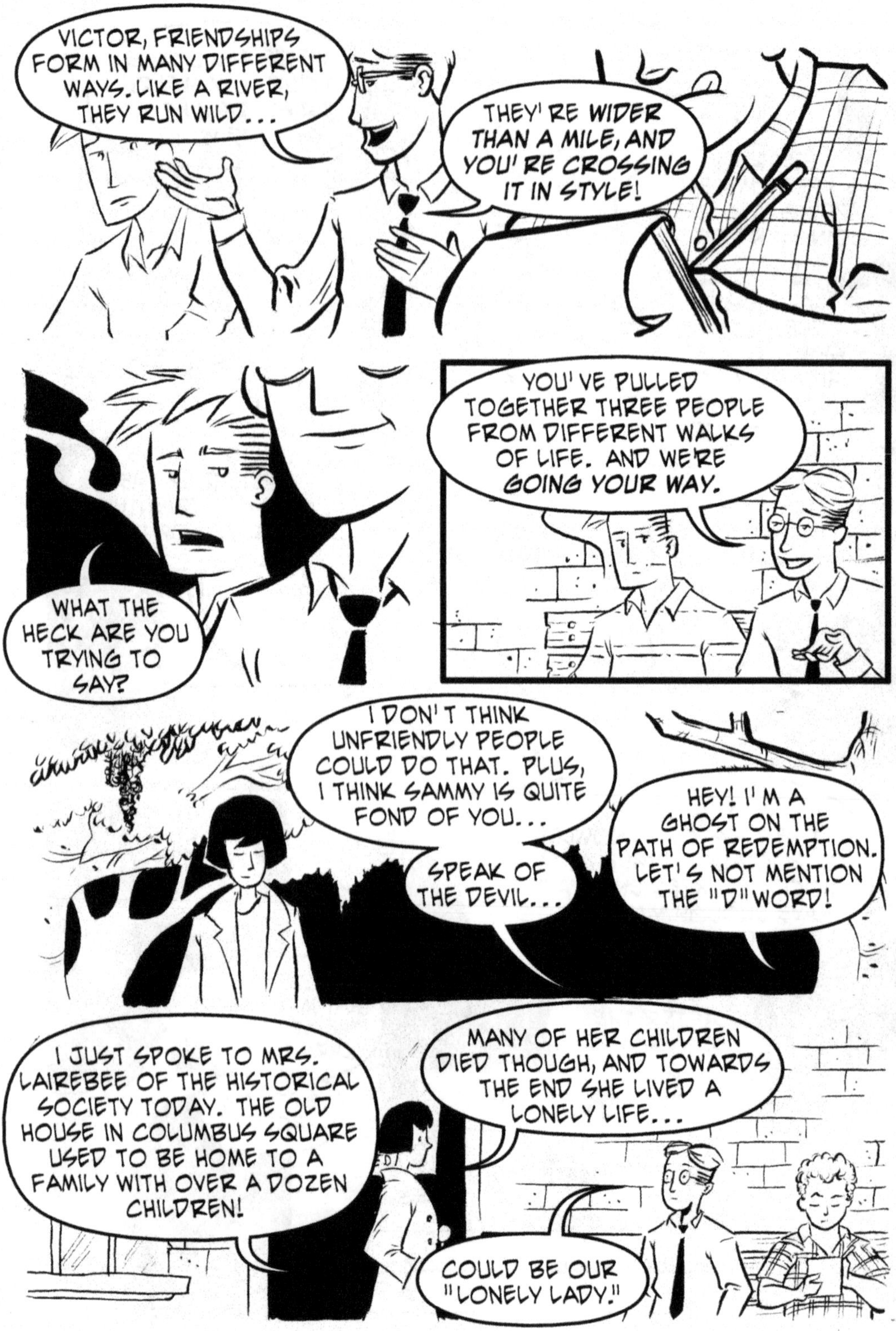
VICTOR, FRIENDSHIPS FORM IN MANY DIFFERENT WAYS. LIKE A RIVER, THEY RUN WILD...
THEY'RE WIDER THAN A MILE, AND YOU'RE CROSSING IT IN STYLE!
WHAT THE HECK ARE YOU TRYING TO SAY?
YOU'VE PULLED TOGETHER THREE PEOPLE FROM DIFFERENT WALKS OF LIFE. AND WE'RE GOING YOUR WAY.
I DON'T THINK UNFRIENDLY PEOPLE COULD DO THAT. PLUS, I THINK SAMMY IS QUITE FOND OF YOU...
SPEAK OF THE DEVIL...
HEY! I'M A GHOST ON THE PATH OF REDEMPTION. LET'S NOT MENTION THE "D" WORD!
I JUST SPOKE TO MRS. LAIREBEE OF THE HISTORICAL SOCIETY TODAY. THE OLD HOUSE IN COLUMBUS SQUARE USED TO BE HOME TO A FAMILY WITH OVER A DOZEN CHILDREN!
MANY OF HER CHILDREN DIED THOUGH, AND TOWARDS THE END SHE LIVED A LONELY LIFE...
COULD BE OUR "LONELY LADY."

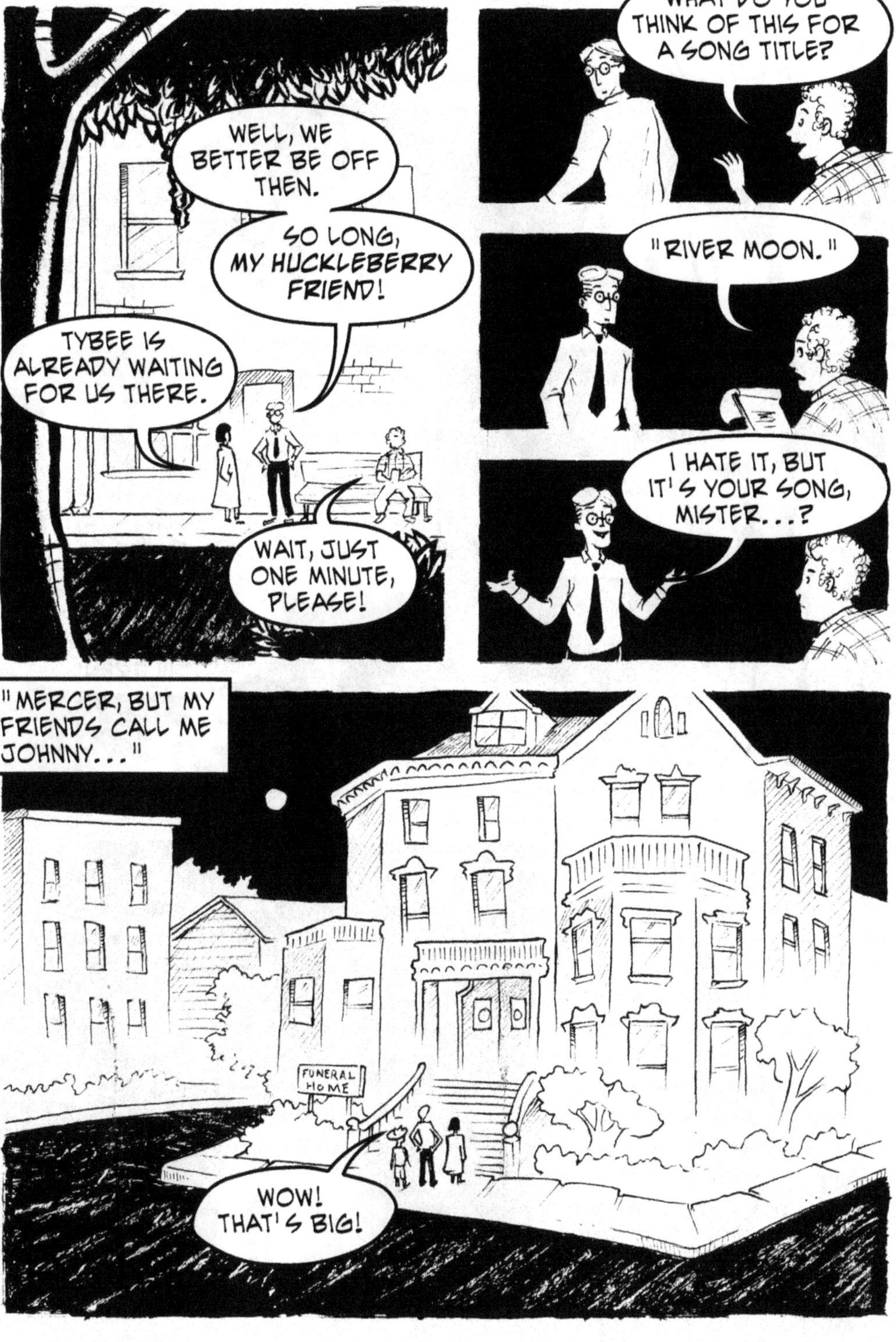
WELL, WE BETTER BE OFF THEN.
SO LONG, MY HUCKLEBERRY FRIEND!
TYBEE IS ALREADY WAITING FOR US THERE.
WAIT, JUST ONE MINUTE, PLEASE!
WHAT DO YOU THINK OF THIS FOR A SONG TITLE?
"RIVER MOON."
I HATE IT, BUT IT'S YOUR SONG, MISTER...?
"MERCER, BUT MY FRIENDS CALL ME JOHNNY..."
FUNERAL HOME
WOW! THAT'S BIG!

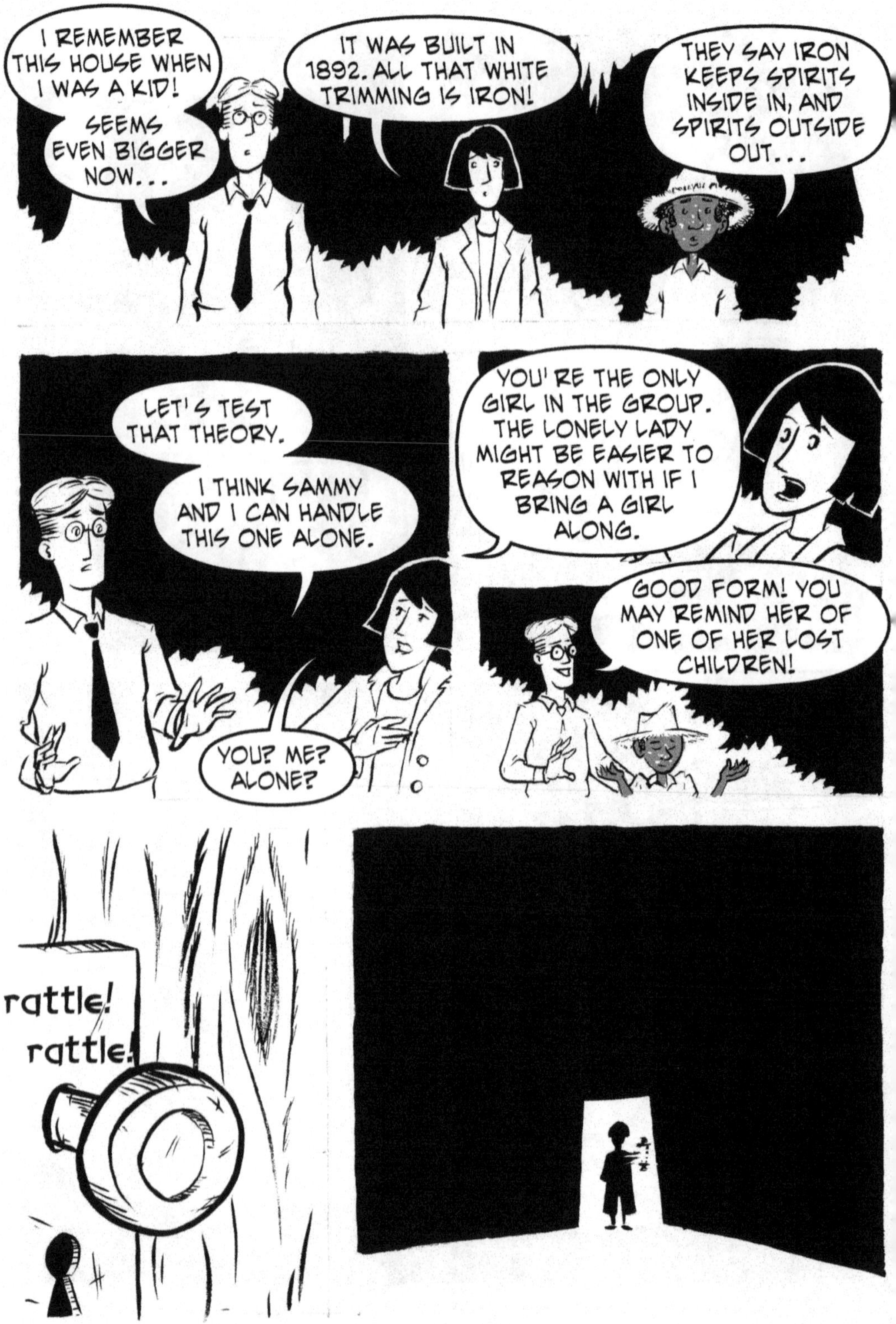
I REMEMBER THIS HOUSE WHEN I WAS A KID!
SEEMS EVEN BIGGER NOW...
IT WAS BUILT IN 1892. ALL THAT WHITE TRIMMING IS IRON!
THEY SAY IRON KEEPS SPIRITS INSIDE IN, AND SPIRITS OUTSIDE OUT...
LET'S TEST THAT THEORY.
I THINK SAMMY AND I CAN HANDLE THIS ONE ALONE.
YOU? ME? ALONE?
YOU'RE THE ONLY GIRL IN THE GROUP. THE LONELY LADY MIGHT BE EASIER TO REASON WITH IF I BRING A GIRL ALONG.
GOOD FORM! YOU MAY REMIND HER OF ONE OF HER LOST CHILDREN!
rattle!
rattle!

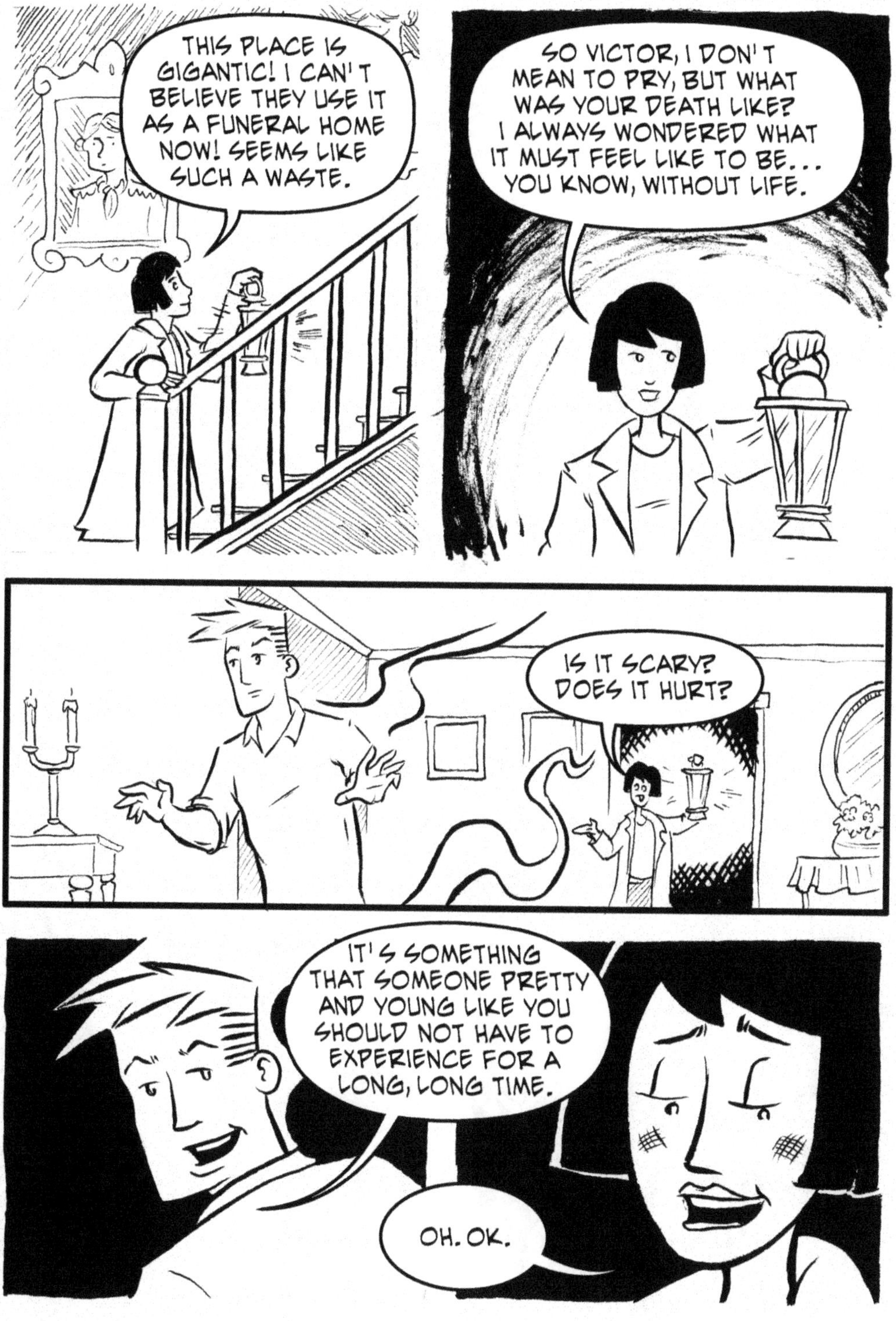
THIS PLACE IS GIGANTIC! I CAN'T BELIEVE THEY USE IT AS A FUNERAL HOME NOW! SEEMS LIKE SUCH A WASTE.
SO VICTOR, I DON'T MEAN TO PRY, BUT WHAT WAS YOUR DEATH LIKE? I ALWAYS WONDERED WHAT IT MUST FEEL LIKE TO BE... YOU KNOW, WITHOUT LIFE.
IS IT SCARY? DOES IT HURT?
IT'S SOMETHING THAT SOMEONE PRETTY AND YOUNG LIKE YOU SHOULD NOT HAVE TO EXPERIENCE FOR A LONG, LONG TIME.
OH. OK.

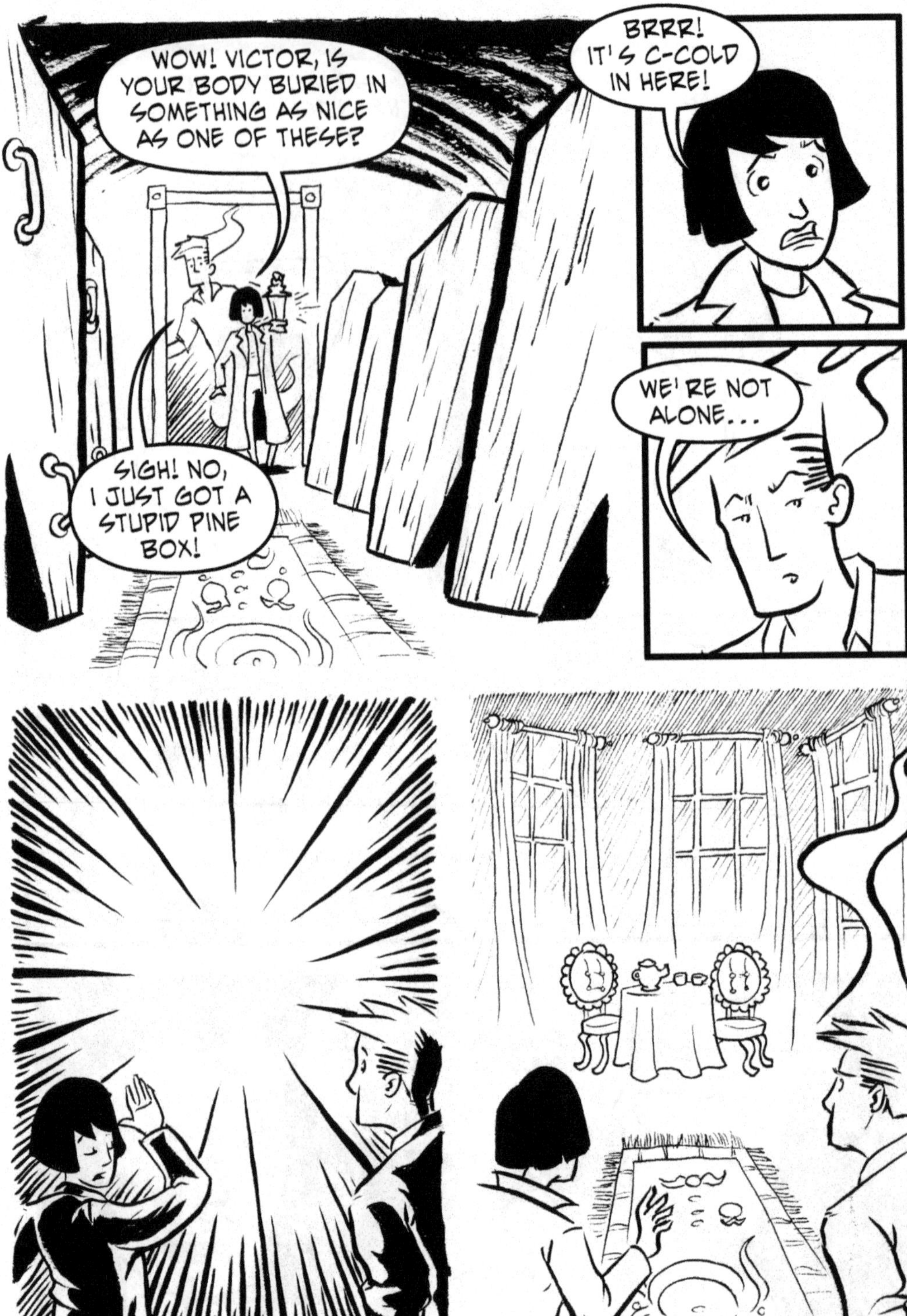
WOW! VICTOR, IS YOUR BODY BURIED IN SOMETHING AS NICE AS ONE OF THESE?
SIGH! NO, I JUST GOT A STUPID PINE BOX!
BRRR! IT'S C-COLD IN HERE!
WE'RE NOT ALONE...

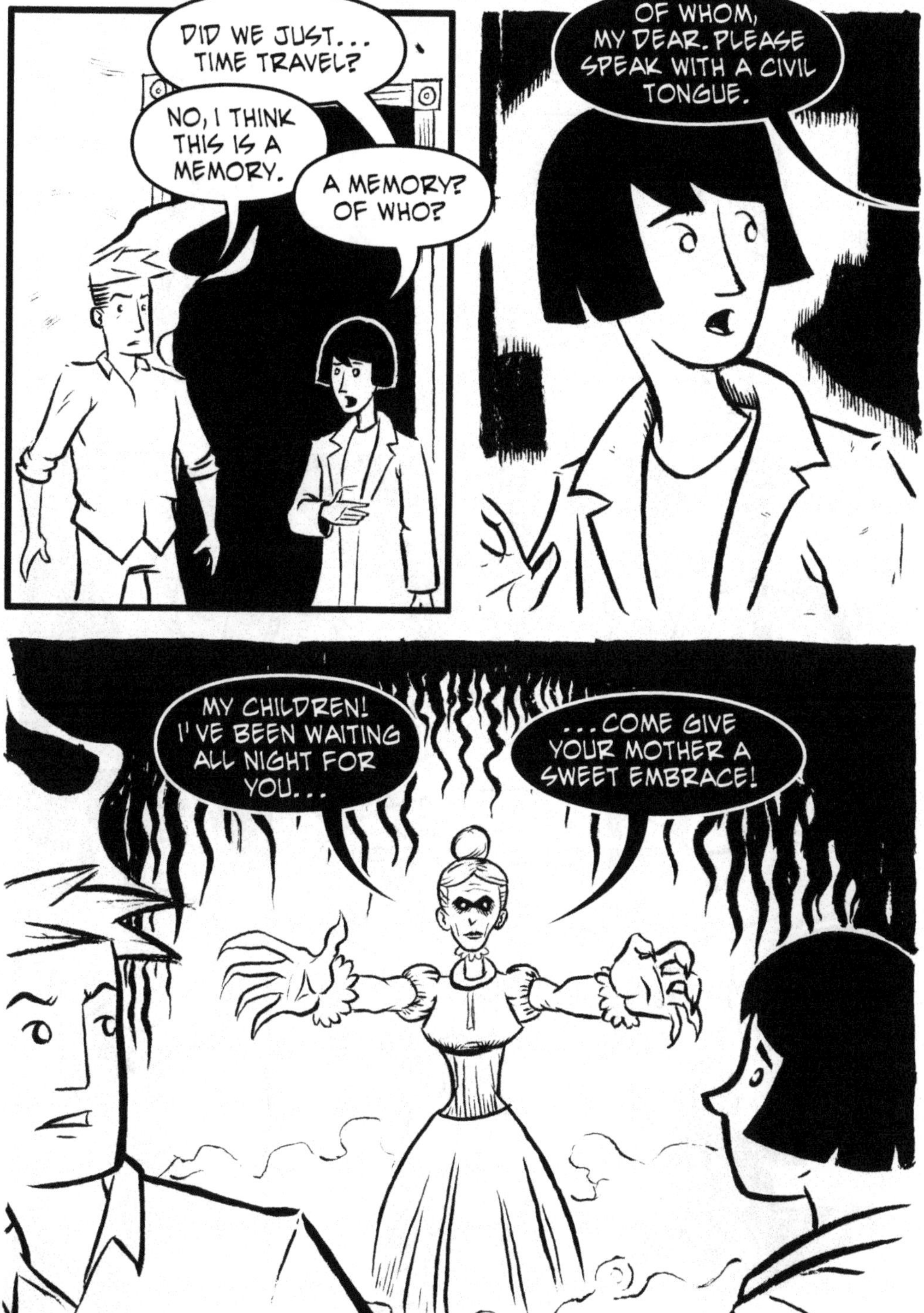
DID WE JUST... TIME TRAVEL?
NO, I THINK THIS IS A MEMORY.
A MEMORY? OF WHO?
OF WHOM, MY DEAR. PLEASE SPEAK WITH A CIVIL TONGUE.
MY CHILDREN! I'VE BEEN WAITING ALL NIGHT FOR YOU...
...COME GIVE YOUR MOTHER A SWEET EMBRACE!

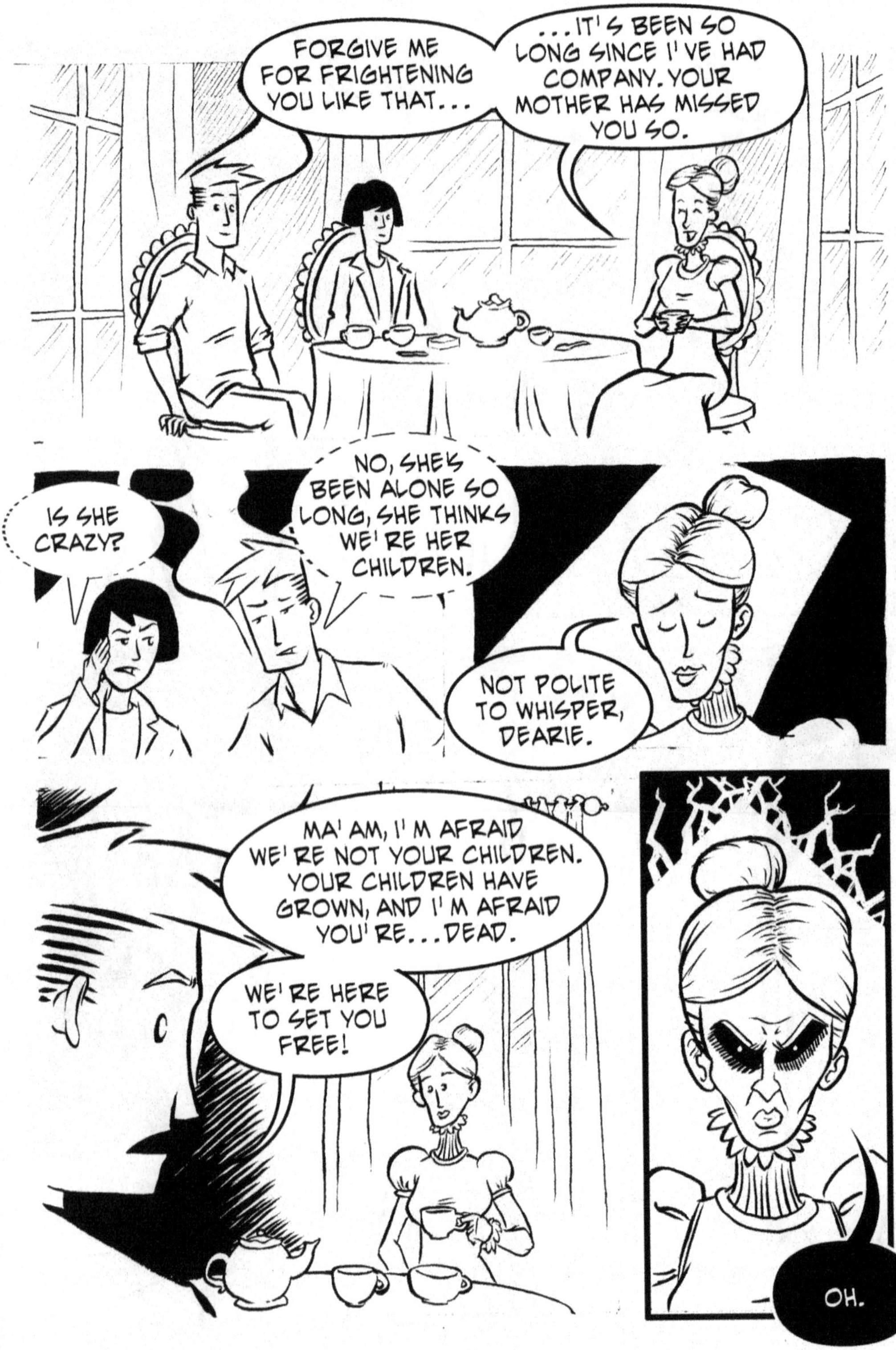
FORGIVE ME FOR FRIGHTENING YOU LIKE THAT...
...IT'S BEEN SO LONG SINCE I'VE HAD COMPANY. YOUR MOTHER HAS MISSED YOU SO.
IS SHE CRAZY?
NO, SHE'S BEEN ALONE SO LONG, SHE THINKS WE'RE HER CHILDREN.
NOT POLITE TO WHISPER, DEARIE.
MA'AM, I'M AFRAID WE'RE NOT YOUR CHILDREN. YOUR CHILDREN HAVE GROWN, AND I'M AFRAID YOU'RE...DEAD.
WE'RE HERE TO SET YOU FREE!
OH.

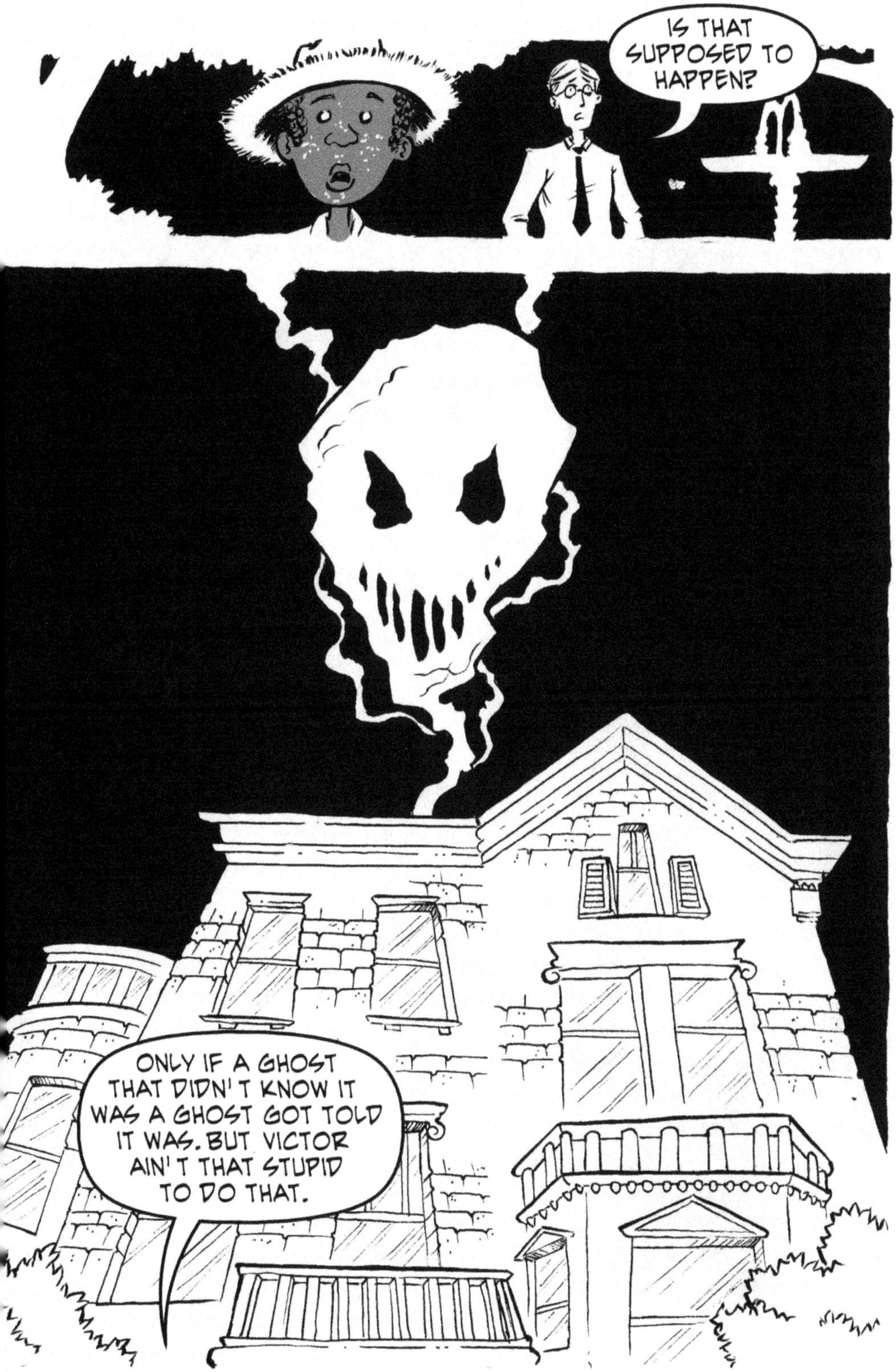
IS THAT SUPPOSED TO HAPPEN?
ONLY IF A GHOST THAT DIDN'T KNOW IT WAS A GHOST GOT TOLD IT WAS. BUT VICTOR AIN'T THAT STUPID TO DO THAT.

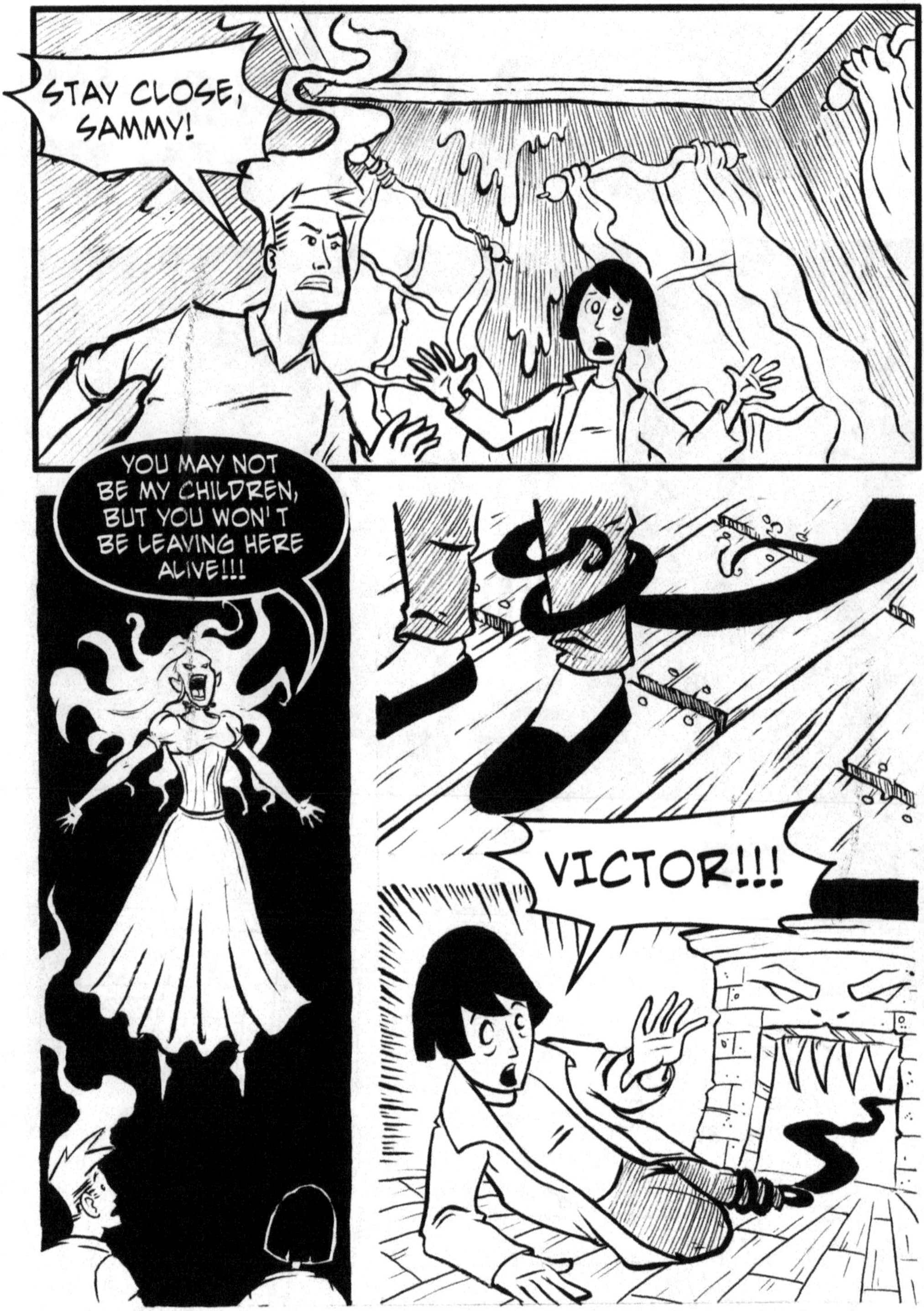
STAY CLOSE, SAMMY!
YOU MAY NOT BE MY CHILDREN, BUT YOU WON'T BE LEAVING HERE ALIVE!!!
VICTOR!!!

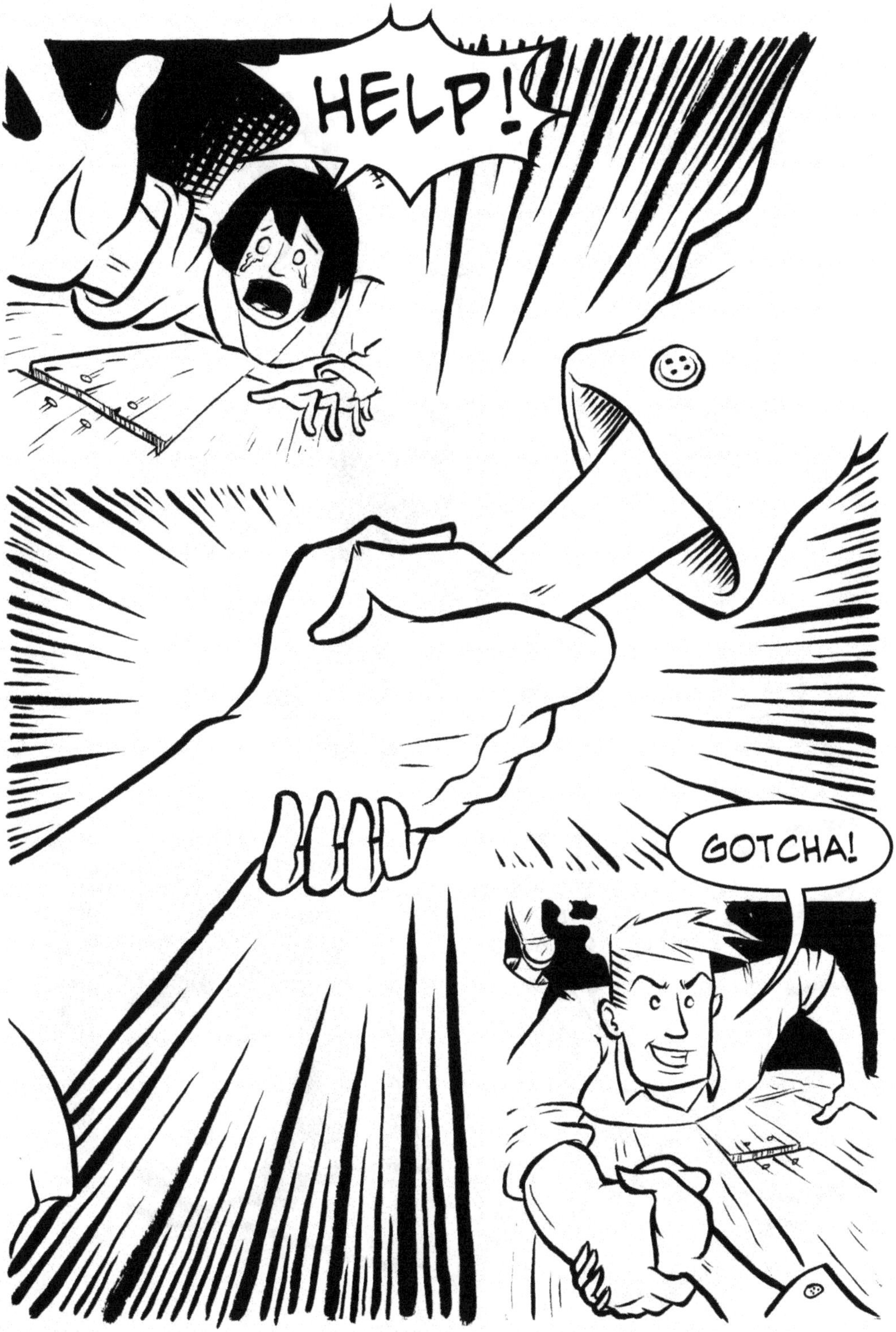
HELP!
GOTCHA!

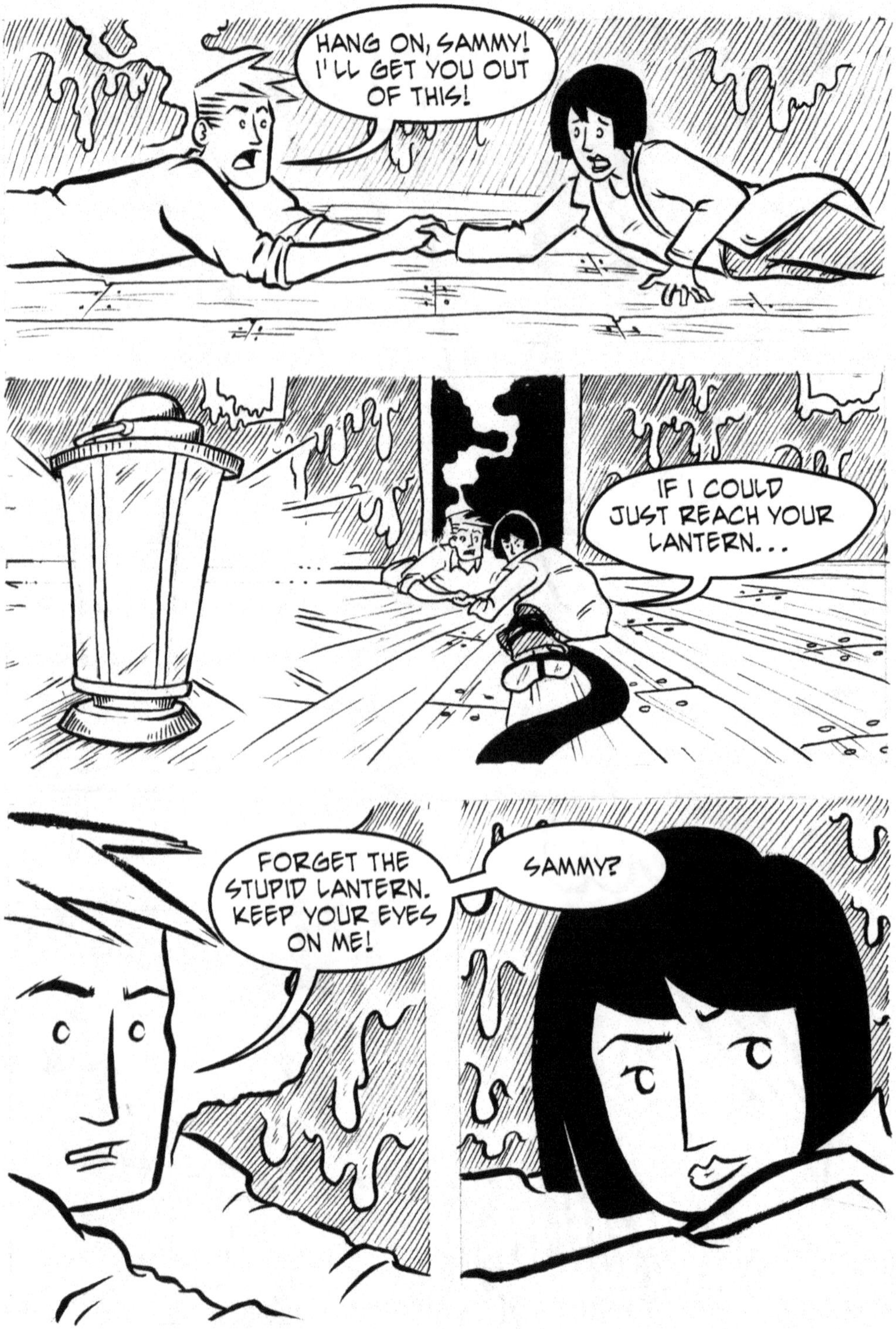
HANG ON, SAMMY! I'LL GET YOU OUT OF THIS!
IF I COULD JUST REACH YOUR LANTERN...
FORGET THE STUPID LANTERN. KEEP YOUR EYES ON ME!
SAMMY?

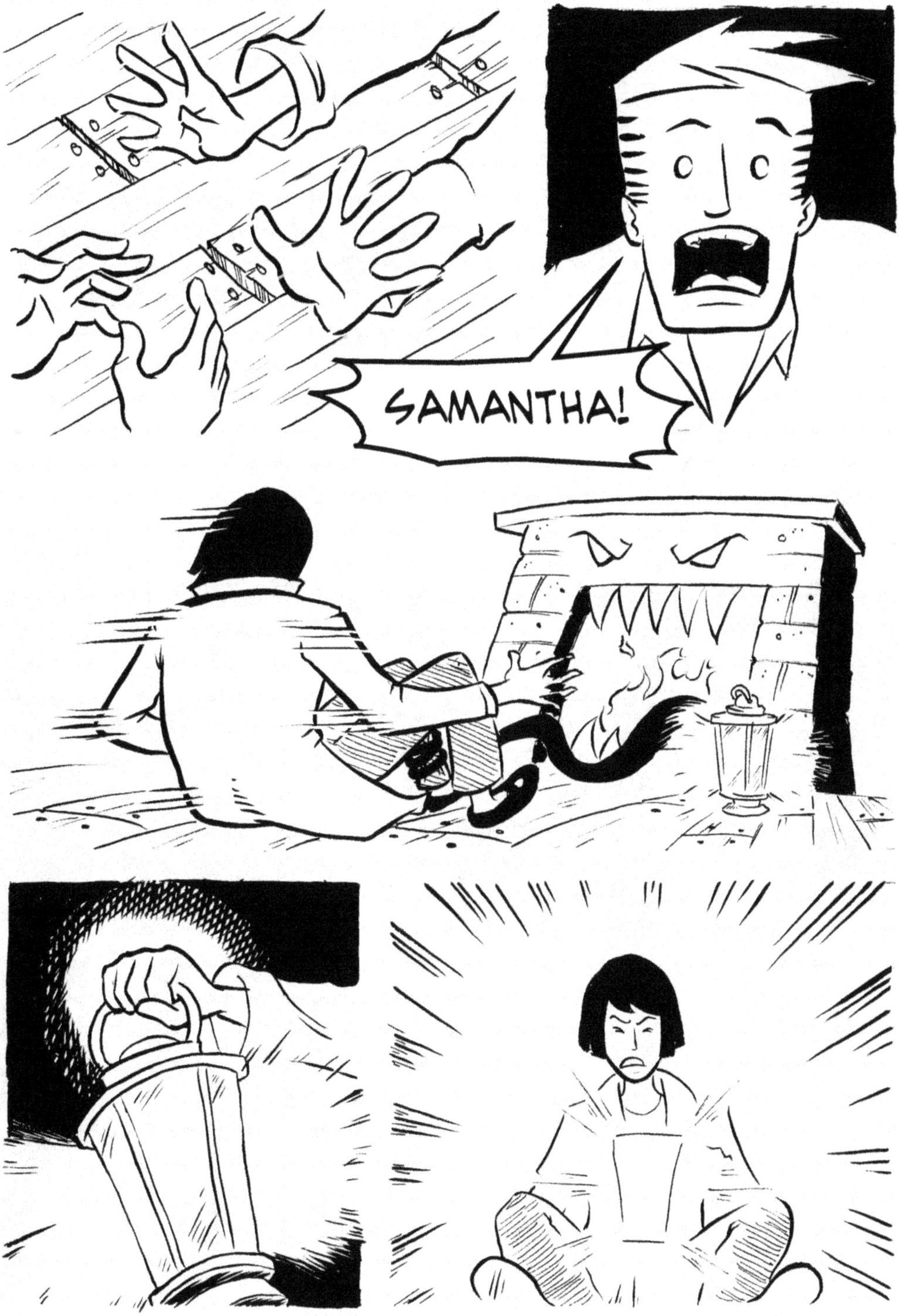
SAMANTHA!

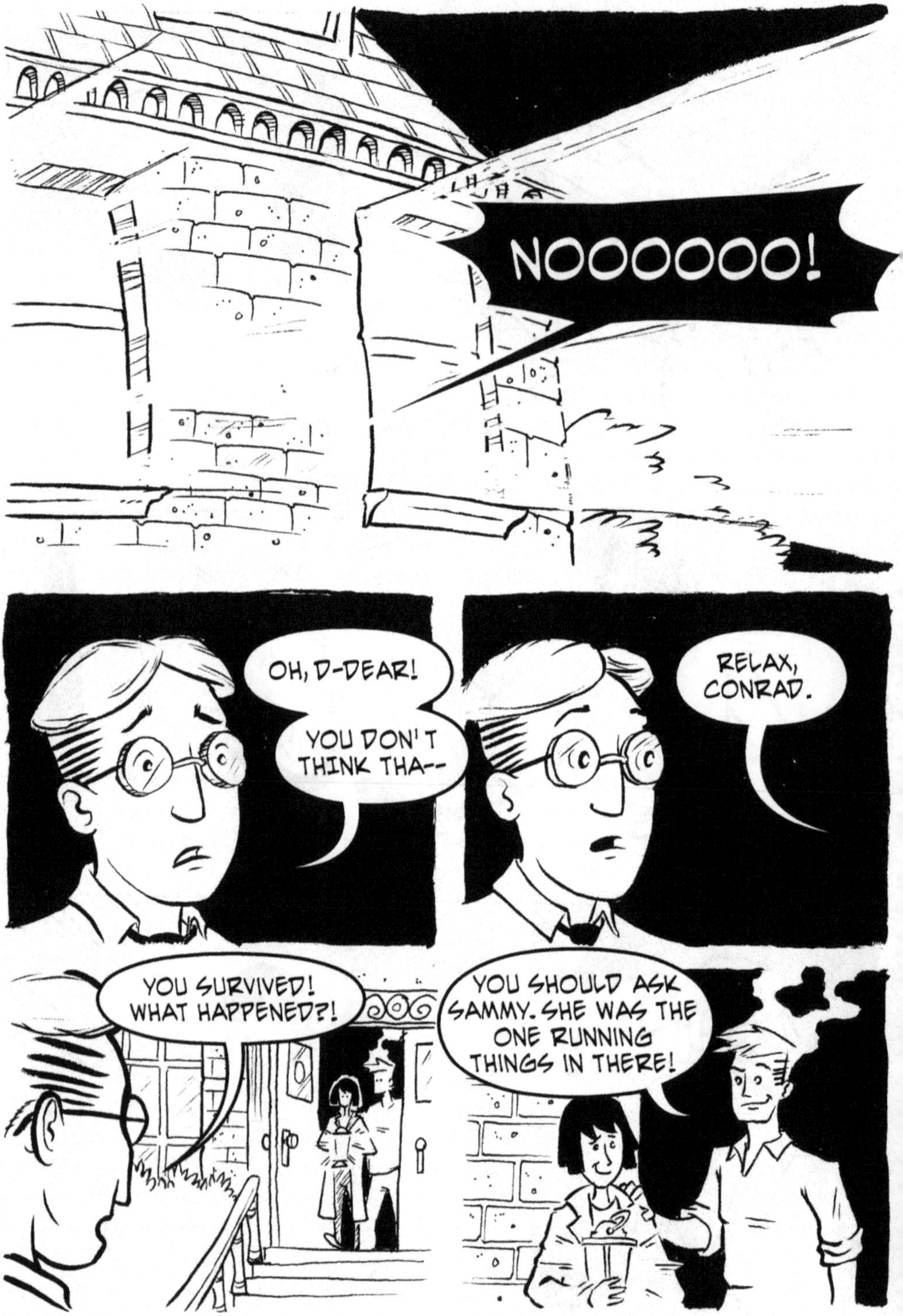
NOOOOOO!
OH, D-DEAR!
YOU DON'T THINK THA--
RELAX, CONRAD.
YOU SURVIVED! WHAT HAPPENED?!
YOU SHOULD ASK SAMMY. SHE WAS THE ONE RUNNING THINGS IN THERE!

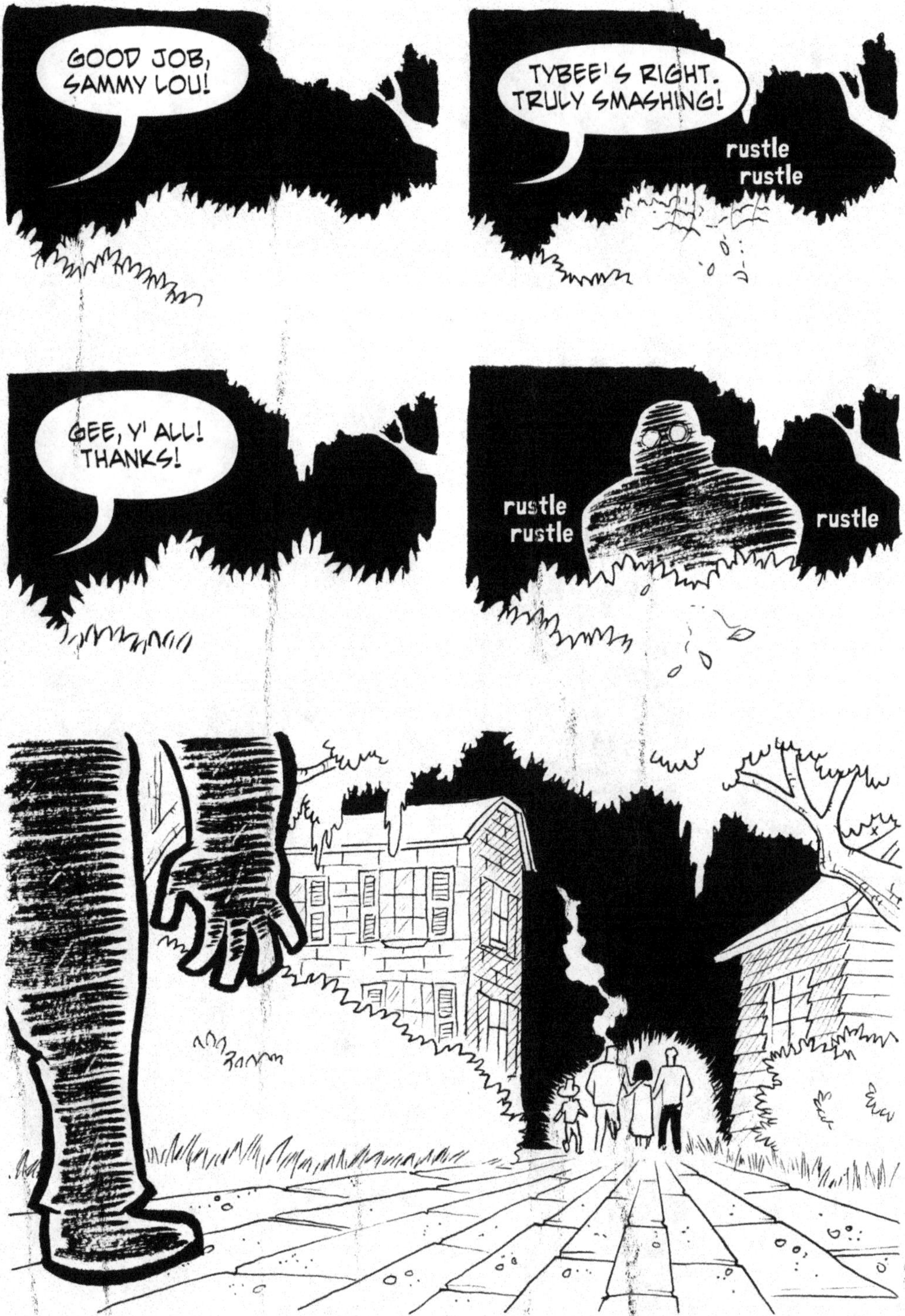
GOOD JOB, SAMMY LOU!
TYBEE'S RIGHT. TRULY SMASHING!
rustle rustle
GEE, Y'ALL! THANKS!
rustle rustle
rustle

CHAPTER

9

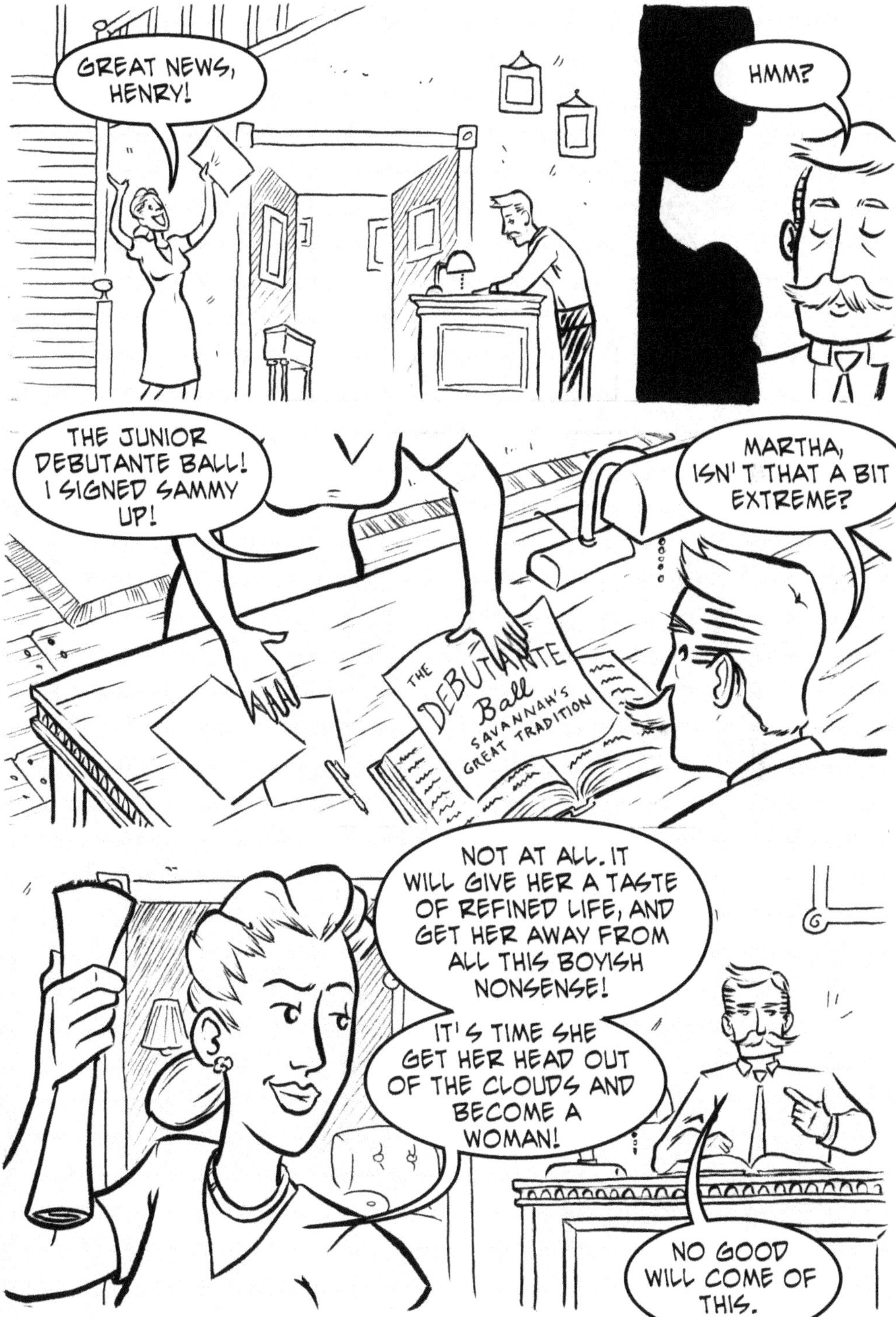
GREAT NEWS, HENRY!
HMM?
THE JUNIOR DEBUTANTE BALL! I SIGNED SAMMY UP!
MARTHA, ISN'T THAT A BIT EXTREME?
THE DEBUTANTE Ball SAVANNAH'S GREAT TRADITION
NOT AT ALL. IT WILL GIVE HER A TASTE OF REFINED LIFE, AND GET HER AWAY FROM ALL THIS BOYISH NONSENSE!
IT'S TIME SHE GET HER HEAD OUT OF THE CLOUDS AND BECOME A WOMAN!
NO GOOD WILL COME OF THIS.

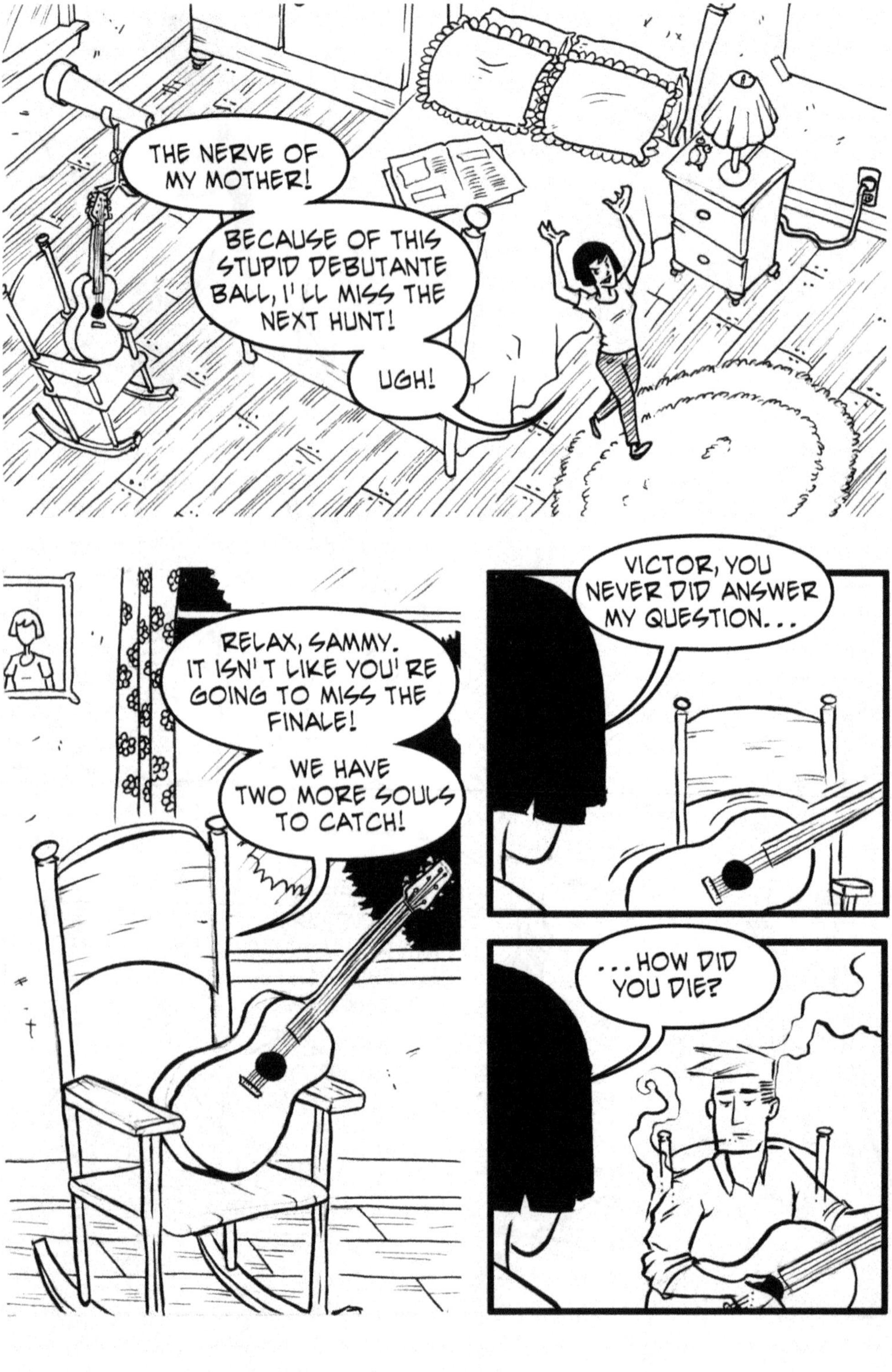
THE NERVE OF MY MOTHER!
BECAUSE OF THIS STUPID DEBUTANTE BALL, I'LL MISS THE NEXT HUNT!
UGH!
RELAX, SAMMY. IT ISN'T LIKE YOU'RE GOING TO MISS THE FINALE!
WE HAVE TWO MORE SOULS TO CATCH!
VICTOR, YOU NEVER DID ANSWER MY QUESTION...
...HOW DID YOU DIE?

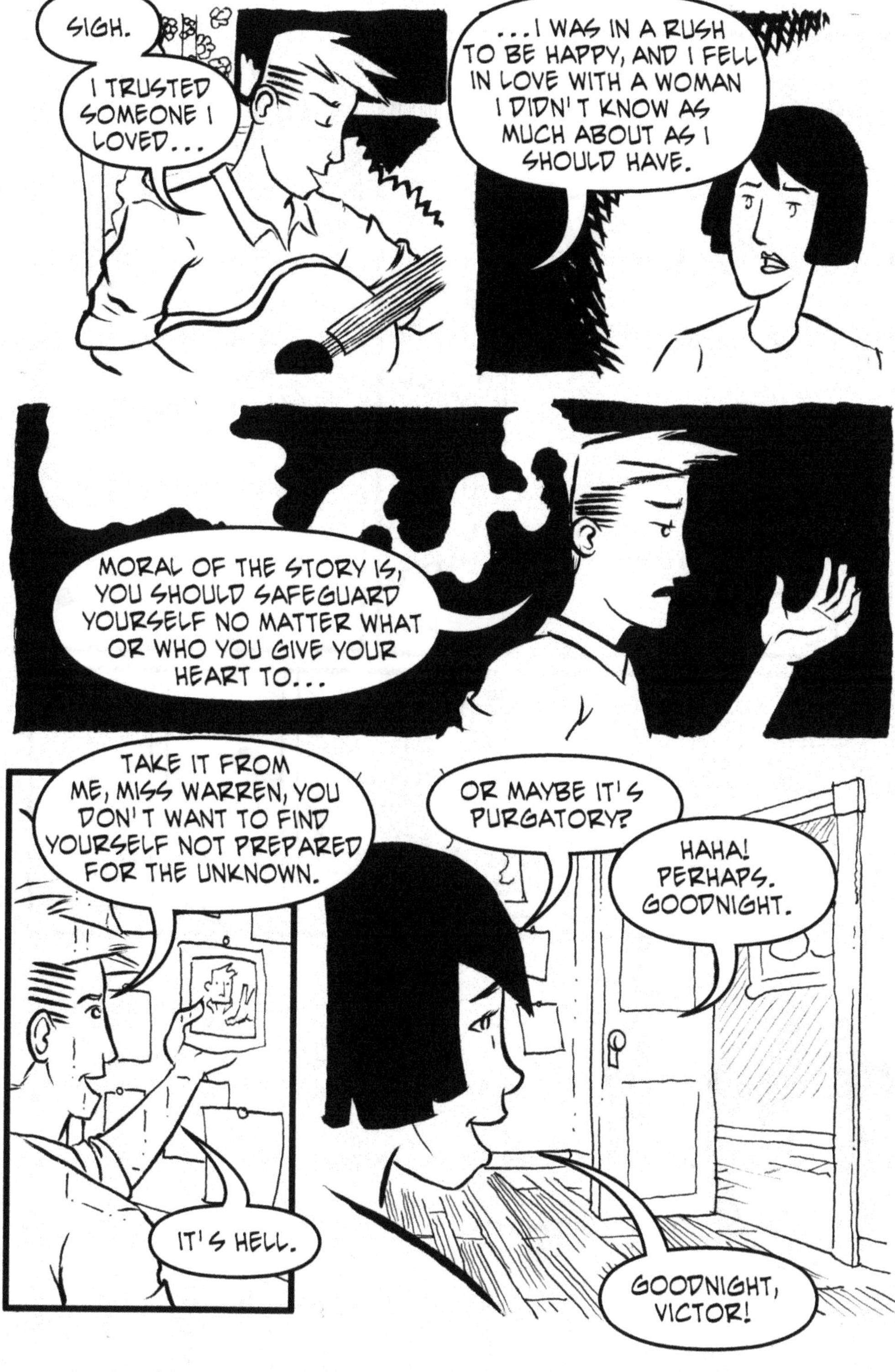
SIGH.
I TRUSTED SOMEONE I LOVED...
...I WAS IN A RUSH TO BE HAPPY, AND I FELL IN LOVE WITH A WOMAN I DIDN'T KNOW AS MUCH ABOUT AS I SHOULD HAVE.
MORAL OF THE STORY IS, YOU SHOULD SAFEGUARD YOURSELF NO MATTER WHAT OR WHO YOU GIVE YOUR HEART TO...
TAKE IT FROM ME, MISS WARREN, YOU DON'T WANT TO FIND YOURSELF NOT PREPARED FOR THE UNKNOWN.
IT'S HELL.
OR MAYBE IT'S PURGATORY?
HAHA! PERHAPS. GOODNIGHT.
GOODNIGHT, VICTOR!

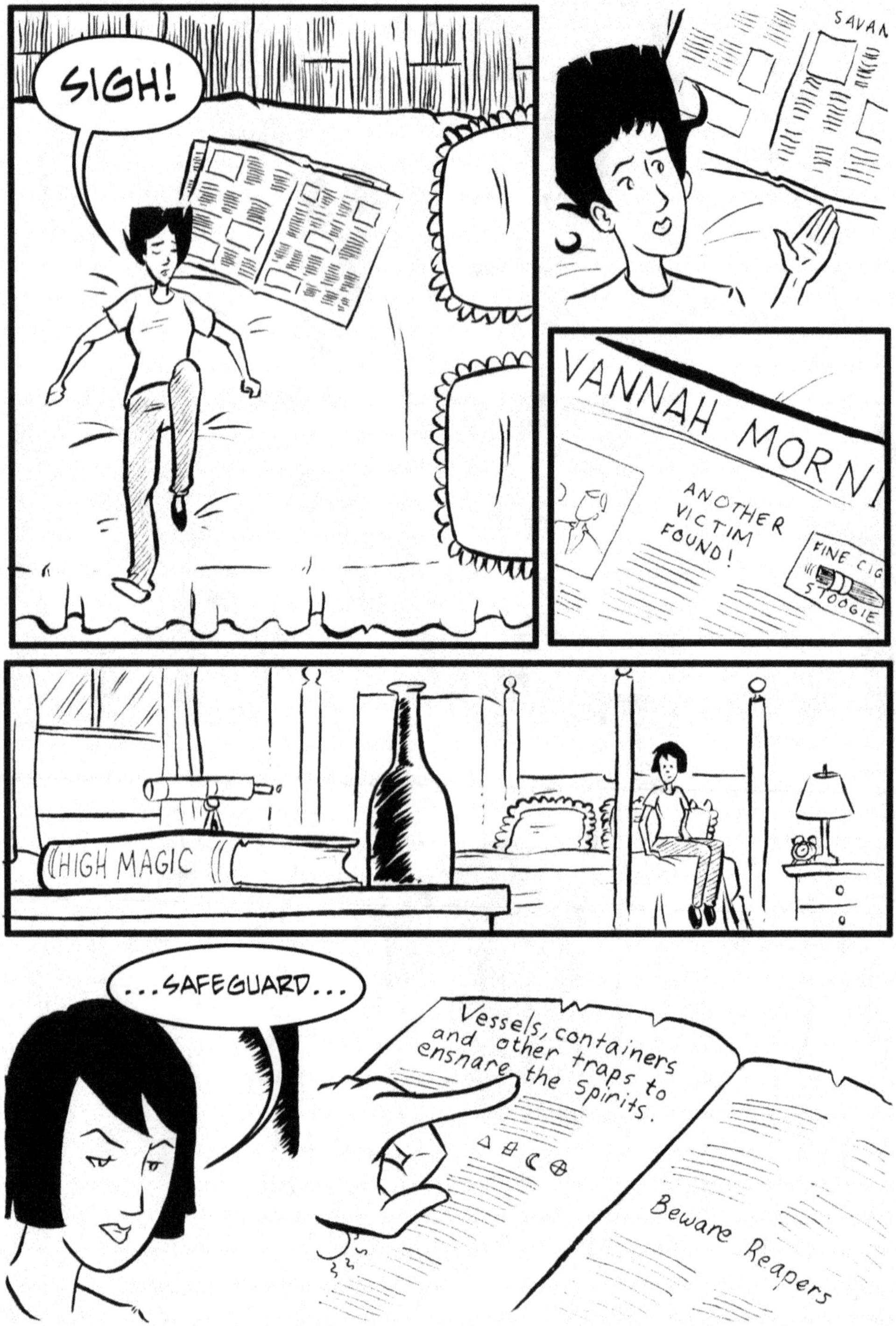
SIGH!
SAVAN
VANNAH MORN
ANOTHER VICTIM FOUND!
FINE CIG
STOOGIE
HIGH MAGIC
...SAFEGUARD...
Vessels, containers and other traps to ensnare the Spirits.
Beware Reapers

CHAPTER

10

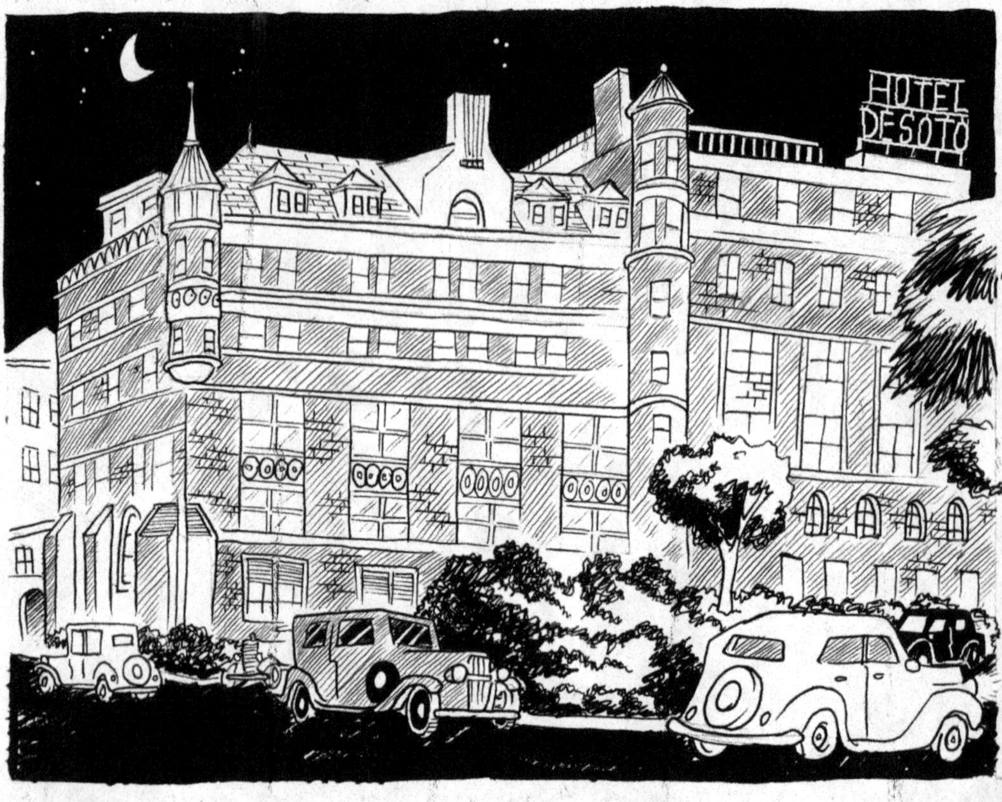
HOTEL
DESOTO

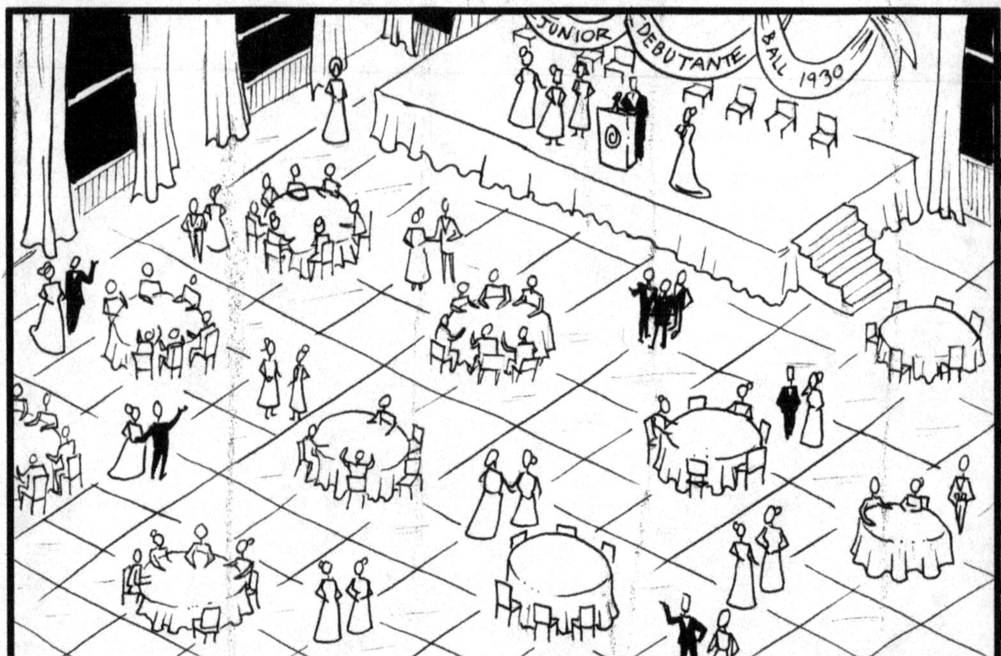
JUNIOR
DEBUTANTE
BALL 1930

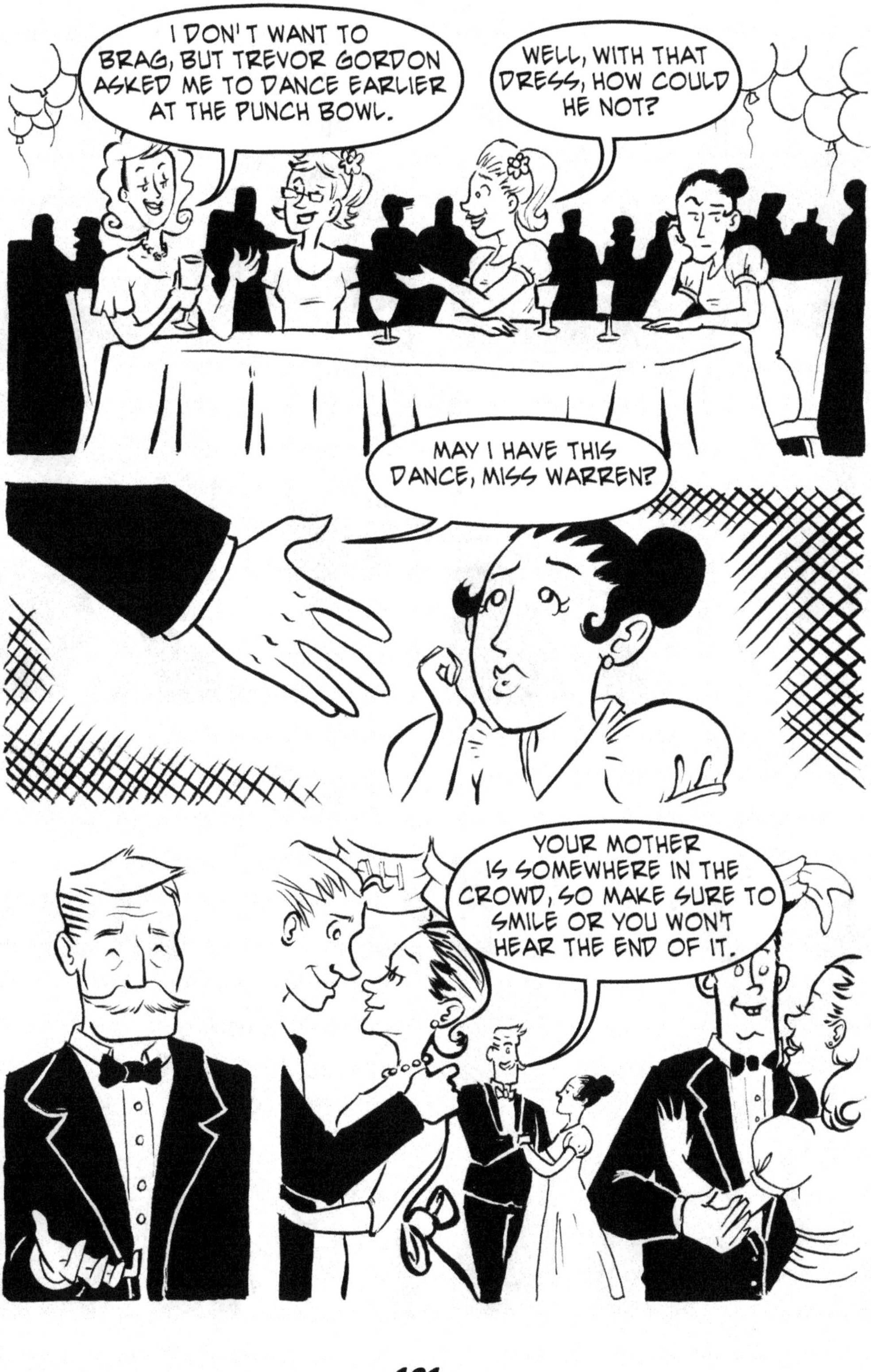
I DON'T WANT TO BRAG, BUT TREVOR GORDON ASKED ME TO DANCE EARLIER AT THE PUNCH BOWL.
WELL, WITH THAT DRESS, HOW COULD HE NOT?
MAY I HAVE THIS DANCE, MISS WARREN?
YOUR MOTHER IS SOMEWHERE IN THE CROWD, SO MAKE SURE TO SMILE OR YOU WON'T HEAR THE END OF IT.

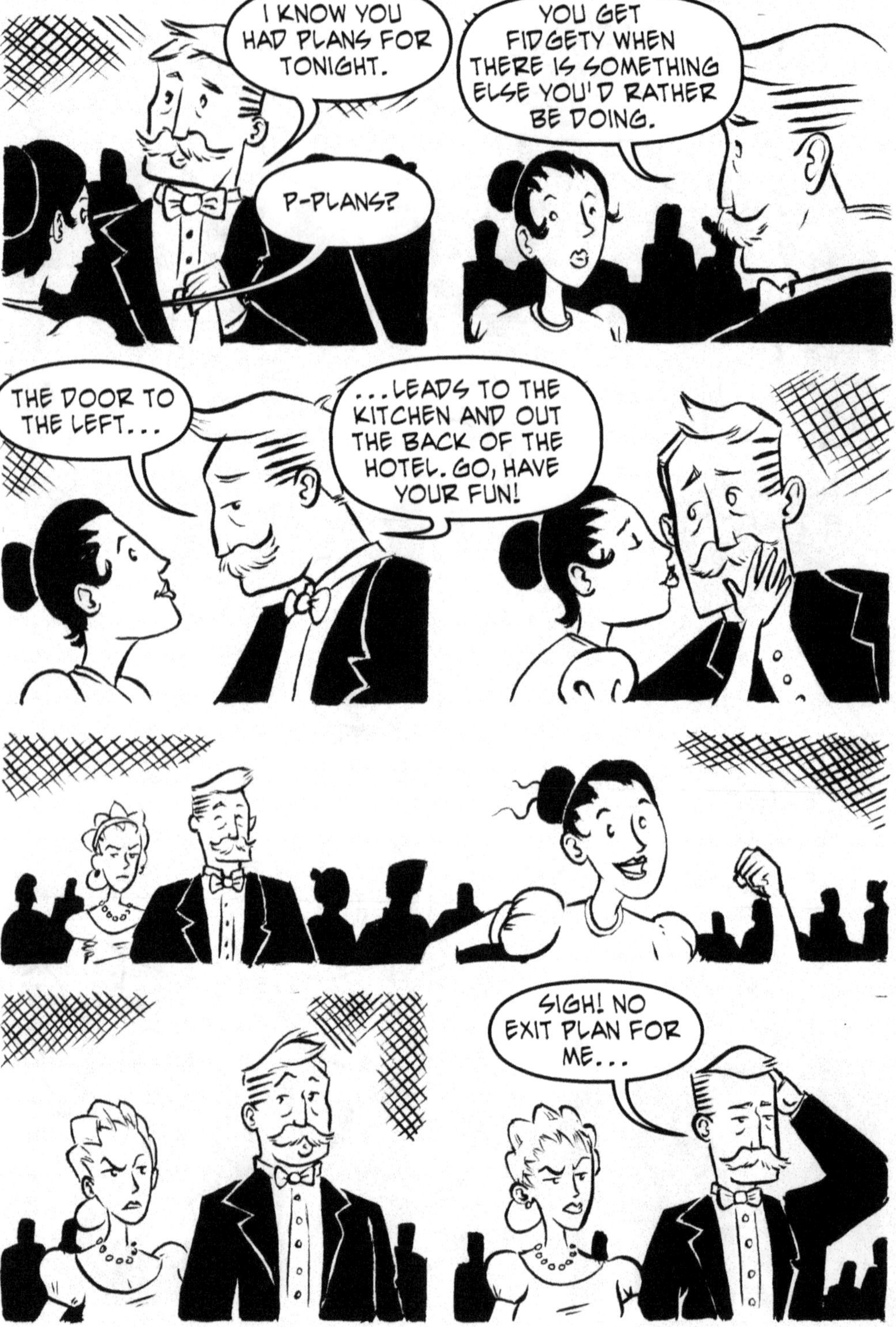

I KNOW YOU HAD PLANS FOR TONIGHT.
P-PLANS?
YOU GET FIDGETY WHEN THERE IS SOMETHING ELSE YOU'D RATHER BE DOING.
THE DOOR TO THE LEFT...
...LEADS TO THE KITCHEN AND OUT THE BACK OF THE HOTEL. GO, HAVE YOUR FUN!
SIGH! NO EXIT PLAN FOR ME...

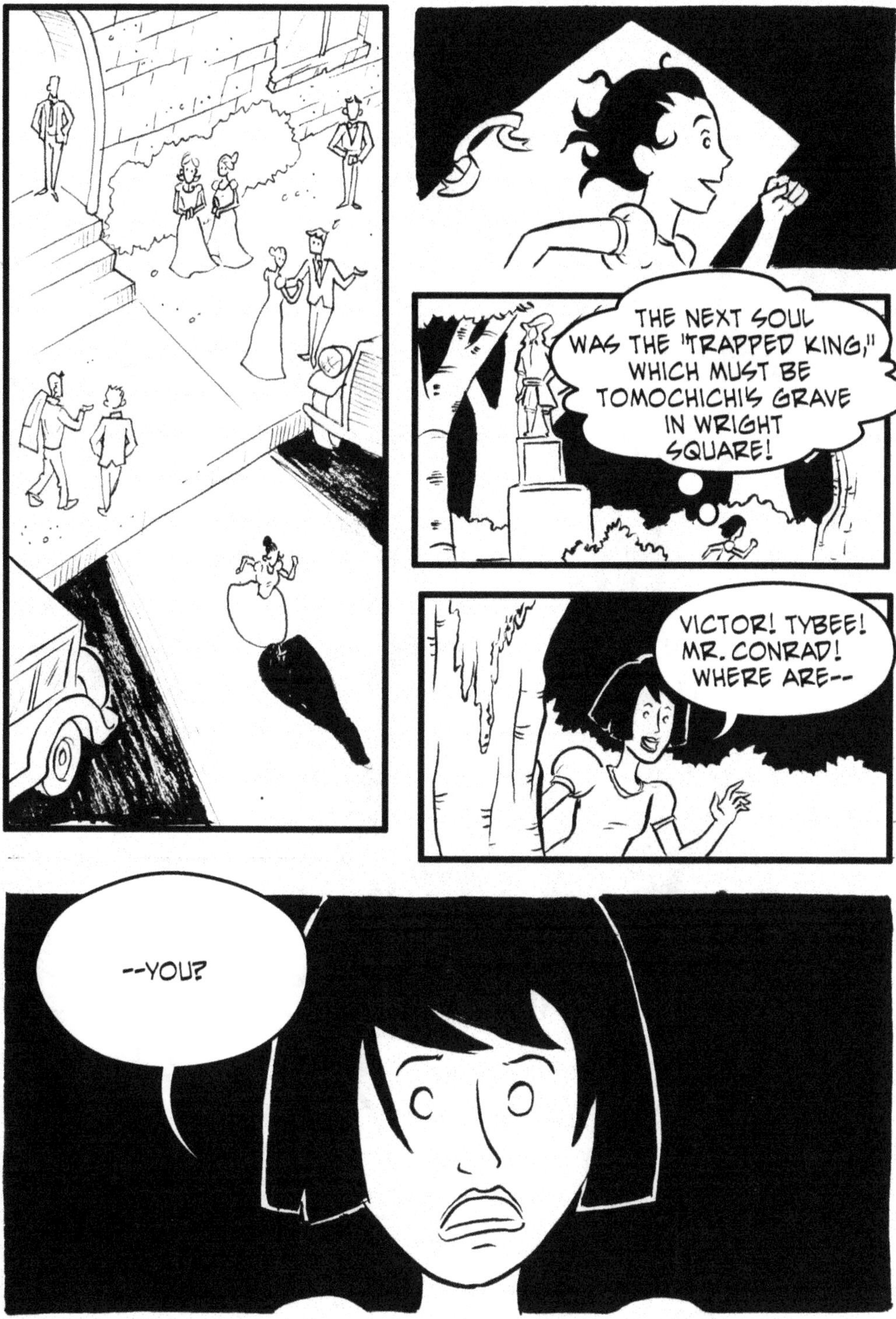
THE NEXT SOUL WAS THE "TRAPPED KING," WHICH MUST BE TOMOCHICHI'S GRAVE IN WRIGHT SQUARE!
VICTOR! TYBEE! MR. CONRAD! WHERE ARE--
--YOU?

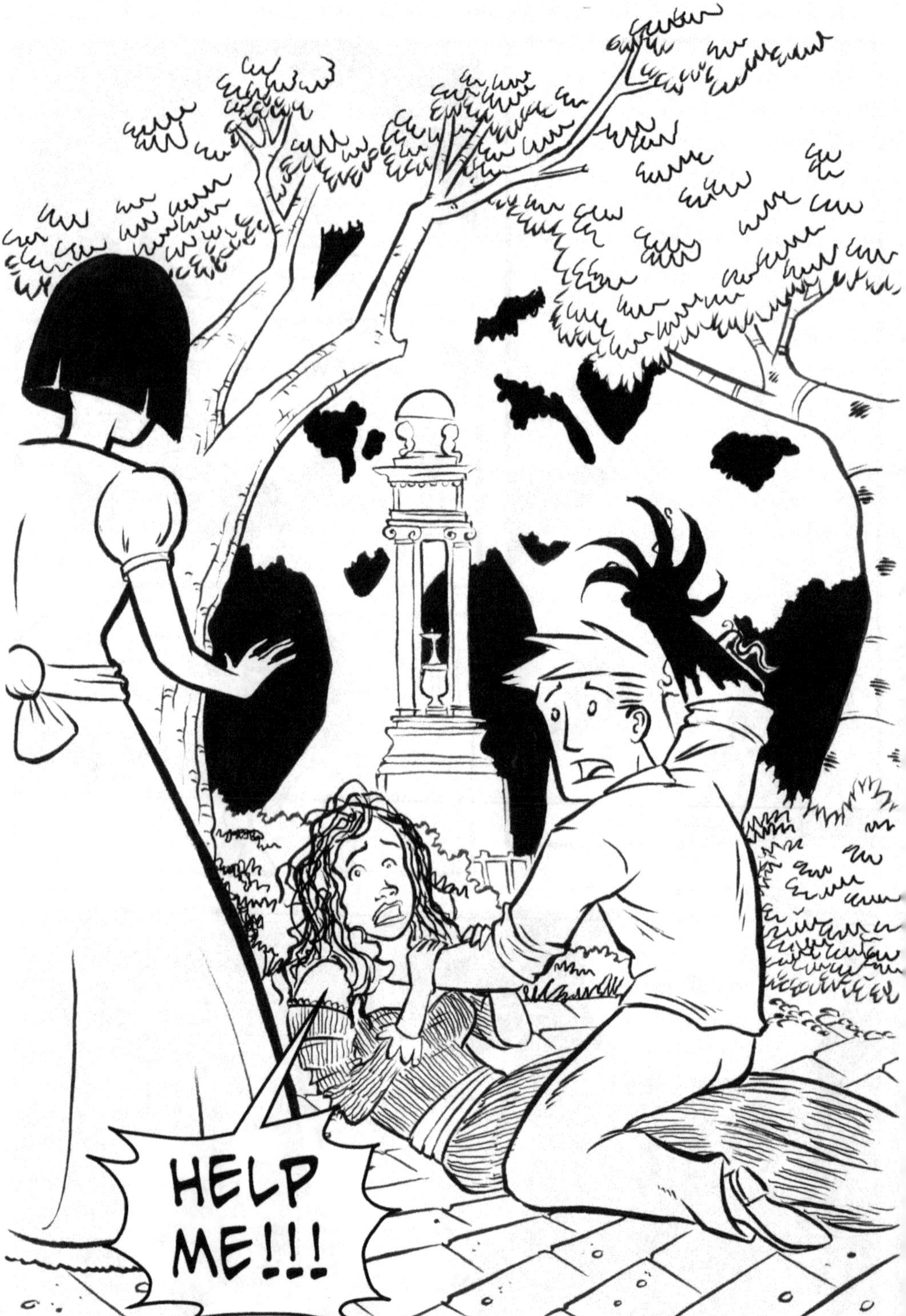
HELP ME!!!

CHAPTER

11

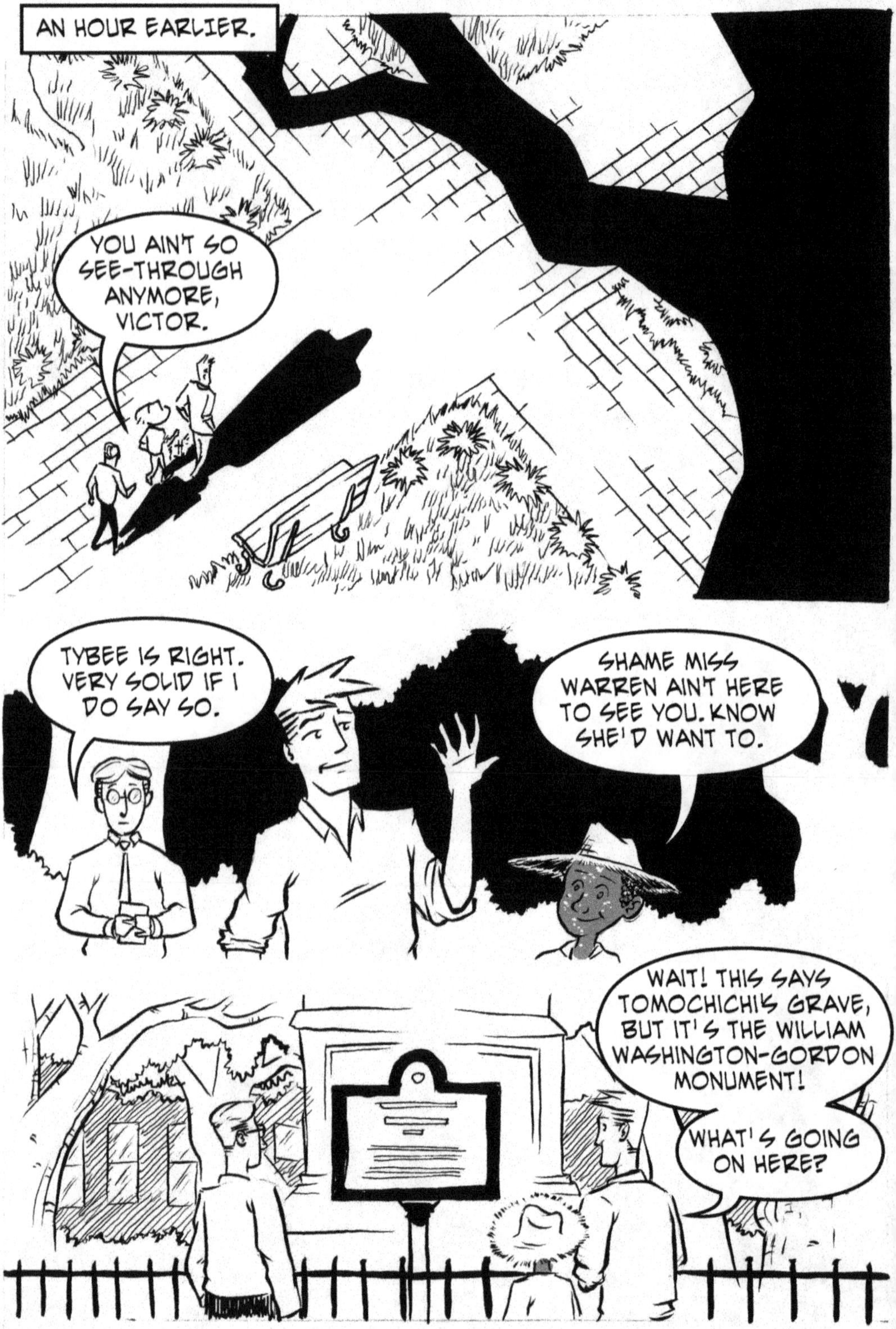
AN HOUR EARLIER.
YOU AIN'T SO SEE-THROUGH ANYMORE, VICTOR.
TYBEE IS RIGHT. VERY SOLID IF I DO SAY SO.
SHAME MISS WARREN AIN'T HERE TO SEE YOU. KNOW SHE'D WANT TO.
WAIT! THIS SAYS TOMOCHICHI'S GRAVE, BUT IT'S THE WILLIAM WASHINGTON-GORDON MONUMENT!
WHAT'S GOING ON HERE?

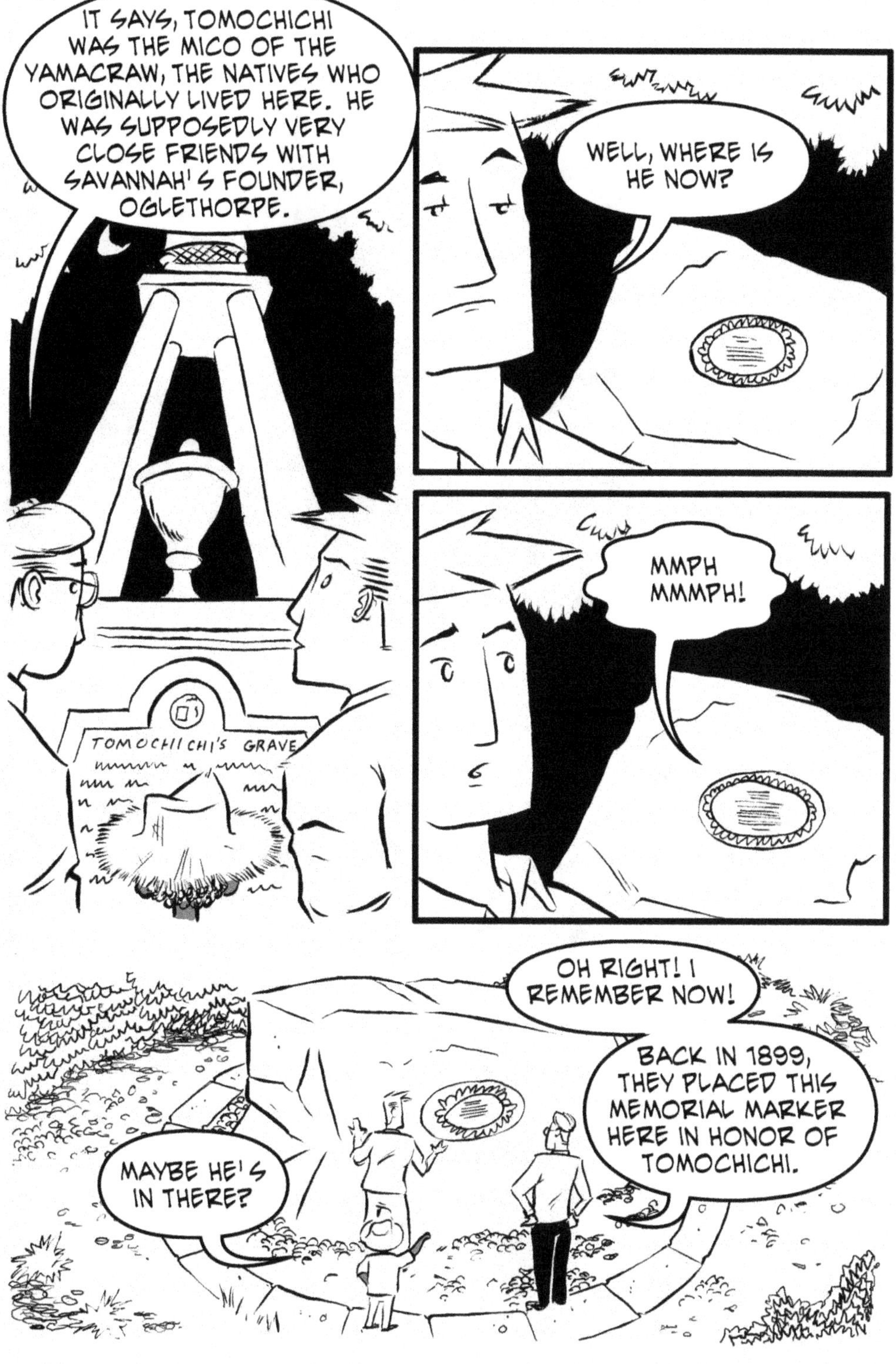
IT SAYS, TOMOCHICHI WAS THE MICO OF THE YAMACRAW, THE NATIVES WHO ORIGINALLY LIVED HERE. HE WAS SUPPOSEDLY VERY CLOSE FRIENDS WITH SAVANNAH'S FOUNDER, OGLETHORPE.
TOMOCHICHI'S GRAVE
WELL, WHERE IS HE NOW?
MMPH MMMPH!
OH RIGHT! I REMEMBER NOW!
BACK IN 1899, THEY PLACED THIS MEMORIAL MARKER HERE IN HONOR OF TOMOCHICHI.
MAYBE HE'S IN THERE?

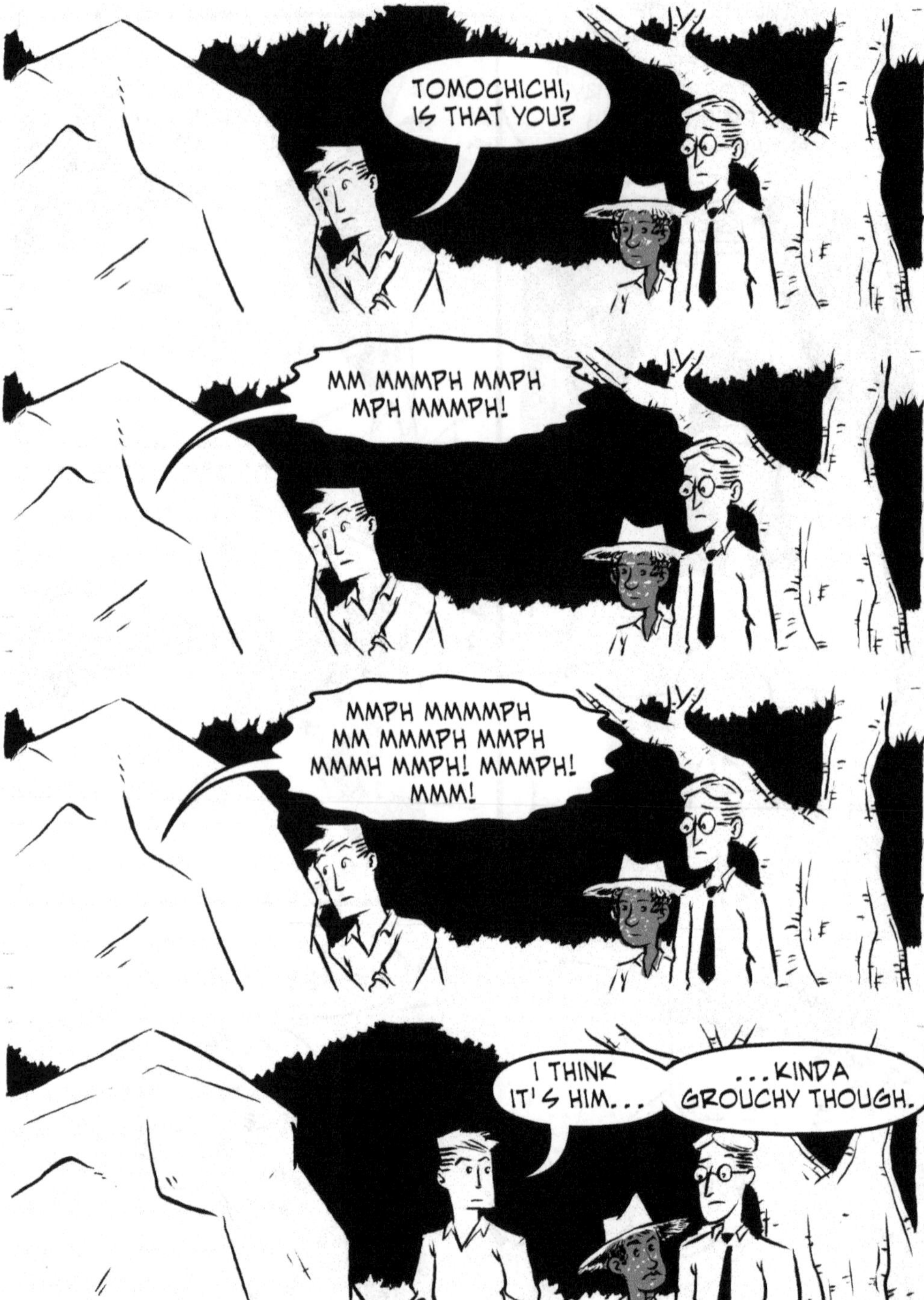
TOMOCHICHI, IS THAT YOU?
MM MMMPH MMPH MPH MMMPH!
MMPH MMMMPH MM MMMPH MMPH MMMH MMPH! MMMPH! MMM!
I THINK IT'S HIM...
...KINDA GROUCHY THOUGH.

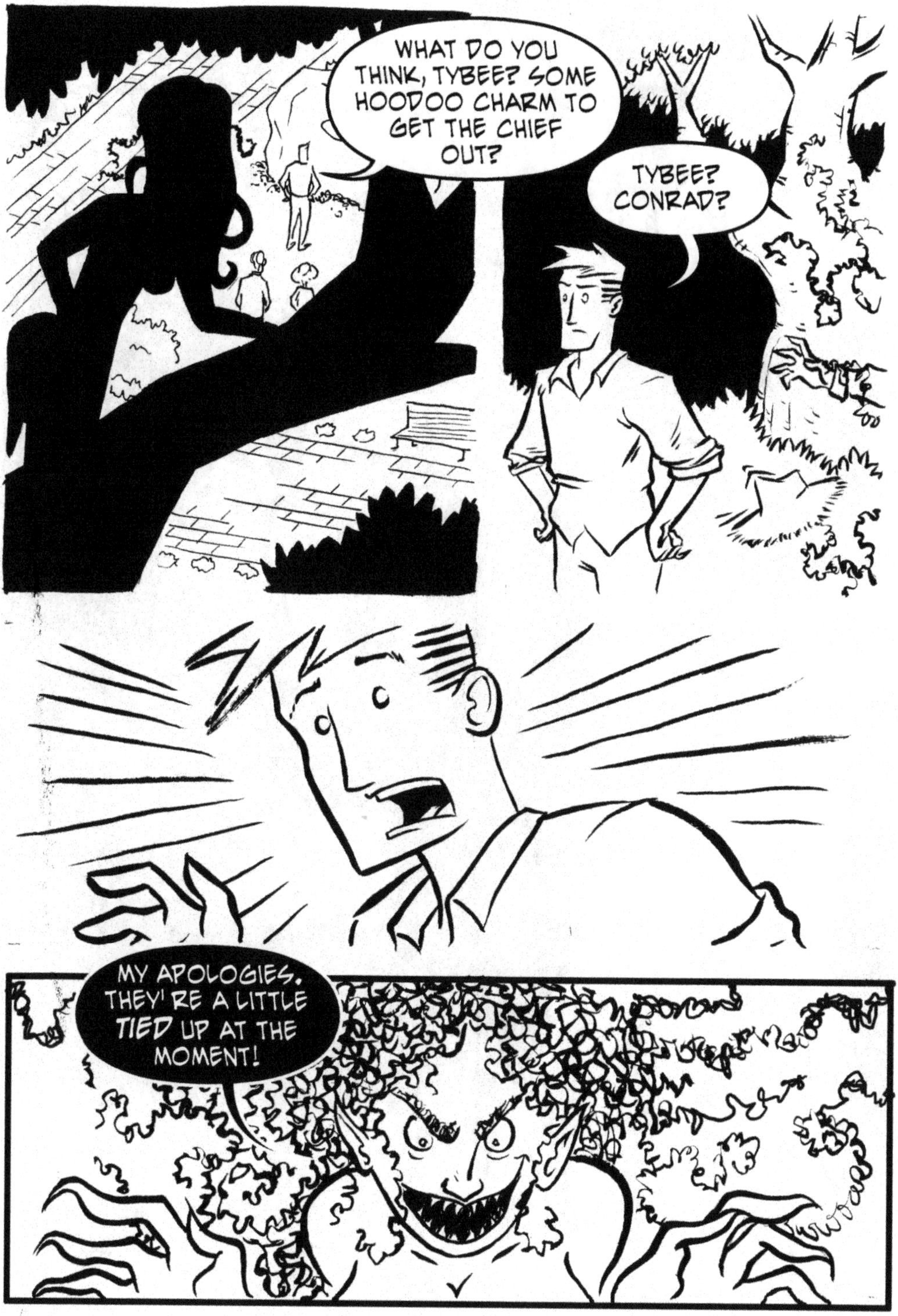
WHAT DO YOU THINK, TYBEE? SOME HOODOO CHARM TO GET THE CHIEF OUT?
TYBEE? CONRAD?
MY APOLOGIES. THEY'RE A LITTLE TIED UP AT THE MOMENT!

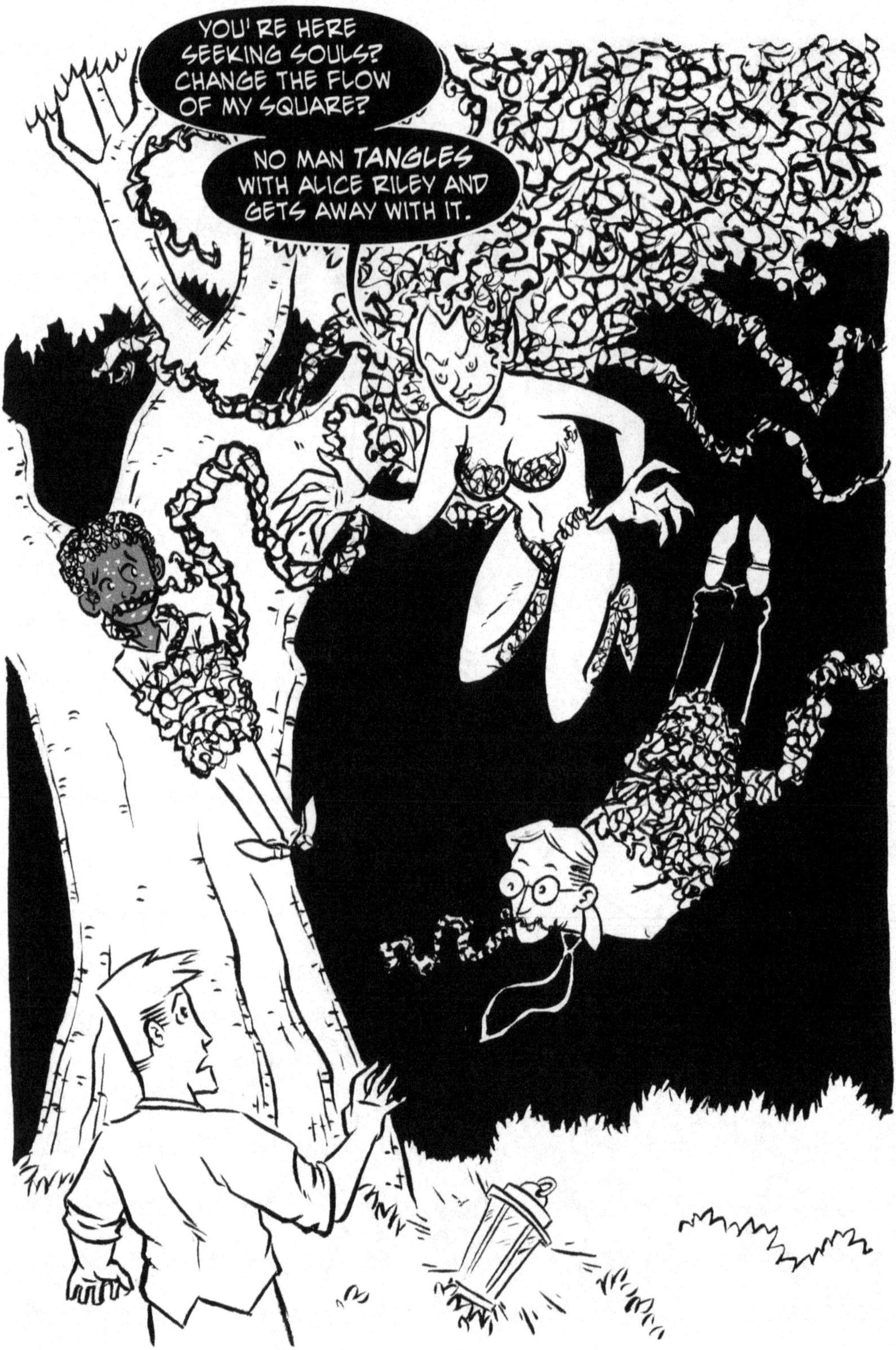

YOU'RE HERE SEEKING SOULS? CHANGE THE FLOW OF MY SQUARE?
NO MAN TANGLES WITH ALICE RILEY AND GETS AWAY WITH IT.

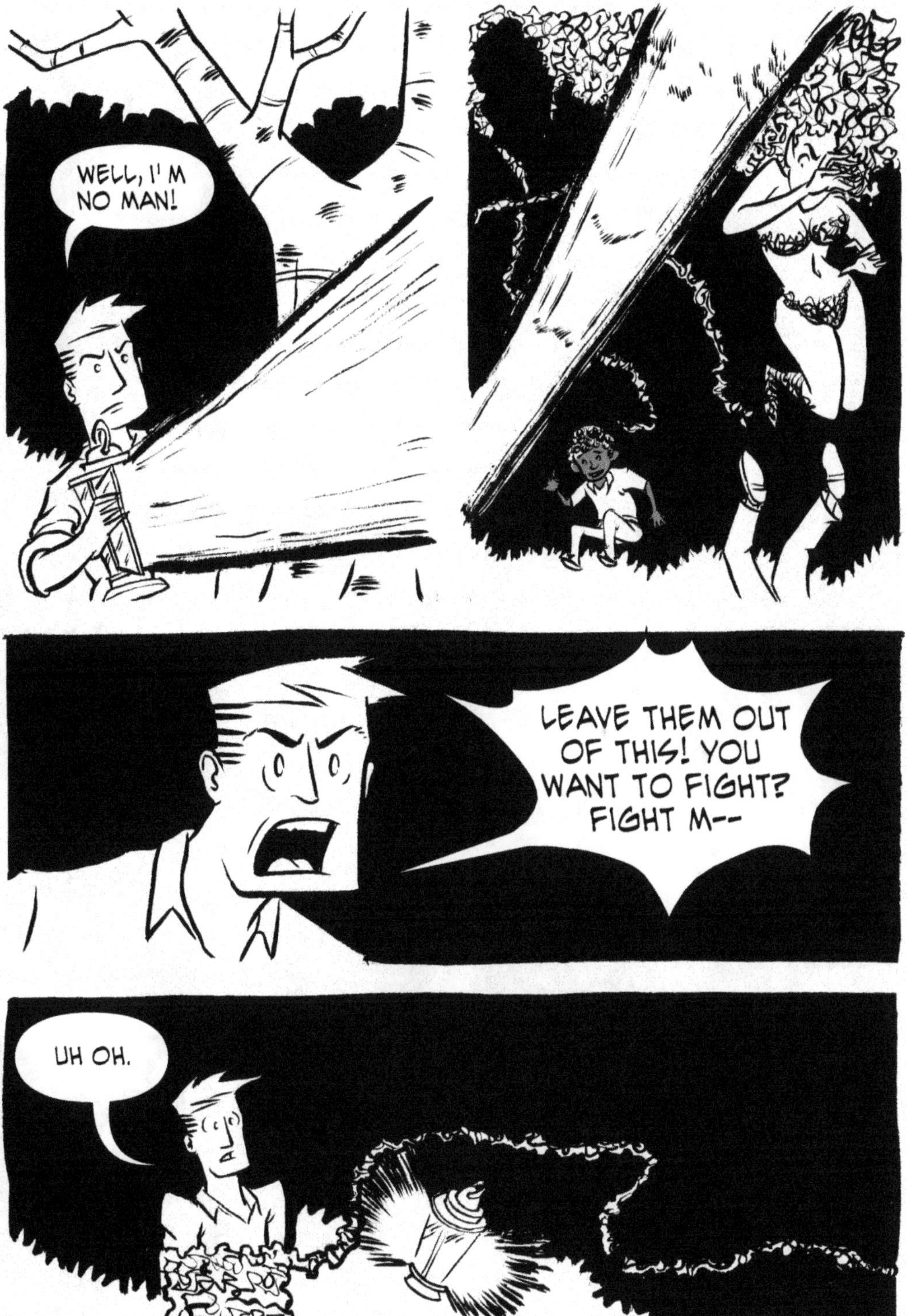
WELL, I'M NO MAN!
LEAVE THEM OUT OF THIS! YOU WANT TO FIGHT? FIGHT M--
UH OH.

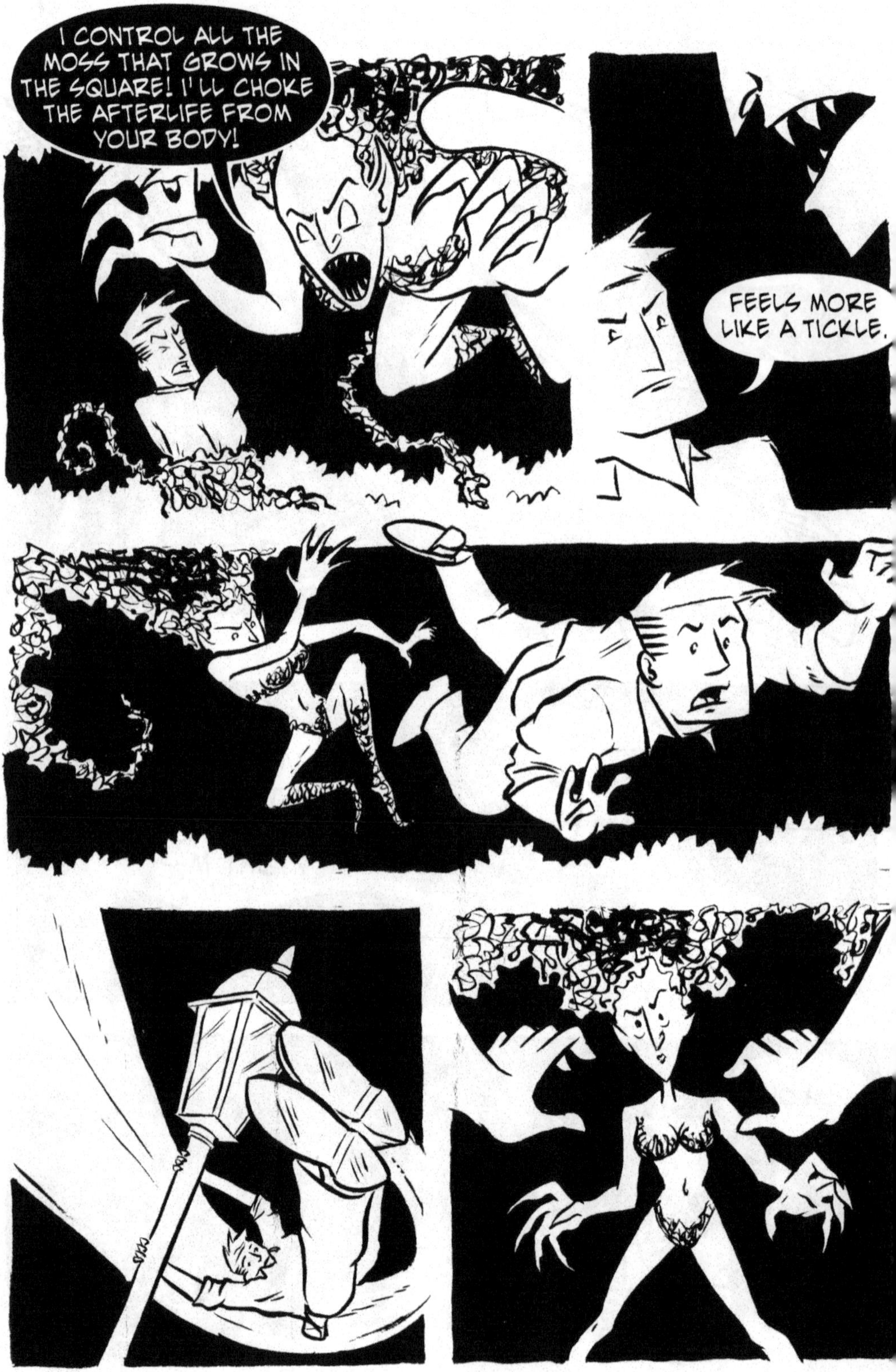
I CONTROL ALL THE MOSS THAT GROWS IN THE SQUARE! I'LL CHOKE THE AFTERLIFE FROM YOUR BODY!
FEELS MORE LIKE A TICKLE.

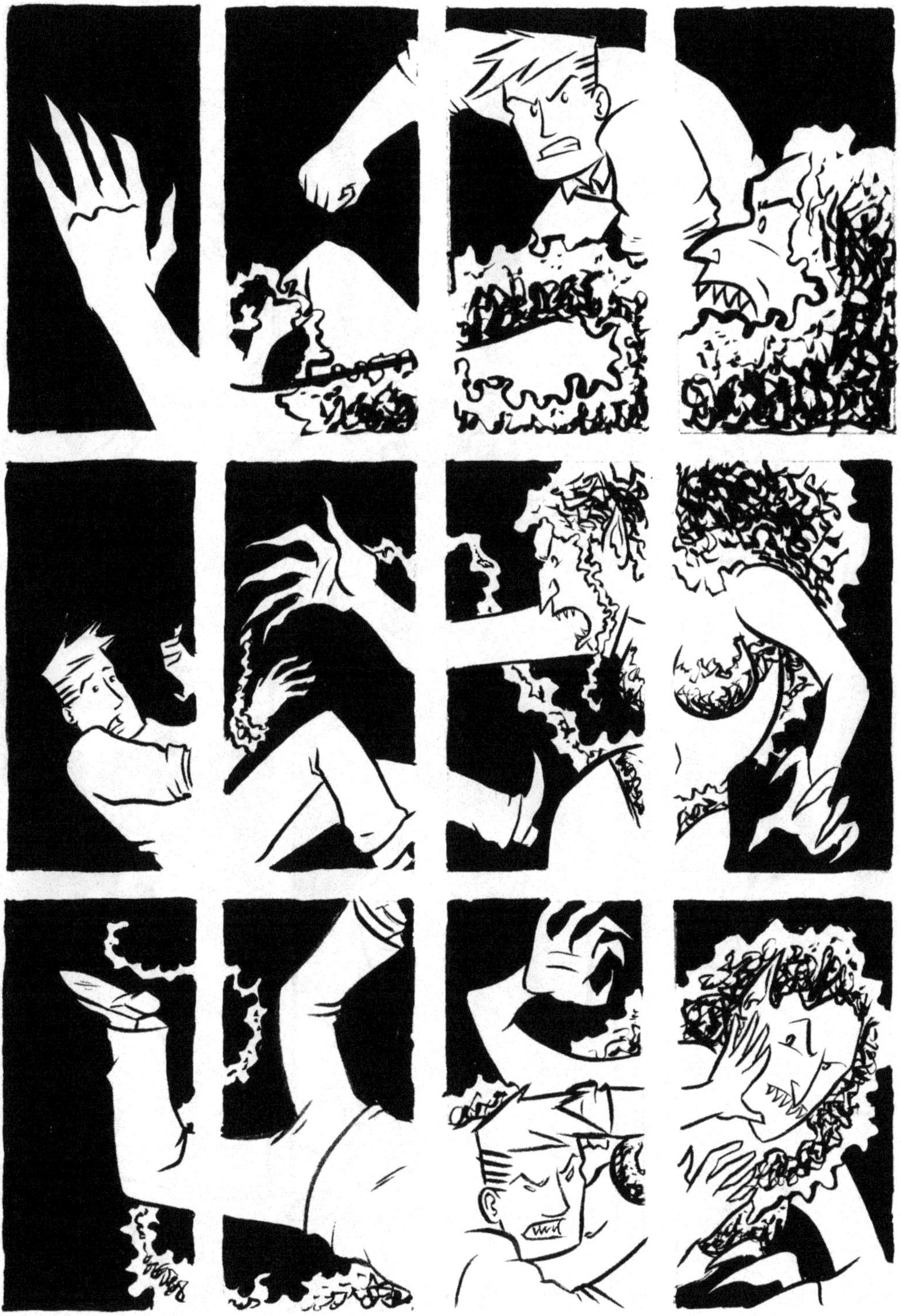

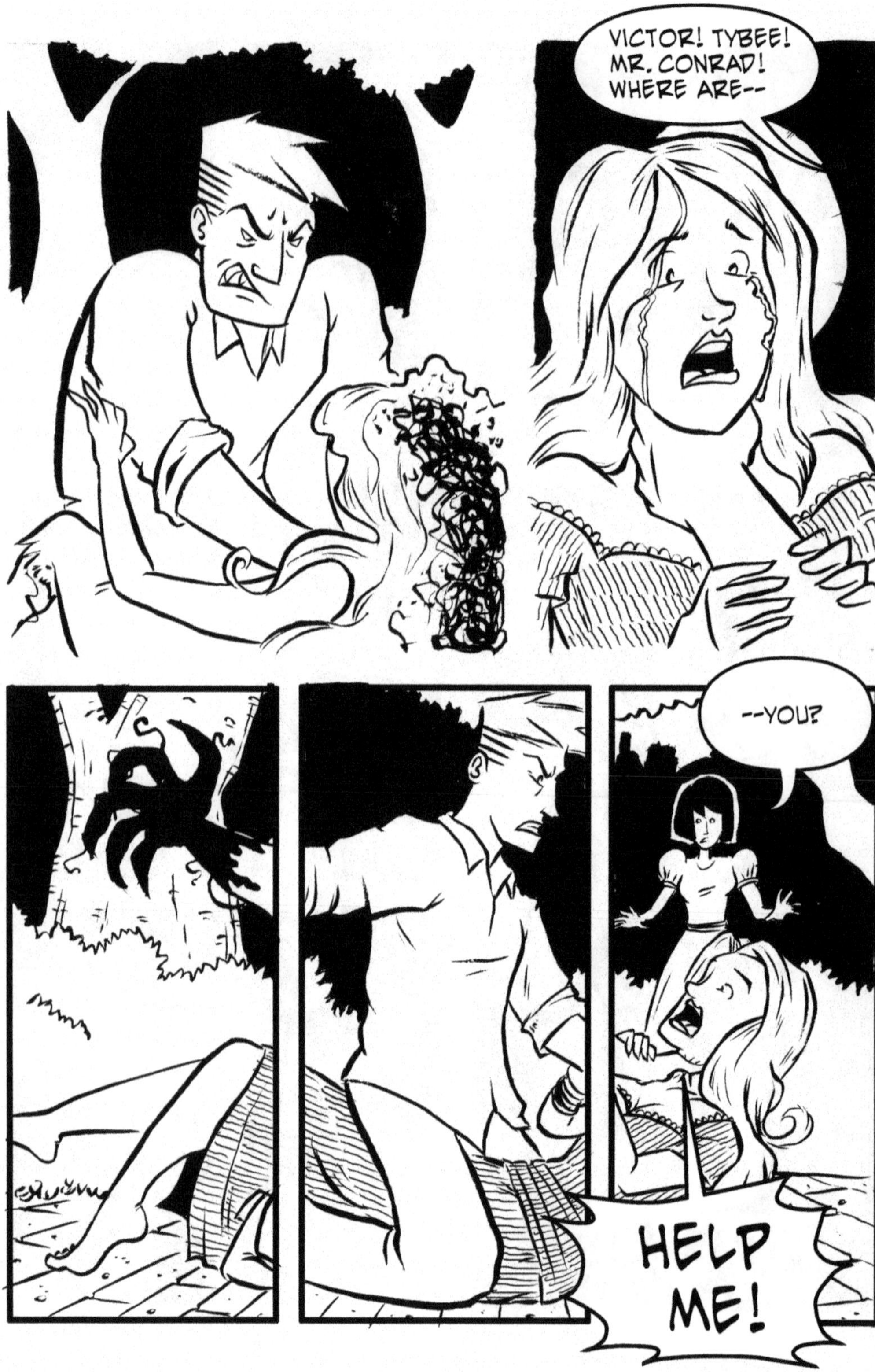
VICTOR! TYBEE! MR. CONRAD! WHERE ARE--
--YOU?
HELP ME!

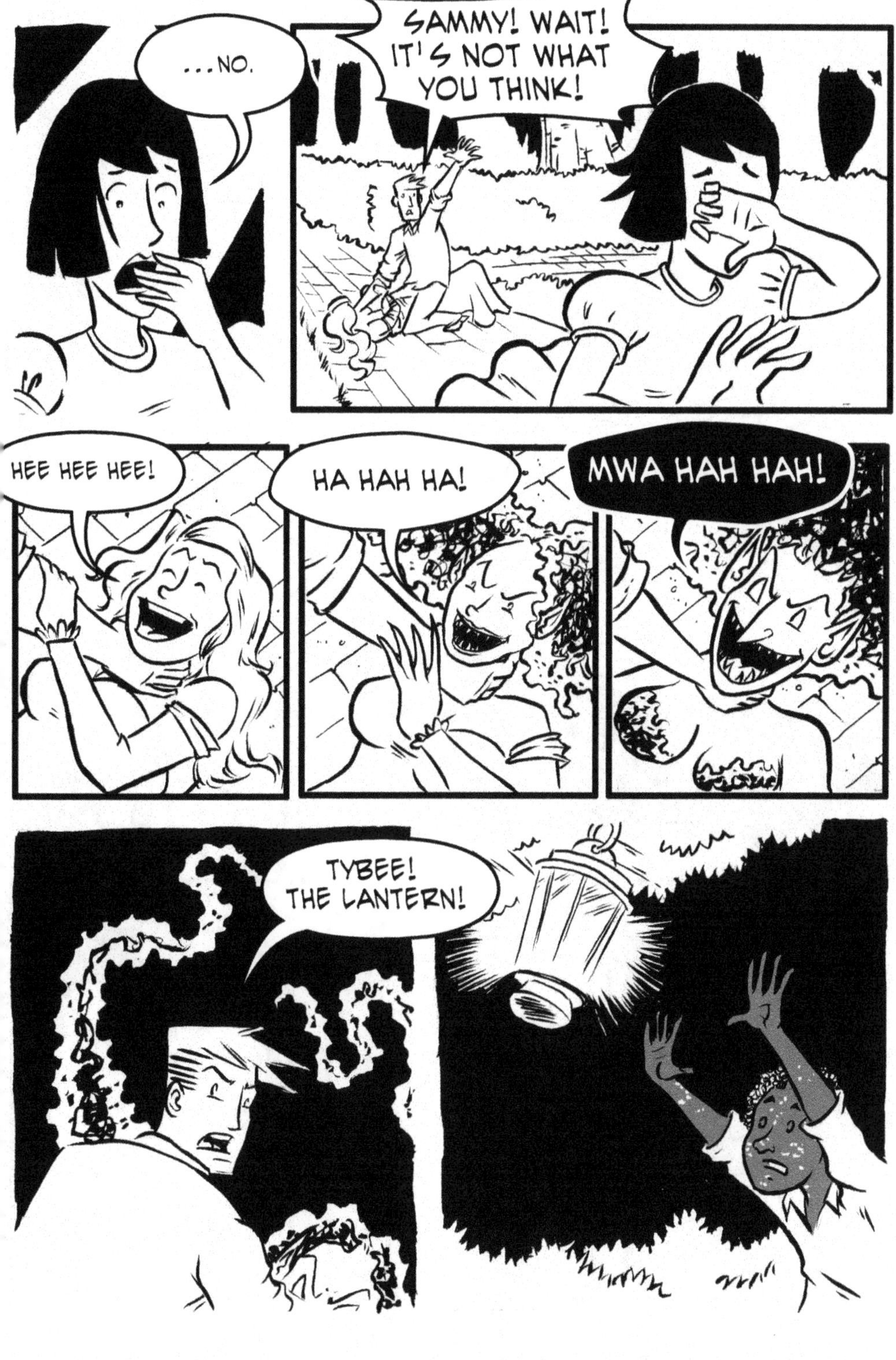
...NO.
SAMMY! WAIT! IT'S NOT WHAT YOU THINK!
HEE HEE HEE!
HA HAH HA!
MWA HAH HAH!
TYBEE! THE LANTERN!

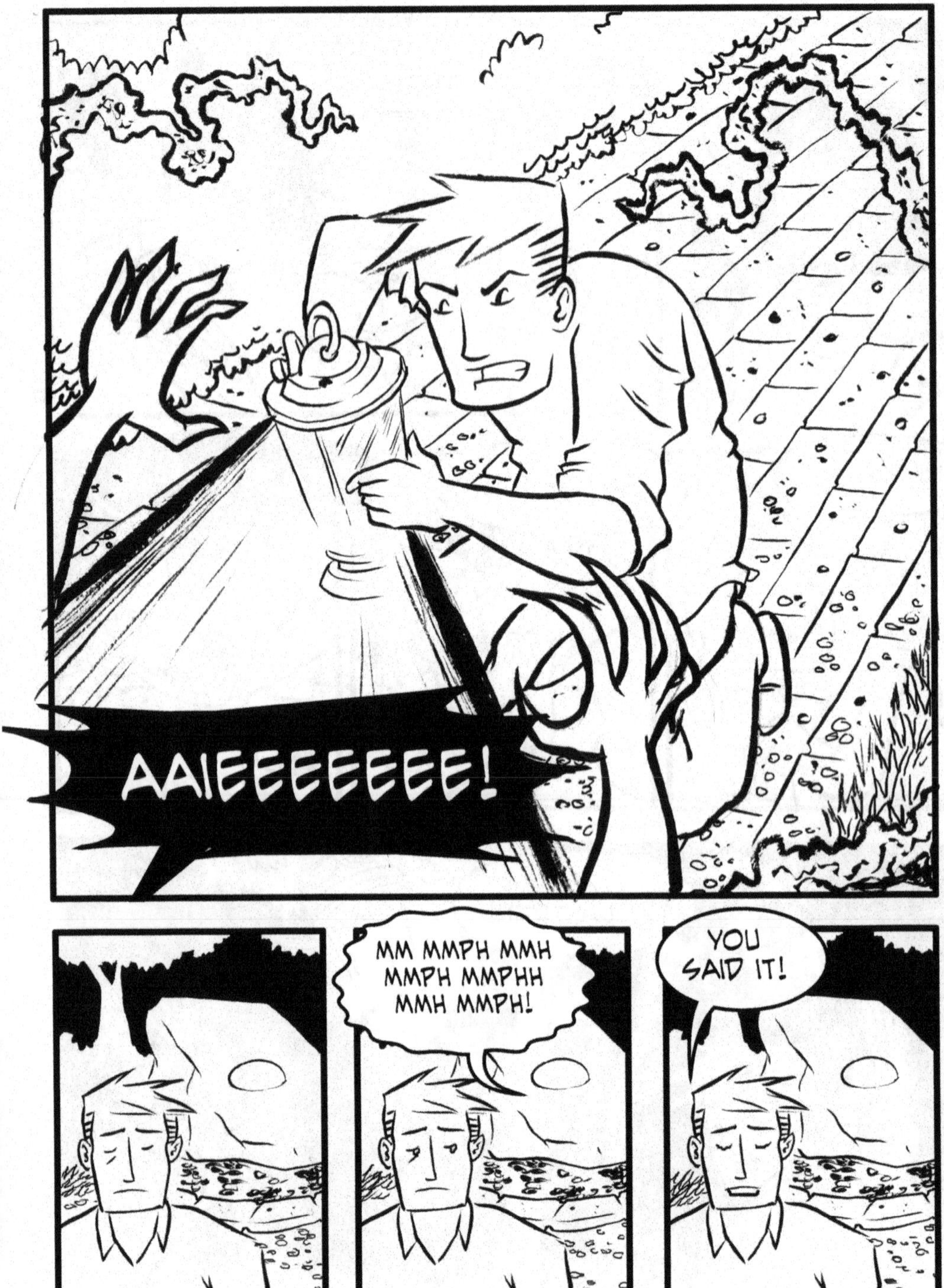
AAIEEEEEEEE!
MM MMPH MMH MMPH MMPHH MMH MMPH!
YOU SAID IT!

CHAPTER

12

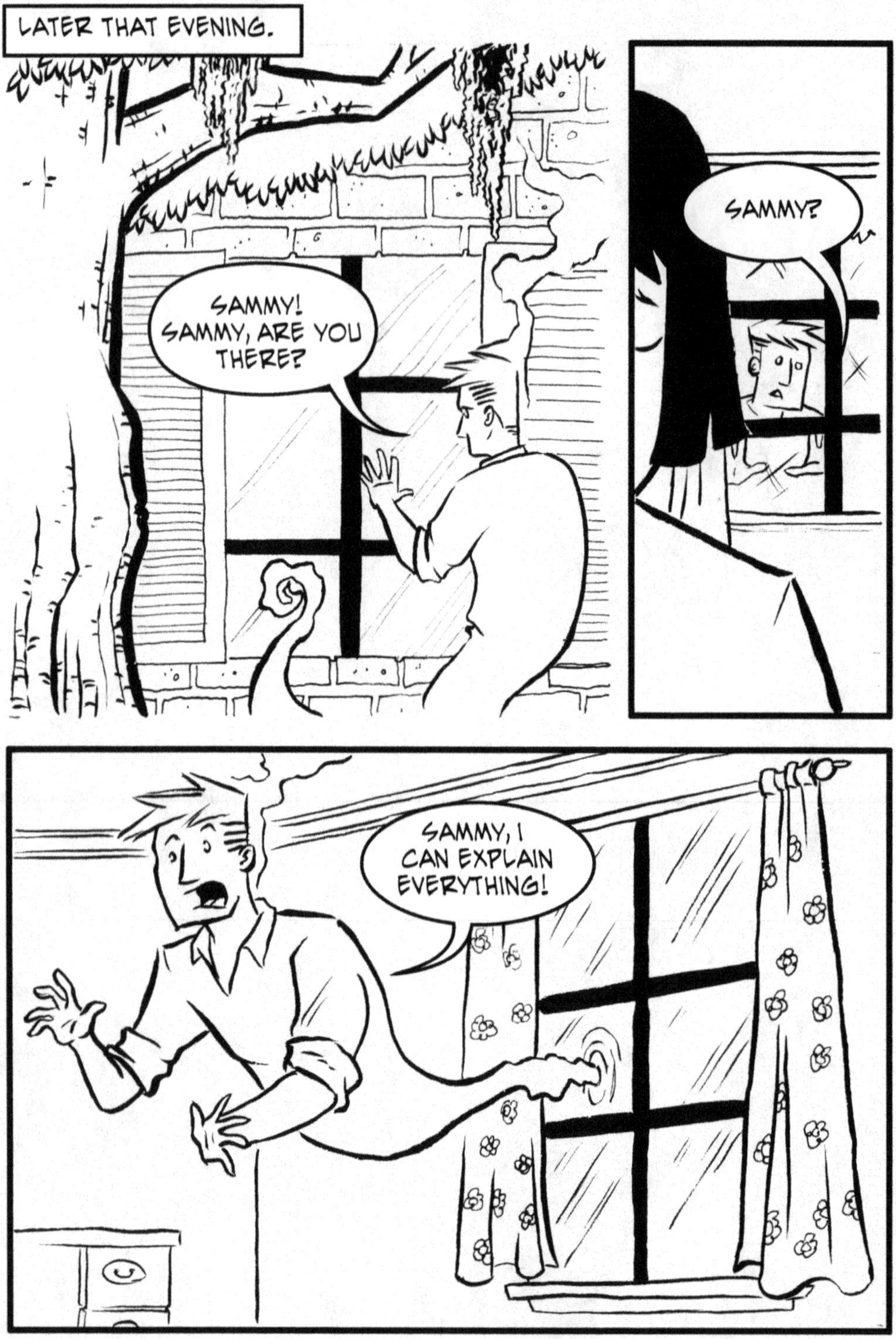
LATER THAT EVENING.
SAMMY! SAMMY, ARE YOU THERE?
SAMMY?
SAMMY, I CAN EXPLAIN EVERYTHING!

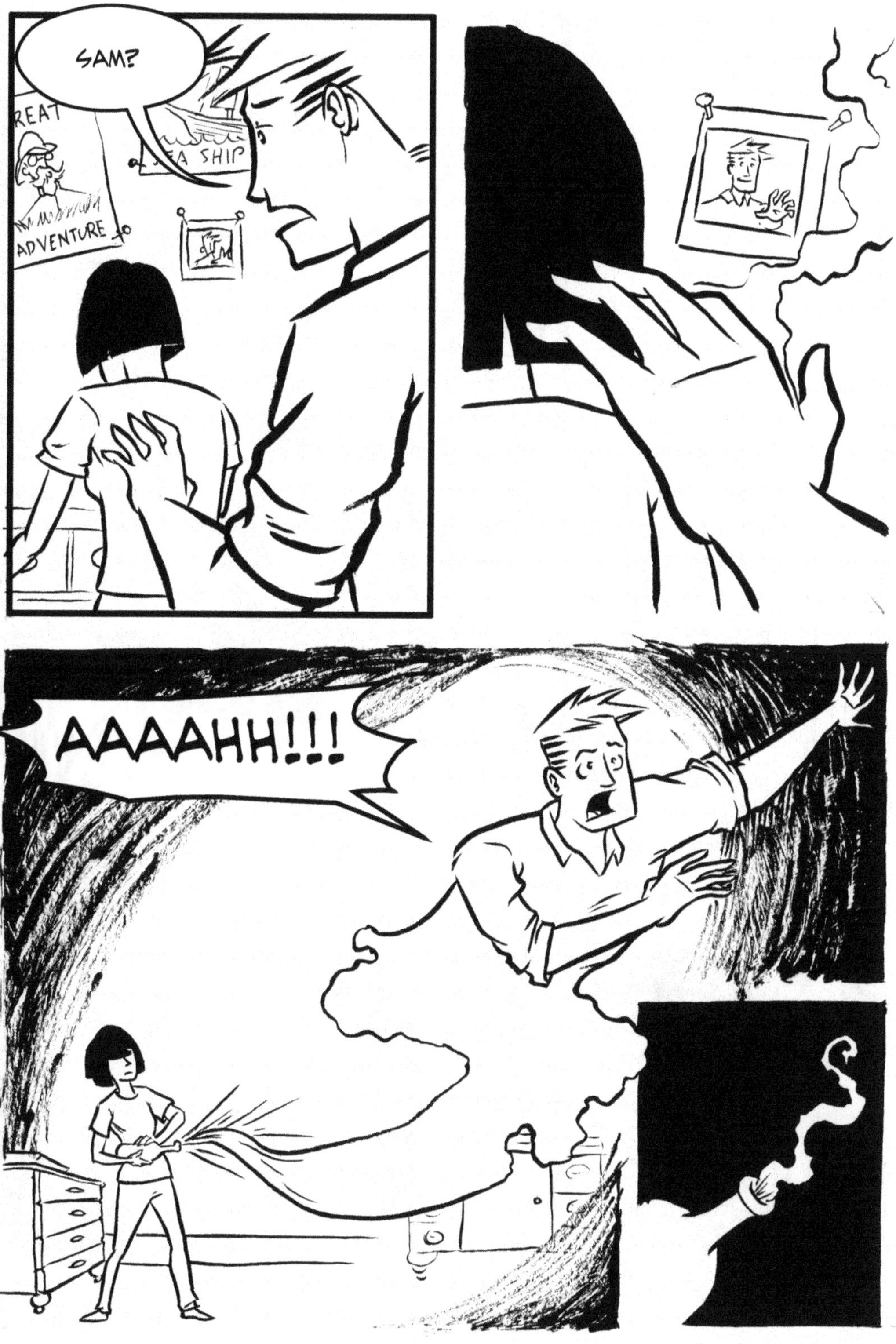
SAM?
REAT
SEA SHIP
ADVENTURE
AAAAHH!!!

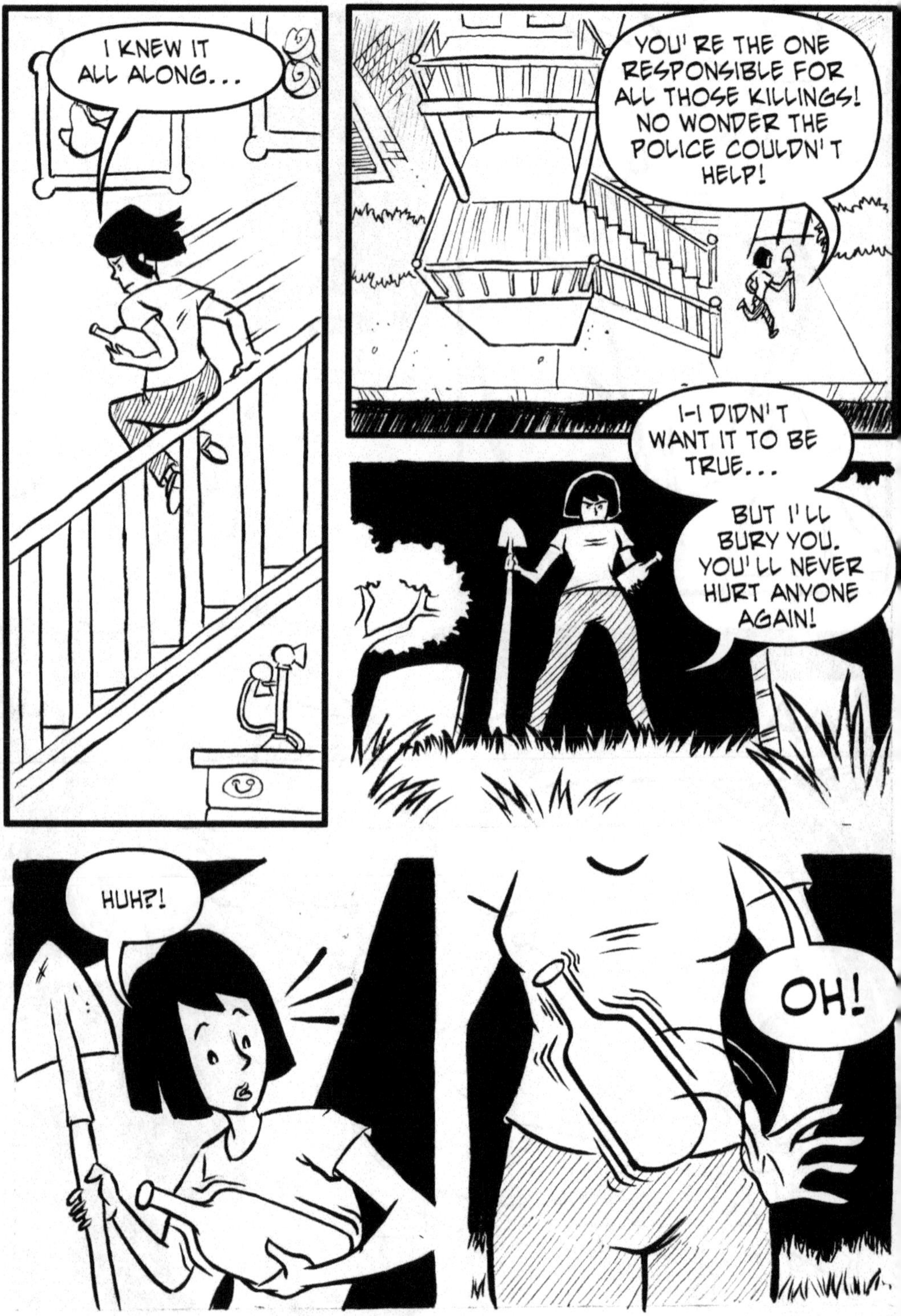
I KNEW IT ALL ALONG...
YOU'RE THE ONE RESPONSIBLE FOR ALL THOSE KILLINGS! NO WONDER THE POLICE COULDN'T HELP!
I-I DIDN'T WANT IT TO BE TRUE...
BUT I'LL BURY YOU. YOU'LL NEVER HURT ANYONE AGAIN!
HUH?!
OH!

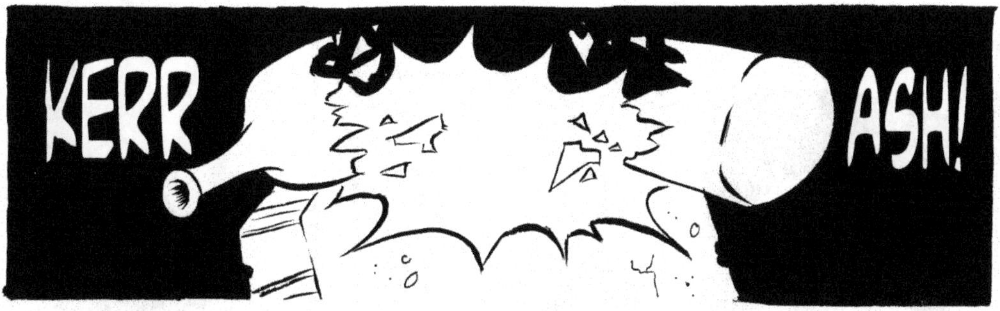
KERR
ASH!

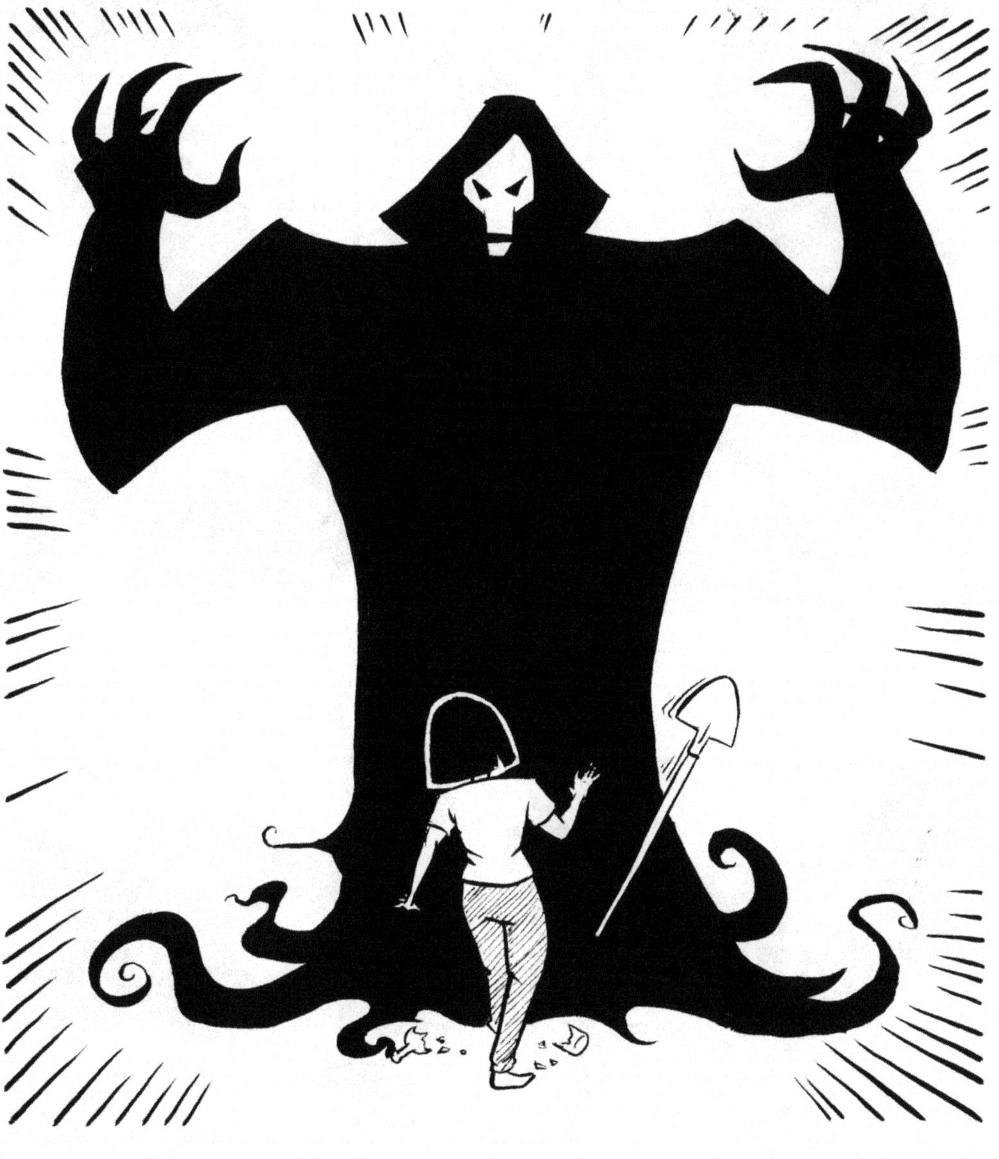

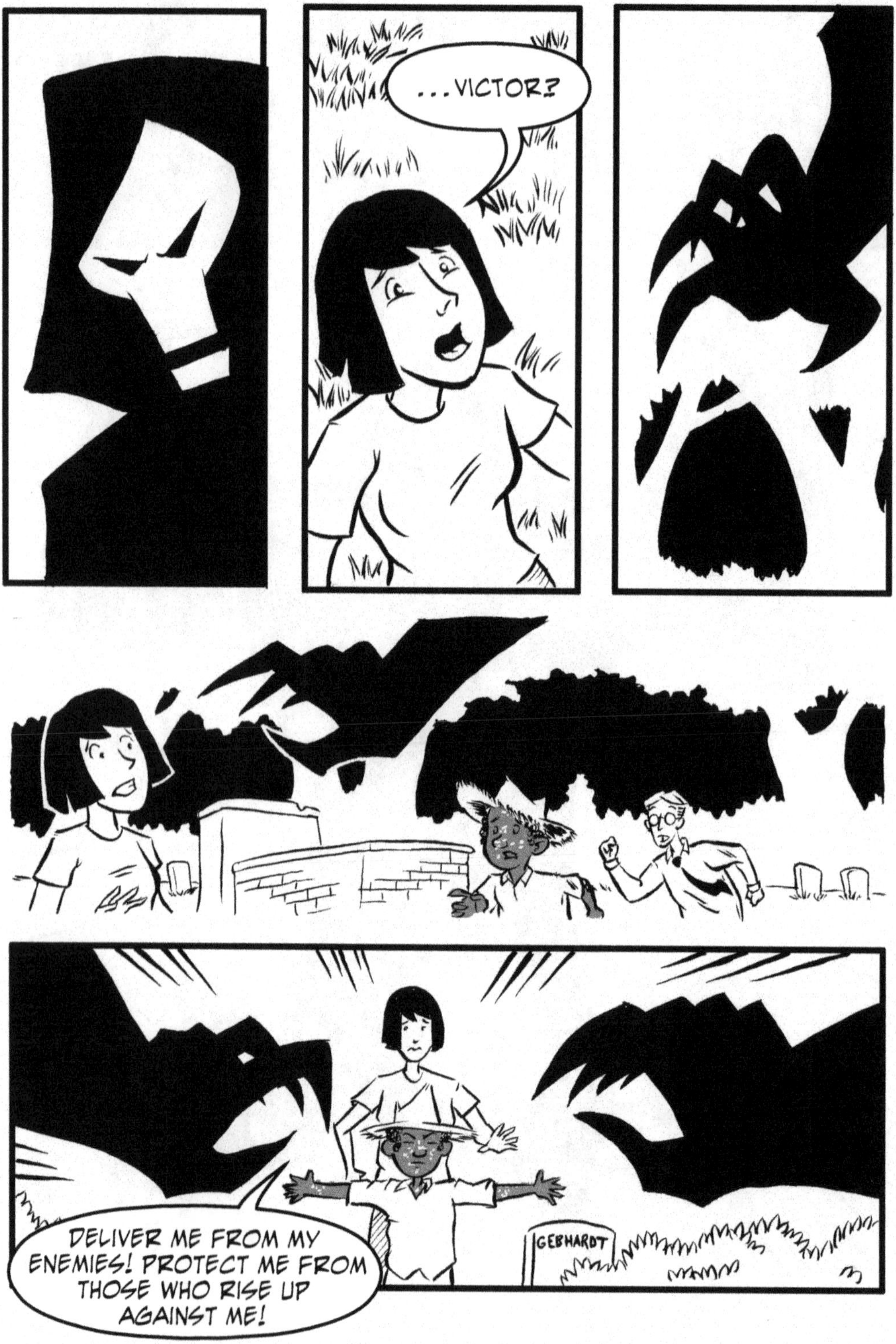
...VICTOR?
GEBHARDT
DELIVER ME FROM MY ENEMIES! PROTECT ME FROM THOSE WHO RISE UP AGAINST ME!

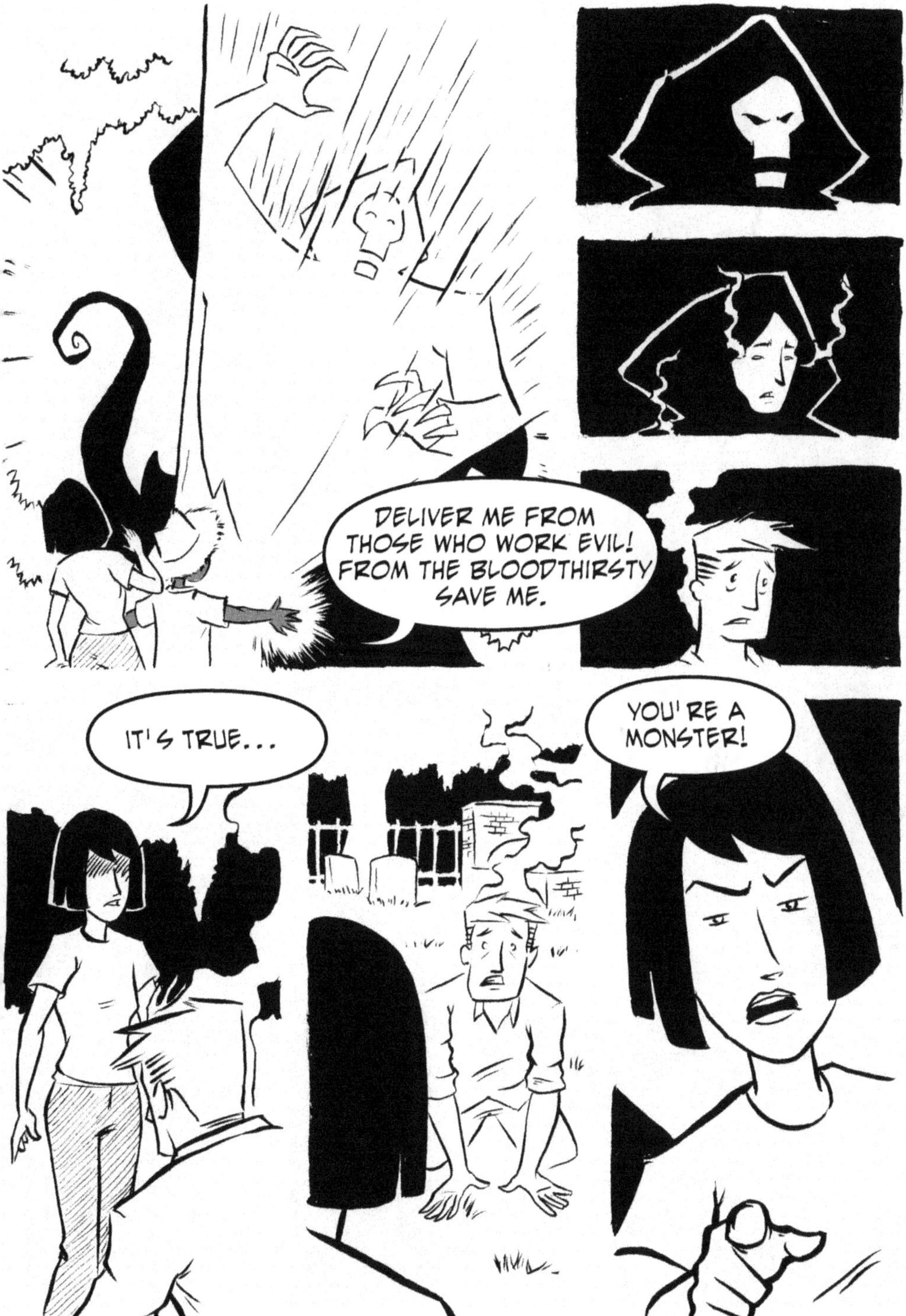
DELIVER ME FROM THOSE WHO WORK EVIL! FROM THE BLOODTHIRSTY SAVE ME.
IT'S TRUE...
YOU'RE A MONSTER!

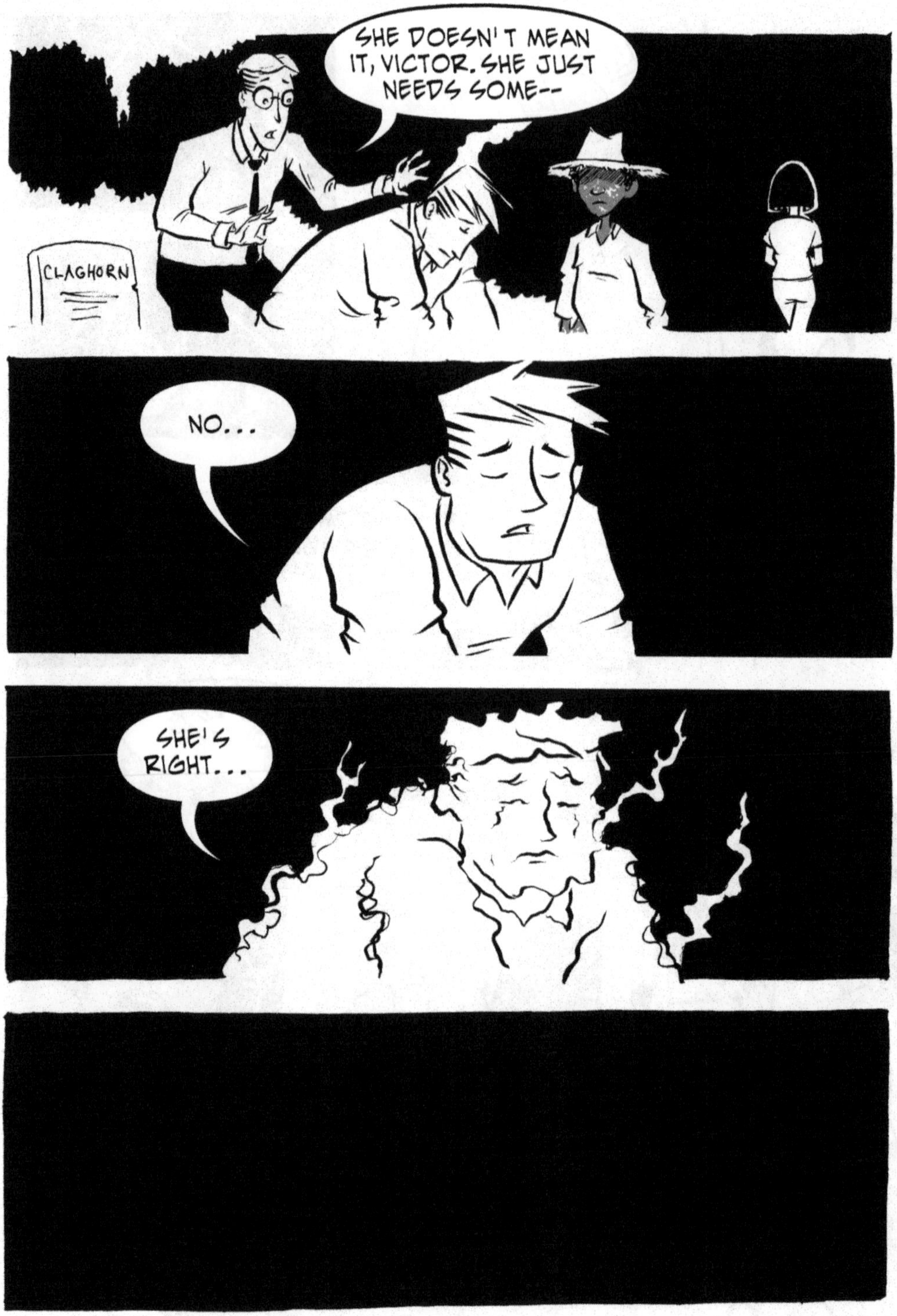
SHE DOESN'T MEAN IT, VICTOR. SHE JUST NEEDS SOME--
CLAGHORN
NO...
SHE'S RIGHT...

CHAPTER

13

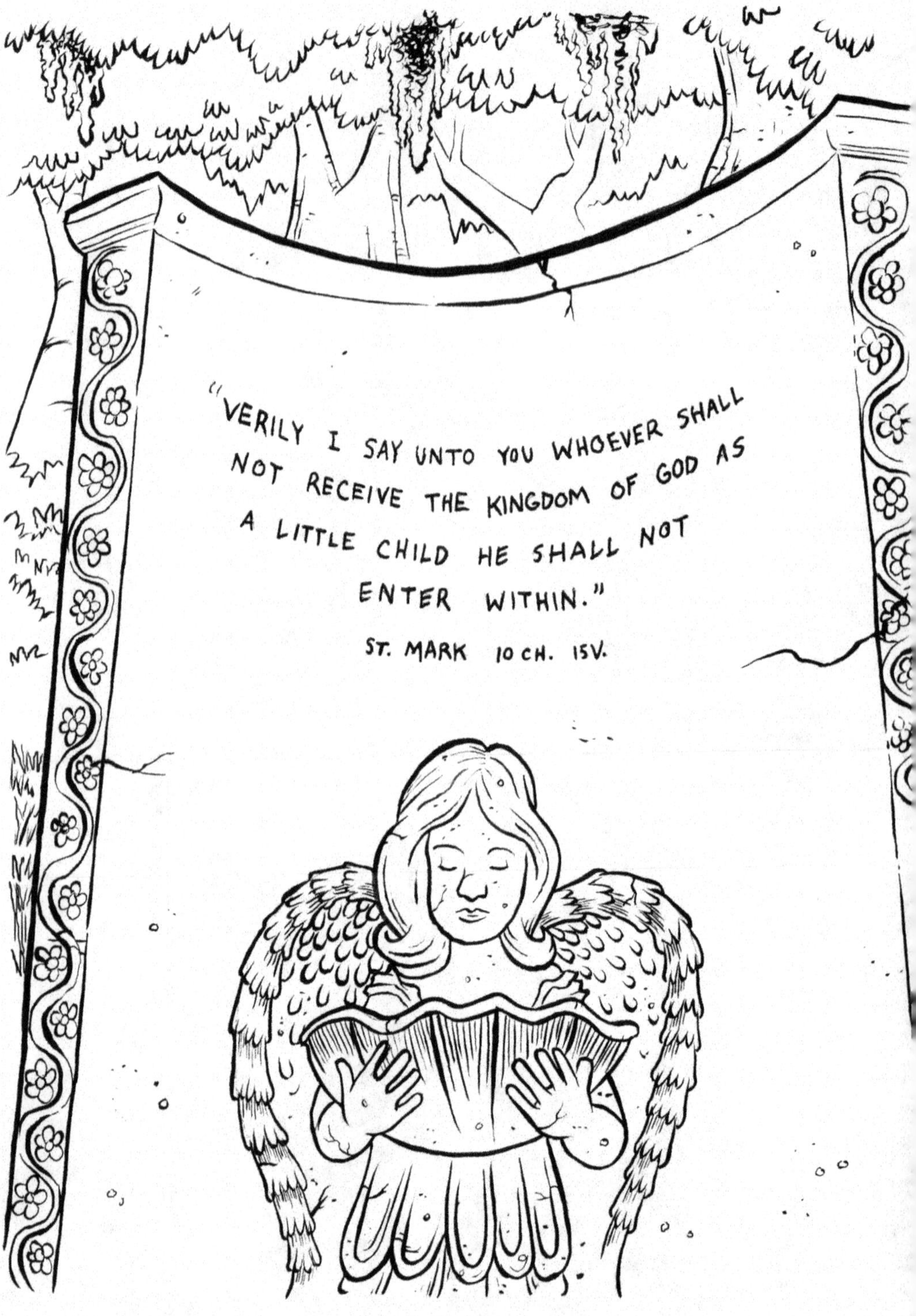
"VERILY I SAY UNTO YOU WHOEVER SHALL NOT RECEIVE THE KINGDOM OF GOD AS A LITTLE CHILD HE SHALL NOT ENTER WITHIN."
ST. MARK 10 CH. 15V.

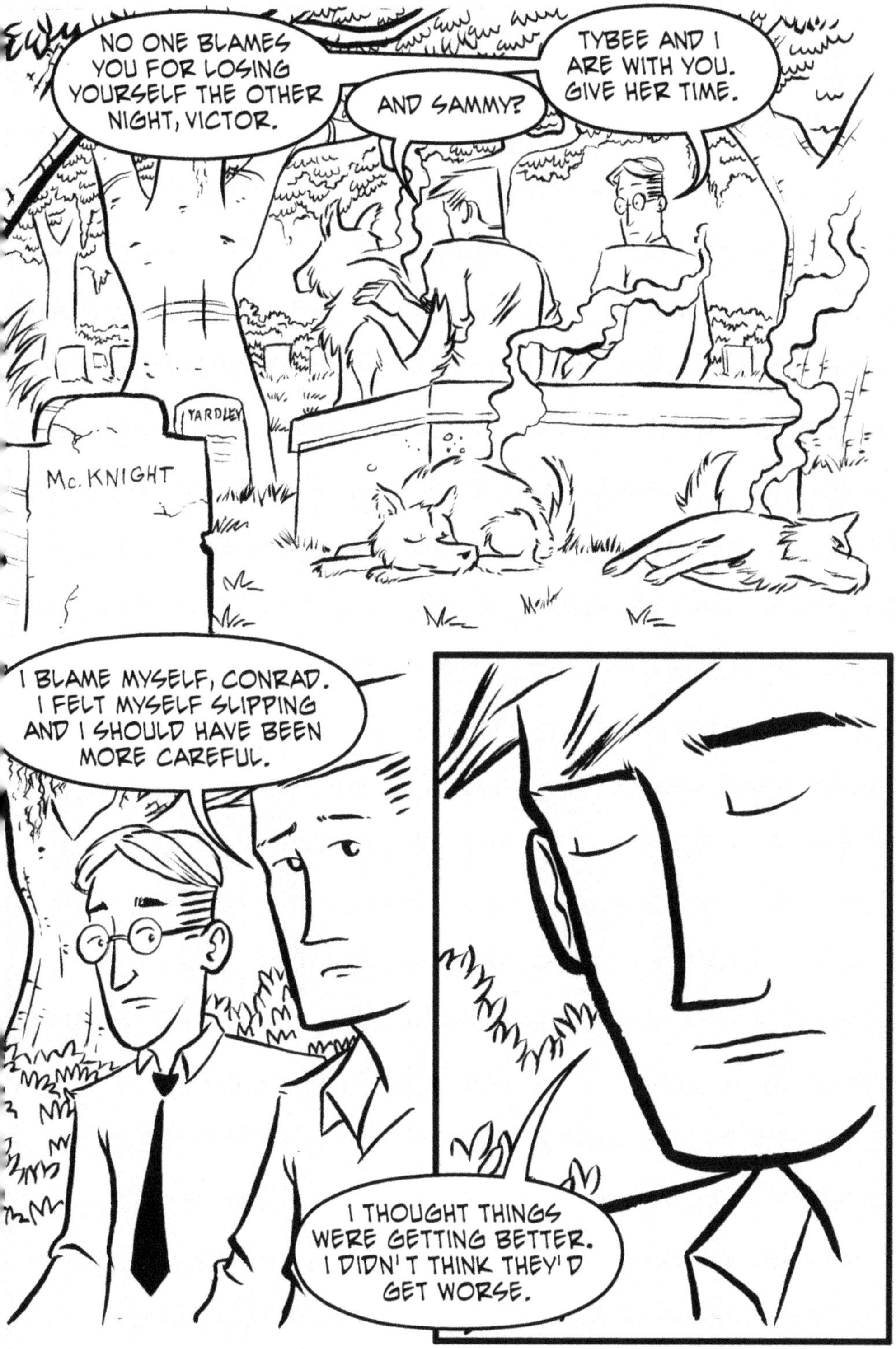
NO ONE BLAMES YOU FOR LOSING YOURSELF THE OTHER NIGHT, VICTOR.
AND SAMMY?
TYBEE AND I ARE WITH YOU. GIVE HER TIME.
YARDLEY
Mc. KNIGHT
I BLAME MYSELF, CONRAD. I FELT MYSELF SLIPPING AND I SHOULD HAVE BEEN MORE CAREFUL.
I THOUGHT THINGS WERE GETTING BETTER. I DIDN'T THINK THEY'D GET WORSE.

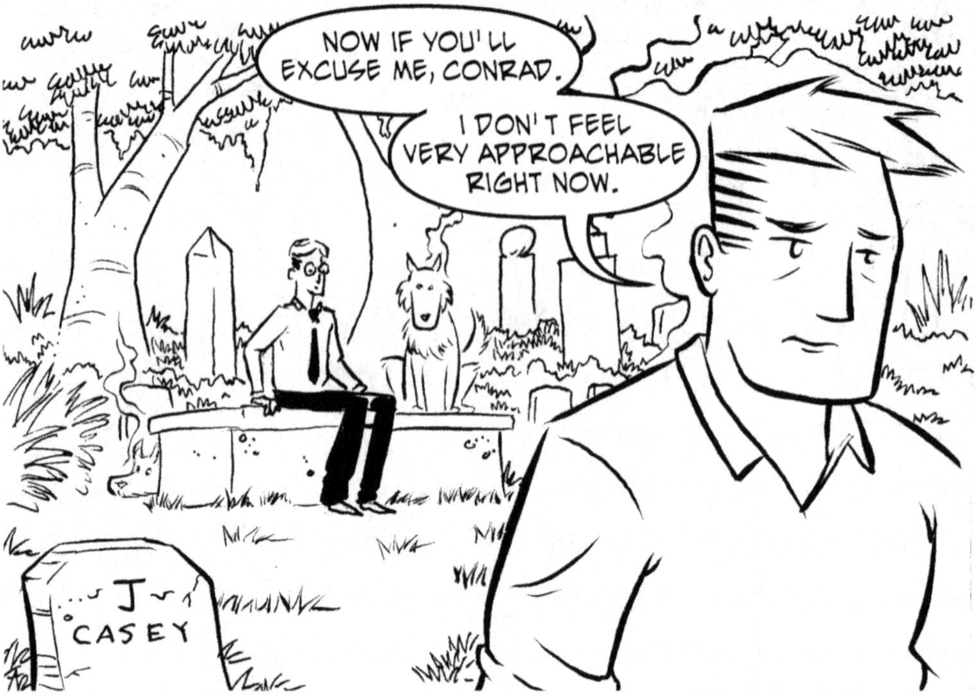
NOW IF YOU'LL EXCUSE ME, CONRAD.
I DON'T FEEL VERY APPROACHABLE RIGHT NOW.
J CASEY

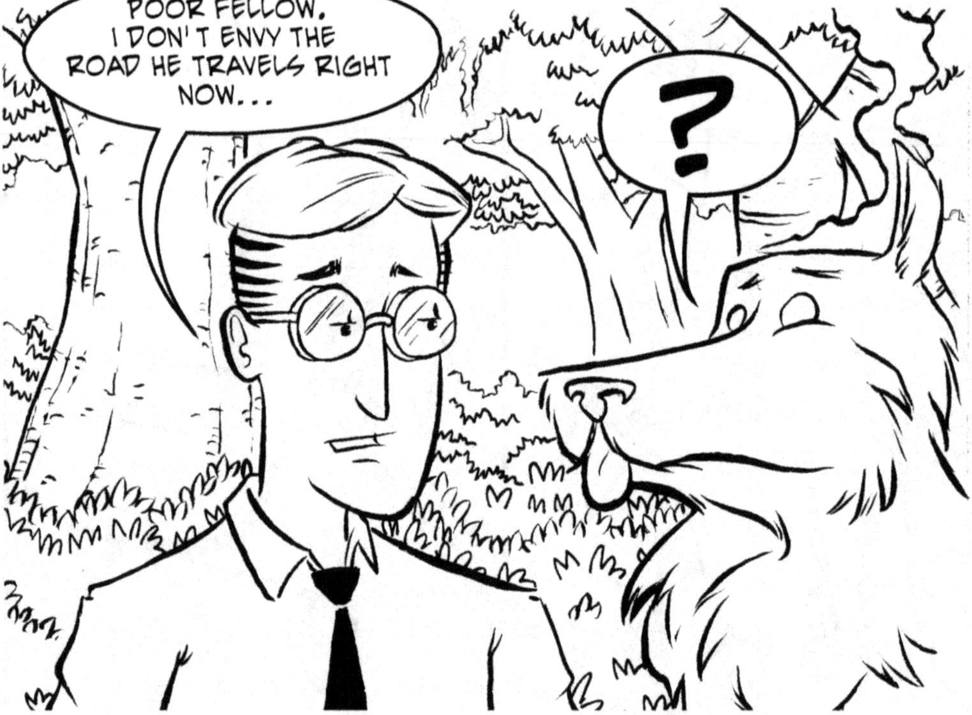
POOR FELLOW. I DON'T ENVY THE ROAD HE TRAVELS RIGHT NOW...
?

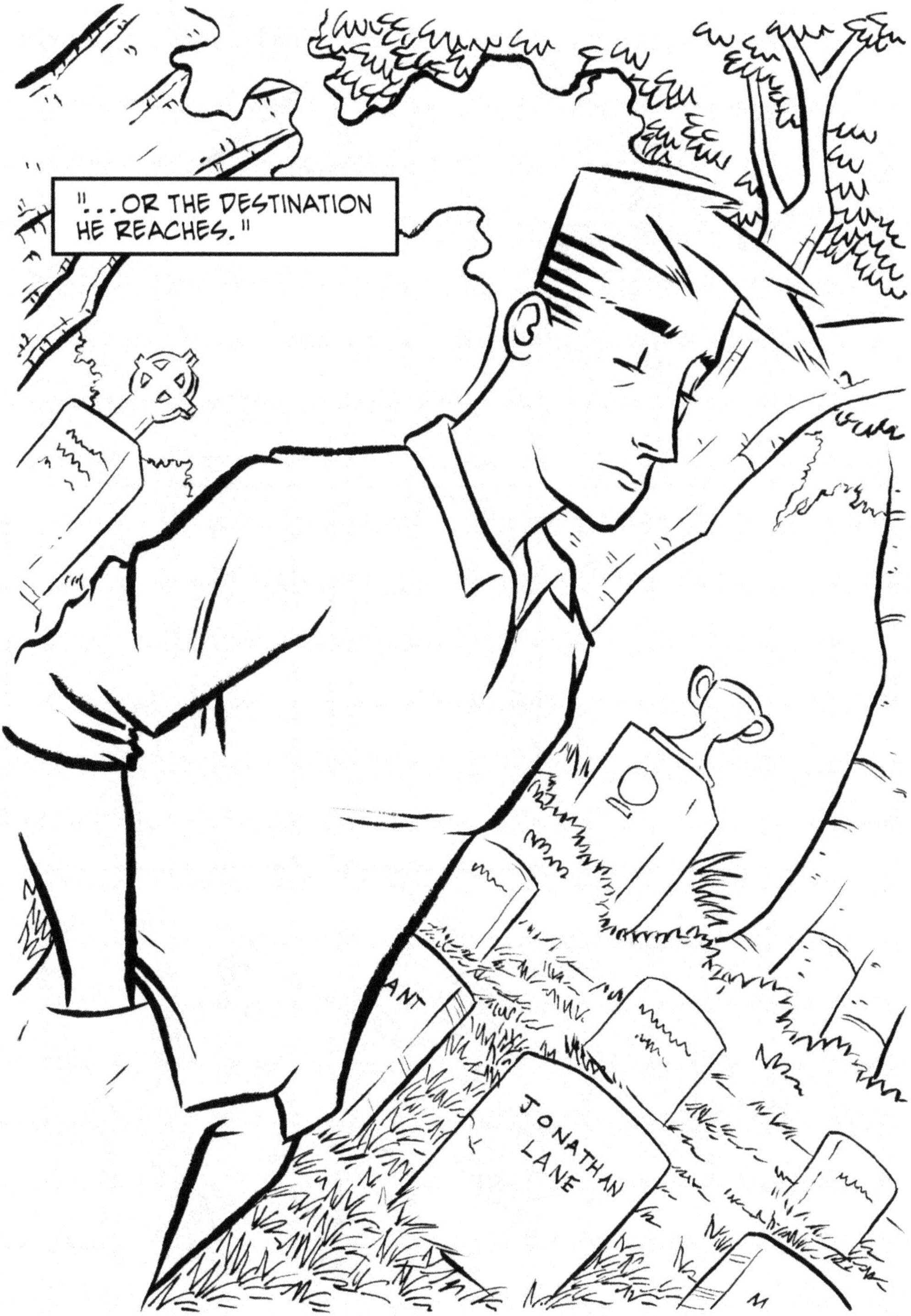
"...OR THE DESTINATION HE REACHES."
ANT
JONATHAN LANE

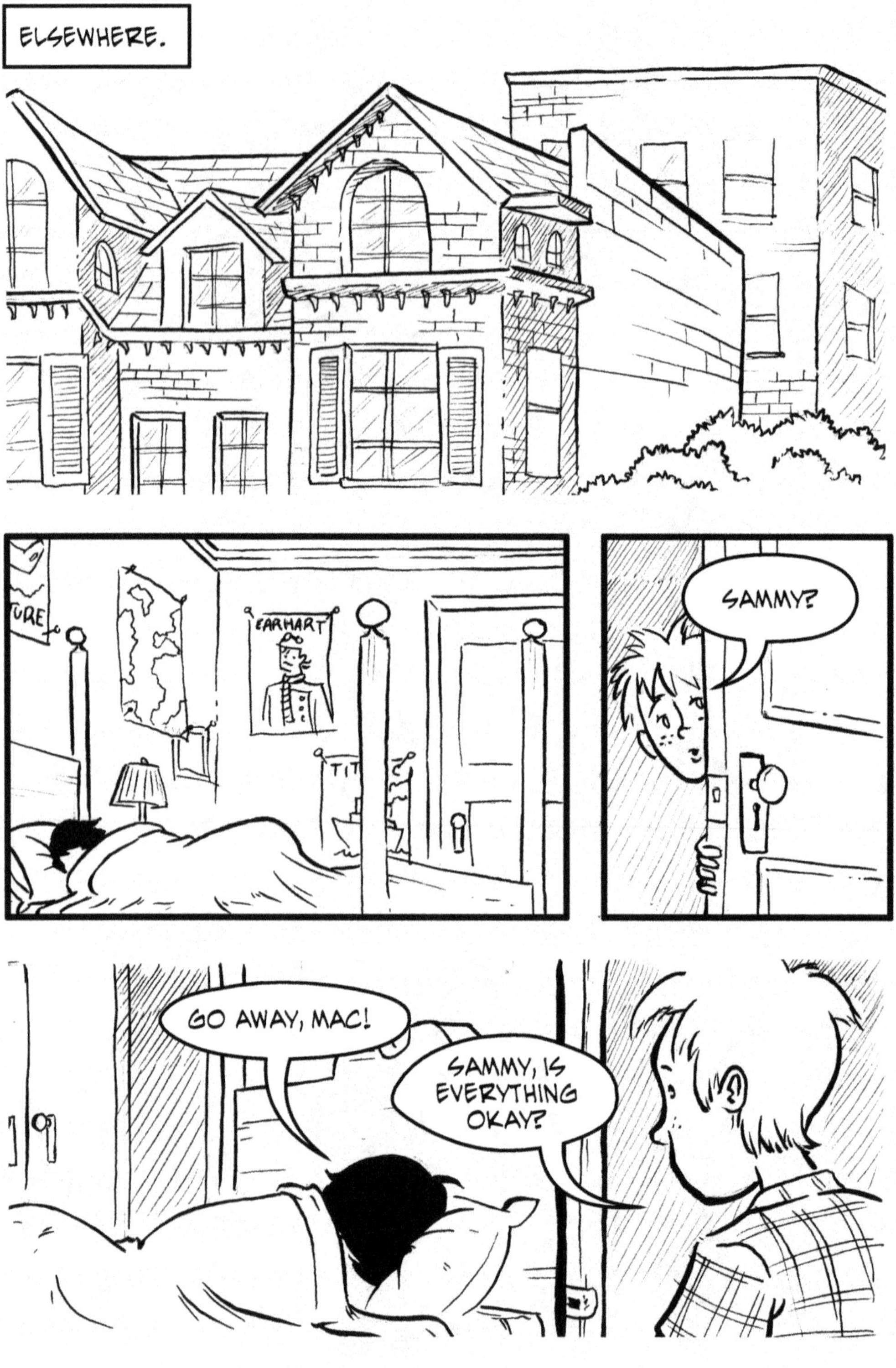
ELSEWHERE.
EARHART
SAMMY?
GO AWAY, MAC!
SAMMY, IS EVERYTHING OKAY?

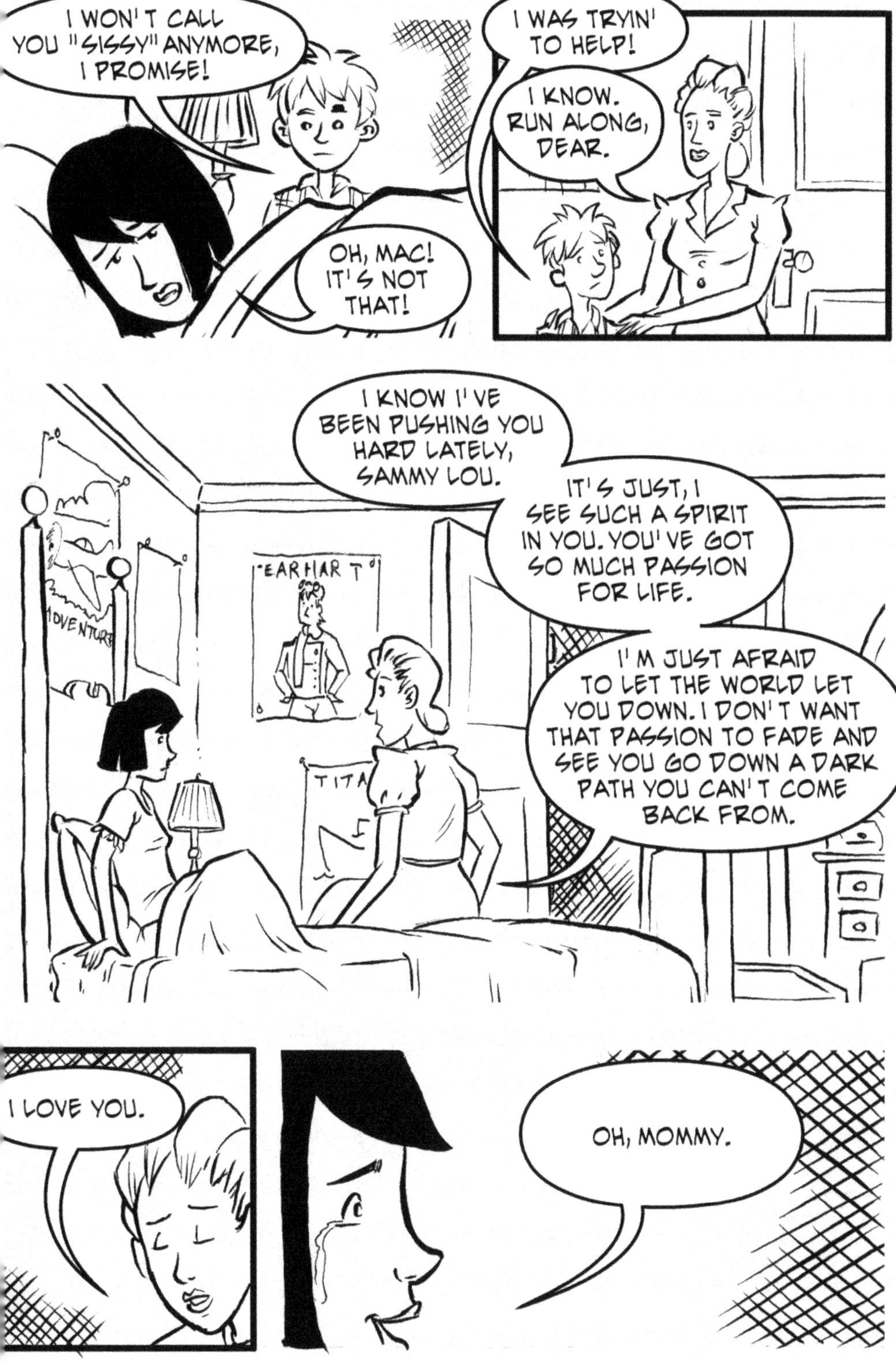
I WON'T CALL YOU "SISSY" ANYMORE, I PROMISE!
OH, MAC! IT'S NOT THAT!
I WAS TRYIN' TO HELP!
I KNOW. RUN ALONG, DEAR.
EARHART
ADVENTURE
I KNOW I'VE BEEN PUSHING YOU HARD LATELY, SAMMY LOU.
IT'S JUST, I SEE SUCH A SPIRIT IN YOU. YOU'VE GOT SO MUCH PASSION FOR LIFE.
I'M JUST AFRAID TO LET THE WORLD LET YOU DOWN. I DON'T WANT THAT PASSION TO FADE AND SEE YOU GO DOWN A DARK PATH YOU CAN'T COME BACK FROM.
I LOVE YOU.
OH, MOMMY.

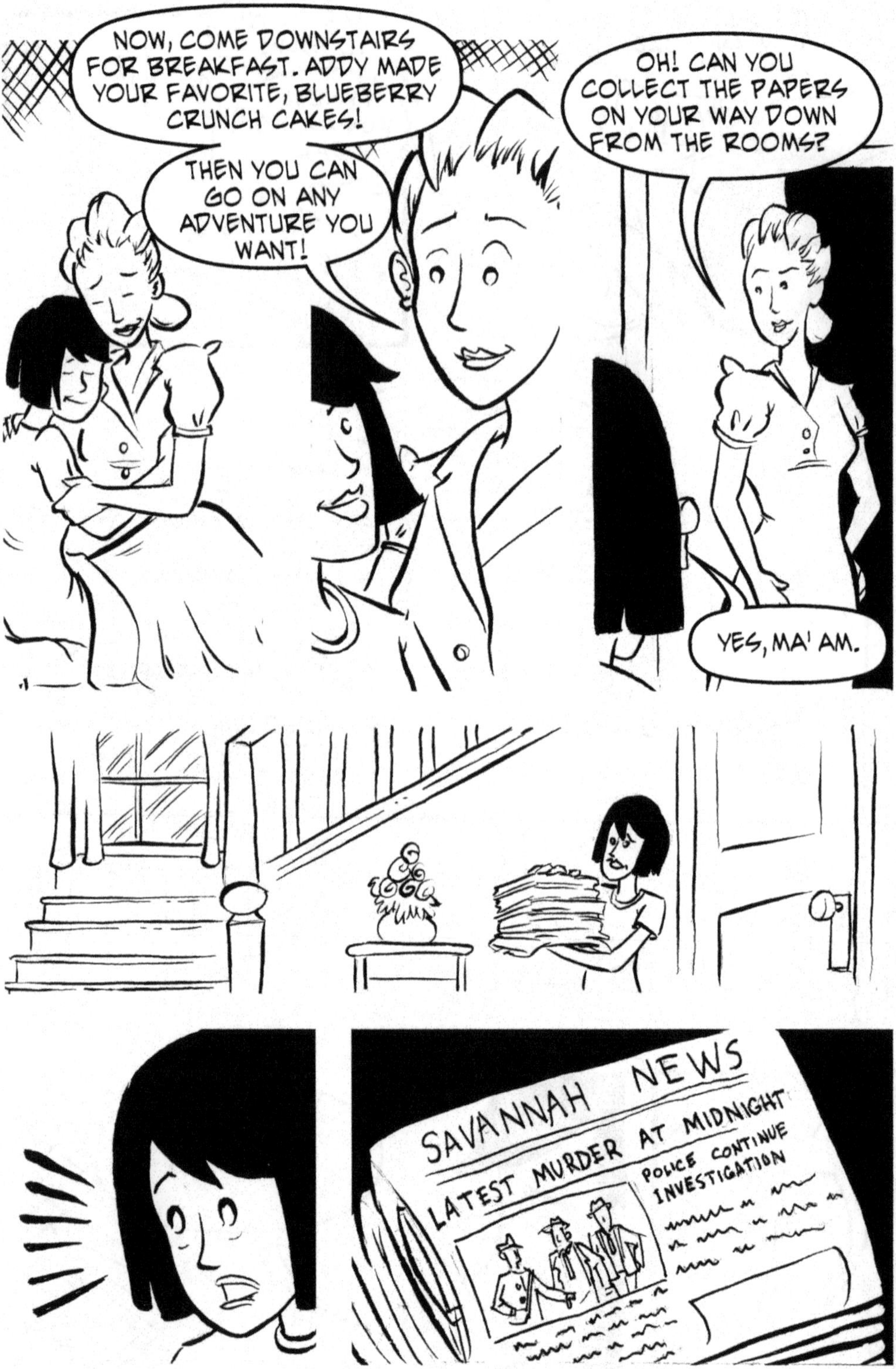
NOW, COME DOWNSTAIRS FOR BREAKFAST. ADDY MADE YOUR FAVORITE, BLUEBERRY CRUNCH CAKES!
THEN YOU CAN GO ON ANY ADVENTURE YOU WANT!
OH! CAN YOU COLLECT THE PAPERS ON YOUR WAY DOWN FROM THE ROOMS?
YES, MA' AM.
SAVANNAH NEWS
LATEST MURDER AT MIDNIGHT
POLICE CONTINUE INVESTIGATION

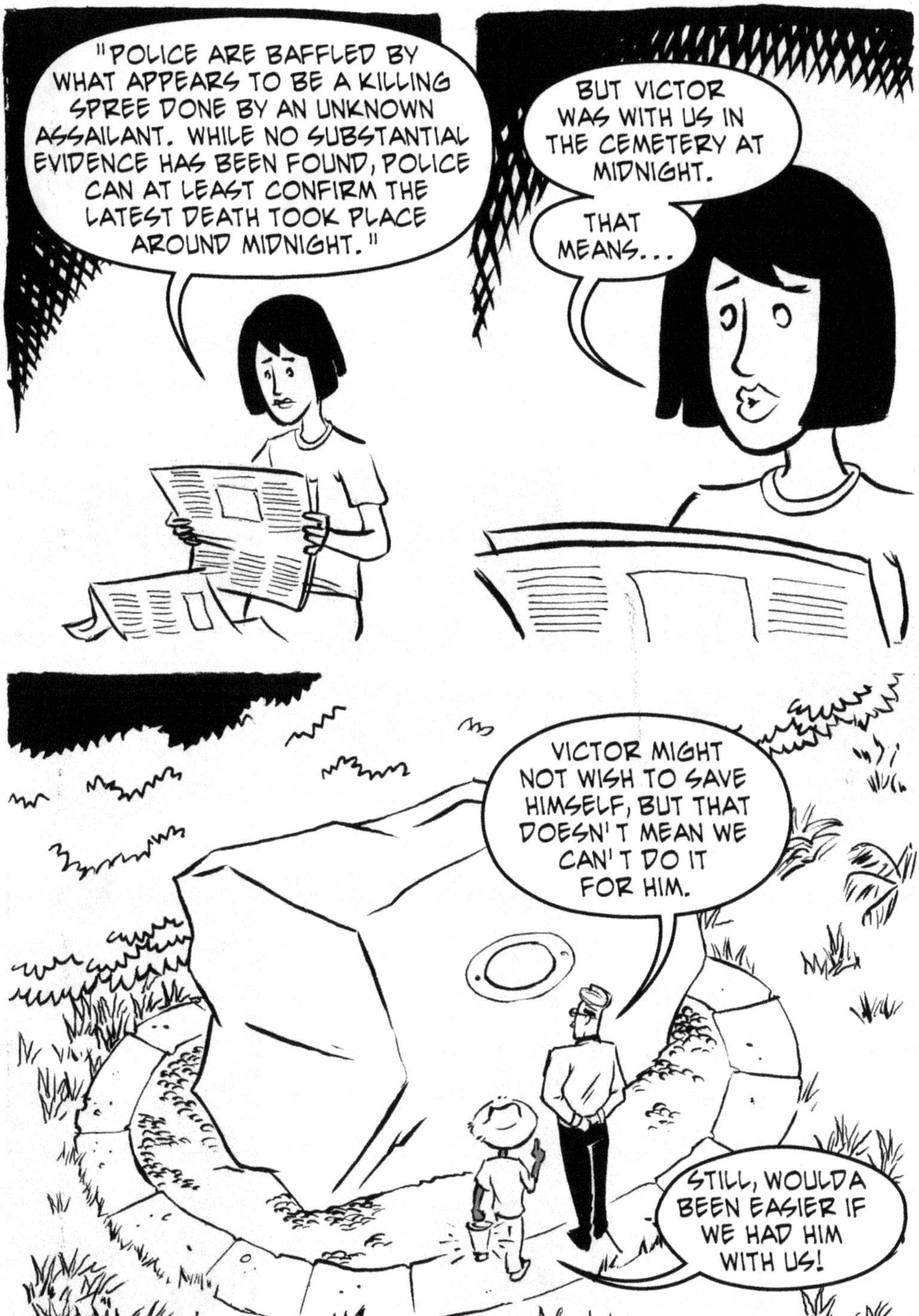
"POLICE ARE BAFFLED BY WHAT APPEARS TO BE A KILLING SPREE DONE BY AN UNKNOWN ASSAILANT. WHILE NO SUBSTANTIAL EVIDENCE HAS BEEN FOUND, POLICE CAN AT LEAST CONFIRM THE LATEST DEATH TOOK PLACE AROUND MIDNIGHT."
BUT VICTOR WAS WITH US IN THE CEMETERY AT MIDNIGHT.
THAT MEANS...
VICTOR MIGHT NOT WISH TO SAVE HIMSELF, BUT THAT DOESN'T MEAN WE CAN'T DO IT FOR HIM.
STILL, WOULDA BEEN EASIER IF WE HAD HIM WITH US!

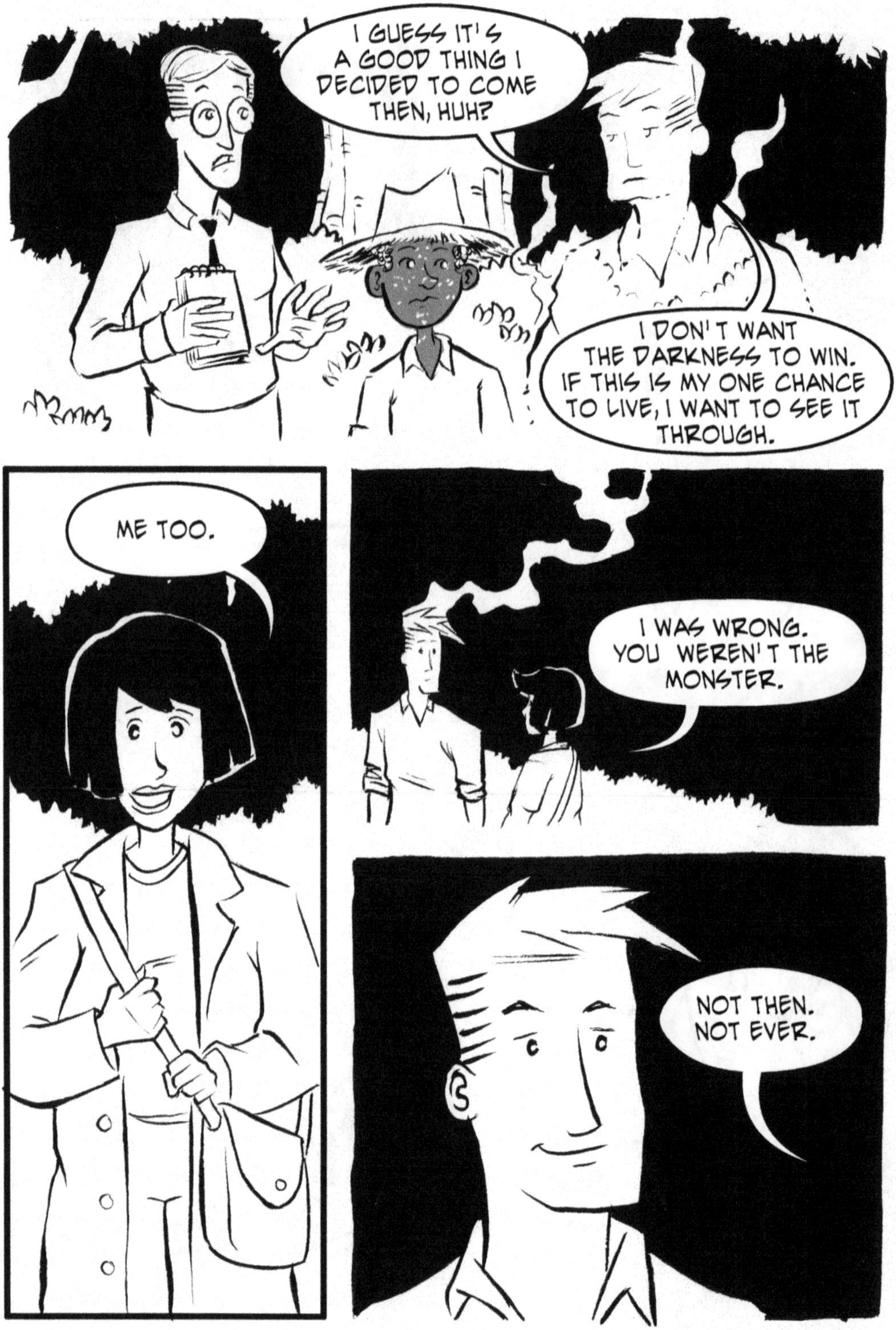
I GUESS IT'S A GOOD THING I DECIDED TO COME THEN, HUH?
I DON'T WANT THE DARKNESS TO WIN. IF THIS IS MY ONE CHANCE TO LIVE, I WANT TO SEE IT THROUGH.
ME TOO.
I WAS WRONG. YOU WEREN'T THE MONSTER.
NOT THEN. NOT EVER.

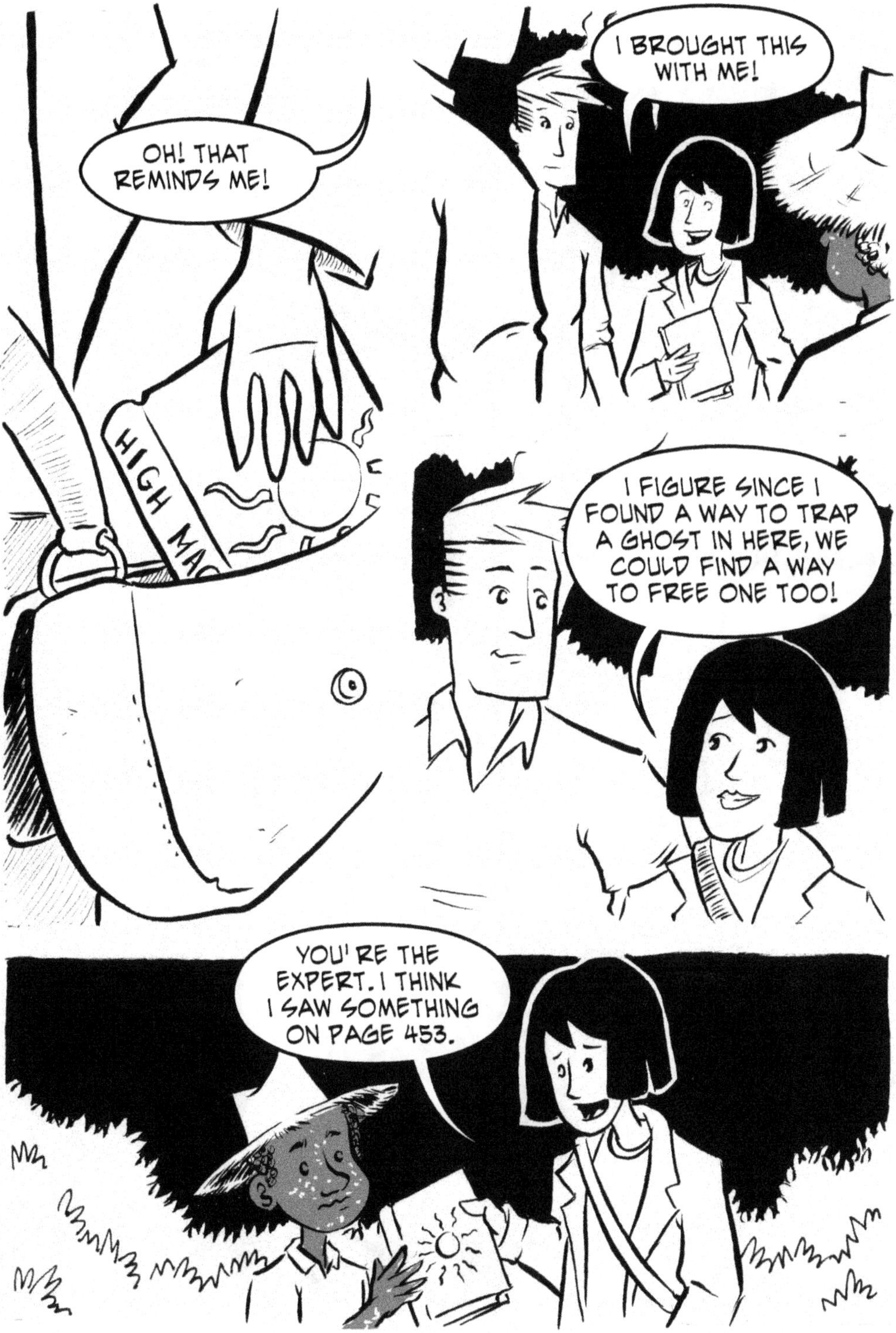
OH! THAT REMINDS ME!
I BROUGHT THIS WITH ME!
HIGH MA
I FIGURE SINCE I FOUND A WAY TO TRAP A GHOST IN HERE, WE COULD FIND A WAY TO FREE ONE TOO!
YOU'RE THE EXPERT. I THINK I SAW SOMETHING ON PAGE 453.

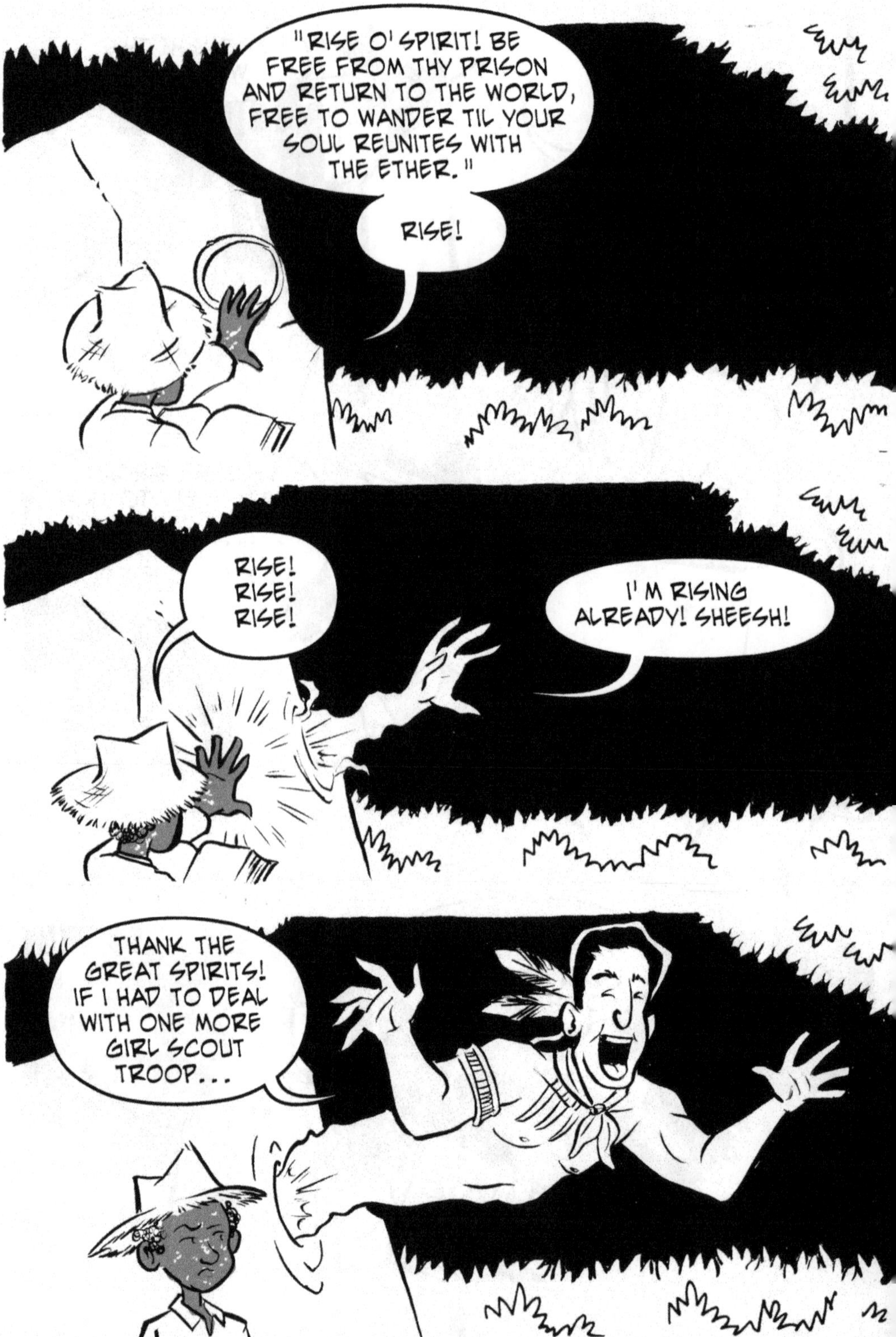
"RISE O' SPIRIT! BE FREE FROM THY PRISON AND RETURN TO THE WORLD, FREE TO WANDER TIL YOUR SOUL REUNITES WITH THE ETHER."
RISE!
RISE! RISE! RISE!
I'M RISING ALREADY! SHEESH!
THANK THE GREAT SPIRITS! IF I HAD TO DEAL WITH ONE MORE GIRL SCOUT TROOP...

CHAPTER

14

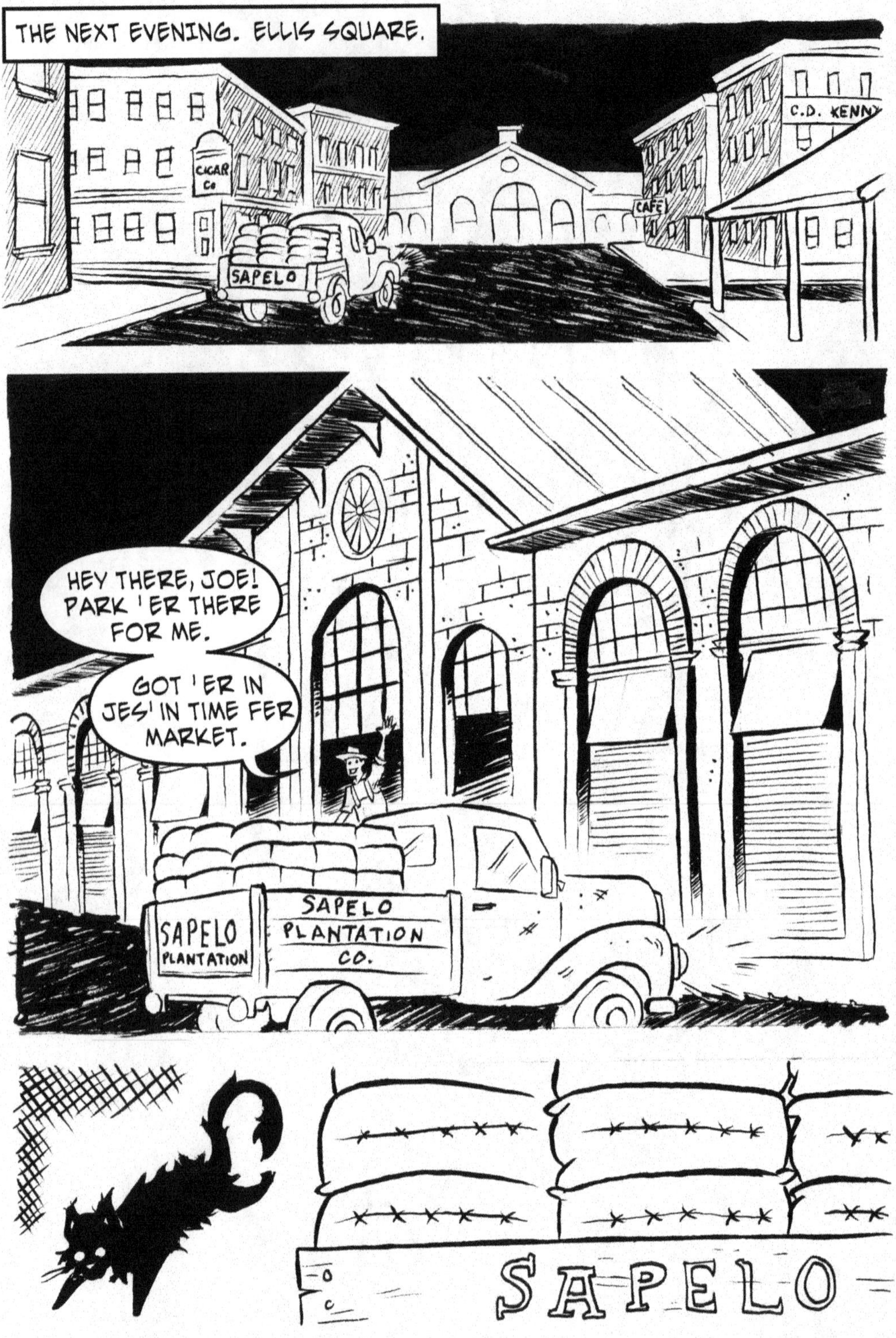
THE NEXT EVENING. ELLIS SQUARE.
CIGAR Co
C.D. KENNY
CAFÉ
SAPELO
HEY THERE, JOE! PARK 'ER THERE FOR ME.
GOT 'ER IN JES' IN TIME FER MARKET.
SAPELO PLANTATION
SAPELO PLANTATION CO.
SAPELO

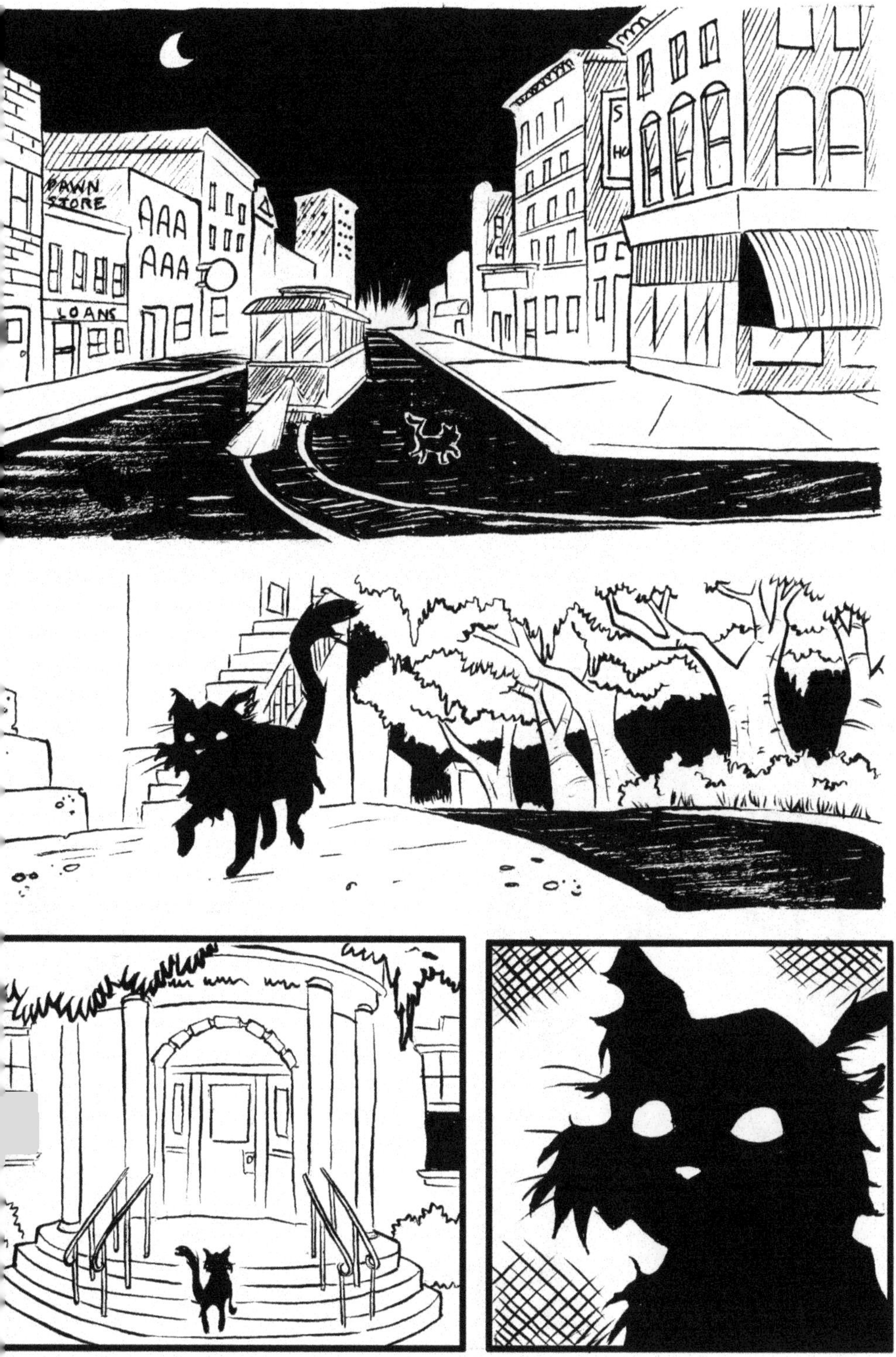
PAWN STORE
AAA
AAA
LOANS

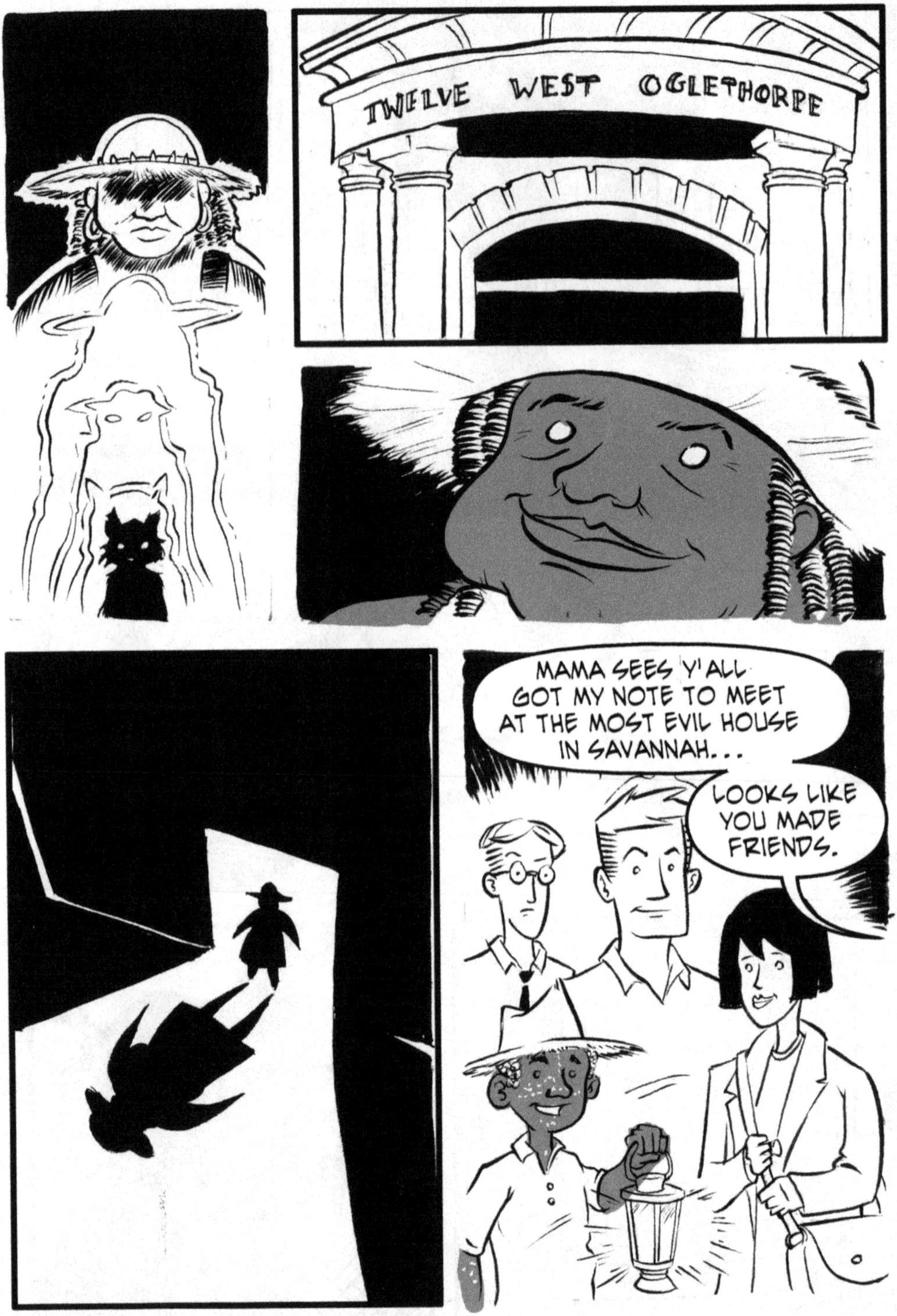
TWELVE WEST OGLETHORPE
MAMA SEES Y'ALL GOT MY NOTE TO MEET AT THE MOST EVIL HOUSE IN SAVANNAH...
LOOKS LIKE YOU MADE FRIENDS.

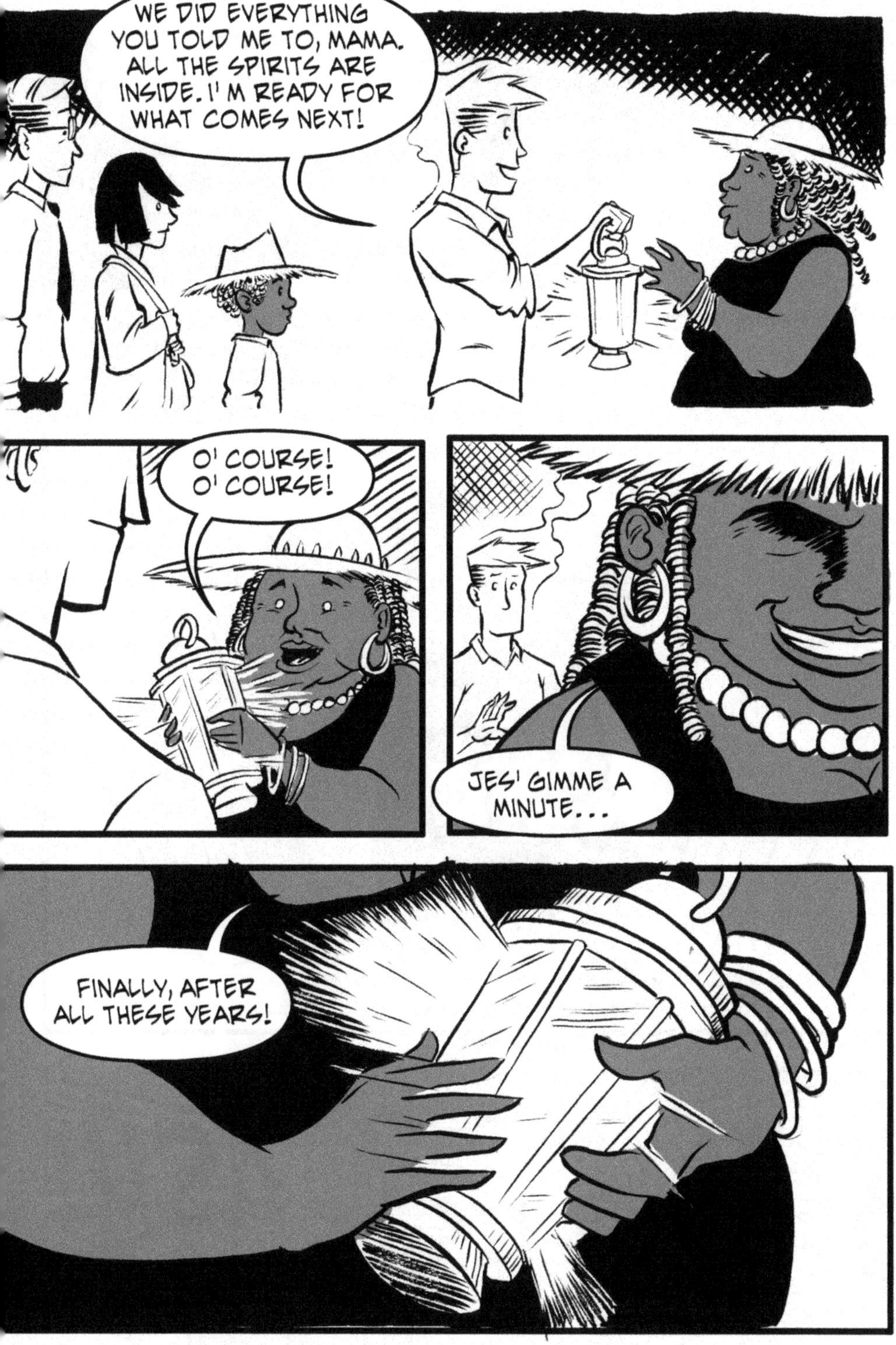
WE DID EVERYTHING YOU TOLD ME TO, MAMA. ALL THE SPIRITS ARE INSIDE. I'M READY FOR WHAT COMES NEXT!
O' COURSE! O' COURSE!
JES' GIMME A MINUTE...
FINALLY, AFTER ALL THESE YEARS!

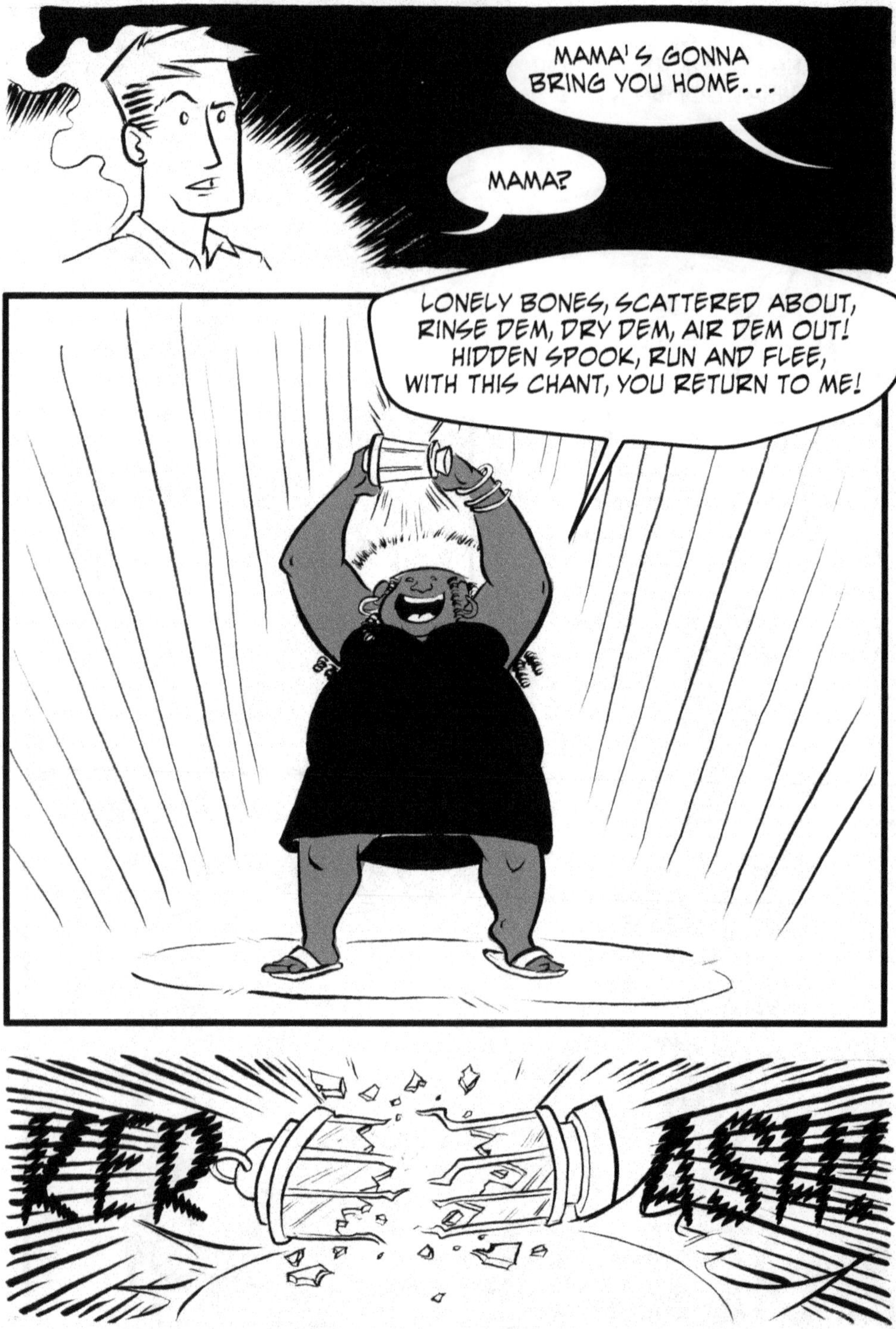
MAMA'S GONNA BRING YOU HOME...
MAMA?
LONELY BONES, SCATTERED ABOUT, RINSE DEM, DRY DEM, AIR DEM OUT! HIDDEN SPOOK, RUN AND FLEE, WITH THIS CHANT, YOU RETURN TO ME!
KER
ASH!

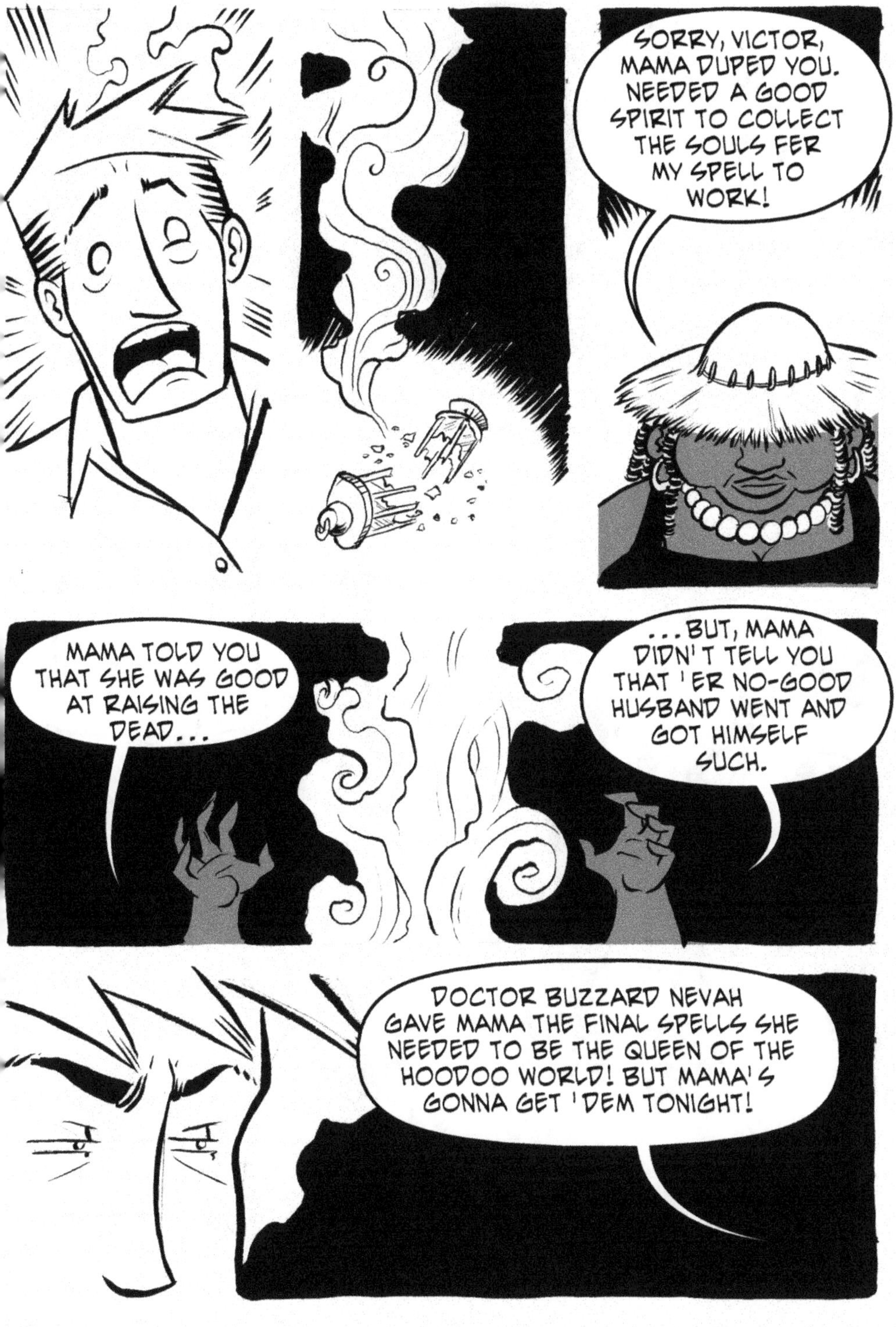
SORRY, VICTOR, MAMA DUPED YOU. NEEDED A GOOD SPIRIT TO COLLECT THE SOULS FER MY SPELL TO WORK!
MAMA TOLD YOU THAT SHE WAS GOOD AT RAISING THE DEAD...
...BUT, MAMA DIDN'T TELL YOU THAT 'ER NO-GOOD HUSBAND WENT AND GOT HIMSELF SUCH.
DOCTOR BUZZARD NEVAH GAVE MAMA THE FINAL SPELLS SHE NEEDED TO BE THE QUEEN OF THE HOODOO WORLD! BUT MAMA'S GONNA GET 'DEM TONIGHT!

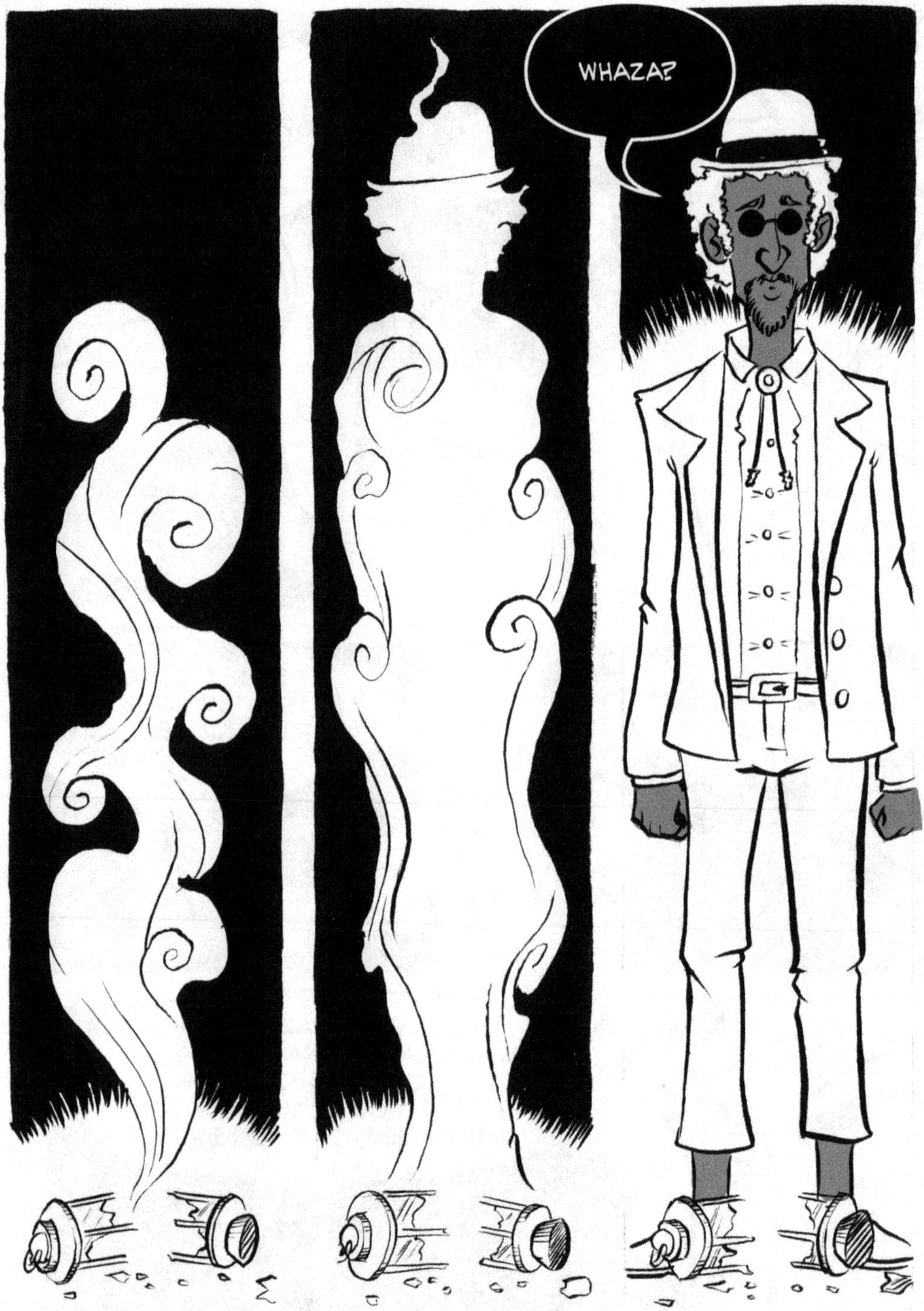
WHAZA?

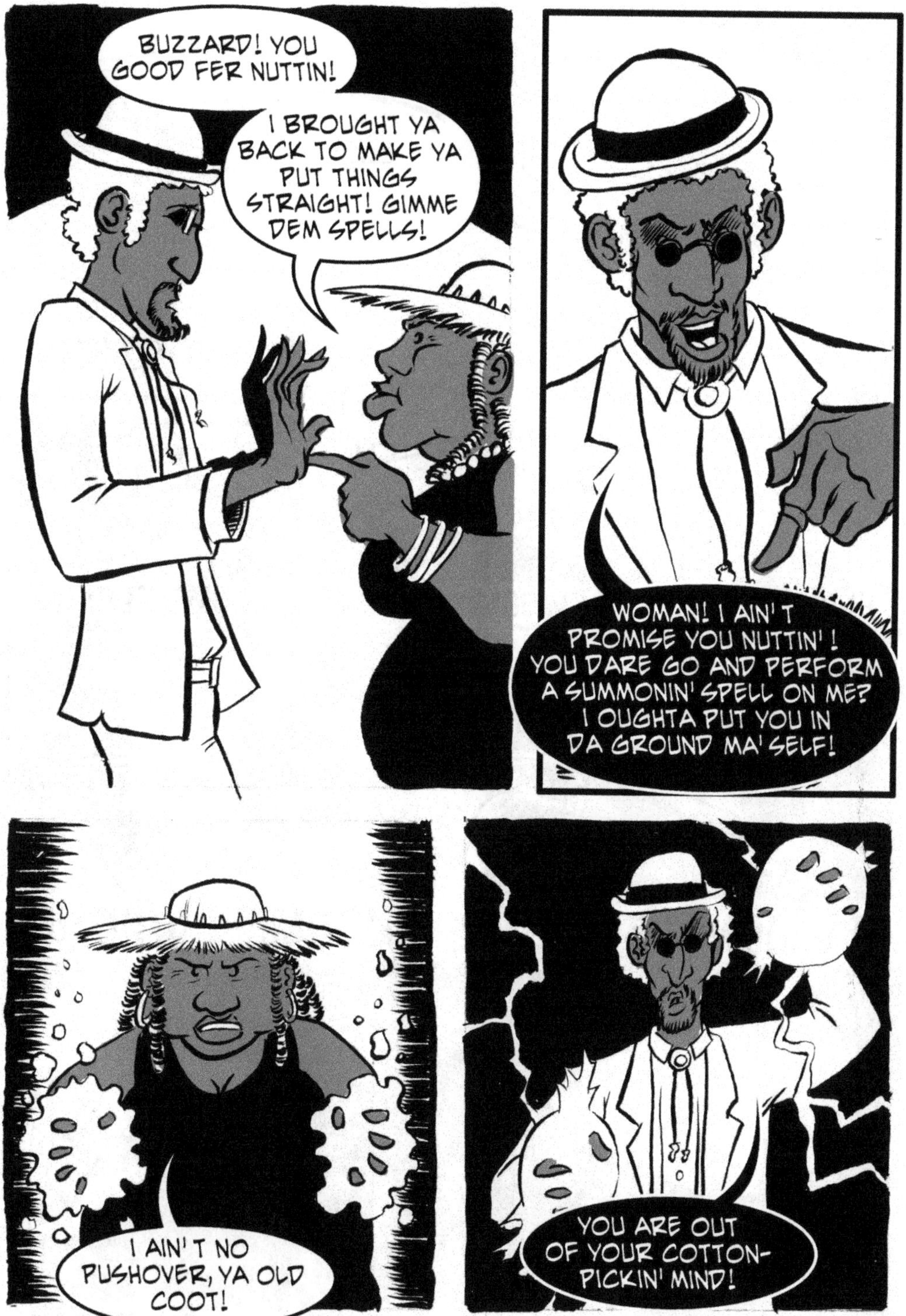

BUZZARD! YOU GOOD FER NUTTIN!
I BROUGHT YA BACK TO MAKE YA PUT THINGS STRAIGHT! GIMME DEM SPELLS!
WOMAN! I AIN' T PROMISE YOU NUTTIN' ! YOU DARE GO AND PERFORM A SUMMONIN' SPELL ON ME? I OUGHTA PUT YOU IN DA GROUND MA' SELF!
I AIN' T NO PUSHOVER, YA OLD COOT!
YOU ARE OUT OF YOUR COTTON-PICKIN' MIND!

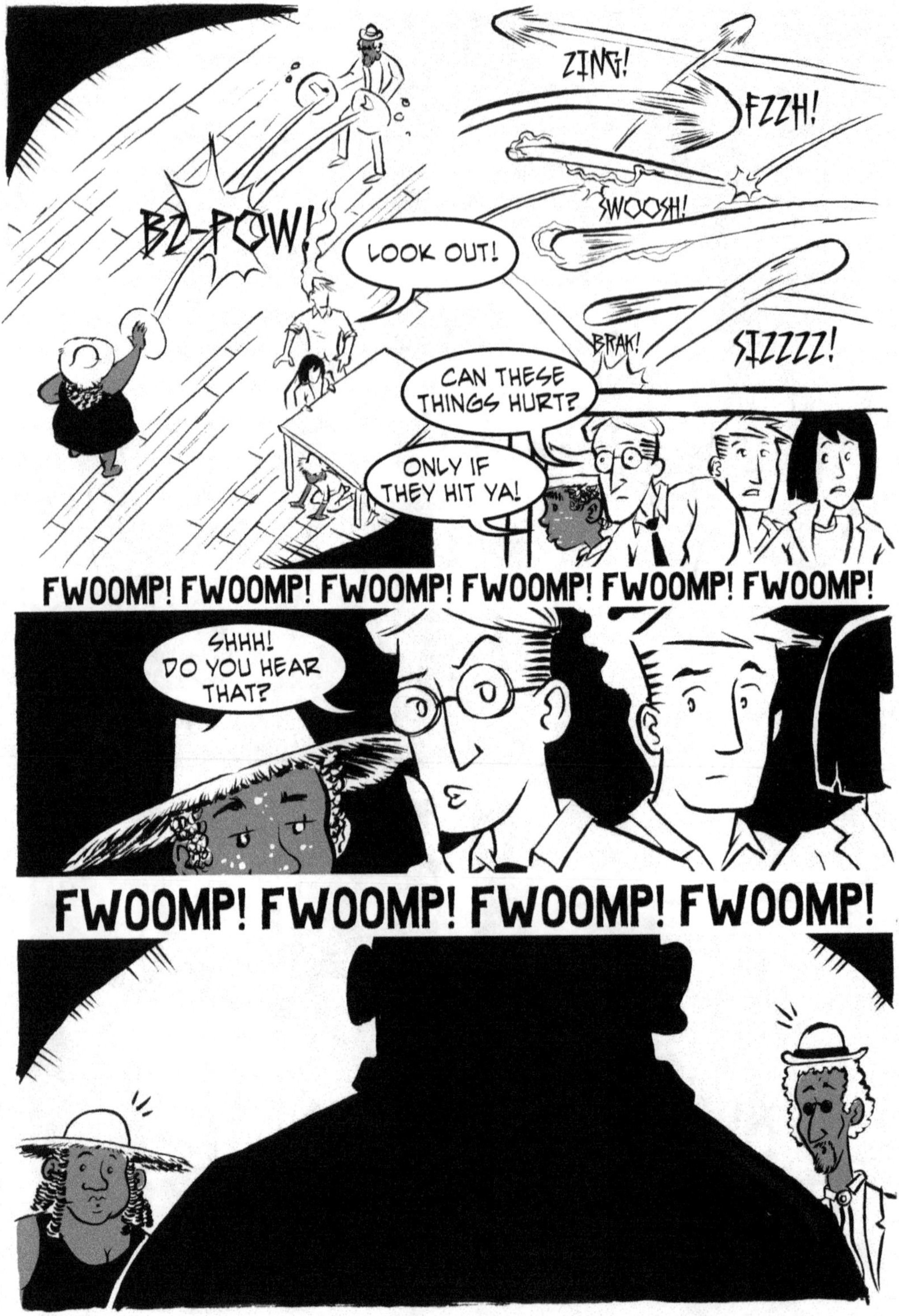
ZING!
FZZH!
BZ-POW!
SWOOSH!
LOOK OUT!
BRAK!
SIZZZZ!
CAN THESE THINGS HURT?
ONLY IF THEY HIT YA!
FWOOMP! FWOOMP! FWOOMP! FWOOMP! FWOOMP! FWOOMP!
SHHH! DO YOU HEAR THAT?
FWOOMP! FWOOMP! FWOOMP! FWOOMP!

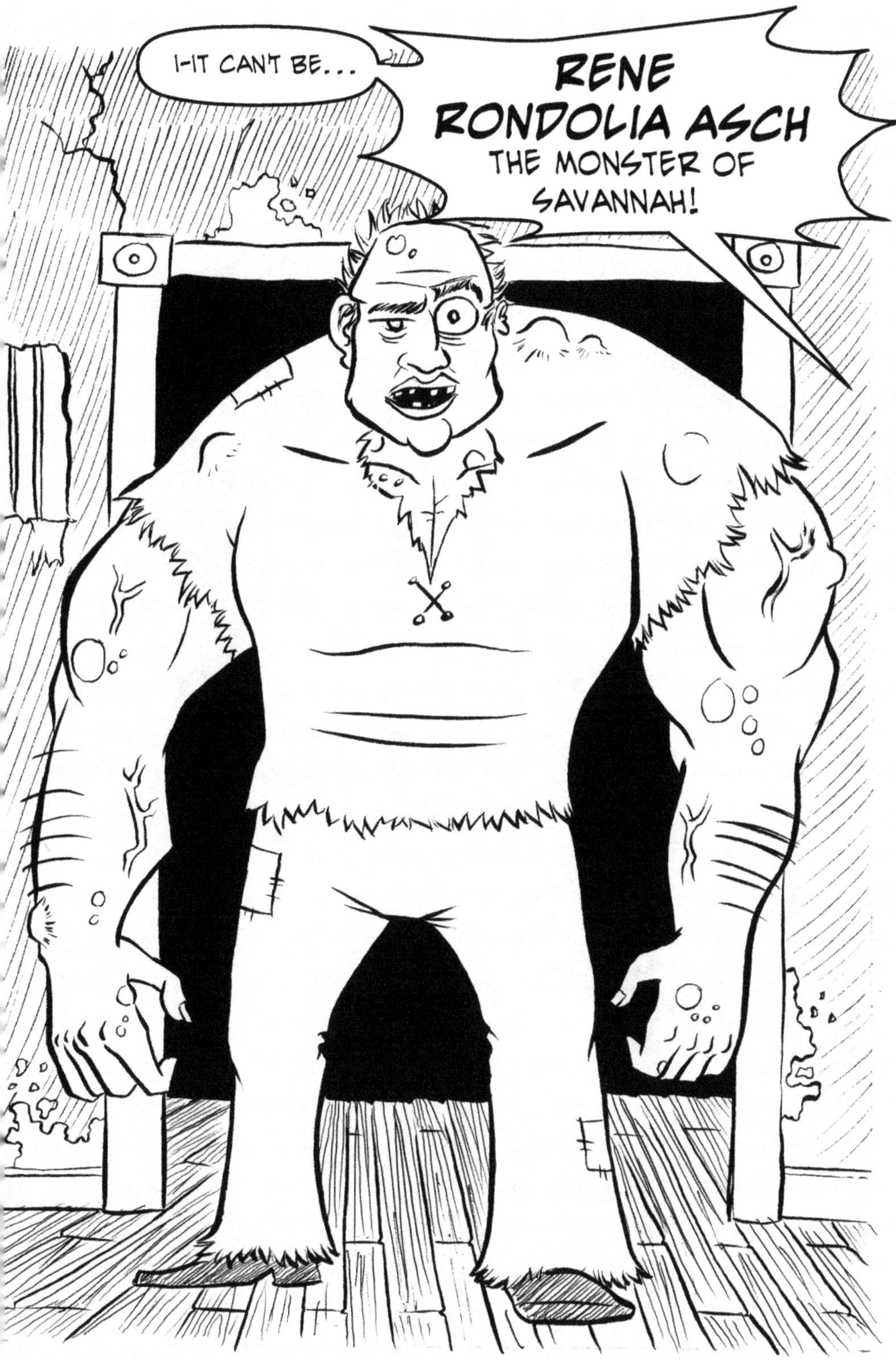
I-IT CAN'T BE...
RENE RONDOLIA ASCH
THE MONSTER OF SAVANNAH!

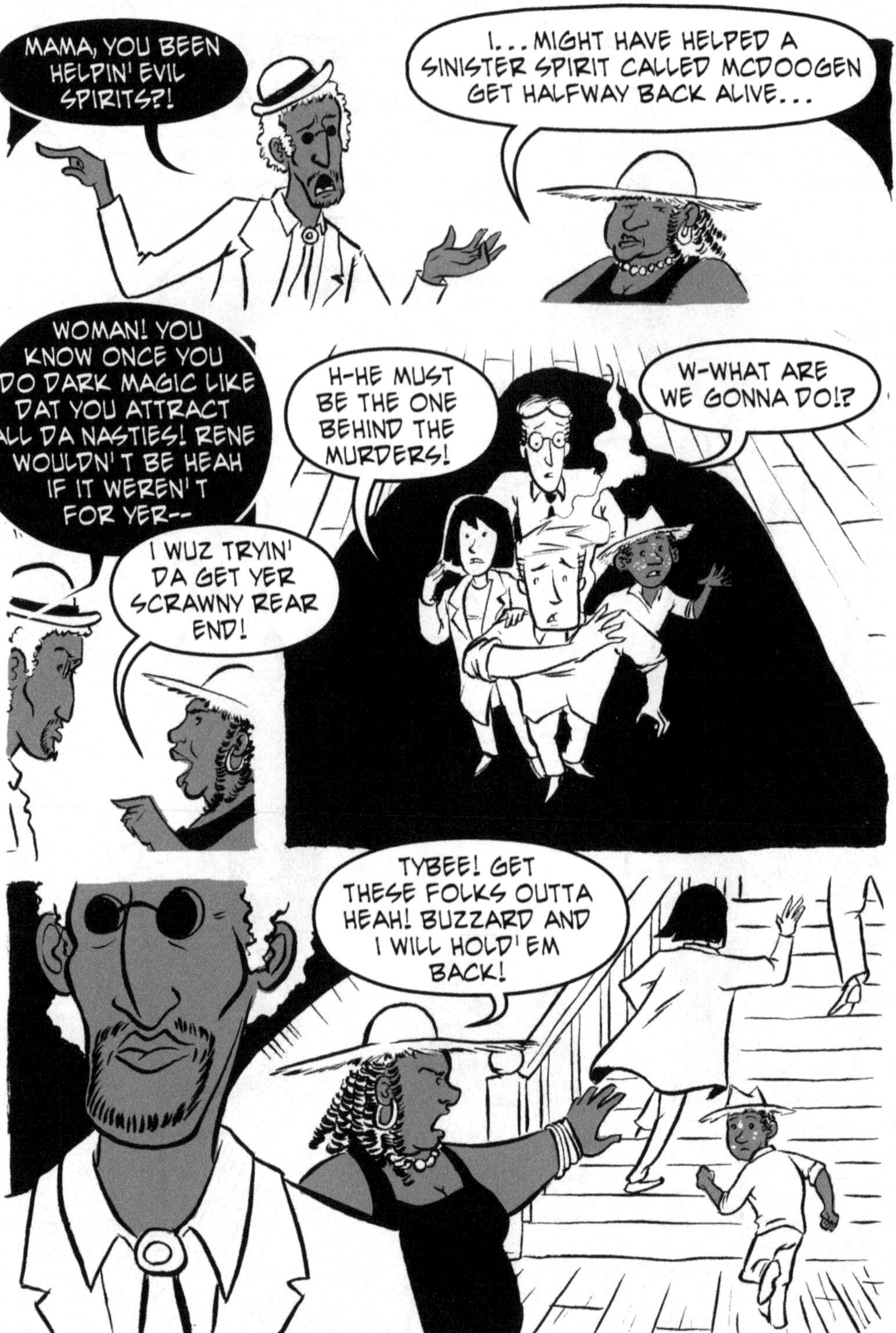
MAMA, YOU BEEN HELPIN' EVIL SPIRITS?!
I...MIGHT HAVE HELPED A SINISTER SPIRIT CALLED MCDOOGEN GET HALFWAY BACK ALIVE...
WOMAN! YOU KNOW ONCE YOU DO DARK MAGIC LIKE DAT YOU ATTRACT ALL DA NASTIES! RENE WOULDN'T BE HEAH IF IT WEREN'T FOR YER--
I WUZ TRYIN' DA GET YER SCRAWNY REAR END!
H-HE MUST BE THE ONE BEHIND THE MURDERS!
W-WHAT ARE WE GONNA DO!?
TYBEE! GET THESE FOLKS OUTTA HEAH! BUZZARD AND I WILL HOLD'EM BACK!

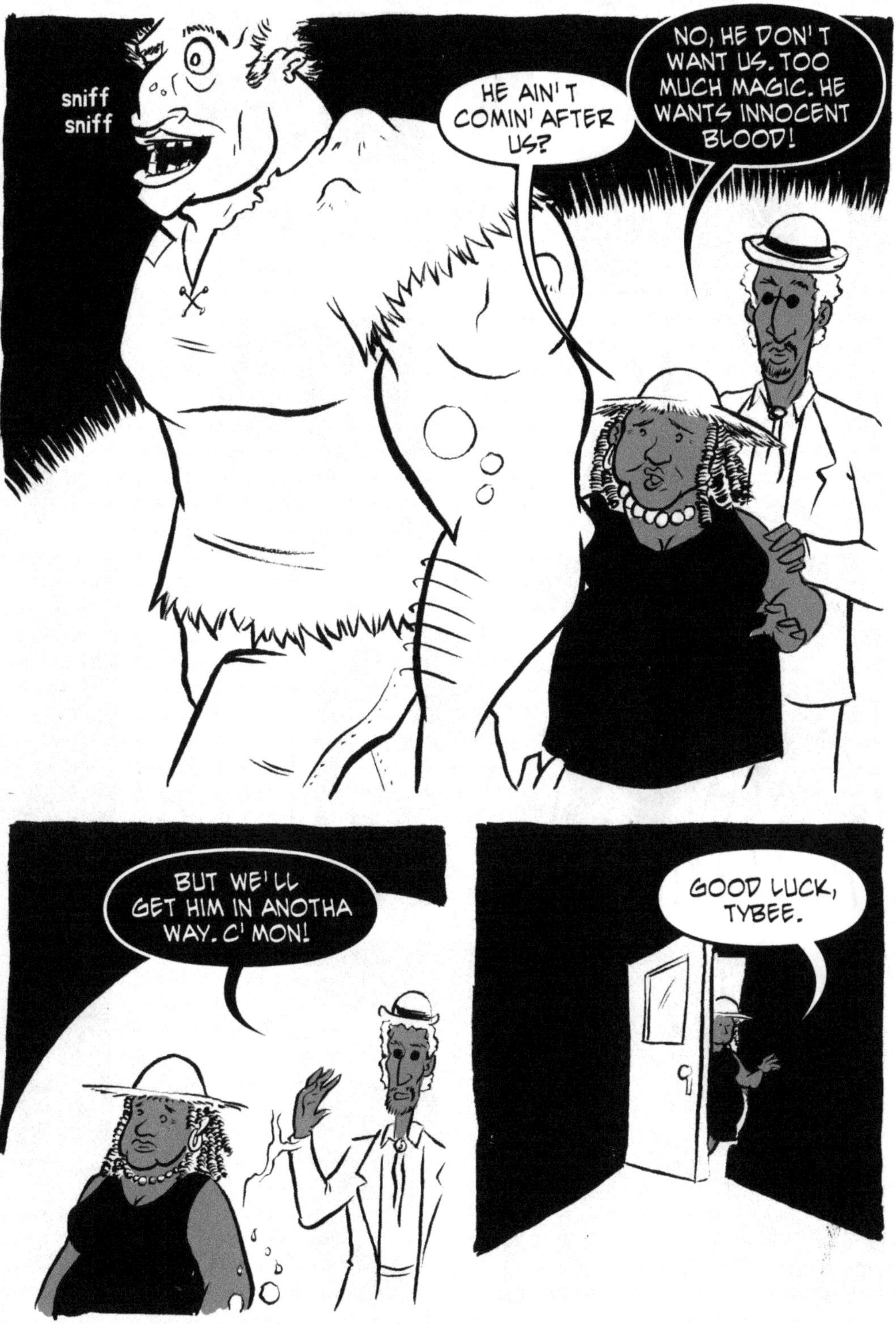
sniff
sniff
HE AIN'T COMIN' AFTER US?
NO, HE DON'T WANT US. TOO MUCH MAGIC. HE WANTS INNOCENT BLOOD!
BUT WE'LL GET HIM IN ANOTHA WAY. C'MON!
GOOD LUCK, TYBEE.

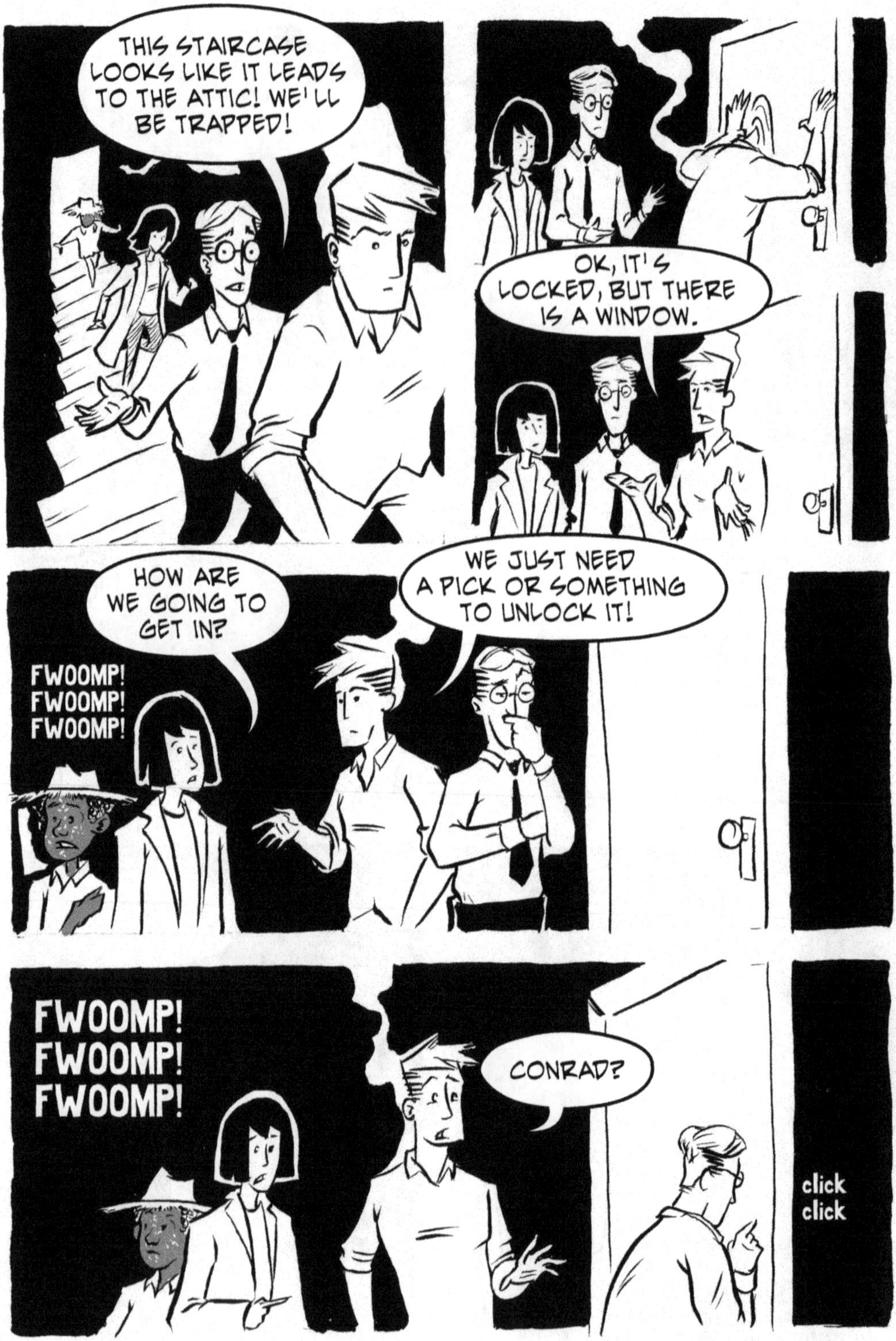

THIS STAIRCASE LOOKS LIKE IT LEADS TO THE ATTIC! WE'LL BE TRAPPED!
OK, IT'S LOCKED, BUT THERE IS A WINDOW.
HOW ARE WE GOING TO GET IN?
WE JUST NEED A PICK OR SOMETHING TO UNLOCK IT!
FWOOMP! FWOOMP! FWOOMP!
FWOOMP! FWOOMP! FWOOMP!
CONRAD?
click click

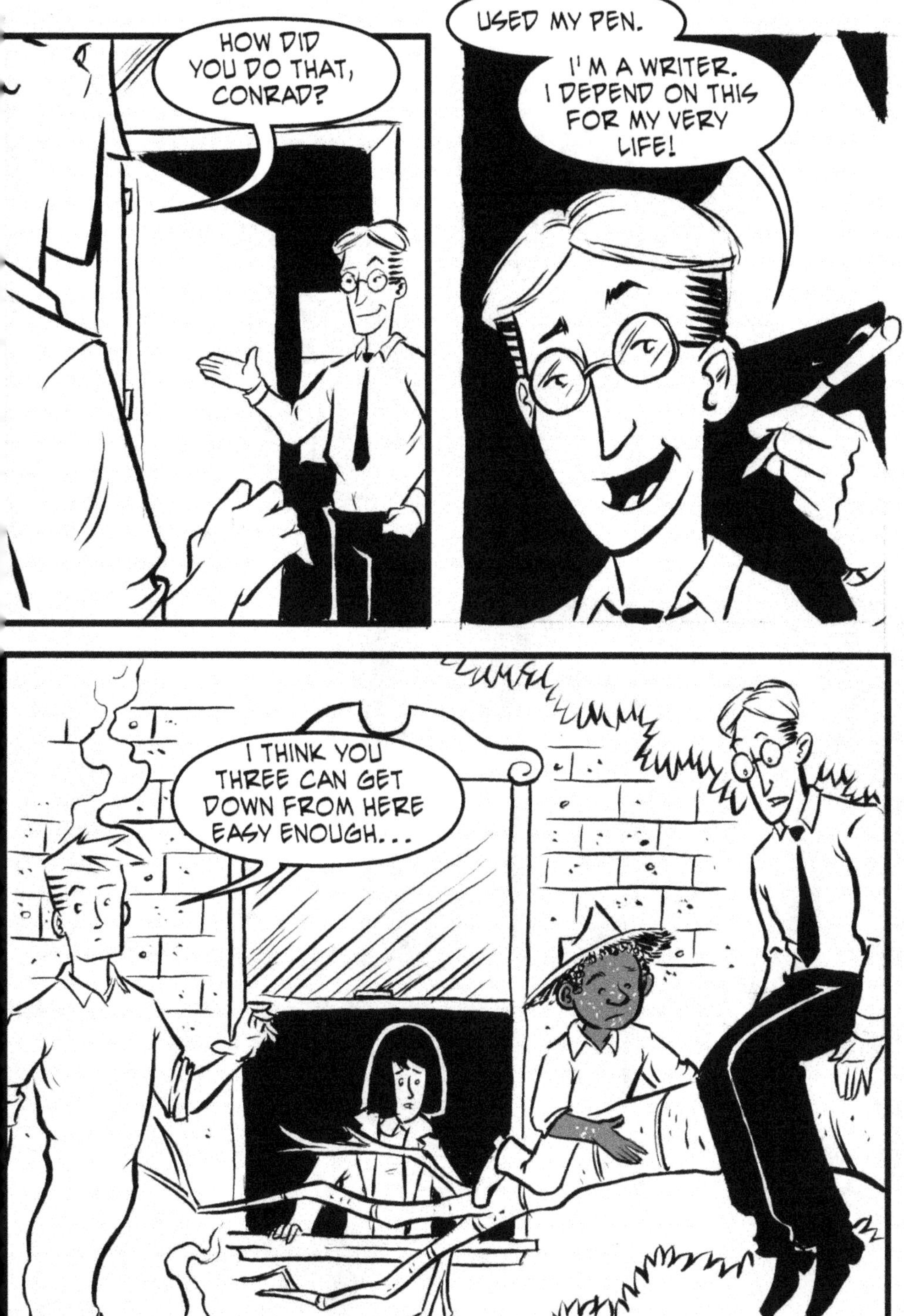
HOW DID YOU DO THAT, CONRAD?
USED MY PEN.
I'M A WRITER. I DEPEND ON THIS FOR MY VERY LIFE!
I THINK YOU THREE CAN GET DOWN FROM HERE EASY ENOUGH...

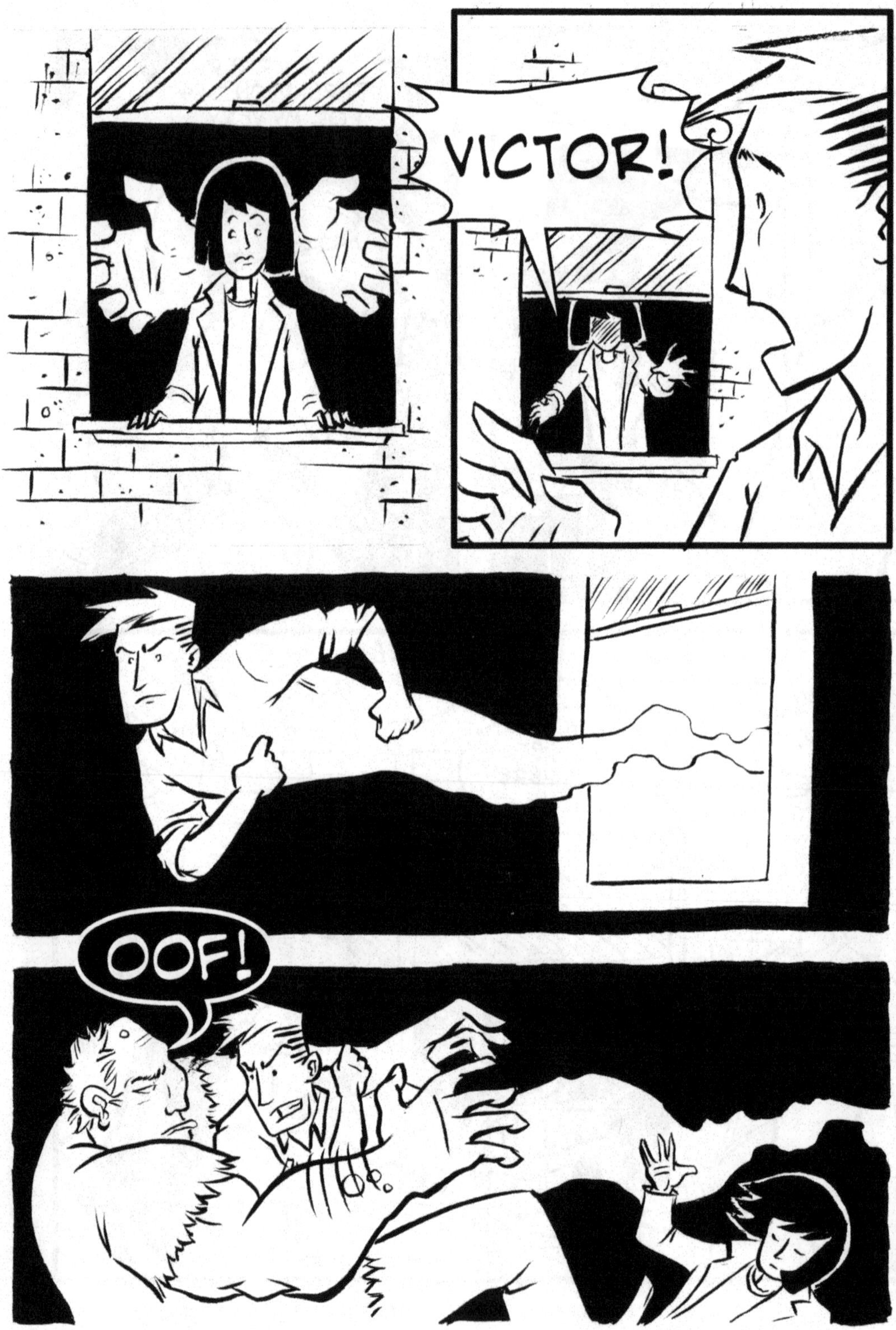
VICTOR!
OOF!

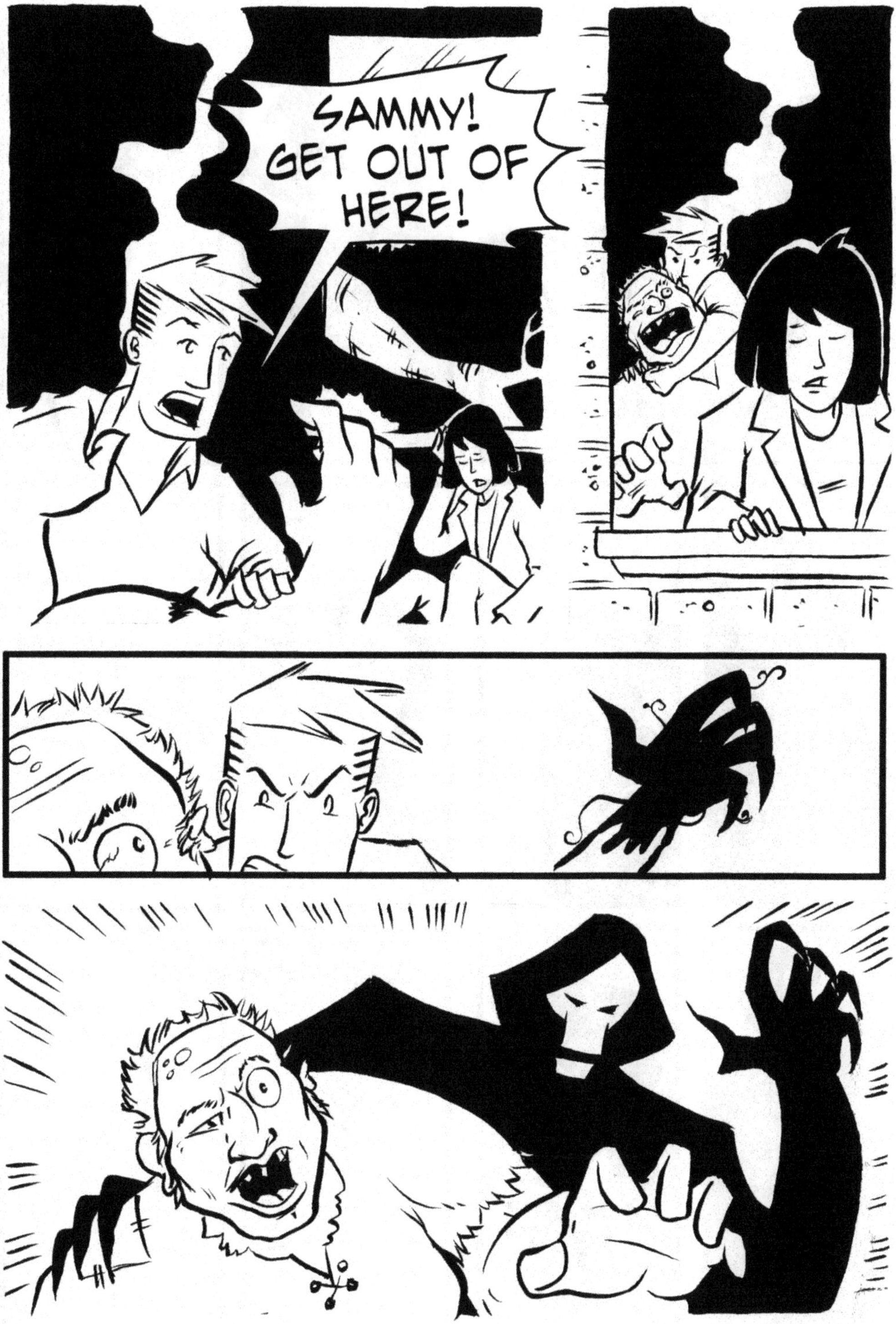
SAMMY! GET OUT OF HERE!

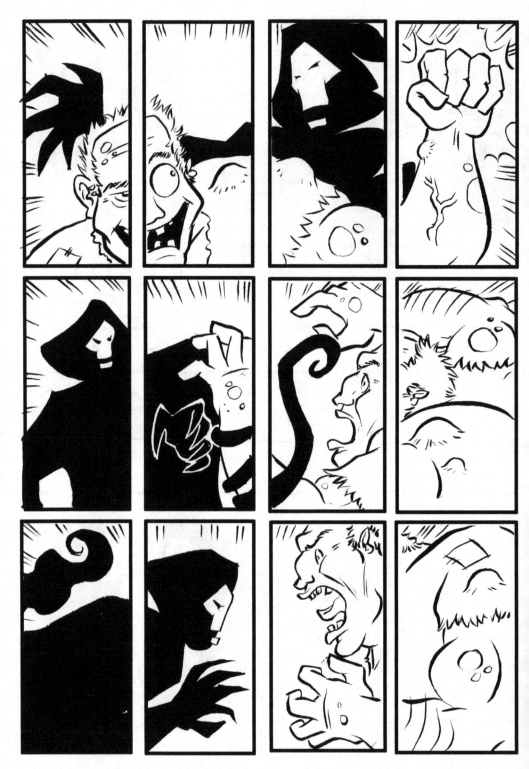

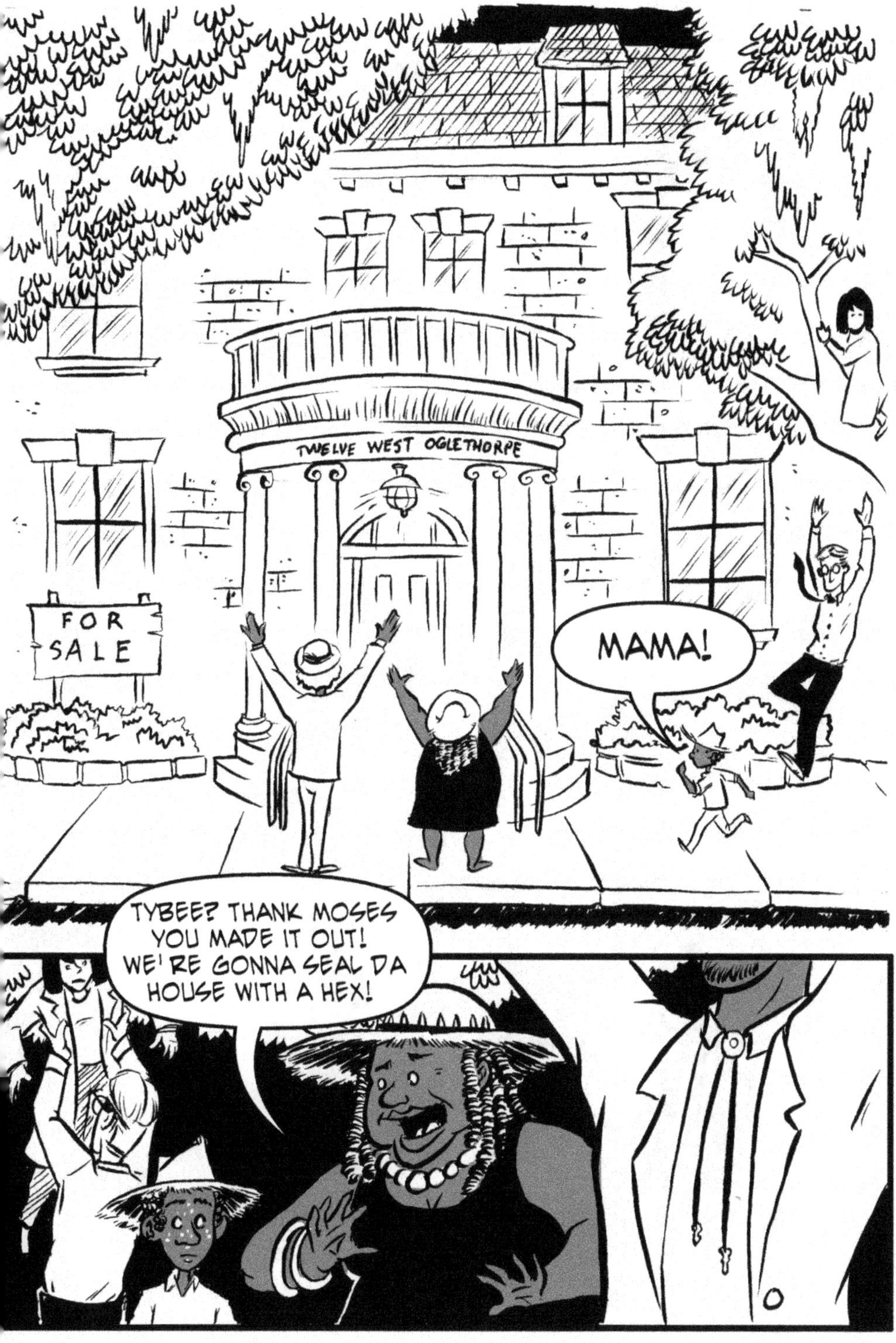
TWELVE WEST OGLETHORPE
FOR SALE
MAMA!
TYBEE? THANK MOSES YOU MADE IT OUT! WE' RE GONNA SEAL DA HOUSE WITH A HEX!

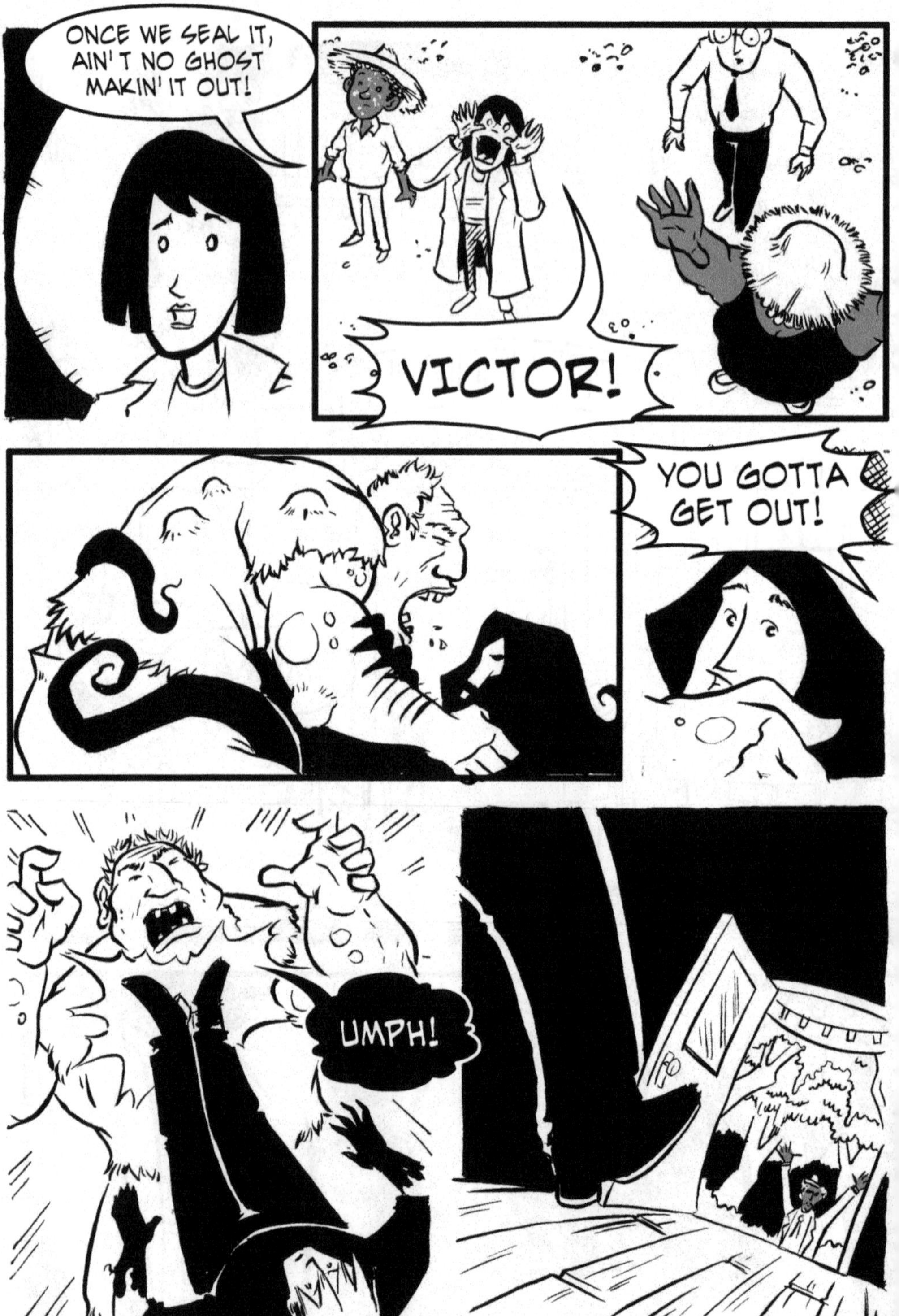
ONCE WE SEAL IT, AIN'T NO GHOST MAKIN' IT OUT!
VICTOR!
YOU GOTTA GET OUT!
UMPH!

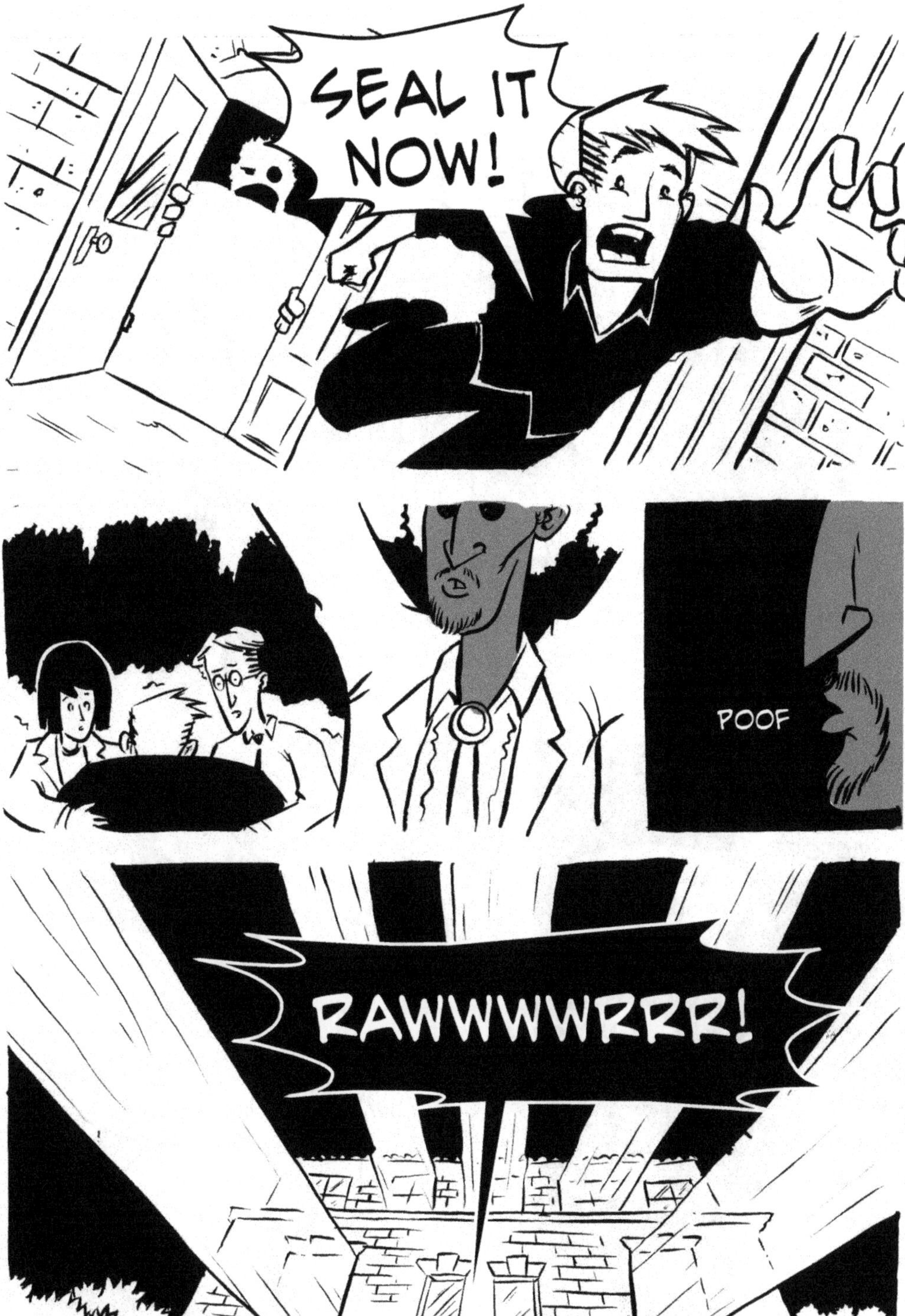
SEAL IT NOW!
POOF
RAWWWWRRR!

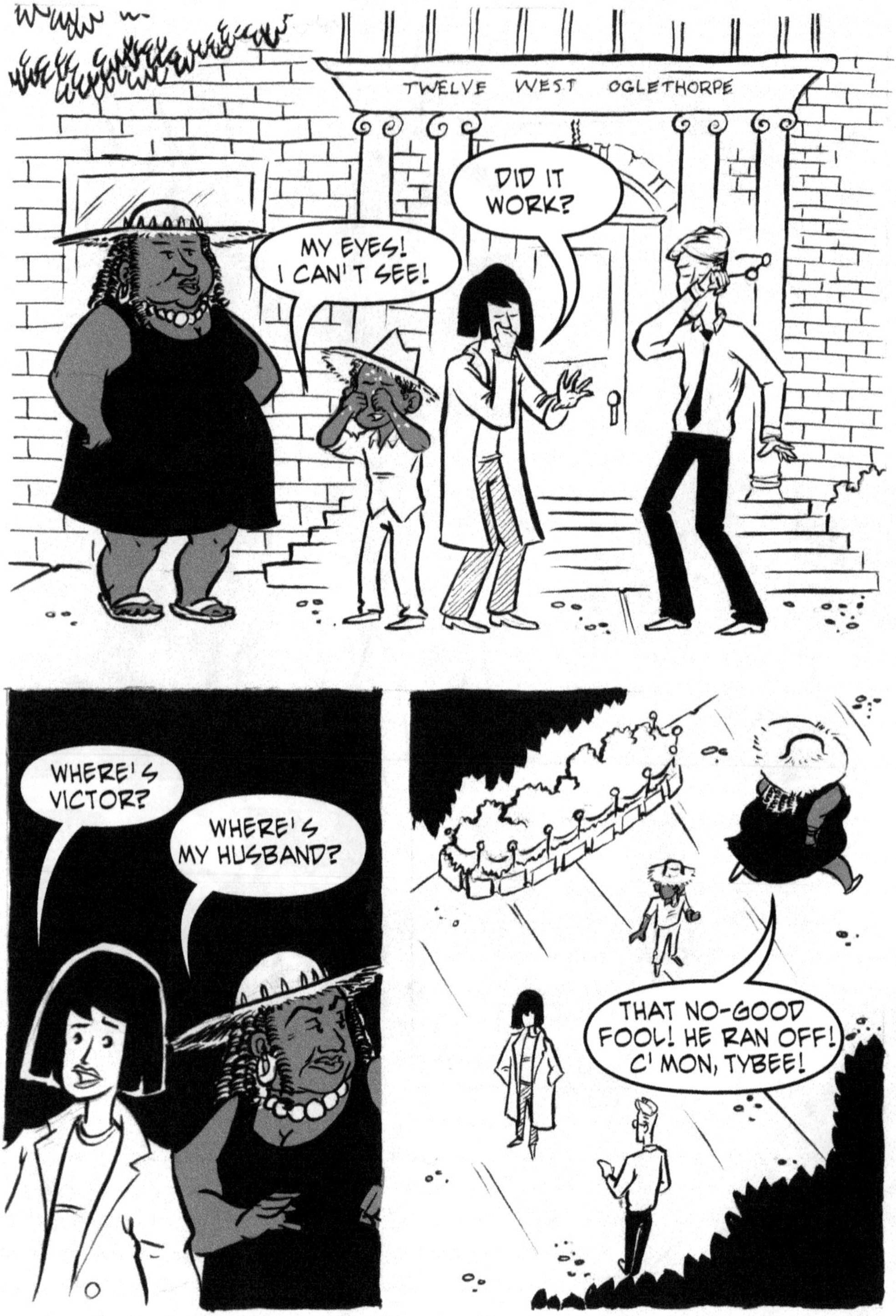
TWELVE WEST OGLETHORPE
MY EYES! I CAN'T SEE!
DID IT WORK?
WHERE'S VICTOR?
WHERE'S MY HUSBAND?
THAT NO-GOOD FOOL! HE RAN OFF! C'MON, TYBEE!

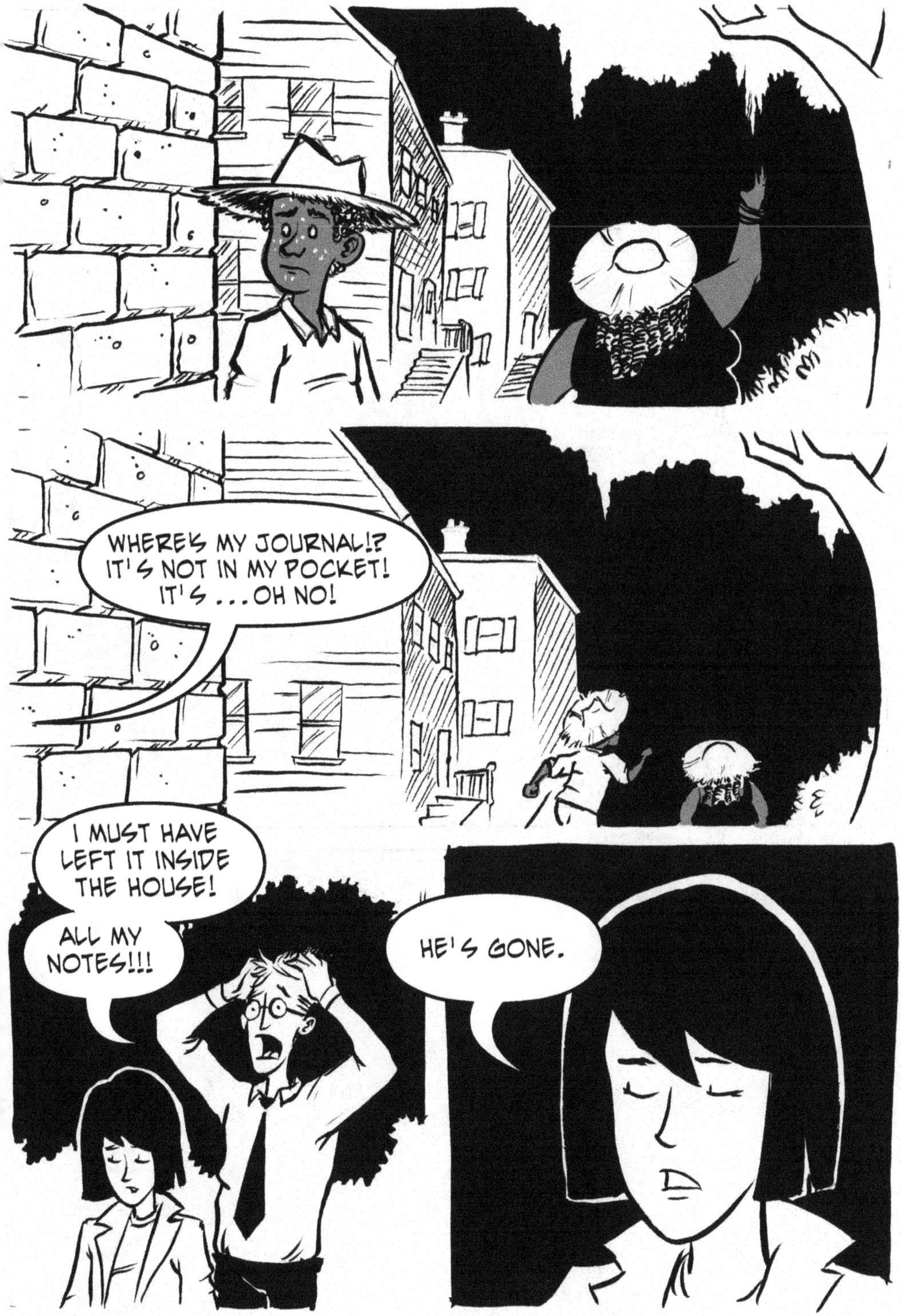
WHERE'S MY JOURNAL!? IT'S NOT IN MY POCKET! IT'S . . . OH NO!
I MUST HAVE LEFT IT INSIDE THE HOUSE!
ALL MY NOTES!!!
HE'S GONE.

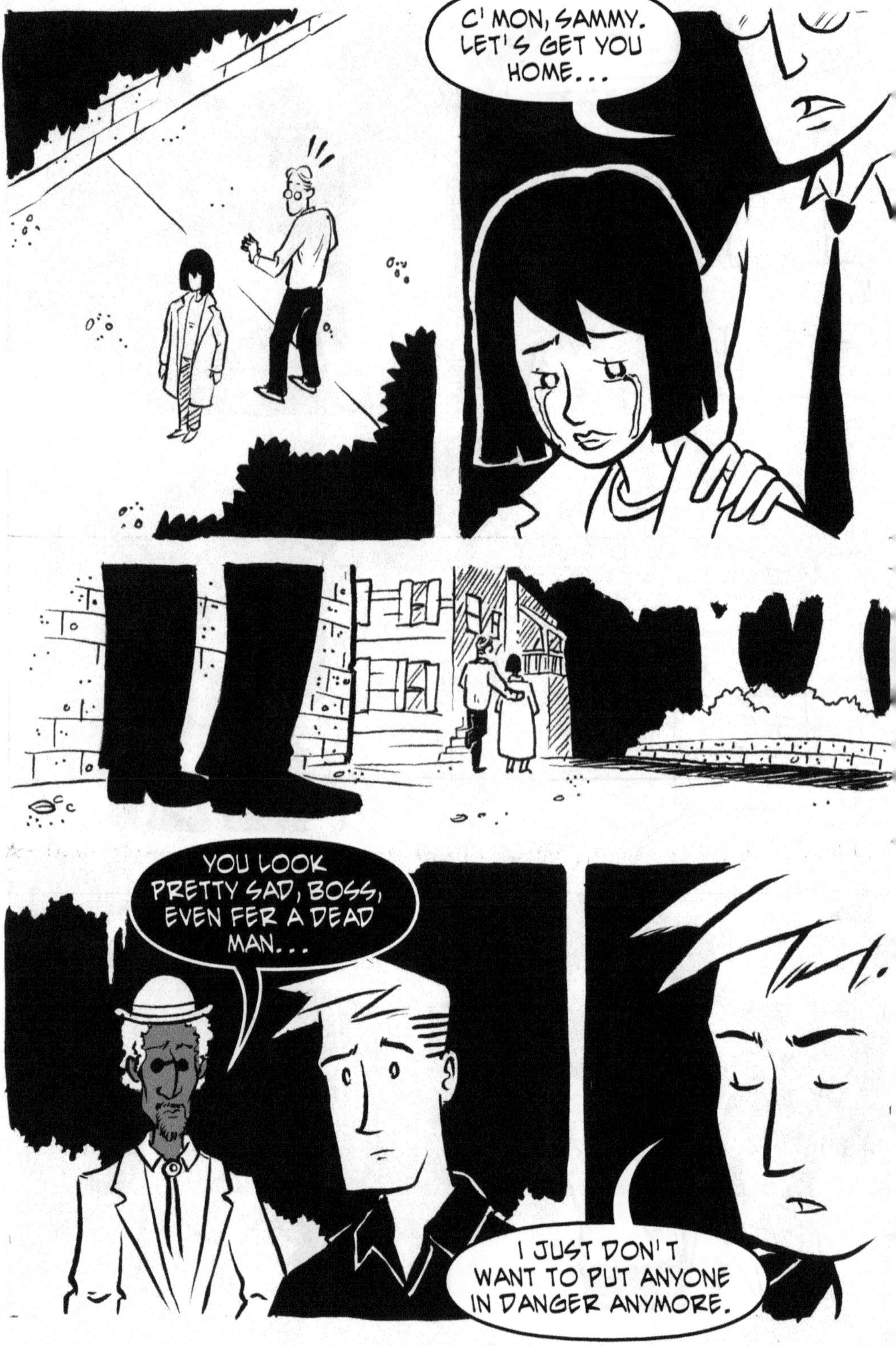
C' MON, SAMMY. LET'S GET YOU HOME...
YOU LOOK PRETTY SAD, BOSS, EVEN FER A DEAD MAN...
I JUST DON'T WANT TO PUT ANYONE IN DANGER ANYMORE.

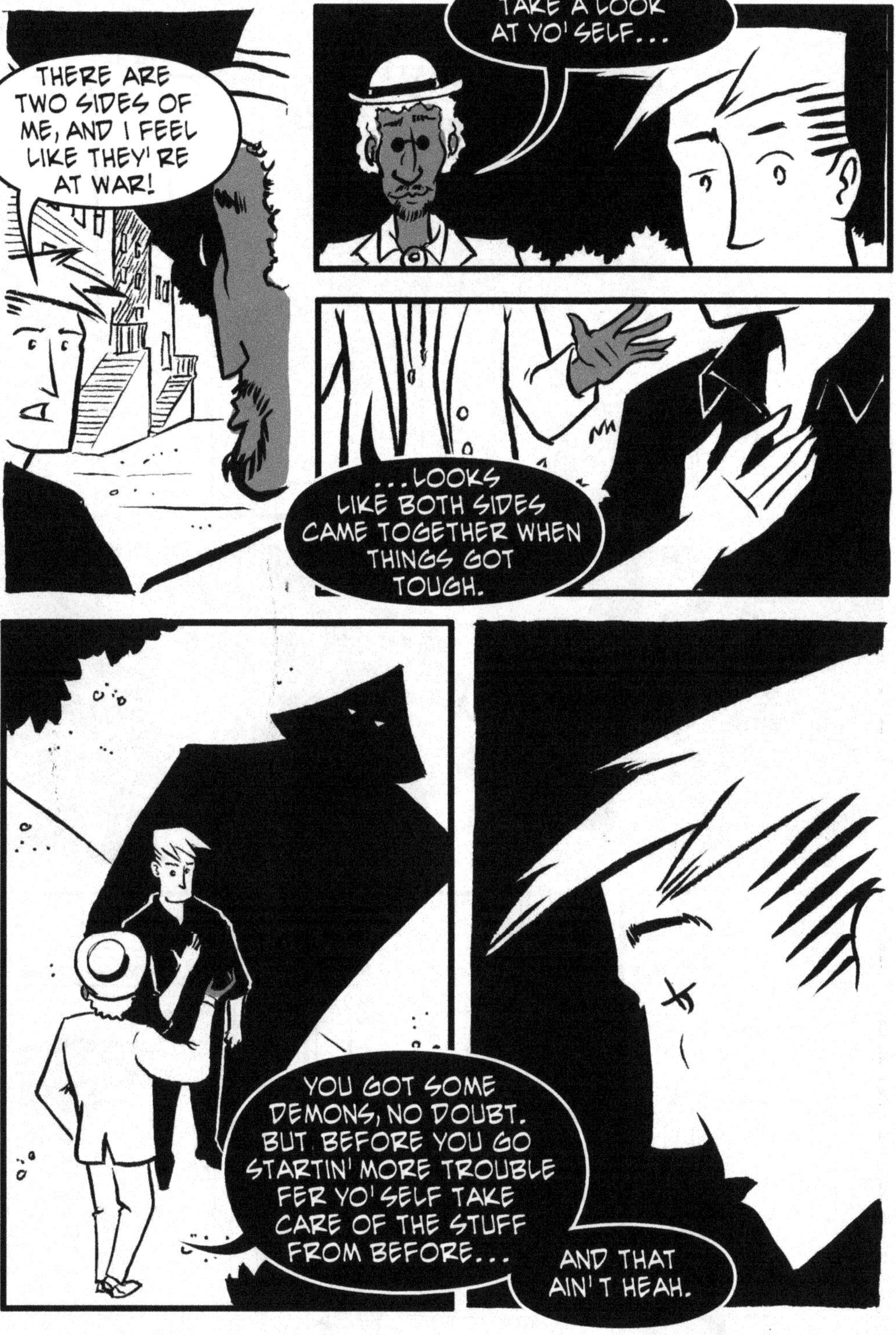
THERE ARE TWO SIDES OF ME, AND I FEEL LIKE THEY'RE AT WAR!
TAKE A LOOK AT YO' SELF...
...LOOKS LIKE BOTH SIDES CAME TOGETHER WHEN THINGS GOT TOUGH.
YOU GOT SOME DEMONS, NO DOUBT. BUT BEFORE YOU GO STARTIN' MORE TROUBLE FER YO' SELF TAKE CARE OF THE STUFF FROM BEFORE...
AND THAT AIN'T HEAH.

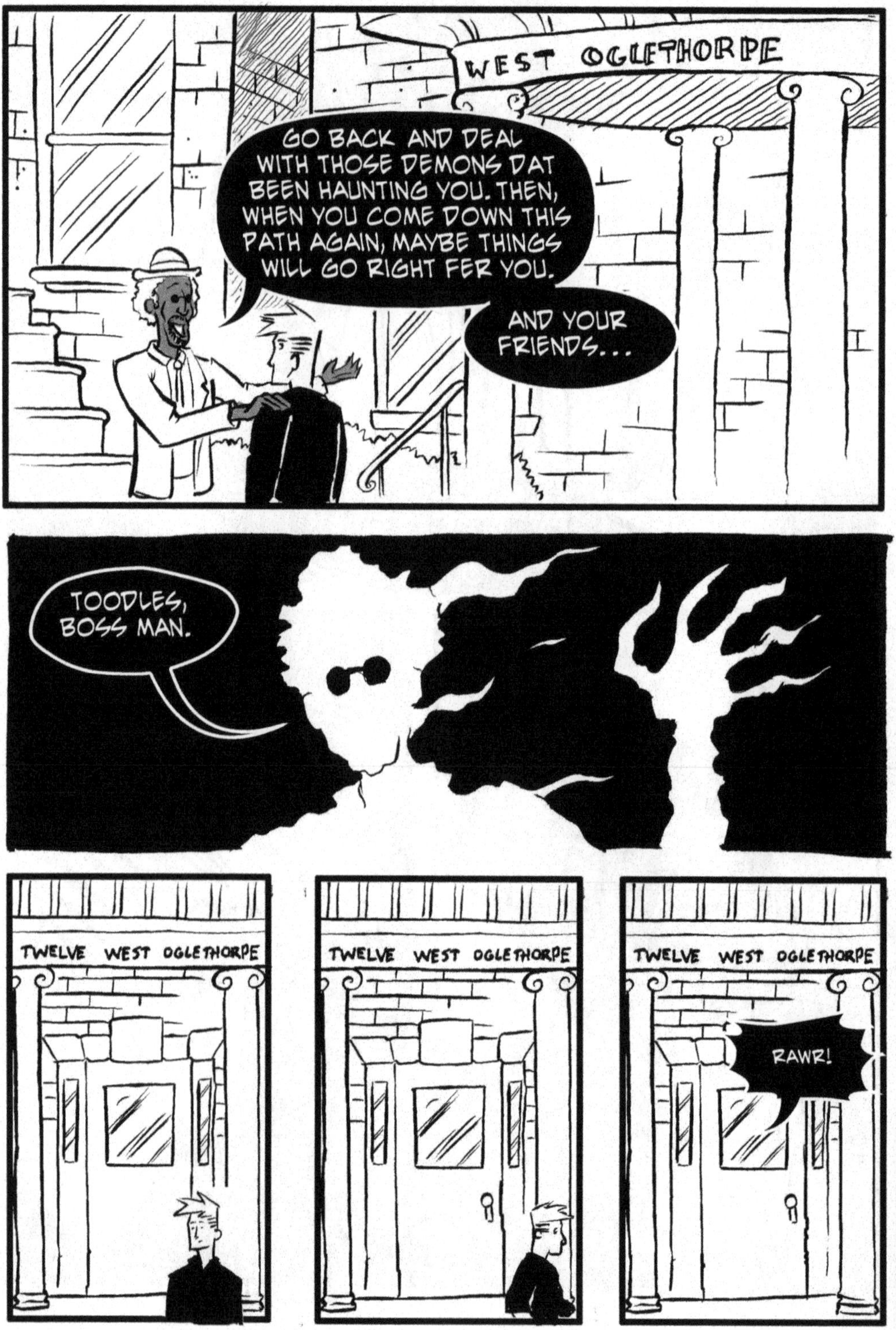
WEST OGLETHORPE
GO BACK AND DEAL WITH THOSE DEMONS DAT BEEN HAUNTING YOU. THEN, WHEN YOU COME DOWN THIS PATH AGAIN, MAYBE THINGS WILL GO RIGHT FER YOU.
AND YOUR FRIENDS...
TOODLES, BOSS MAN.
TWELVE WEST OGLETHORPE
TWELVE WEST OGLETHORPE
TWELVE WEST OGLETHORPE
RAWR!

CHAPTER
15

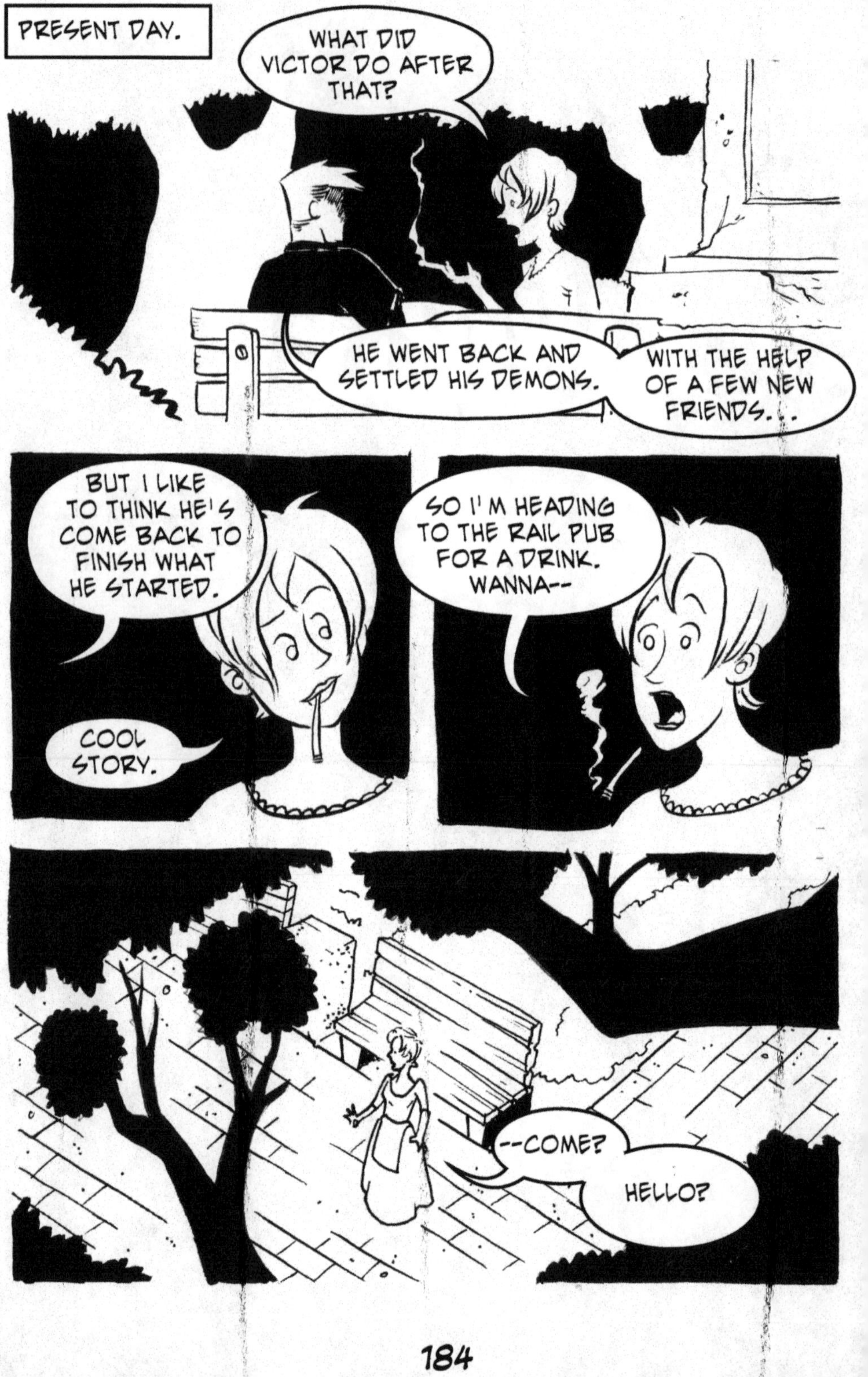
PRESENT DAY.
WHAT DID VICTOR DO AFTER THAT?
HE WENT BACK AND SETTLED HIS DEMONS.
WITH THE HELP OF A FEW NEW FRIENDS. . .
BUT I LIKE TO THINK HE'S COME BACK TO FINISH WHAT HE STARTED.
COOL STORY.
SO I'M HEADING TO THE RAIL PUB FOR A DRINK. WANNA--
--COME?
HELLO?

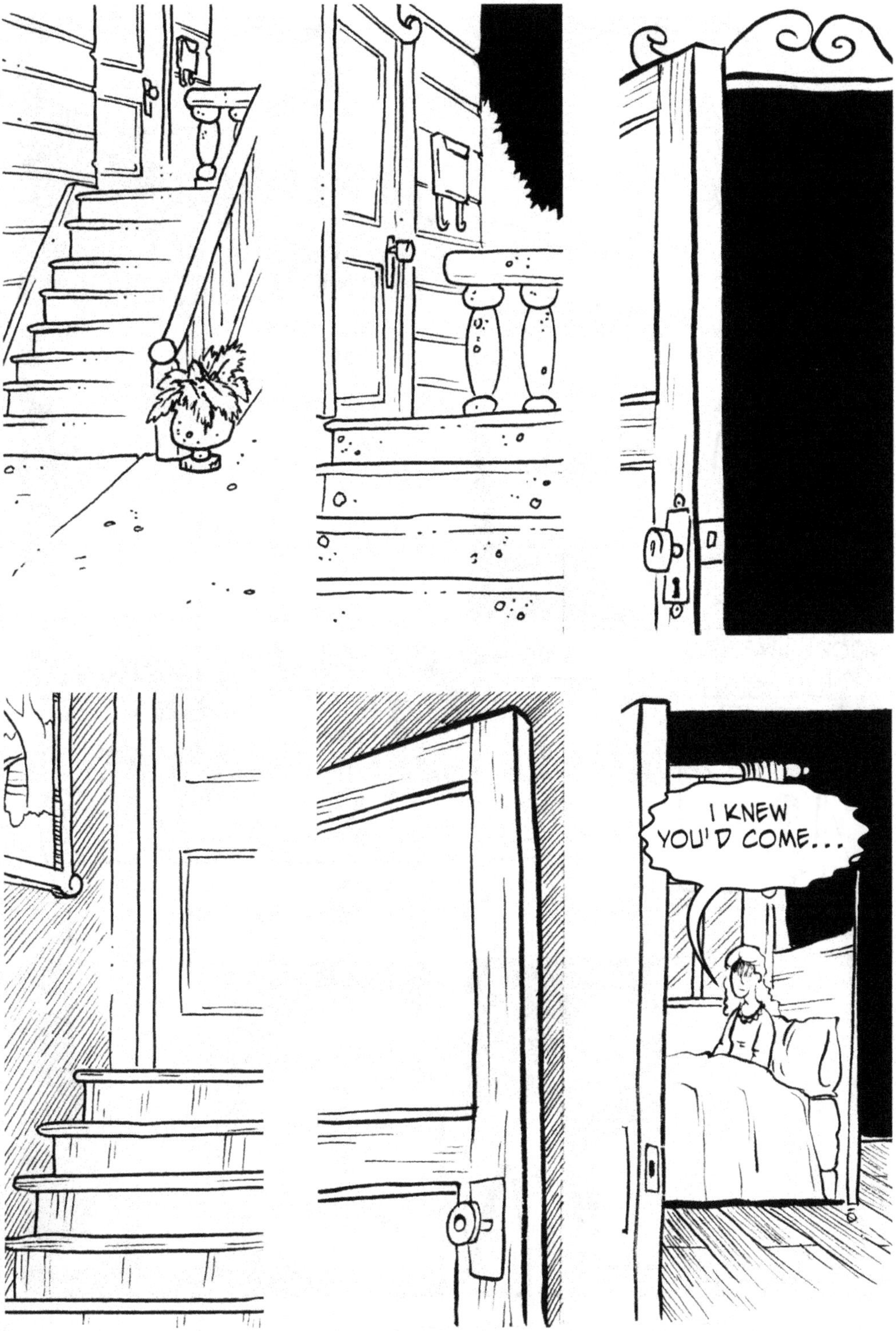
I KNEW YOU'D COME...

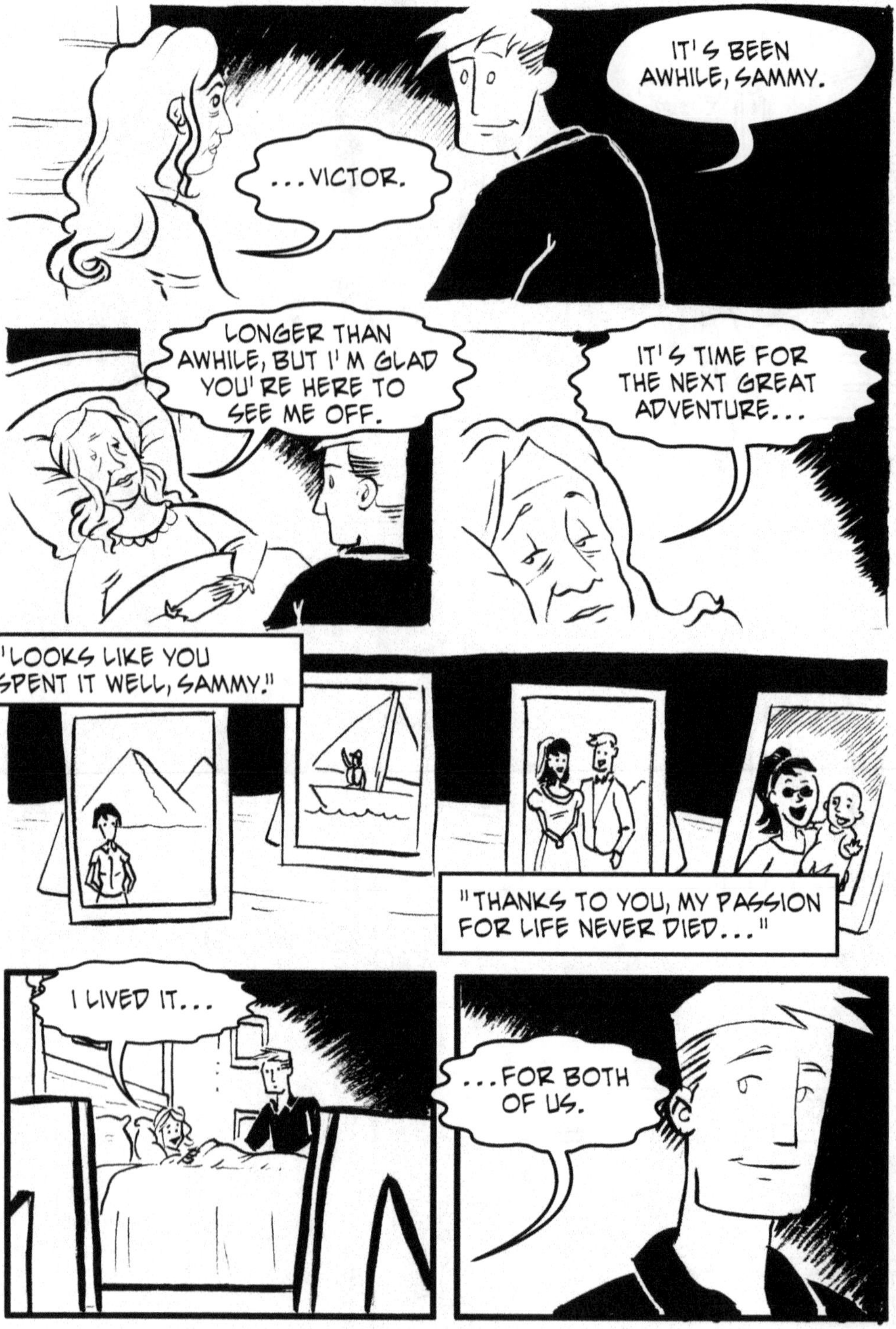

IT'S BEEN AWHILE, SAMMY.
...VICTOR.
LONGER THAN AWHILE, BUT I'M GLAD YOU'RE HERE TO SEE ME OFF.
IT'S TIME FOR THE NEXT GREAT ADVENTURE...
"LOOKS LIKE YOU SPENT IT WELL, SAMMY."
"THANKS TO YOU, MY PASSION FOR LIFE NEVER DIED..."
I LIVED IT...
...FOR BOTH OF US.

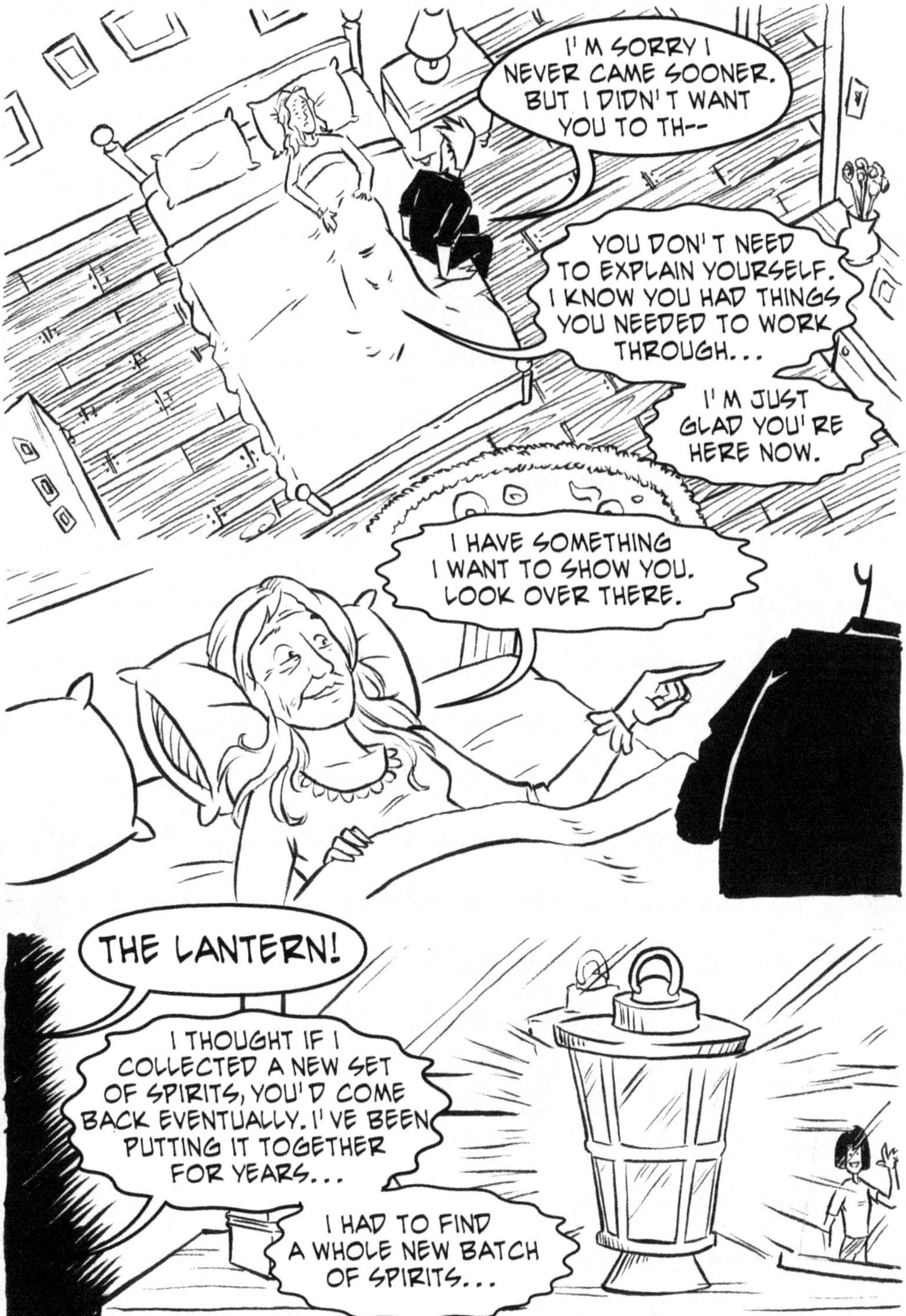
I'M SORRY I NEVER CAME SOONER. BUT I DIDN'T WANT YOU TO TH--
YOU DON'T NEED TO EXPLAIN YOURSELF. I KNOW YOU HAD THINGS YOU NEEDED TO WORK THROUGH...
I'M JUST GLAD YOU'RE HERE NOW.
I HAVE SOMETHING I WANT TO SHOW YOU. LOOK OVER THERE.
THE LANTERN!
I THOUGHT IF I COLLECTED A NEW SET OF SPIRITS, YOU'D COME BACK EVENTUALLY. I'VE BEEN PUTTING IT TOGETHER FOR YEARS...
I HAD TO FIND A WHOLE NEW BATCH OF SPIRITS...

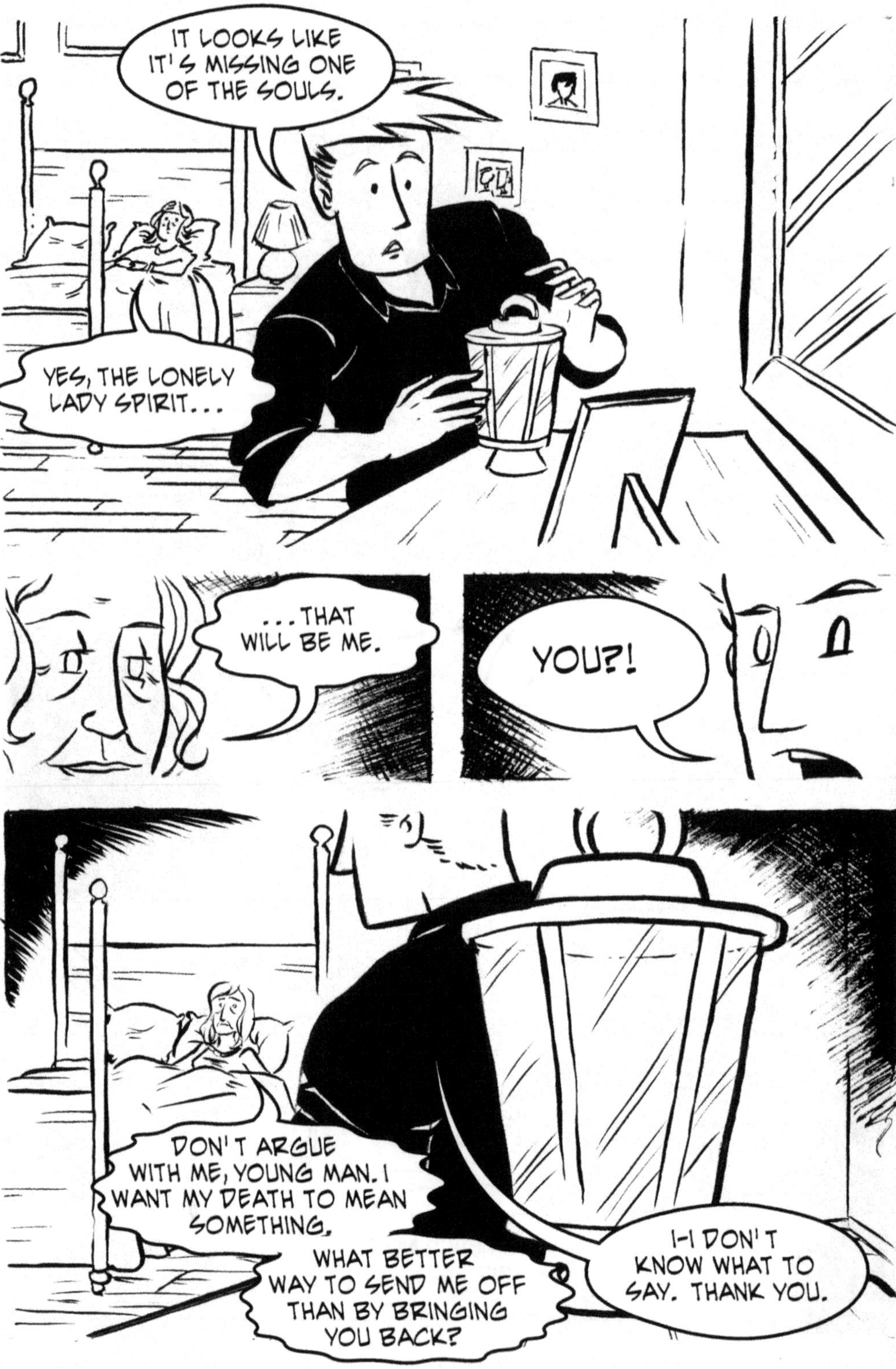
IT LOOKS LIKE IT'S MISSING ONE OF THE SOULS.
YES, THE LONELY LADY SPIRIT...
...THAT WILL BE ME.
YOU?!
DON'T ARGUE WITH ME, YOUNG MAN. I WANT MY DEATH TO MEAN SOMETHING.
WHAT BETTER WAY TO SEND ME OFF THAN BY BRINGING YOU BACK?
I-I DON'T KNOW WHAT TO SAY. THANK YOU.

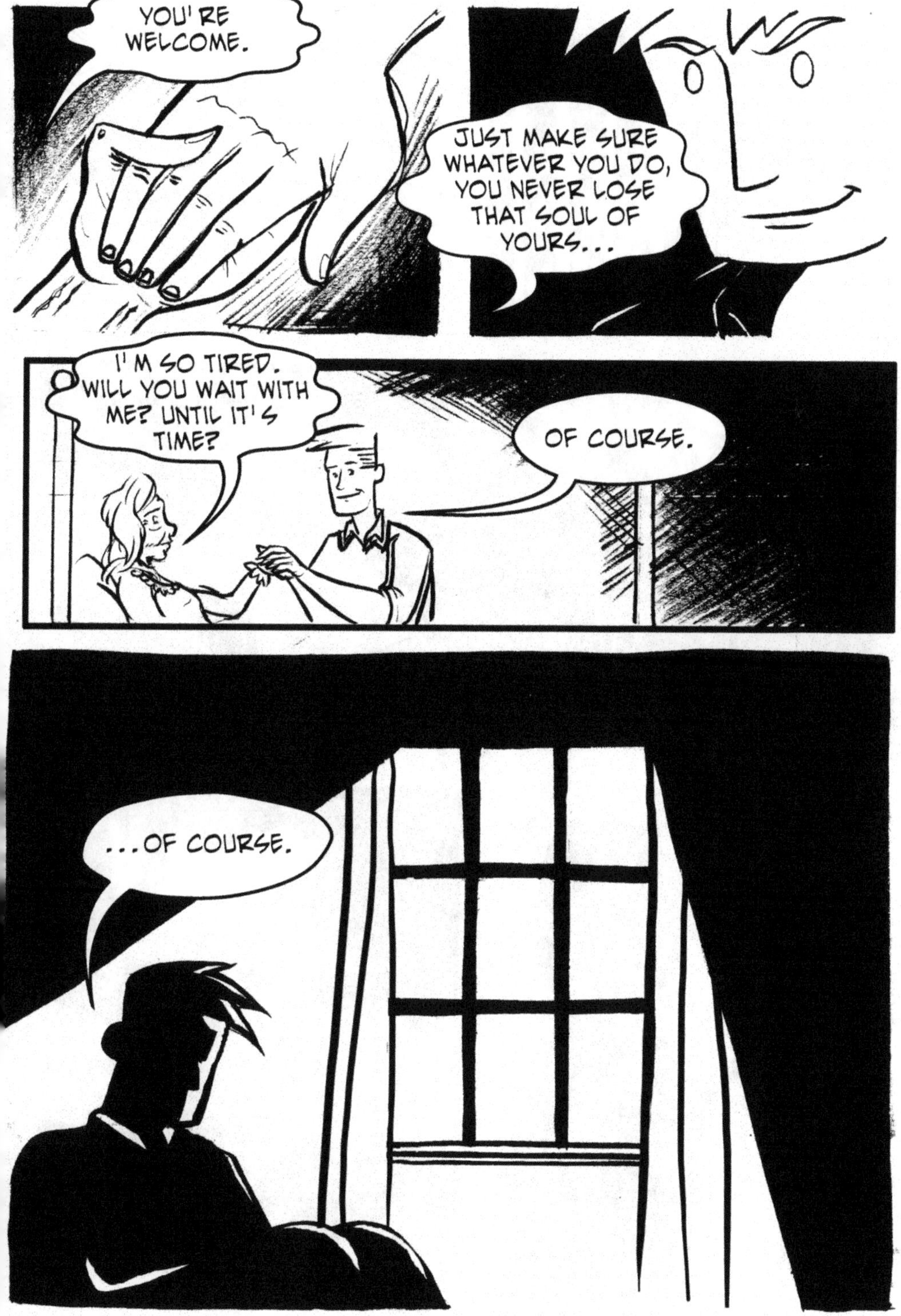
YOU'RE WELCOME.
JUST MAKE SURE WHATEVER YOU DO, YOU NEVER LOSE THAT SOUL OF YOURS...
I'M SO TIRED. WILL YOU WAIT WITH ME? UNTIL IT'S TIME?
OF COURSE.
...OF COURSE.

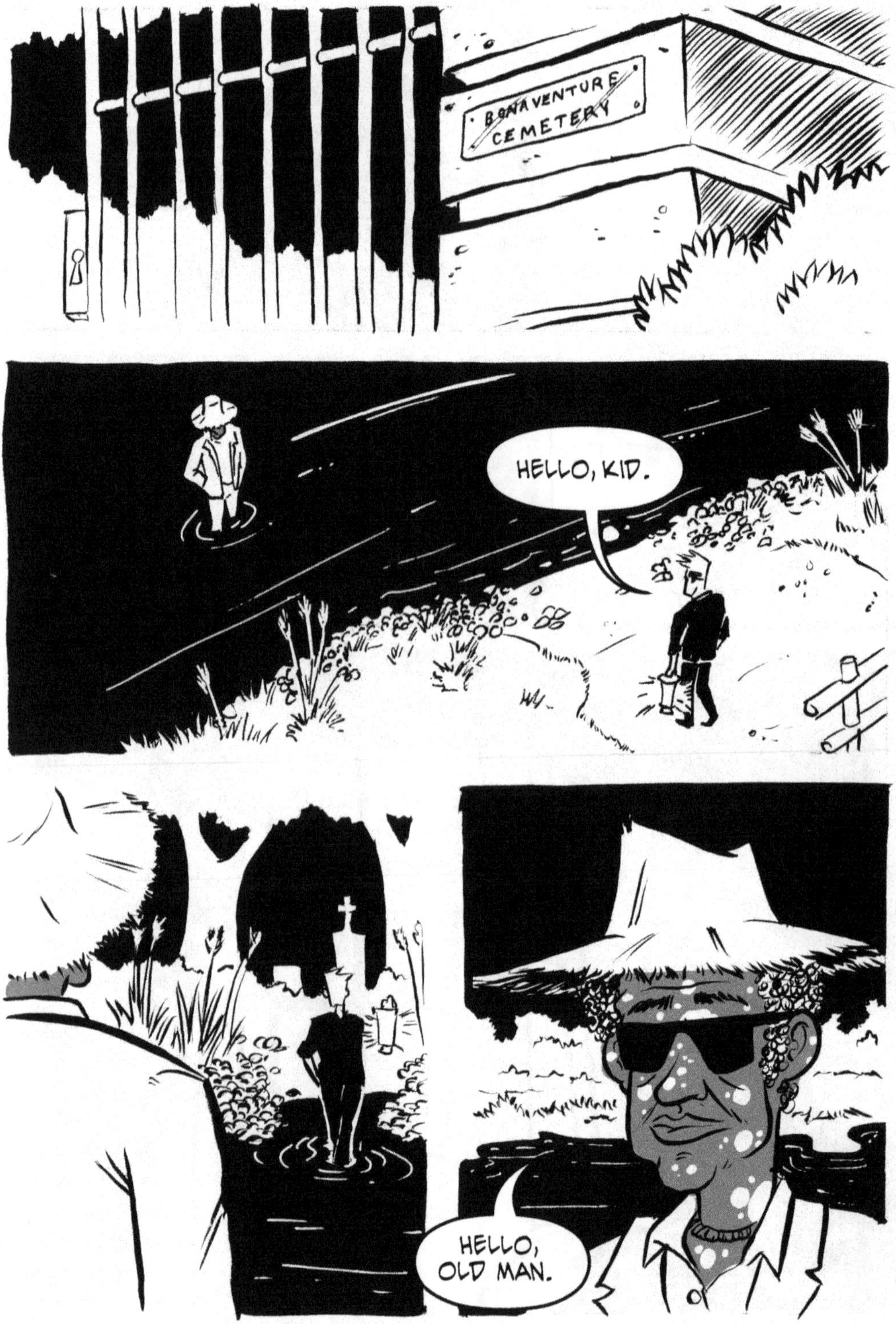
BONAVENTURE CEMETERY
HELLO, KID.
HELLO, OLD MAN.

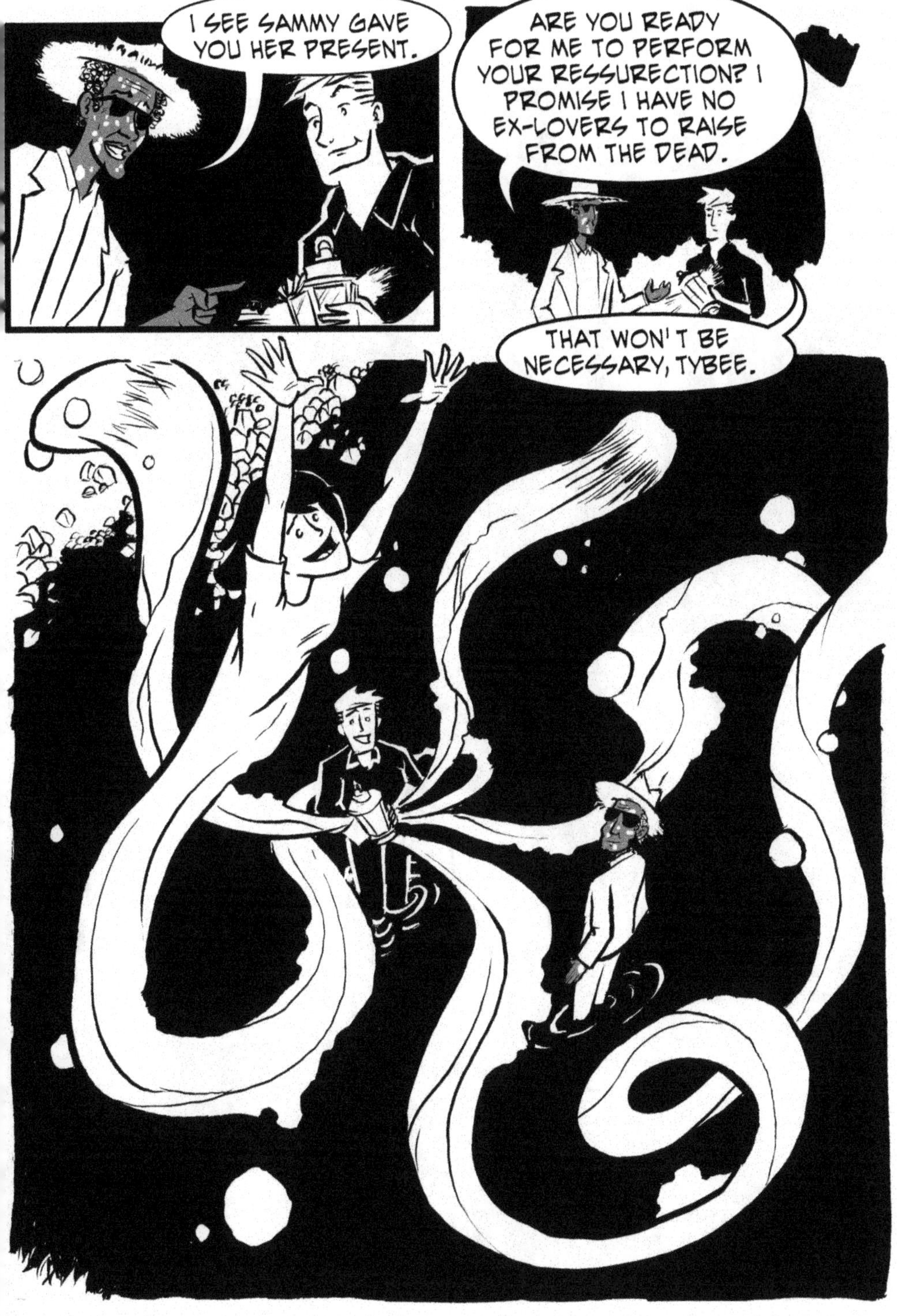
I SEE SAMMY GAVE YOU HER PRESENT.
ARE YOU READY FOR ME TO PERFORM YOUR RESSURECTION? I PROMISE I HAVE NO EX-LOVERS TO RAISE FROM THE DEAD.
THAT WON'T BE NECESSARY, TYBEE.

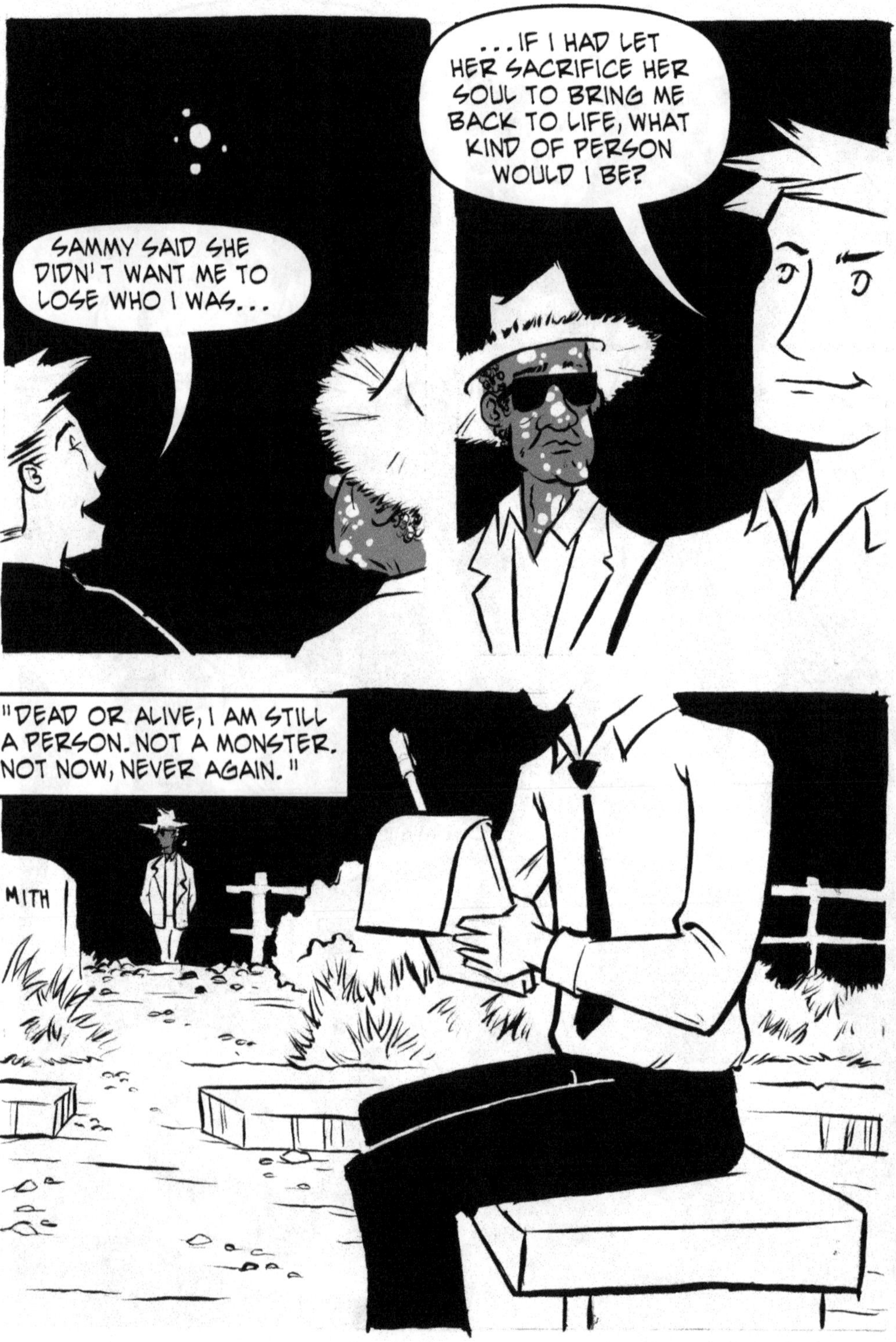
SAMMY SAID SHE DIDN'T WANT ME TO LOSE WHO I WAS...
...IF I HAD LET HER SACRIFICE HER SOUL TO BRING ME BACK TO LIFE, WHAT KIND OF PERSON WOULD I BE?
"DEAD OR ALIVE, I AM STILL A PERSON. NOT A MONSTER. NOT NOW, NEVER AGAIN."
MITH

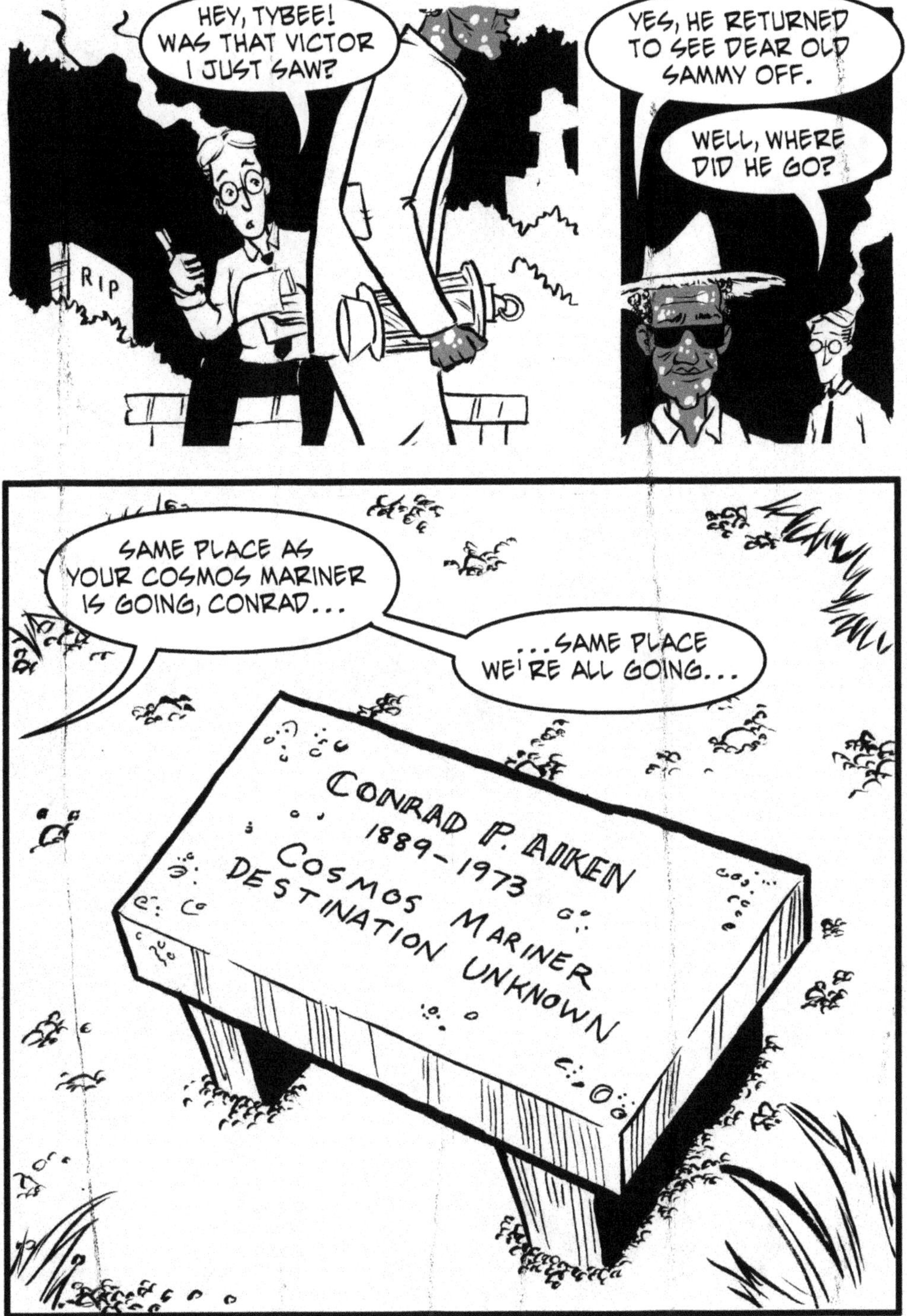
HEY, TYBEE! WAS THAT VICTOR I JUST SAW?
RIP
YES, HE RETURNED TO SEE DEAR OLD SAMMY OFF.
WELL, WHERE DID HE GO?
SAME PLACE AS YOUR COSMOS MARINER IS GOING, CONRAD...
...SAME PLACE WE'RE ALL GOING...
CONRAD P. AIKEN
1889-1973
COSMOS MARINER
DESTINATION UNKNOWN

THE

END

Bibliography

Bailey, Cornelia W. *God, Doctor Buzzard and the Bolito Man.*
New York, NY: Anchor Books, 2005.

Bird, Stephanie R. *Sticks, Stones, Roots and Bones.*
St. Paul, MN: Llewellyn Worldwide, 2004.

Capozzola, Connie. *Images of America: The Savannah College of Art and Design. Restoration of an Architectural Heritage.*
Charleston, SC: Arcadia Publishing, 2004

Caskey, James. *Haunted Savannah.*
Savannah, GA: Bonaventure Books, 2005.

Cobb, Al. *Savannah's Ghosts.*
Atglen, PA: Schiffer, 2001.

Cobb, Al. *Savannah's Ghosts II.*
Atglen, PA: Schiffer, 2007.

DeBolt, Margaret W. *Savannah Spectres.*
Virginia Beach, VA: DeBolt Publishing, 1984.

Gunther, Justin. *Images of America: Historic Signs of Savannah. Photographs from the Collection of the Georgia Historical Society.*
Charleston, SC: Arcadia Publishing, 2004.

Johnson, Michele N. *Images of America: Sapelo Island's Hog Hammock.*
Charleston, SC: Arcadia Publishing, 2004.

Jones Jr., Charles C. *Gullah Folktales from the Georgia Coast.*
Athens, GA: The University of Georgia Press, 2000.

Stavely, John F. *Ghosts and Gravestones of Savannah, Georgia.*
Key West, FL: Historic Tours of America, Inc., 2006.

Andre Frattino

Born and raised in Gainesville, Florida, Andre Frattino graduated from the Savannah College of Art and Design in 2009 with a BFA in sequential art and has worked as an illustrator for various clients. He is also an active contributor to *The Independent Florida Alligator* and is pursuing a master's degree in fine arts at the University of Florida.

Besides his devotion to the arts, Andre's other passion is the paranormal. He has conducted more than fifty haunting investigations along the East Coast and even worked as a consultant for SyFy's *Ghosthunters*. He continues his pursuit of both the arts and the paranormal and hopes to continue to bridge the gap between them.

Mr. Frattino is also the author of the graphic novel *The Reaper of St George Street*, also published by Pineapple Press.

Here are some other books from Pineapple Press on related topics. For a complete catalog, write to Pineapple Press, P.O. Box 3889, Sarasota, Florida 34230-3889, or call (800) 746-3275.
Or visit our website at www.pineapplepress.com.

The Reaper of St. George Street by **Andre Frattino.** In this first graphic novel published by Pineapple Press, Andre Frattino has created unforgettable characters and a spooky story that centers on an evil spirit. Arriving in haunted St. Augustine to attend college, skeptic Will is soon thrust into a mystery he wants no part of. But the girl he's falling in love with needs his help to rid her of the nightmares plaguing her sleep. Aided by a motley crew of ghost hunters—a pickpocket, a modern-day witch, a retired pirate, and a comic book nerd—Will must discover why a murderous poltergeist named the Reaper of St. George Street is wreaking havoc. Filled with characters you'll come to love and some laugh-out-loud humor, *The Reaper of St. George Street* will keep you turning pages until this mystery is solved.

Ghosts of St. Augustine by **Dave Lapham.** The unique and often turbulent history of America's oldest city is told in twenty-four spooky stories that cover four hundred years' worth of ghosts.

Ancient City Hauntings by **Dave Lapham.** In this sequel to *Ghosts of St. Augustine*, the author takes you on more quests for supernatural experiences through the dark, enduring streets of the Ancient City. Come visit the Oldest House, the Old Jail, Ripley's, the Oldest School House, all the many haunted B&Bs, and more.

Oldest Ghosts by **Karen Harvey.** In St. Augustine, the Ancient City, ghostly apparitions are as intriguing as the city's history.

St. Augustine and St. Johns County: A Historical Guide by **William R. Adams.** More than eighty of the oldest historic sites in the U.S. are found in and around the Ancient City of St. Augustine, Florida. Includes color photos, maps, and directions, as well as visitor information and an accurate historical narrative for each site.

The Houses of St. Augustine **by David Nolan.** A history of the city told through its buildings, from the earliest coquina structures, through Colonial and Victorian times, to the modern era. Color photographs and original watercolors.

Florida Ghost Stories **by Robert R. Jones.** Stories of ghosts and tall tales of strange happenings will give you goose bumps and make your hair stand on end.

Haunting Sunshine **by Jack Powell.** Take a wild ride through the shadows of the Sunshine State in this collection of deliciously creepy stories of ghosts in the theaters, churches, and historic places of Florida.

The Ghost Orchid Ghost and Other Tales from the Swamp **by Doug Alderson.** Florida's famous swamps—from the Everglades to Mosquito Lagoon to Tate's Hell—serve as fitting backdrops for these chilling original stories. Who but a naturalist can really scare you about what lurks in the swamp? Doug Alderson has been there and knows. From the author's notes at the end of each story, you can learn a thing or two about Florida's swamps, creatures, and history, along with storytelling tips.

Florida's Ghostly Legends and Haunted Folklore, Volume 1: South and Central Florida; Florida's Ghostly Legends and Haunted Folklore, Volume 2: North Florida and St. Augustine; and Florida's Ghostly Legends and Haunted Folklore, Volume 3: The Gulf Coast and Pensacola **by Greg Jenkins.** The history and legends behind a number of Florida's haunted locations, plus bone-chilling accounts taken from firsthand witnesses of spooky phenomena. Volume 1 locations include Key West's La Concha Hotel, the Everglades, Stetson University, and the Sunshine Skyway Bridge. Volume 2 locations include Silver Springs National Park, Flagler College, and the St. Augustine Lighthouse. Volume 3 covers the historic city of Pensacola and continues southward through the Tampa area, Sarasota, and Naples.

Haunt Hunter's Guide to Florida **by Joyce Elson Moore.** Discover the general history and "haunt" history of numerous sites around the state where ghosts reside.

CPSIA information can be obtained
at www.ICGtesting.com
Printed in the USA
BVHW01s0536091018
529437BV00010BA/13/P